Son of Astoria

Book Two of the Astoria Series
J.B. Wright

Content Warning

Hello friends,

Welcome to the second installment of the Astoria Series. Please be advised moving forward that this book will include the following topics; grief, loss, unwanted advances, discussion of off-page SA, coercion, cliffhanger, infertility, having to give up infants, off-page blood kink, blood, SA by introduction of a substance, degradation, emotionally abusive and manipulative relationships, violence, drugging, capture, deep-rooted family issues, a little sprinkling of murder.

I think that's all...unless sassy shadow daddy is a trigger because, yeah, he's in there too.

As always, be kind to yourself.
Your mental health matters, and if you have any questions about the content, do not hesitate to reach out.

xX JB

Dedication

For those who feel trapped in the circumstance of
their birth:
This world can be cruel
and sometimes all we can do is survive it.
If that means you have to play the villain...
Play. The. Damn. Villain.
We can't all be heroes.

PROLOGUE
DeLuca

I'M VAGUELY AWARE THAT there is something I should be doing. Someone needs me. My consciousness drifts in an odd void that appears infinite, and trying to navigate it is agonizing. Someone needs me. That small thought is what I cling to. I'm fighting to regain control of my body, my limbs, my mind. Anything.

Open your eyes, DeLuca.

Just open them.

Come on, damn it.

My thoughts halt as I strain to hear the muffled voices breaking through the endless nothing.

Aislinn.

I'd know her hypnotic voice anywhere. The way it sends off little bells in my ears each time I hear it. Like a symphony the Weavers wrote for me.

Who is she talking to?

Open your eyes, DeLuca.

My head threatens to split down the middle, but whatever has been holding me captive within my own mind subsides and I'm able to grasp the small threads of reality. My eyes are impossibly heavy as I slowly open them. Everything around me is a blurred mess.

Where am I? I was just in the water when...Audrina.

My hand curls around the Siphon Stone lodged in my abdomen. I grunt as I pull it out. My flight suit is torn around the wound, and there's a good amount of blood surrounding it. The wound is deep, but I've had worse. It will heal. It always does.

I examine the thumb-sized crystal. It swirls blue, like waves of water are trapped within, but that can't be right. It was clear...wasn't it? Once my vision returns to normal, I realize I'm at the entrance of a cave. A glowing cave. Silver is scattered through the air. The walls light up with writings in the language of gods. A beam of dark moonlight shines through a hole above and—

Wait. Is that...

"Aislinn?" I say quieter than I mean to while still getting my bearings on my consciousness.

She is wearing a shadow of a dress. The black slip beneath is barely visible through layers of gray. When did she change? I've never seen her in anything like it. She looks like some kind of beautiful nightmare.

Her arms are wrapped around another man, their lips touching. She noticeably twitches, but the man pulls her harder against him.

That bastard got her.

Erebus fucking got her.

"Aislinn!" I shout up to them, and the ground begins to shake as my control slips.

I failed her. I couldn't protect her.

That thought shatters what little hold I have left. The blood in my veins boils. All the rage, all the pain, everything I've suppressed is unleashed. My vision burns red. Flames erupt from every inch of me. My fingertips. My eyes. My legs. Even my godsdamned toes. My entire body is alight. Nothing on this island is safe. The fire grows and grows, and I continue to push it farther. It surrounds me completely as far as I can see. I'm a dying star, and this is my supernova. Nothing else exists. My blaze burns until I remember how to breathe.

With a final frustrated yell, I stop the flow of power and begin to walk through the flames engulfing the area. Nothing will be left of this cursed island by the time the fire snuffs out.

My fire. It came from within *me*. I didn't have to manipulate it from something else. It's mine.

I go to stick the Siphon Stone into the pocket and curse with the realization my clothes are gone. Burnt off along with everything else around me. I head back for the water. Our boat is still safely floating near the shoreline, far enough away that it is untouched by my destruction.

After I climb in, I place the stone in a small jar and call upon a wave to push me to Sutton's shore.

Nothing. Not even a ripple.

Fucking Audrina.

I row as quickly as my arms will allow. The adrenaline helps to push me faster.

Charging through the doors of the palace, I'm calm enough not to burn it down but not enough to stop the prickle of power from rising to the surface. A serv rushes toward me with a towel, and I wrap it around my waist without breaking stride.

"DeLuca." Lady Soleil's eyebrows raise to her hairline. "Where is Aislinn?"

A line of fire ignites between my shoulders as that control slips again, but I know I can't lose it completely. There are innocents in this house, and I refuse to let them become casualties in a fight that is not their own. Her mouth drops and her eyes widen.

"He took her," I say. My fist tightens around the jar containing the Siphon Stone. "You seem surprised to see me, Lady Soleil. Is it because I'm supposed to be dead? Because you and your treacherous daughter had planned to kill me?" The anger feeds the flames, and they dance violently around me. It takes everything I have to rein them back in, to not level this ocean-side obnoxiously large house until it's nothing but another old ruin to gape at.

"I'm *surprised* because you're nude, bleeding, and slightly aflame in my entryway. I've never seen an element created." Her hands fall to her hips. "What about my daughter? She snuck out shortly after you left. Where is she? What happened?"

"*Your daughter* stabbed me with a Siphon Stone. I don't know after that because I was knocked out. When I came to, Erebus was floating away *with* Aislinn."

Lysette comes down the stairs. She only needs to look at me to know I failed. Her eyes well up, and she covers her gasp with her hands.

"Get your things, Lysette. We're leaving," I order.

"Leaving? Where?" There's a hint of panic in her tone.

"I'm taking you back to Caeliss, to your brother. You're not safe here."

"Not safe?" She looks at Lady Soleil with a pinch between her brows.

"Audrina betrayed us. Lady Soleil is her mother. We can't trust her. We can't trust anyone." My fingers tingle with the power begging to be released.

"You are perfectly safe here. I know nothing of a betrayal." Lady Soleil folds her arms. "When Audrina shows up, we will sort all of this out. It has to be a misunderstanding."

"I doubt it." I hold her gaze. "She's dead."

She pales in an instant. "Dead? Aud-Audrina?" Her voice cracks. "My Audrina?"

"I would assume by Erebus or Aislinn. If not by them, then when I laid waste to the Isle of Shadows. There's nothing left of it."

Lady Soleil drops to her knees as if she can no longer bear her own weight. Her breathing comes out in short, ragged puffs before she lets out a high-pitched shriek. Aurelia is quickly by her side, but honestly, there's not a lot of comfort you can give someone who just lost the only person in the realm they care about.

I start toward the stairs. "We are leaving. *Immediately.*"

"DeLuca, wait," Lysette calls.

The flames along my shoulder blades flicker a little higher as I turn around, digging my nails into the banister.

"We should stay. The transport from Caeliss will be here in a few days. It would be quicker to wait than to go on foot through a hostile country."

"We're *not* staying here."

"Go without me then. I'll wait for the transport." She folds her arms.

I groan and run my hands over my face. "I can't leave you."

"Why?"

"I promised Aislinn. I promised if something happened to her, I'd look out for you, for all of you."

"Oh." She stares somewhere beyond me as if those little gears in her mind are working in overdrive.

"I can't stay here. I have to go after Erebus...after Aislinn."

"I know," she says quietly, "but you don't know how to get into the god's realm...and we don't have any way off this island. Think, DeLuca, look past the emotion and really think about the best options here."

Gods damn it, she's right.

Lysette's hand reaches for my arm, but I shake my head in warning—knowing I'm burning too hot right now, and she would certainly get burned. The awkward silence passing between us gets interrupted by another of Lady Soleil's wails.

"I can't just do nothing, Lysette."

"Then don't do nothing. We have a room full of information about the gods. Maybe we can find a lead to getting into their realm."

"There wasn't anything in there!"

"We weren't looking for a way in before!" Her voice raises to match mine, which I would find amusing on a regular day. Not that we have ever had one of those.

An unamused laugh sticks in my throat. "I don't have much of an alternative at the moment."

The stairs bow beneath my heavy steps. Lysette is right. I hate that she's right, but she is. It makes the most sense to wait here for the transport to take us back to Caeliss. If anyone knows where to find a portal, it would be Priestess Alis. In the meantime, I will read every godsdamn text and tome ten times over until I find something of use.

After I dress, I begin pulling clothing from the drawers and march across the hall, throwing them in an empty drawer in Aislinn's room. If I'm going to be stuck here, I'm going to damn well stay where I feel closest to her.

While throwing my things in the closet, I spot the blue dress she wore on our first day on this cursed island. My fingers trace the straps—bringing the memory of her skin beneath it. My fist tightens around the fabric and burns beneath my fingers before I can rein in the heat.

Fuck. Fuck. Fuck!

I back away from her things towards the bed to avoid completely annihilating what's left of Ailie. The backs of my knees bump against the bed frame and I sink to the floor in front of it—pulling her quilt down with me. I can still smell Aislinn on it as if she were here with me now. Lunalilies and freshwater, not like that of the ocean, but like the waterfalls in Caeliss, completely pure.

My gaze turns toward the window. A single star shoots across the night sky. I straighten up, remembering who I am.

I am the son of Astoria. Born of shadow and light.

A descendant of both Haile and Egon.

Life and Death.

I *am* the god of vengeance.

And I am coming for you, Erebus.

I'm coming for you, Aislinn.

Part One
EMPTY

ONE

NEW PLAN

DeLuca

FRUSTRATION IS AN UNDERSTATEMENT.

It has been three months, and we are still no closer to finding Aislinn.

We have practically lived in Caeliss's silver temple, going through every book or scroll available, and nothing.

Slamming another useless tome closed, I groan. "This is a waste of time, Lysette."

She looks up at me with a sigh. "I'm beginning to think you're right. We have been through all of these, and while it provides us with histories of Children and some gods, there is nothing about the other portals or ways to cross into the gods' realm."

With a careful hand, she places another leather-bound book back onto the shelf. It's a snug fit; the shelves are at capacity, and it's a wonder they haven't built an entire library yet with the amount of knowledge they've procured. Somehow, with the hundreds of books they have, there's still no mention of Erebus.

It takes a lot of effort to keep the flames at bay. Ever since the ability manifested, it's been nearly painful to repress them. But I don't want to burn all of Caeliss like I did the Isle of Shadows, so repression is the best option for now.

I run my hands through my overgrown hair. The feeling I've so desperately tried to push out is creeping back in. Absolute hopeless dread that burns through me with a vengeance, seeking to destroy all in its path.

"I have to get her back, Lys, I *have* to." I sit against the wall and hang my head down while I try to calm my racing thoughts.

What good is being a fucking god if I can't even protect one person?

"We will."

"You can't know that."

"I don't know it, you're right, but I do *feel* it. I know this is not how it ends for her—or for you."

I can't help but scoff at how ridiculous she sounds. *'Feel it,'* right. We're just going to follow our feelings to get Ailie back from the god of shadows. Maybe chase a fucking rainbow while we're at it. I'm going to say as much when Lysette comes and sits beside me, keeping a careful distance to avoid being burned. I shut my mouth, swallowing the added guilt of almost being an ass to her.

The scar near her white eye hasn't faded much; the skin is still a pinched angry red which gives her a hardened look. A fitting match for her hardening personality. There have been a few instances where it has scared off some of the little kids. Lys has taken to wearing a leather eyepatch whenever walking about the village because of it. She only removes it when she's comfortable in her surroundings and company. I don't know when *I* became someone she is comfortable with. Even with my rigid attitude and trouble keeping my emotions at bay, she always removes the patch in my presence, and I find that I do not hate the time I spend with her. Lysette has proven herself a loyal friend and her mind is incredible, as is her patience.

Being the quick learner she is, she has all but mastered her gift as a Bottinial—surpassing the Bottinials here in such a short time.

In the last few weeks, when we're not in the temple researching, she has been mentoring me in the same ability. It's a trade off with the self-defense lessons I've been giving her. We both realized quickly after Ailie was taken that we are severly outmatched.

If I'm being honest with myself, I wouldn't have come as far with any of my gifts without Lysette. I've learned I can control just about anything that comes from the ground, as well as fire and air. The loss of my water ability has me feeling less than whole, but the familiarity of the other elements is comforting.

I blow out a breath. "We should have just stayed in Sutton. At this point, the Shadow Moon is due to return in the next few weeks. We could have tried to use the portal there."

She inches closer, testing the heat of my skin with the tip of her finger before placing a hand carefully on my arm. "You know why we couldn't. Using another god's portal would tear us apart without their escort."

"Don't remind me. I don't want to think about the way he took Ailie through it."

The memory of her being taken by Erebus, god of shadows...*my father*, through his portal. In his arms. Their lips touching. His arms wrapped around her.

Fuck. I'm losing it again.

4

Lysette moves her hand quickly as my skin begins to burn. The lick of flames prickle between my shoulder blades. I hop up and move towards the door.

"Where are you going?" she asks.

"I need air."

The rain pelts my face as if it's mocking my failures. My hand tightens around the blue stone I carry in my pocket, the one filled with my ability to manipulate water. The Siphon Stone Audrina stabbed me with. Her betrayal took me by complete surprise, and I am *not* someone who is easily surprised.

When she jumped in the water, I was afraid something had gone wrong. I dropped my guard. My thoughts were only on Aislinn and her safety. I'm sure that's exactly what Audrina was counting on as she shoved that small stone into my gut with all her might. Striking fast, her eyes wide and apologetic before a shadow appeared at her side and everything went dark.

And cold.

And empty.

I have never known emptiness like that.

That's probably what Aislinn endures every single day as I fail to find a way to get to her.

There's a hissing noise as the rain makes contact with the flames rising off my body. Soren must be pissed about something. It hasn't stopped raining in weeks. Priestess Alis believes it to be a blessing, but what kind of blessing is drowning?

My fingers are still curled around that small blue stone when the rain above stops falling on me. I am untouched, yet it still falls in the same rhythmic patterns around my feet. I unclench the stone to reach my hands out for the drops, and the second my fingers leave my pocket, the rain continues to soak through my shirt.

I grab the stone again and focus on how much I hate the feeling of the water dropping on me.

It stops.

I let go of the stone.

It rains.

I grab the stone.

It stops.

Holy shit.

"Lysette!"

She rushes out, concern sprawled across her face and half-breathless. "What is it?"

"Just watch." I show her how the water obeys while I hold the stone. "My power must recognize me," I whisper.

I have never cared to be powerful, but it feels like I'm missing a limb. There's always this vague itch, but when I try to scratch it, it's just...*gone.*

"Hmm." I see her mind work at a fierce pace. "Let me try." I place the stone in her opened palm. She then closes her eyes and focuses. The water above her halts. She opens her eyes, and they widen in surprise. "This is dangerous." Her voice is hushed.

"Dangerous? I don't see how."

"How could you not? Do you understand? Whoever possesses this stone can control water; they become a Voda even if they weren't born one."

I try to follow her train of thought, but I don't see the danger. "It actually seems fair, like it could create a balance in the realm."

She sighs. "Or disrupt it completely. A mortal with a grudge could gain an ability...or another of Astoria's Children could gain more power... Even a wayward god could gain *more* power. Can you imagine if there are more infected stones in the realm? If they all are able to give power? Can you imagine what someone like Pierce would have done with that information?"

Lysette visibly shudders at the thought and hands the stone back to me. We go back inside of the silver temple where it's dry.

"Shit." I rake my fingers through my wet hair. "There *is* more, Lys...at least one."

"One what?"

"An infected Siphon Stone. Remember the story Lady Soleil told us in Sutton? About the Guardians of Astoria and how one of the guardians went crazy? Sorena was her name. She could call upon lightning. They had to stab her with a stone."

Lysette is silent for a moment. Then her voice is quiet when she finally speaks. "I remember. I also remember she lost her mind from being separated from her ability." She looks at me with pity.

I loathe being looked upon with pity. It is a look I have received all of my life. Found as an orphaned baby. Dead parents. Lost siblings. *Dead* siblings. Being the sole survivor of a tragic explosion in the mines under the Obsidian Mountains. A life in service to others.

It wasn't until I became a spy for the Liberators under Pierce Decatur's leadership that I felt I had stepped out from the cycle of pity. Only to fall in love with the future lady of the house, one I was supposed to be spying on...and to rescue her from the very rebellion I had joined. The weeks since have been a blur. Finding out that I am the son of Astoria and Erebus—two gods—making me a god as well. Discovering Caeliss, a safe haven for the Children of Astoria. Assassinating the leader of the Liberators...and my own sister. Facing Erebus on the Islands of the Sons...and him beating us before we even had a chance.

Losing Aislinn was losing everything for me. Now I have nothing more to be taken. Nothing more to hold me back. I am consumed by a need for vengeance. I feel it prickle beneath my skin every second of the day. It's building stronger with each show of restraint. I will use every ounce of power I have to take Erebus down.

Even if it kills me.

"Do not look at me with pity in your eyes, Lys. I can't take it, not from you," I say.

She turns away quickly. "I'm sorry. I just—I just worry for you. You have been *so* angry since the island. I'm afraid you will erupt again."

So am I. But she doesn't have to know that. "I promised Ailie I would protect you and those she cares for. I intend to keep that promise. You don't have to worry about me burning you."

"I'm not worried for me, you idiot." She smacks my shoulder.

A smile tugs the corners of my lips. "You don't need to worry for me. I have been taking care of myself for a long time."

She raises a brow. "If I don't, then who will?"

I try not to let those words sink below the surface because of the truth they hold and the pain that comes in acknowledging them.

Lysette drums her fingers along the table thoughtfully and says, "I think we should talk to Alec about the stones."

The fire in my veins ignites, and I step away so that Lysette doesn't feel it. "No."

I curl my hands at my sides, trying to control the raging inferno within me. I still have not forgiven Alec, the Sanguist, for using his control on Aislinn. Watching her choke on her own blood as I returned from scouting the Capital was the first time I had a taste of that out-of-control rage. I nearly took down the entirety of the Silver Hills. It was the first manifestation of real power I had, and I would have traded all of it if I could've saved her from the pain.

"DeLuca," Lysette starts as if she is about to try reasoning with me.

"I said no, Lys. Leave it."

"Fine. At least tell Priestess Alis or Demetrius...or *any* of the Elders about the stones."

"We'll see." I cross my arms and look down at her.

"Will we? Or are you just saying that to placate me?" Her tone matches my own.

"You're my most agitating friend, you know that?"

"I'm your *only* friend, Lucy."

9

"I told you not to call me '*Lucy.*'"

"And I told *you* I. Don't. Care." She smiles and wrinkles her nose in a way that reminds me of a rabbit. But Lysette is no rabbit. She's more in line with a wolf...or bear...if her father's lineage has any hold in her blood.

I roll my eyes and nod to the door. "Let's go home. It's time to make a new plan."

Since coming back to Caeliss, Lysette has taken Audrina's old room. She thought Rett and Iris could use some space of their own...at least that's what she said. I'm more inclined to think that after everything we have all been through these last few months that she doesn't know how to be around her brother. She is not the same sister he had at the beginning of summer. The loss of her twin hardened her heart. I think she feels she has to be one way for him, but it's no longer who she is at her core.

She is not delicate. She is not a lady. She has become a force of nature. She is strong—of body and mind. Yet, whenever Lysette is near her brother, she seems small. Rett and Iris may be enjoying their own space, but it is as much for Lysette as it is for them.

"What are you thinking?" Her gaze fixes on me with the question scrunching her brows. I bring her a steaming cup of tea, brewed using the tulsi and alora she helped me grow in tiny pots placed on our kitchen's windowsill.

"I'm thinking I'm going to leave Caeliss," I say calmly.

She nods as if she expected the answer. "You mean *we*." Lys takes a deep inhale of the steam coming off her cup. Her face is set in a way that says "*end of discussion*" but to Haile with that.

"I don't."

The mocking laugh that comes from her mouth has my jaw clenching. "Lucy, how far do you expect to go without me?" Her amused expression is getting under my skin. I open my mouth to speak, but she puts up a hand to stop me. "*Without* burning down entire provinces."

My teeth grind. As much as I hate to admit it, I would be lost without Lysette. Her knowledge of gods and her skills as a researcher far exceed my own. Not to mention, she can read and understand some Old Daeil, the language of the gods. A dead language that most of the old texts seem to be written in.

As if reading my mind, she adds, "And, as an added incentive, I know where we have to go."

I arch a brow, leaning back in my chair with my arms folded. "You do?"

"I do."

"Are you going to tell me?"

"I don't know. Are you going to throw a fit about me going home?"

"Home? You mean Obsidian Manor?"

"Yup."

"I don't like it."

"Sure you don't, but I believe my father has a secret archive, like the one in Sutton." Her shoulder drops in a shrug. "It makes the most sense."

I run my hands down my face. It's probably worth a look if it is even half as big as Lady Soleil's. "Fine, you can go for research *only*. You can't follow me beyond that."

She smiles deviously. "Try to stop me."

TWO
GRAVELY ILL
Erebus

EVERYTHING ABOUT THE SUN Palace offends me. Every gold engraving. Every white pillar. Every window bursting with false light.

It's so open and so unnecessarily bright. My shadows scream each time we come to this side of Kaoket, as if the obnoxious glow coating the Olvi distresses them in the worst of ways. They protest and pull back as they ache to get back to the Shadows, but they answer to *me* and go where I go. Today, we must endure this torture together.

I've been putting off this visit for days. I can't put it off any longer. He's bound to already know of a mortal presence given his many spies around our realm. He may be the biggest bastard of us all, but he is still the king, crowned by Kato himself. Therefore, he needs to be informed of my unlikely visitor. My neck cracks as I roll out my shoulders and expel some premature agitation.

The favored son, Soren, leads me through the long hallways. Haile *always* greets those seeking council in his throne room. Pious to a fault. His throne is an exaggerated chair made of solid gold with white cushions. There are small suns engraved around it between filigree swirls. Directly beside his throne is a much smaller one, designed similarly but with a representation of each season and nowhere near as grand. It is meant for Queen Isela, but I have not seen her use it in hundreds of years—presumably because they finally came to see how horribly lacking the other is and found company in the arms of others.

Soren tucks his gray falcon-like wings so he fits through the doorway. It is a large doorway, and he could most absolutely make them fit or have them vanish all together, but enjoys making us gaze upon the monstrosities. At one of the tamer parties thrown by Millena, each of the winged gods lined up to measure their wingspan. Soren came in first and has been a smug little shit ever since. He always fails to mention how my half-sister, Helena, was just the tip of a feather shorter.

I cast an illusion over his wings, making them appear no larger than his shoulder blades and changing the gray to a shimmering lavender. I'd laugh if my shadows weren't wailing so loudly.

We finally arrive before Haile's throne. I kneel even though my body fights against it. Soren begins to shout obscenities as he realizes what I've done to his mighty wings. The smirk on my lips betrays me as the culprit—not that there were many suspects. No one can cast illusions like I can.

Haile clenches his jaw. "Fix it."

With a shrug and what I intend to resemble a pout, I snap my fingers, and the illusion is gone, leaving Soren's wings exactly as they were...maybe the tip of a feather shorter. "Happy, King?"

"Ecstatic," he says, though his face is anything but. "Tell me, *trickster*, why should I allow this mortal into our realm? You had to bend quite a few rules to get her here. In fact, I'm not entirely sure how you did it, but I am immensely interested in finding out. Why do you believe we will benefit from her presence? Especially after Kato forbade mortals journeying to our realm in the First Battles?" Haile's condescending voice makes the shadows beneath my skin hiss.

I take a controlled breath and try to keep the bite out of my tone. "You know as I do that our realm is gravely ill. Without new shadows passing through to the Afterlands, there is nothing sustaining our lands. Yours and mine—"

Haile interrupts me. "They are all *mine*. I am king. The Shadows is just your domain. I find it depressing and do not care to tend to it."

Every shadow inside me stirs, aching to lash out, but by some kind of miracle, I remain calm. "That's neither here nor there. The fact is the realm is dying. We need to break down the barrier to get the shadows through. You know as well as I do that if we do not solve our barrier problem soon, it puts a risk to the whole of *your lands*. I believe she may be able to open a portal... I believe she is the reincarnated Utikalo...perhaps one third of Millena's children. I also believe she can help restore Astoria's sanity."

Haile sits a bit straighter in his throne. "How will any of that help my daughter?"

"If I can see what broke her, how she broke, I can fix her. And with Utikalo's ability to not only see the past but travel through it...I could even stop her from breaking in the first place."

"Alter the past..." He's mumbling to himself. "Alter the present and the future...a portal to the mortal lands." Some kind of plan formulates as he continues his mutterings. After a few unbearable seconds in his presence, he finally says, "Yes. Keep your pet. Do what you must to help my daughter and open the barrier."

"One request. Let's keep Agnar out of it. If he finds out who she is, he will try to keep her in Kaoket. I won't be able to guide her as I can from the Shadows. Agnar is good at what he does and not much else."

"Yes, fine, fine." Haile waves his hands lazily.

I bow in thanks, and I'm about to turn away when he stops me.

"You're *sure* she's here of her own volition?" His eyes narrow.

There is a stirring in my chest at the question. "Yes, I am sure."

"Good. You know the enchantment Kato put on the realm to any of those who force another to do anything against their will."

"*I know*," I say with little restraint over the annoyance. "And the fact that I am standing here well and intact should tell you I did not take her against her will."

"Very well. Bring her to Kaoket later. We will hold court and introduce her to the others."

"If I bring her to Kaoket, Agnar will know of her presence. As will the rest of the gods." It takes almost all the resolve I have left to keep my voice even. "Do you not believe that will be counterproductive?"

"What do you think they will say if they find out you have a mortal plaything that you hid? Especially after the barrier went up and no one else has been able to go between realms. No, best to share her before they suspect you of some kind of plot."

I can't rein in the snarl. "I do *not* share."

The shining bastard fucking laughs. "Be a good god and bring her to court, *today*." And then he waves his hand to dismiss me.

I am still seething as I enter my palace that rests on the border between the Abyss and the Shadows. The sounds of my heavy footsteps echo down the empty halls. We do not have live-in help as the rest of the gods do. Considering my shadows are capable of fetching anything we need or completing any task, we do not need the added warm bodies getting in the way. Astoria and I are the only living beings in this house, but since my wife lost her mind, it has felt like only me. Now my little pet is thrown into the mix and has thrown off this energy. Even the shadows that serve me seem riled by her presence.

When I reach her room, I find myself pacing in front of it. Hesitating and wondering how I got myself tangled so deep into the web of schemes and fate. With a hiss, I shake away the thought. There is no going back, and I have committed to this course. I reach for the door that's charmed to only open for me, to keep others out as much to keep her in. I've been watching this problematic creature for weeks and know she would run at first chance.

I will not give her that chance.

Her door opens with a soft creak, and I close it behind me. She looks so at peace when she sleeps. Her dark hair is all over her face and her features are messed up into that tight scowl she always wears around me. It's nice to have this moment of quiet.

She responds to anything I say with such hostility and defiance. My little pet is an infuriating creature, but she is necessary, and despite my attempts to push her out, she has a draw over me I can't quite explain. I release a sigh, knowing this quiet peace will be short lived when I wake her. But Haile wants her at court, and the king gets what the king wants.

THREE
MUNDANE
Aislinn

"I'M SORRY. I'M SO *sorry.*" *Audrina's voice seems to come from nowhere and everywhere at once.*

"*I don't deserve a friend like you.*"

"*I betrayed you.*"

There's no way to block it out. It's like it lives within my head. Like she lives within me. My hands are shaking and my chest hurts. I look down and realize there's a blade sticking out of my chest.

My heart.

She's taken my heart.

"*I'm so sorry.*" *It's Audrina's voice...but the words pass through my lips.*

It's raining now. The drops are thick and heavy. I'm soaked in an instant. The rain is red. Blood. All around me is blood. Coating everything and drenching me until there's nothing left. There's a shadow in the distance and I run from it towards a strange golden sun. The farther I get from the shadow, the heavier the blood rain falls. The ground is so slick I can't keep my footing.

"*I'm so sorry.*"

The shadow hovers over me, the crimson rain running from its presence and the strange sun shriveling. I lean into the darkness and let it wash over me.

"Wake, pet." His voice curls around my body like a chain.

For a moment, my nightmare bleeds into my reality, but then I remember my reality *is* the nightmare. There's no reprieve. This is my life. Imprisoned by a monster. Killed my best friend. Found love only to lose it. Yes, this is the true nightmare.

Sitting upright in the bed—holding the plush blankets close to my chest—I narrow my eyes at the shadow god standing by the foot of the bed.

"What?" I say on an annoyed exhale.

He tsks. "Such a rude greeting. You must not waste the day sleeping. I am going to present you before the other gods today." His eyes catch mine and his voice becomes ice as he says, "I expect you will be on your best behavior."

"As your *pet*?" I spit the accusation.

"As my *guest*." His voice is softer, less commanding and borderline sweet like a carnivorous plant luring its prey. I know if I'm not careful, he will consume me whole.

"Is that what I am now? A guest?"

"It's what you have always been."

I gasp with an overdramatic hand covering my mouth. "How could I not have known? Your hospitality is overwhelming." I roll my eyes, pointing to the door of my room that only opens for him.

"I could not have you exploring this realm until you have been introduced. We wouldn't want you to get lost amongst the Abyss." He winks.

A chill slides down my spine, but I try not to visibly shiver. "What do you want from me, Erebus?"

"You ask this question each day, and the response is always the same. There is something inside of you that I desire. Now, let me ask *you* a question." He comes to the side of my bed and touches the mark visible from the slim material of my nightgown, sending a cold and hollow feeling through the whole of it—wrapping around my torso and spreading out along my shoulder blades like wings made of shadow.

He exhales as I recoil from his touch.

"This could be simple if you would stop fighting my every word. Why are you so determined to hate me, pet?"

I snort—I can't help it. His question seems so absurd. "Are you joking?"

"That is not something I tend to do. Trick? Obviously. Jokes? Rarely. Now, answer me."

"Because you ruin everything you touch. You have taken everything from me. You have taken *me*, against my will," I reply with acid in my voice.

"It was not *against* your will. If it were, we would have been shredded when passing through the portal."

"Semantics. I was willing because I had no other choice." I was so ready to argue back that I almost missed it, but then the realization comes through. "Wait, did you say *we*?"

Erebus ignores the question. "Tell me, pet, was your truest desire not to live a life of adventure? Have I not provided just that? Is exploring a new realm not adventurous enough for you? If it wasn't for me, you'd be married to that *mortal,* living a mundane existence high in those lonely mountains. Did you want that life?"

The answer is no, but I won't give him the satisfaction of admitting it. He smiles at my silence, taking it for an answer anyway, a wicked gleam shining in his dark gray eyes.

He toys with a lock of my hair. "You may think of me as your villain, but surely, you must know everyone is someone else's villain. Even you."

With a shudder, I yank my hair away from him. "That doesn't make any sense. Not everyone can be a villain, and *I* most certainly am not."

"With time, I feel you may understand. For now, I must attend to some things around the Shadow. I will be back within the hour. *Behave,* my pet."

Erebus snaps his fingers. At the same moment that he disappears into a mist of shadow, a tray containing breakfast lands seamlessly on my lap in the outrageously oversized bed. If I am being honest, it is the most comfortable bed I've ever slept in, with dark gray silk sheets and a soft mattress that feels better than a hug. I refuse to like anything about it, but my body betrays me each time I lay to rest. Perhaps the luxury is compensation for containing me within this one room for days. Completely secluded and alone, aside from his spontaneous and brief visits.

Left with memories.

Audrina seems to swim to the top of them. Each thought of her radiance and light is tainted with the dark clouds of coercion. It has been impossible for me to face her memory. They're too painful. I don't know what was real and what wasn't. She did so much for me...but took so much from me.

Like DeLuca.

There is a large window that overlooks darkness. An endless void of nothing that I can only assume is the Abyss. If I were to try to escape that way, I would surely be lost to it, and even from the little I know of it, I can say with certainty it is not somewhere I want to be lost in. I could use the front door and perhaps find myself in the gods' realm. Amongst gods who may or may not be worse than Erebus. Not that I have been able to test that for myself.

I open the dome lid to find smoked ham, fresh fruit with a strange glow, and toasted bread beside a cup of coffee. I take a sip and throw the cup across the room. It shatters on impact with the wall.

A splash of cream—exactly how I like it. It reminds me of that day in my room at Obsidian when I dropped the cup and DeLuca cut his hand. The memory widens the already hollowed out pit in my stomach. My breathing comes out in short, hard bursts. I toss the dark bedding off my lap, not caring that the tray gets thrown with it— launching it all across my glorified prison. The spilled coffee continues its slow drip down the wall, and for a second, it looks like blood.

Pierce's blood.

Valera's blood.

Audrina's blood.

All the blood on *my* hands. *Mine.*

A deep rage seeps through my veins and I kick over the bedside table. Not stopping there, I start throwing, ripping, and shredding—destroying everything in sight.

Erebus returns shortly after. He is not at all surprised by the disarray of my room. I knocked over everything I could. Vases. Shelves. The breakfast dishes. Tore the covers off the bed. Attempted to push the mattress off but failed with it halfway off the frame due to its weight. Pulled down the black velvet curtains. I broke everything I possibly could. My hair is smothered across my face, stuck in places with my sweat. The tiny nightgown is wrinkled and a strap is falling off my shoulder.

I'm still breathing heavily from my fit of rage, seething as I stare at him in his pristine charcoal suit. His laugh is malicious as he waves his hand, returning everything to its place. There's a shard of broken vase hidden behind my back. While Erebus is distracted by his amusement, I lunge towards him and wrap my legs around his waist—stabbing at his chest over and over. I pull back a final time and smile with pride as his wounds weep blue and blood drops all over his suit. He looks at me with a smirk while adjusting the buttons on his shirt. In a blink, it is back to its pristine condition. My proud smile drops into a scowl and my shoulders sag in defeat.

"Your temper is delightful, pet, but you look like a deranged mouse which will be most unacceptable at court."

There's a pause before I answer, taken aback by the last word. "Court?"

"Oh, that's right, mortals are incredibly simple-minded. How do I explain this?" He leans against the wall and crosses his arms. "Court is where someone of royal stature—"

"I know what a court *is*. I didn't realize gods had them." I roll my eyes.

"Yes, unfortunately. The king has really dug his heels into it for the last few centuries or so. It is incredibly dull. Everything must be voted on by his small council. Sometimes a single session can last years."

"*Years*?!"

He straightens his suit. "Indeed."

I can't stay here for years. I simply can't. "Why am I going?"

"To entertain me, of course. *And* because I, unfortunately, need approval for you to stay." There's a bite in his voice.

He is unhappy.

Good.

"So they can send me back?" I feel the first swell of hope since I arrived.

"They could. It would take some maneuvering, of course, between the barrier and the finicky portals. They could force me to take you back the way you came. We'd have to wiggle through some rules, but it's not impossible. But then again, if you did get sent back, how would you restore your relative's shadow?" His eyes dance with the words.

My heart drops.

This is a game to him.

And I'm losing.

"Heidon?"

"Yes. I still have him, part of him at least, and if you'd like that part to return to his decaying body, you will be on your *best* behavior tonight." He hisses in my ear.

Of course he'd have some contingency to keep me compliant, the slimy trickster that he is. What choice do I have when he holds Heidon's fate over me?

I force "fine" through a tight jaw and roll my eyes.

Erebus waves his shadows to me and they begin to dance around my body. Cold and caressing every inch of exposed skin. They flow through my hair and all the way down to my toes, weaving from nothing. When they finally stop, I'm so dizzy from the constant spinning that I falter in step. A frigid hand wraps around my arm to steady me.

"You look divine, pet." Erebus's expression twists with amusement as if he's keeping a secret while admiring his handiwork.

My hair flows in loose waves and has an ethereal shine in this realm. My eyes also somehow shine brighter here, resembling an emerald stone that has been tossed atop a fire. Erebus has put me in a black dress that embodies a dark metal and trails behind me as

I walk. It hugs my curves yet the fabric is pliable and gives when I move. It's extremely comfortable, and I would have picked it for myself if I had been presented with it as an option.

I hate him.

"Of course, you like it. You picked it." One of my hands instinctively holds the locket around my neck, the one containing DeLuca's ruby. I feel calmer the second my fingers touch the cool gold. It's one thing Erebus hasn't taken from me, unlike the Child Blade and my scrap of bloody lace. I haven't seen either since he took me from the cave, yet for some reason, he hasn't thought to take the locket.

He slithers across the floor in the form of a shadow and reemerges in front of me, his face less than an inch from mine, and I shiver from his cold breath. "You can pretend you do not like it, but I *see* you, my pet. I *know* you."

My heart lurches and I suck in a breath. "You know nothing about me." My words are filled with as much venom as I can muster, but I'm silently cursing myself for falling prey to his intimidation.

He reaches for the locket I keep around my neck. I quickly smack his hand on instinct and clench the locket in my fist like it's my only lifeline.

His eyes glow and his smile turns predatory. "*I* know you, Aislinn. *You* do not know yourself."

I shiver again, this time not from the cold.

Being called 'pet' makes my skin crawl, but somehow, my name on Erebus's lips is so much worse.

"Come, there is something I wish to show you before we leave for Millena's palace." Erebus puts out a hand in offering.

"Millena's palace? I thought we were going to court?" I stand still, silently rejecting his offer.

"Millena was the Goddess of Balance. She was between life and death, between dark and light. She was the essence of equality. We gathered at her palace since the beginning of time. Neutral territory that sits right in between Etalo Olvipo'at and the Shadows. In her absence, Agnar keeps the peace...yes, *that* Agnar, god of war. It's actually mildly entertaining to watch him strain against his very nature. Now come, pet. I will not ask again."

Erebus grabs my hand as we are swarmed by his shadows and cast into icy darkness. It's like everything around us is morphing and twisting into perverted versions of reality cloaked through a veil of smoke.

We appear before a large uncut stone basin that shines with a pearlescent liquid in an otherwise empty room. Room might be too generous; it's more like a gutted-out closet, repurposed to conceal whatever it is that the basin is used for. The walls are made of gray unfinished stone, and there's a cold, stale air that has goosebumps instantly rising along my arms.

"What is that?" I rub the chill away and nod towards the basin.

He smirks. "A portal of sorts made from pure imperialite. It's called an isvipotale." Erebus opens his palm and a mist of shadow produces something that resembles a Siphon Stone. Instead of clear, the inside swirls with a golden mist.

"And what is that?"

His teeth grind, and he speaks through tight lips. "Your lack of patience is wearing mine thin. *This* is the Opari Stone."

The Opari stone...one of the three stones that turned the Utikalo mortal. It's a struggle to keep the surprise out of my voice as I ask, "How did *you* get it?"

"I took it."

Of course he did.

As part of the three heads of the Utikalo, Opari had the sight of what was happening anywhere at that given moment. Forbis could see the past and Viitor the future. The Utikalo was Millena's only child, and therefore, was more inclined to seek balance. They grew tired of the fighting in the realm of gods and gave up their gifts to pursue mortal lives. They stabbed themselves with Siphon Stones to accomplish this. The Opari Stone must grant the ability to see anything as it is currently happening.

"Why do you have it?" I ask, reaching to take it from his hand.

He clenches his fist around the stone and his words are sharp. "If you stop asking questions, you will find out."

"Well, by all means, continue," I grind out with annoyance as I wait for his explanation.

"This Opari Stone allows me to see anything happening in our realm—and also yours. Anything that is *currently* happening. I can not see what has yet to happen. I can not see what has passed. This, my dear pet, is how I was able to communicate with you." His eyes flash with an emotion I can only describe as smug. "As I was checking in on something earlier, I came upon a rather unexpected turn of events that may be of interest to you." He smiles with anticipation, sending dread slithering down my spine.

Erebus takes the Opari Stone and lets it sink into the basin that is already filled with shimmering liquid that is lapping up around the rough edges of the imperialite. The pearlescent colors begin to shimmer and shift, mixing with the gleaming gold of the stone, until it shows an image of a place I am vividly familiar with—my home in Caeliss, my little dining table to be exact, the one where I shared meals with Audrina. Sitting at the table, in the exact seat he always picks, is DeLuca. A swell of longing painfully blooms in my chest. My breathing becomes shallow as I try to reach into the basin only to be stopped by a cold hand.

"Watch, but *never* touch."

With a small nod, I turn back to the scene in the basin. DeLuca is sitting at the table and talking. His words are muffled through the liquid, and I can't make them out. There are two steaming cups of tea laid before him. He's talking to someone with blonde hair, but I can only see the back of her head. He's laughing...a light reaching his eyes. She puts a familiar hand on his shoulders as she tosses her head back, joining in. That's when I notice all the fresh plants in the room that weren't there before. The blonde moves her head to the side slightly, revealing a scar from temple to cheek, narrowly avoiding a white eye...Lysette.

"I don't understand." I squint and wait for the scene to change, for something else to happen, something that will shine a light on their interaction, but the constricting in my belly tells me what I need to know. Lysette is living there. In *my* house. With DeLuca.

And they've gotten close. It's clear to anyone with eyes. The way their bodies shift toward each other. The familiarity of being able to casually touch one another. And those smiles. They've been growing impossibly close, all while I've been taken by Erebus. Anger replaces the longing in my chest, threatening to consume me from within.

Erebus is smiling. "Moving on didn't take long, did it?"

I hate him.

"Whatever this is, it's wrong. You're wrong. DeLuca loves me. Lysette would never betray me like that." I seethe. "I tire of your games, Erebus."

His smile only widens at my words. A light flaring behind the shadows in his eyes. He leans down, hovering over my shoulder while I continue stare at the image. "Just like your dearest friend, *Audrina*, would never betray you? Do you not see what is so plainly before you, Aislinn? Time works differently between realms. It has been days since you've arrived *here*. But it has been *months* in the mortal realm. They have already mourned you."

"Liar." I feel the bite of repressed tears as I again watch the familiarity pass between the two. I try to press down the jealousy, to tell myself it is not what it seems, but the longer I look, the more it hurts. Even if it has only been days, I miss him. I miss him like I'd miss a limb, and to see this—whatever this is—hurts, because it should be me beside him.

I should be the one sitting at the table. I should be sharing a home with him, that's supposed to be my life.

But I'm stuck here.

With *him*.

"You see? It is time to stop fighting *me*; they have stopped fighting *for you*."

The words DeLuca spoke before we left for the Capital sear into my memory; *Don't you understand if something happened to you I'd have to burn the whole realm?* He meant it. I didn't know for sure then, but I know now. After all, didn't I beg him to watch over my friends? Especially Lysette? I'm jealous, sure, I can admit that to myself. But not in the way Erebus assumes. I know DeLuca. I know he won't give up so easily. I don't care what kind of tricks Erebus has planned.

I know *my* god.

But Erebus doesn't.

And he doesn't know me.

It's time I start playing his game by *my* rules.

He only has to *think* he's the one in control.

I lift my chin, letting him see the fury in my eyes, allowing him to believe he's won.

"What would you have me do?"

He smiles in vicious victory. "We begin with your indoctrination."

FOUR
PLACE FOR US
DeLuca

THIS MIGHT BE MY least favorite room in all of Caeliss. The council chamber—a building dedicated to meetings with the Elders and occasionally the people of Caeliss. Paintings depicting old stories of the gods cover nearly all wall space. They're crammed together so close that there's barely enough of a gap for a finger between each of the ornate frames.

My gaze snatches on one of the portraits of Erebus. He's cloaked in shadow and standing in front of a moon, nearly extinguishing all of its beauty. Probably one of the more realistic depictions, in my opinion. The rest are all greatly embellished.

Six chairs head the front of the room, and rows of benches spread out before them. The way seating is designed, we—as the guests—are forced to look up at the members making up the small council charged with the safety of Caeliss.

This doesn't work for me. I will not be made to feel small. Not by cowards who hide from threats rather than fight them.

"I'm leaving, Lysette too. We've already decided, so there is no point in trying to talk us out of it." My voice is stern and unwavering as I stride toward the six eldest of Children of Astoria.

On the council is Alec, Demetrius, Priestess Alis, an eikvidalis named Lyle, Wrenna—who aside from being a pain in the ass is also a grounder, and the last position is filled by an illusionary named Kainon. Leighra also sits in on Elder business as Kainon's translator and as his eventual successor. He is deaf and needs someone fluent in the language of hands, and considering she is his granddaughter, she has been taught since birth.

I make a point to ignore her. Ever since Leighra attempted to throw a knife in Aislinn's chest while in Sutton, I haven't been able to look at her without seeing it. She would have done it without a second thought. Acting on outdated orders. Caeliss might not have an army, but she's a soldier at her core.

We haven't spoken since she and Cass, along with Wrenna, came to retrieve me and Lys from the island. Tensions have been thick. She is too proud to apologize, and I won't accept it if she does. Blind loyalty is dangerous.

"Where are you to go?" Priestess Alis asks. She seems genuinely curious and not suspicious like I would have thought.

I roll out my neck, feeling the tension gathering there and begging for release. "We will start by going back through the Obsidian Mountains. To Lysette's home...or whatever is left of it."

Lysette speaks up, her voice strong. "When we were on Sutton Isle, Lady Soliel showed us her private archive, a room filled with histories of Children and gods. My father had a similar room, but I was never able to access it before. I believe I may have an idea of how to do it now."

I admire how resilient she has grown in the last few weeks. A far cry from the spoiled governing daughter I'd met when I was nothing more than a serv in her manor. Well...a spy and a serv.

"Our rules are clear. Once you come to Caeliss, you can not leave," Wrenna says, her jaw set and eyes hard.

Rules. There is always some *rule.*

I am growing weary of living by the rules of others, especially when they stand between me and Aislinn. It's time I leave this place.

"Fuck your rules," I say with a rumble burning my throat.

The brash words stun the Elders. Lysette takes a few deliberate steps away from me in case I spontaneously ignite.

"DeLuca, you forget yourself," Wrenna says. Her voice is so bitter it's a wonder she doesn't choke on it.

"No, *Wrenna*, you forget *yourself*. I am a *god*. Are you not here to live by the will of the gods?"

Wrenna scowls and folds her arms, but has no retort.

"He has a point, Wren," Lyle says, placing a hand tenderly on the woman's shoulder.

She turns her grueling gaze to him. "He is not a god worthy of our worship. Gods are meant to build, not destroy. He is no better than the one who sired him."

Kainon starts moving his hands swiftly to convey his thoughts, none of which I am able to decipher. I haven't known many people well-versed in the language of hands and never had a reason to learn it. I'm beginning to think I should have taken the time to learn all the languages, even the dead ones.

Leighra translates on behalf of her grandfather. "We do not get to choose which gods are worthy of worship. We honor each for a purpose."

"If you ask me—" Alec begins but stops short when he notices the heat of my stare.

"We *didn't* ask you," I say, letting the flare of my temper bring the temperature even higher.

"Enough." Priestess Alis finally interjects. "Here's truth of the matter: DeLuca *is* a god, and we are to bend to the will of the gods. There is also the truth that we do not allow anyone to leave to *protect* the families within Caeliss."

"You have such little trust in us after everything?" Lysette asks.

"We have reason not to," Wrenna says.

"They must go," Demetrius says calmly, earning the spotlight.

"What do you see?" Lyle asks.

"It is not what I currently see, it is what I have seen. This is the path DeLuca must take for all of our sakes." His ambiguous response only brings more questions.

"Will we be safe, Demetrius?" Priestess Alis asks.

"Everyone has a role to play. Things are murky beyond his departure, but I feel the tug of fate calling him," Demetrius responds, avoiding the question.

Always non-answers and vague prophecies with him. I wonder if he really is as talented a seer as everyone thinks he is. If so, how did he not see Aislinn being taken? My eyes narrow on him. I study his face, feeling a muscle in my cheek feather. He looks back at me with sorrow. A trail of fire swims up my spine as a thought clicks into place.

"*You knew.*" My gravelly tone shakes the walls.

Demetrius says nothing, not needing me to elaborate before he nods once. A silent confession.

"Knew what?" Lysette asks, looking between us in confusion.

"Tell them. Tell them all what you knew." I'm seething. I feel the flames flicker beneath my skin.

Demetrius looks around calmly, serene even. *The bastard.*

He clears his throat and speaks without a hint of remorse. "I knew Aislinn would be taken to the gods' realm. I knew Erebus wanted her. I know she has a larger role to play even if I can no longer see her. I know she is on her woven path."

No one looks surprised other than Lysette and Leighra.

The prick of fire between my shoulder blades begins to itch as it begs for release. "You *all* knew," I say with realization.

Priestess Alis at least has the decency to look remorseful, fiddling with her robe and keeping her head down.

"It was the *best* path," Demetrius explains.

"She's your blood, your granddaughter!" I'm losing the inch of control I held. The flames ignite between my shoulders.

Demetrius raises his voice. "And Heidon is my grandson! I knew what sacrifices had to be made. I am responsible for keeping all the people of Caeliss safe. *All* of them. Not just my blood. The good for the many is more important than the few. As a god, that is a lesson you will soon learn, of that I have no doubt!"

The heavy steps of my boots headed toward his chair echo throughout the room. I'm close enough to see the beads of sweat forming at his hairline when I grab him by his shirt and pull him forward so our noses almost touch.

"Let me make this very clear, *Demetrius.* The only reason you will live beyond this day is because of your relation to Aislinn. I will leave it in her hands what happens to you *after* I have rescued her from the god you *sacrificed* her to."

Alec clears his throat. "We should put it to a vote."

I lose it. The ground shakes and winds shriek past in fierce gusts, knocking all their precious paintings to the ground. The flames stretch from either hand and across my back like wings of fire.

I push Demetrius back into his seat. The prickling need to expel the chaos in me increases.

"Fuck. Your. Vote."

The windows around the room burst as I let the feeling consume me, letting go of any reasonable thought. All I feel is rage. It is as much a part of me as I it, and we will burn cities.

"DeLuca...DeLuca, stop. You will bring the building down. You're going to *kill* us!" Lysette's shaking voice worms through that wall of anger built around me like a shield and calls me back to sensibility like a beam of pure light.

On an exhale, the ground stops shaking and the winds stop blowing. The fire extinguishes, leaving plumes of smoke in its wake. The entire room is in disarray, but the look of horror imprinted on each of the Elder's faces is worth the momentary slip of control.

I may have felt guilty for it once, before I knew they deserved this and so much worse.

"Come, Lys, we are leaving this place." I grit out the words, using everything within my power to reign in the tsunami of emotions.

"You can't," Wrenna says, standing on shaking feet and lifting her chin to regain some dignity.

I snort out an unamused laugh. "How do you plan to stop me?"

"Was that the best way to handle that?" Lysette asks once we've made it back to our house to pack our things.

"Probably not, but this is no longer the place for us. I grow tired of the games people play when seeking control. They should not have withheld the information about Ailie. If we had more of a warning, we could have planned better."

"If they told you, would you have let her go?"

"No," I say without hesitation.

"Maybe the alternative was much worse."

Lysette is ever the rationalist. Sometimes it drives me crazy. Sometimes, it's exactly what I need.

I drop my head into my hands and take a few deep breaths before I'm able to speak calmly.

"I'm suffocating without her. Everyday, I feel as though I am dying." I say quietly, "I don't care about anything else right now."

"Ouch," she says with a playful smile.

"You know what I mean."

"That you'd let the realm dissolve into chaos as long as Ailie's safe. Yeah, I get it, dramatic, but I guess sort of romantic at the same time."

I give a half smile and continue packing our leather rucksacks. "Are you sure you want to follow me on this path? Once we go, there is no turning back. I don't think I will receive a warm welcome here after my little show."

"I'm sure. But we are going to have to work on your power outlet so we don't destroy the rest of Katova...and we have to tell Rett. Prepare yourself because I'm absolutely positive he is not going to like it."

He is an overprotective brother on his best day. I can already see the scene play out. He's going to try to come with us. And then Iris is going to beg him not to. Then he will argue with her and Lysette, then more than likely threaten me. Ultimately, he won't come because Iris has such a hold on him that he might as well be chained to her.

"Is that something we *really* have to do?"

"Yes." She pats my arm and strolls past me with a victorious smile.

I pull her bag over my shoulder with my own. "Alright, let's get it over with then."

FIVE
KAOKET
Aislinn

EREBUS'S PALACE IS SURPRISINGLY simple and decorated in various shades of gray. The wallpaper is a swirl of damask designed to resemble his shadows. The ceilings are extravagantly tall. From our spot in the foyer, I can see three floors up. There's a crystal chandelier hanging over our heads, probably the size of a standard transport back in Stellera. The dim light is refracted all around us and creates an illusion of shadows moving. It's strangely beautiful.

"I still don't understand why I have to be introduced formally in the first place. I've already been here for days."

He breathes out, and I swear he says something on the breath, but it's indiscernible. "We have discussed this, pet. We all must follow rules. No one may enter the realm without the blessing of Haile's precious council."

"But why the rules? Aren't you all gods? What's the worst that can happen if you choose not to submit?"

He turns to me with glowing eyes. "Do you plan to annoy me until I let you go? Is that your grand plan?" I hold my ground and look up at him innocently, not balking from the intensity of his stare. His eyes shift between mine before he deflates. "That is just how it is. Those are the rules, set into place by beings able to inflict a wide variety of punishments upon those who do not follow them."

"I am surprised you follow anyone's rules but your own."

He smiles wickedly. "You have much to learn about me—and this realm. Even gods are not spared from a hierarchy, and ours tend to be a tad on the ruthless side. In fact, you may find you favor *me* over the others. A delightful twist that would be, wouldn't it, pet?"

"I highly doubt it."

He smirks as he brushes the mark he bestowed upon my right arm using the back of his fingers. "Do you know why I placed my mark upon you, Aislinn?"

"To mess with DeLuca?"

I rub the sides of my dress down, pretending to smooth it out, just to give my hands something to do instead of fidget. My nerves are alight from thinking about meeting the other gods...especially Haile...but I don't want to show Erebus how the anticipation is affecting me. I won't give him any weakness to latch onto.

His eyes crinkle in the corners as if he's trying to smile but has forgotten how. "No. I placed it upon you to show that you belong to the Shadows. That you belong to *me*. Among other reasons."

"Ah, labeling me as—what is the word you're so fond of? Oh right, *pet*." I roll my eyes.

He ignores me and continues. "As a mortal belonging to me, you will be under my protection. No one will be able to harm you without answering to Haile."

"Unless you are the one causing the harm, right? Isn't that how this works? As your property, you can handle me however you see fit?" I raise my eyebrow.

"Even by me. I told you, we *all* must follow the rules."

This confession is unexpected, and I step back, trying to assess his sincerity. I believed wholeheartedly that Erebus's intentions were sinister. Never did I imagine that I'd be *safe* in his presence. Not that I believe a word that comes out of his mouth. But, he hasn't touched me yet even though he has had ample opportunity, and I suppose that is something.

"Come now, pet, we mustn't be late. The king absolutely detests waiting. I'm going to need you to hold onto me and not break contact. I'm going to shadow us there."

"We don't have to kiss again, do we?" Bile rises at the thought.

He leans in so that his breath caresses my ear. "Only if you want to."

"Absolutely not."

There's a small chuckle in his throat. "Just take my arm."

With a small grunt of annoyance, I loop my arm through his and close my eyes. It feels as if we are flying against a blizzard. My insides twist. There's nothing solid around me. We are particles moving through space. I tighten my grasp on Erebus. I may despise him, but he is the only thing keeping me from spinning out into a void of endless nothing. After the longest minutes of my life, my feet land on hard stone. My eyes are still shut tight while I move my feet around—testing the stability.

Erebus's icy breath makes the skin along my neck rise. "Open your eyes, Aislinn," he whispers. "We are here."

I blink in the majesty of the palace before us. We are standing in a courtyard. To the left of us is a lush green garden with a glowing aura, freckled in vibrant flowers and trees with perfectly ripened fruits. To the right is in direct contrast with the left. It's as though someone drew a line directly down the center and stole all the life from one side to push it into the other.

There are skeletons of dead trees stretching as far out as the eye can see, spaced so tightly together they create an almost wall-like effect. The palace is just as divided; the left side is entirely white with a slight iridescent sheen that sparkles in the strange sunlight. The right side of the palace is a range of gray, completely colorless, yet still beautiful in the same way that the Obsidian Manor once was.

A line of people...no, *not* people—gods—are walking into the grand entry doors that sit directly on the line between gray and white. There are dozens of them, each one better looking than the last. There are a few other beings I can only describe as *creatures*, some humanoid, some unlike any animal I've ever seen.

When I look up at Erebus, I notice his entire demeanor has hardened, and there's an obvious reluctance.

He must sense my eyes on him because he rolls a shoulder, releasing some of that tension in his stance and says, "Welcome to Kaoket."

I pull my arm out from his.

"Millena's palace?" I once again take in my surroundings. It's awe-inspiring, each side its own kind of beautiful, and it makes perfect sense that Millena would live between two vastly different lands as the goddess of balance. "It is so...literal."

One side of Erebus's mouth quirks and seems to relax a fraction more. "Indeed. The left is the side of life. It is called Etalo Olvipo'at. Some simply call it the Olvi. I, of course, prefer *proper* names." He points out the skeletal forest. "And there lies the Imorti Woods, the border between Kaoket and the Shadows. So, you see, we stand directly between the light and dark. Kaoket translates to *center*. The Creator was not very creative."

I take everything in with a pinch of my brows. "The Creator?"

"Do you always ask so many questions?! Katoeieut, *Kato*, is the *Creator*. It gave life to Haile, Egon, and Millena as well as the Weavers and a handful of other gods, most of which perished as a result of the God's War. Utterly ridiculous."

I want to ask more about Kato and the war, but I can see I am already testing Erebus's patience, not that I don't love pulverizing his restraint, but I also am enjoying not being secluded to my room, so I decide not to push him.

The Weavers I have heard of, though not much. While we were researching in Lady Soleil's archives, I remember coming across a passage on them. Quintuplets who decide the fate of, well, everything. They weave destinies from the threads of fate. Though I have to admit the idea that each event in *every* life is determined by five shut-ins sounds a little more than unlikely.

Look where you are, Aislinn.

Nothing is unlikely.

I'm chewing the inside of my cheek and lost in thought when I look up to find Erebus's gray eyes piercing my skin.

"What?" I meet his gaze with what I hope is the same intensity and a bite in my tone.

"I expected another question." He shrugs.

"Don't expect anything from me. You don't know who I am."

He chuckles, and though his voice is hardly above a whisper, I swear I hear him say, "You have no idea."

The inside of Millena's palace isn't what I expected. The harsh contrast of the outside led me to believe the inside would be just as divided, but somehow, there is a perfect synergy instead. A large sculpture of balanced scales serves as a fountain in the grand foyer. The sound from the cascading water is soothing and peaceful. Soft cream walls pair beautifully with the large windows giving an aura of light and airy. The majority of the decorations are darker shades like maroon or forest green, a perfect compliment to the muted base. The overall effect creates a harmonious aesthetic. Agnar may reside here now, but there is not even a hint of his rumored wrath and temper. It feels comforting...and familiar.

The halls are mostly empty, odd considering I watched dozens of gods shuffling through the doors just before us. We don't go far before we find a large set of double doors. The frame is engraved with swirling filigree and ancient writing that looks like...Old Daeil, maybe? But because I can't read Old Daeil, it looks like pretty swirls and lines to me.

Erebus leads me into the large room and I find it similar to one we'd see in the king's court. There is a raised platform with five chairs; one large in the center ornately decorated with leaves made of some kind of metal I am unfamiliar with, but it is comparable to opal-gilded iron; strong and beautiful.

The others on either side are smaller and more simply decorated with a small sigil unique to each at the head. A moon, bolt of lightning, skull, and dagger. The benches that surround the room are at staggered height to allow all occupants an unobstructed view of the stage, and it reminds me of a kind of theater which makes sense because if this court is anything like the king's court in Stellera, it's all just a show.

The gods talk amongst themselves in the already filled seats. I am so far out of my depth here. I swallow, trying to remind myself to not show weakness. Never would I have expected to be in a room with so much divinity. Especially because I believed them to be nothing more than beautiful myths only months ago.

I recognize two from visions I have had. Cintamarri, the god of desire, is dressed in low hanging gold pants and a loose fitting cream shirt. Even from across the room, my mouth waters and skin begins to tingle at the sight of him.

The goddess of love and art, Edwissa, has a crown made of flowers and wears a flowing gown with every color I've ever seen...and some I haven't. Two tiny creatures resembling women with almost clear wings fly beside Edwissa. I take them to be her muses, but they are much smaller than they are in the old text depictions.

Many of the gods cease their conversations as they spot us. I'm not sure if it's me or Erebus that draws their faces into sneers. Especially the one standing directly next to the podium with red hair and yellow eyes which seem almost serpentine. I look elsewhere—at the pillars, the molding, the maroon curtains flowing on a phantom breeze. But I still feel her stare.

I'm so caught up in trying to avert my gaze that I jump slightly when Erebus touches the line he's left in my skin. It turns so cold it burns and returns the sense of hollowness through my body, causing me to shiver.

Leaning down so I can almost feel his chin on my shoulder, he whispers, "You will be fine, pet. Avert their gazes. Come, follow me." His hand wraps around my wrist. His grasp is firm and burns like cold stones in winter.

He leads me close to the raised platform and instructs me to sit in a row close to the floor. I do as commanded because, honestly, I am completely overwhelmed. I have no idea what is happening, nor the temperament of these gods that can end entire civilizations on a mood swing.

"Stay," he commands.

I scowl but nod as he turns and disappears behind a curtain hanging from the raised platform. My wrist still burns even in his absence, so I look down to examine it.

"Bastard," I say under my breath when I see a shadow cuff placed upon me. There is no visible chain, but I am sure if I were to test it by wandering, I would feel the effects of a tug.

Maybe this is how he keeps Astoria at bay.

My spine straightens. Realization hits me that I have not seen the goddess of beauty and night. Not in Erebus's home. Not here. I scan the crowd for familiar white hair, her painted skin, her familiar eyes she gifted to her son that I'd be able to spot from miles away because his are forever burned into my heart.

I hold my locket and try not to imagine what he and Lysette are doing right now.

Searching for me.

They're trying to find a way to me.

You know this, Aislinn. In your bones.

I will not let Erebus's mind games find their hold in my thoughts; I *know* DeLuca.

"You're new," a female's voice says from the row of benches behind me. I look up to see a pair of intense violet eyes staring back at me from a goddess with raven hair, who appears to be much younger than her peers.

"I am," I say quietly, unsure of who I am talking to or the best way to do so.

"We don't get anyone *new* often. It's been—" She taps on her chin with long pink fingernails as she thinks—"maybe six hundred years or so, probably longer."

She seems friendly enough. A little conversation won't hurt...it might piss Erebus off. Actually, I'm not seeing a downside. "Probably because the portals are so finicky."

Her brows shoot up until they're hidden beneath her curtain of bangs. "You're from the realm of mortals?" I nod, and she lets out a noise that's almost a laugh. "How? Why?"

I lift my wrist and show the shadow cuff, hoping it will give her the answer I don't feel like vocalizing. Her face changes to sympathetic with a fake pout.

"I'm Helena." She offers a genuine smile.

"Helena?" My words come out in an obvious tone of disbelief. "The Reaper?"

Helena's smile falls. "I prefer to think of myself as a greeter."

"Oh, I didn't mean to offend you. You're just referred to as the Reaper back home," I say with a sliver of guilt.

This is starting off well.

"Oh believe me, I know, I have heard it every time I returned. Back when we went between realms freely, before the Gods' War when everything changed. They called me Reaper then as well. I was blamed for the deaths of their loved ones...as if *I* had any control over it." She scoffs. "I am a *messenger* goddess. I have no control over who lives or dies. In fact, I never was intended to escort the shadows of the dead at all...I did it so they wouldn't have to be alone. My father's methods lacked a certain decorum, and my brother...well, you've met him. Erebus isn't the most considerate." She nods to the cuff around my wrist.

I snort. "No, he is not."

When reading about the Reaper...about Helena...she was always depicted as a monster. Cruel and dark, with claws that she used to rip the shadows from mortal bodies. Never would I have guessed this beautiful, welcoming woman could be the same Reaper of children's nightmares.

She shifts slightly and I notice she has giant white wings folded behind her. They're beautiful, so beautiful it's almost painful to look at. She is not at all the monster she is made out to be.

I have a suspicion that I don't know nearly as much as I thought I did about the gods...and what little I do know...is wrong.

"So, why did the lord of brooding and darkness bring you here?"

"If you find out, let me know."

A loud bang makes me jump as the door behind the raised platform opens. I recognize some of the gods who storm through. The air radiates with so much power and in such an extreme amount I can taste it—like a storm waiting to be unleashed.

The room silences as Haile takes his seat in the center, followed by Agnar in the dagger chair. A god with large falcon-like wings and a head full of chestnut curls sits in the chair with the bolt, and Erebus beside him in the moon chair. The skull chair remains empty, and Helena stares at it with tight lips.

"Who sits there?" I ask.

"It's supposed to be Egon."

"Is he still imprisoned?"

"Yup. For a few hundred years now."

I lean closer to Helena and lower my voice. "Where is Astoria?"

She looks at the place where Astoria should sit with a heaviness. "Broken." Her voice is full of regret.

Broken.

Erebus told me as much when we were in the cave on the Island of Shadows: *She's not dead, just broken,* were his exact words. What do they do with a broken goddess?

"Erebus gets to sit in for her?"

Helena nods.

"Who sits for Egon?"

"No one."

"Why don't you?"

"Because my mother wasn't a god. She was Claudia, harbinger of madness. I'm lucky Haile allowed me to be called a goddess at all. He wanted to make me a guardian because of my half-breed blood."

I don't miss that she uses the term '*was*' when speaking about her mother. I've, of course, heard of harbingers, but they're usually unnamed entities. I'm about to ask her more when Haile clears his throat, and his voice booms, echoing off the walls. "Potoevikpois lolluy pouais, yo poeietalot eu aviiskaisis el koy wviisvieut." Whispers and gasps from the crowded room punctuate his words.

"What did he say?" I ask Helena.

"Greetings, fellow gods, we gather to discuss a new visitor," she translates.

She climbs down to the seat beside me. Haile continues to speak in Dailliot while Helena continues to relay his words in the common tongue.

"It has been centuries since we have allowed a mortal into our realm. My nephew thinks this one may be able to cure my daughter, Astoria. She is to be welcomed and is not to be harmed. She will remain in the Shadow Palace with Erebus until her role has been fulfilled. No one is to touch her—no one is to speak with her, not without first asking Erebus for permission. She is under his care for as long as she remains in our realm."

I fold my arms and lean back in my chair, annoyance tugging my face down. "Why is he so possessive?"

She winces. "Erebus is complicated, but believe me when I tell you that you will need his protection in our realm. You mortals only know a fraction of our truth, and your stories are usually terribly wrong. I mean, they're really, *really* wrong about almost everything."

"I don't believe they're wrong about Erebus." I risk a glance in his direction. He looks like a pompous ass sitting in his mini-throne.

She laughs. "Maybe not, but if he hasn't harmed you yet, he probably won't."

Probably.

"What do you think he means by 'I can cure' Astoria?'"

She shrugs.

Erebus stands. "Aislinn Theodora Delphia, rise so all may look upon you and know what is mine."

What is mine. I can't decide whether to roll my eyes or barf. Oh, wait...Aislinn Theodora Delphia...that's me. I shudder at the use of my full name. It no longer feels as though it suits me, and I hate the way it sounds coming from his mouth.

The gods are staring at me. I don't need to rise for them to know I am the piece that doesn't belong. Taking a controlled breath, I stand and keep my eyes on the four gods, not wanting to look at the others—though I feel their gazes burying beneath my skin. Erebus watches the three gods beside him. Soren and Haile look me up and down with mild interest. But Agnar, his reaction is peculiar. He is squinting and rubbing his eyes as though he has seen a ghost.

SIX
NOT ON FIRE
DeLuca

THE SICKLY SWEET HERBAL aroma turns my stomach. This vile smell screams Iris. We have only just walked in through the threshold of Rett's place, and he already has a deep scowl. I can tell this is going to go exactly as I thought it would. I don't even pretend with pleasantries. Instead, I lean against the wooden doorframe with my arms crossed and wait for Lysette to say her piece. Rett and I have a strained relationship on our best day, and I'm pretty sure this isn't going to be one of our best days.

"Absolutely not," Rett says as soon as he spots our packs resting by my feet.

"You don't even know what we came to say," Lysette says with an uncharacteristically childish whine.

Iris continues to eye me uncomfortably. She keeps one hand protectively over the small bump of her belly. I can't help but roll my eyes as she side-steps further behind Rett. Playing at being a frightened helpless girl, but she forgets...I lived in that manor too. I see her for what she is. What she's *done*.

"Word travels fast in Caeliss. Alec told Sylvie while Iris was with her, training to be a midwife—she told her about your outburst with the Elders. You're *not* going back to Obsidian."

"We're going," I say with enough fire to have Rett's beady eyes flare. "Your sister was offering the courtesy of informing you. Not asking permission."

"*You* can go wherever the Haile you want. You don't need Lysette. As the lord of Obsidian, I forbid her to go back." The muscle in his jaw ticks and he folds his arms.

Something snaps in my resolve. "You're no longer a lord, Urson, let it go."

"I'm going to help him save Aislinn." Lysette's voice is far too soft for the severity of her features. "You can't stop me...but you're my brother, and I don't want you to worry. I'll be okay."

"If you're going, then I'm coming too." Rett huffs.

"No," all three of us say in unison.

It's almost worth the trip here to see his face right now. With a clenched fist, he looks at Iris. She places a gentle hand on his arm in what I can only guess is an attempt to placate him. He knows he's not going to win this fight. "When do you leave?"

"Now," I reply. Rett opens his mouth to say something, but I cut him off. "I *know*, if anything happens to her—I've heard it before."

If eye contact could be wielded as a weapon, I'd be dead beneath his glare, but as luck would have it, dirty looks hit about as hard as a summer breeze.

"And yet, where *is* Ailie?" Rett's jab strikes its mark. The familiar prickle of heat rises along the bridge of my shoulders.

"Why don't you go outside?" Lysette suggests. I can only grunt in response. I'm using all my focus not to burn the place down.

Outside, I take a few calming breaths. I summon a small gust of wind to cool my temper off. I haven't mastered the elements yet. They're definitely tied to my emotions. My affinity for fire is not lost on me, especially when each time I feel something passionately—like anger—I release actual flames.

My control is slowly getting better with all the help Lys has given me. Her lessons in bottinial abilities apply to all of my elements. I just have to find the thread of which one I want to use. Even with the lessons, the fire is still unpredictable. It's like it's always flickering, and the second my blood begins to heat, the flames take over.

I look at the lines of identical houses on either side of the path. Lately, I have felt too large for them. Too large for Caeliss and too large for Katova, like I no longer belong here...but maybe it's because I miss Aislinn so godsdamn much. Nowhere will be home without her. I just pray to whatever gods are listening that she's alright and that I won't be too late.

Whatever gods except Erebus.

He can go fuck himself.

"Ready?" Lysette smiles as she shuts the door to her brother's house, hopping down the steps and causing the flowers to bloom behind her as she walks towards me. I admit it's slightly endearing.

"Mhmm." I shrug our bags over my shoulder.

"We should say goodbye to Cass too," she says while picking some of the freshly bloomed flowers and tying them at the stem with a thin vine to make a bouquet.

"I don't know if she will want to see me." I rub my hand on the back of my neck.

Lysette shoves the bouquet into my hands. "It's Cass, she's the most understanding person I have ever met."

"Okay...she's probably in the infirmary...with Heidon."

"That's what the flowers are for." Lysette agrees with a sad nod.

We walk the cobblestone path leading through town. The wet stones echo beneath each footstep. You can smell the impending winter on the brisk air. I'm using the Siphon Stone to keep the rain off of us.

As we pass the spot where I found Aislinn all those months ago, the memory of finding her floating above the ground sends another bolt of panic to my chest as if it's happening all over again. Her first real encounter with Erebus. When he first marked her. The same air-sucking helplessness that made me want to cleave this realm apart with my bare hands.

"You're heating up," Lysette says, bringing me back from my swirling thoughts.

I shrug the packs over my shoulder and tighten my hold on their straps. "Sorry. I was thinking about when Erebus first marked Aislinn."

Her face turns a little green at what I can only imagine is the image of Aislinn being marked up by that disgusting pervert. "Why do you think he's so obsessed with her?"

"Isn't it obvious? To get to me. He knew how I felt about her. He took her to punish me. He continues to punish me for living."

"Erebus could have messed with you in other ways." She sticks her tongue in her cheek as if she's holding back words.

"What are you not saying?"

"I'm saying it's entirely possible he took her for another reason."

Flashes of skin and shadows colliding push into my imagination. They turn my stomach so severely it causes actual pain. It's making me sick.

His mouth on hers...his *mouth* on *hers*. *Gods, what if he's forced her to do something unspeakable? I'll kill him.*

I will fucking kill him.

Even if it destroys me.

The infirmary is small and so rarely used it gets forgotten. The stone walls are overrun with cracks from the ground settling below it, and the inside is cold—and depressing. Except Heidon's room which has fresh flowers brought in each day and cheery yellow curtains hanging in front of the window. They leave it open so the air doesn't become stale. His mother, Maegora, knit him a quilt of yellows and blues she keeps high up to his neck. She has a hard time being in the room. She mostly stays in the meadows praying to gods. I'm not sure which ones. They probably don't listen anyway.

Cass still comes. Every day, for hours. Sometimes she brings his little sister, Hadleigh. Today is one of those days. Lysette secures her eyepatch in place—afraid she will frighten the young girl.

"You're leaving." It's not a question as Cass observes the bags slung over my shoulder.

I nod and place the flowers in the vase beside the others, noticing they're the exact same. I should have known the daily flower delivery would come from Lysette.

Cass doesn't speak, just holds Heidon's hand tighter and inhales deeply.

"We just wanted to say goodbye," Lysette says. "We don't know when, if at all, we're coming back."

"Hmm," is all she replies.

"Are you okay?" I ask. Cass has been just about the only one of us who has seemed relatively unchanged by our trip to the Capital and Sutton. For her to be this quiet and void of emotion is unusual.

"I just—" Her voice breaks. Then she forces the words through the heartbreaking crack. "I've never lost anyone like this, and it's hard to see him here...but not here...I thought he'd be okay by now."

"If we make it to the gods' realm, we will try to find a way to release Heidon's shadow," Lysette says, placing a comforting hand on Cass's shoulder. I don't want to bring them down even more by reminding her she made a promise I'm not sure we can keep.

Hadleigh chimes in, "You'll make it."

We turn to her in question.

"Have you seen something, Hadleigh?" I ask quietly, trying not to scare her with the intensity of emotions I am feeling.

Her lip quivers. "I don't want to see it again. Don't make me see it again."

"Please, Hadleigh, do you know something that can help us?" I ask with pleading eyes.

She reluctantly nods. "I see cousin Aislinn, and I see you. You're fighting off creatures and people...there are so many people fighting...so many have abilities, strong ones. I think maybe they're gods...but they're here in our realm. Fields are covered in blood, red and blue, and bodies."

"Hadleigh!" Cass snaps her attention to her little cousin. "Why have you not told anyone?"

"I told Grandpapa," she admits. "He told me not to tell anyone else, that I'd only worry them, especially Mama. She's been so sad since Heidon went to sleep. She cries all day. "

That's too much to put on a nine-year-old girl. My heart breaks for her. For what Aislinn must have seen as a girl too—without anyone to talk her through it. I feel heat behind my eyes, not fire this time. This burn comes from the threat of tears. I take Hadleigh into a tight embrace. Both to comfort her and myself and maybe a version of Aislinn I never got to know.

"I'm sorry you saw something so horrible," I say as I pull her back from me. "But know if I was there, you would have been safe because I would never, and I mean *never*, let any harm come to you."

She smiles, but the youthful smile she had when we first arrived in Caeliss has been replaced by one that doesn't ever reach her purple-rimmed eyes. Another pull at my heartstrings for I've seen the same haunted look on Ailie more times than I can count.

"DeLuca?" her little voice whispers.

"Yes, Hadleigh?"

"She dreams about you...almost every night. She has nightmares, and then she sees you, and the bad things are gone."

"Who?" I say, already knowing the answer when my blood runs cold.

"Aislinn," she answers.

I close my eyes and take a deep inhale. Aislinn is still alive. She has to be if Hadleigh can still connect to her. I hug the little girl once again. She will never know what a gift she has just given me.

"Thank you," I say with renewed strength—and something dangerous...hope.

"Well, now I know I can't convince you to stay," Cass says with a sad laugh.

I pull her and Lysette into a hug. "You couldn't have anyway."

Raindrops are falling through the cracks in the woven treetops. Not as bad as being in the open like in Caeliss, but the sporadic drops are more than a little annoying as we trudge through the sticky mud-covered ground. I'd use the stone, but I'm using both hands to clear a path from the brush and trees and can't risk dropping it.

"Last chance, are you sure?"

Lysette swats my arm. "Stop checking on me. I'm just as determined to see this through as you are."

"Alright, I won't ask again. But if you need to turn around, be honest with me. I will take you as far back as Vristra's bog where I know you will be safe."

"You're worse than Rett sometimes." She rolls her eyes and climbs over a fallen tree. She has to use branches as steps to get over it because the trunk is so large, and even though I know she'd never admit it, it looks as if she is struggling with the climb.

"Why didn't you just move the tree?"

"It's already been uprooted from the ground. Its connection to life has been severed, therefore any connection I would have had to it has been cut off."

"Mmm." I nod and climb over the same tree with ease." It probably wouldn't be a good day for anyone if any of us found ourselves able to control dead things."

"No, it seems only one god is able to do that, and he is, thankfully, locked away."

"Egon...you think Haile still has him as a prisoner for killing their sister?"

"Would you let him go if you were Haile?"

I answer without hesitation. "Never."

The look she gives me says *"and you think he would?,"* but she doesn't vocalize it and continues trudging through the damp brush.

"Do you think the Liberators are still there?"

"At Obsidian?" She pauses. "Probably. I wouldn't be surprised if most of Ashe were there now."

My foot sloshes through a puddle, and I look up toward the hidden sky, cursing the wet weather. "We will have to play it safe. Pretend we are in league with them or maybe seeking refuge. It will be easy enough for me to blend in. Do you think you can?"

"I'm not sure...do you think they will recognize me from the family portraits?"

I study Lysette. Her one blue eye is now completely white, and she has a scar extending from above her eye to the corner of her mouth, but she is still recognizable. It's her hair—shining like the first ray of sunlight and falling in waves around her.

I sigh. "Yes. I'd still be able to pick you out easily by your hair—it screams *highborn*."

"My hair?" She takes the ends of it, examining the strands between fingers. "Easy enough, cut it."

"The color too, Lys."

She stops walking and closes her eyes with her head tilted back as if she's trying to recall something. She takes a deep inhale—and with her exhale, opens her eyes. "We can find some ennis root. It will change the color to red temporarily, and it thrives in the Thickett Woods." She shrugs and continues on as if it's nothing.

I laugh. I don't know why I am surprised. Lysette is not at all what I expected her to be. Each day is a reminder of how little I actually knew about the highborns I had hated my whole life.

The drizzle of rain sneaking through the trees turns into fluffy white flecks of snow. Lysette holds her hand out and watches the snow melt against the warmth of her palms. Her lips part, and her breathing deepens.

"First snow," she whispers.

"It's early." I don't really understand why she seems so sad about it.

Sad might even be an understatement. She looks like someone has stolen her still beating heart from her chest. Yes, snow is annoying, but with my ability to create fire, we won't be cold. I've become pretty skilled at raising my body temperature just enough to keep the chill away. So that's not something we will have to worry about too much. I can't help but feel as though I'm missing the significance of this moment, but looking at the pain so clearly written in her features, I decide not to press her on it. We've endured enough pain.

"Gods, I hate these woods," I say, trying to bring her out of whatever memory she's lost to.

Lysette chuckles and pats me on the shoulder. "At least you're not on fire."

SEVEN
DREAMING
Aislinn

IF MY MOTHER HAD been a good person, this is surely what her version of the Afterlands would've been. The gods know how to throw a party. Everything is coated in shimmering dust, creating a dreamlike atmosphere, paired with the lull of beautiful music that seemingly hovers around us. Even the air smells like...well, the air smells like laughter, which doesn't make any logical sense, but that's the only way to describe it.

Trays carrying a range of hors d'oeuvres and colorful spirits float in and out. The gods mingle amongst themselves, ignoring my existence. A few times, I caught eyes wandering to shadows around my wrist. I can't be sure if it's pity or amusement in their gazes before they are back to whatever conversation they were in.

The gods are not unlike the highborns of Stellera. I'd measure their personalities and temperaments to be much the same just from the behavior I've observed. They hold the same undeserved pride and arrogance.

I swallow thickly as I think of what Audrina would make of this. She'd probably excel at navigating the gods. Thrive in their presence instead of watching from outside. Perhaps she'd even be running things around here given enough time. I catch myself smiling at the thought before my memory catches up. My chest tightens at a vision of her laying in the sand surrounded by blood. The same image I've revisited again and again since I killed her.

She betrayed me.

She *betrayed* me and deserved the end she got.

She did deserve it.

I am again filled with the same anger that took control of my senses. The same anger that made it possible for me to kill someone I loved.

Deep, controlled breaths, Aislinn. Deep, controlled breaths.

"Exhausting aren't they?" Helena appears by my side. I raise my brows in question. "All of them, each and every one, think they're better than everyone else in this room. All of this is fake, a facade. Unnatural. Don't trust anything here."

"Does the warning extend to you as well?"

"Yes." She smiles deviously. "We gods are all bound by our duty assigned by Kato and the Weavers. You could be my best friend, but if it was my destiny to rip your still-beating heart from your chest, I would, no questions asked."

Fitting. "I stabbed my last best friend, so maybe it would be deserved." My voice doesn't hint at the whirlwind of emotion I'm feeling.

Helena's eyes sparkle and she grabs a drink off a tray floating by. "I *must* hear the rest of the story immediately."

A silky voice interrupts us. "Another time, Helena. I require Aislinn." Erebus appears at my side. Every place his shadows mark, my body cools, not like the frozen burn I've grown accustomed to; it's more like a snow-kissed breeze blowing against exposed skin.

"I am at your will, master." I mock bow, and Helena fails to conceal her amused smile behind her drink as she walks away.

"Adorable. Remember, *best* behavior."

"Of course, Lord Erebus." I roll my eyes.

Amusement rolls over his features before he replaces his stoic mask. "I am taking you to Haile, and then we are leaving this place as quickly as we are able. Did anyone talk to you?" His gray eyes narrow and quickly shift to Agnar, then to a god with large falcon-like wings before his jaw tightens. "Did anyone *touch* you?"

"No one touched me, and aside from Helena, it seems as though the gods are avoiding me like my mortality will rub off on them."

He seems satisfied by my answer and leads me to where a golden throne sits high above the rest of the party. I remember Haile from my visions. Somehow, they didn't quite do him justice. He has this glow, and in his presence there is a stirring beneath my skin. It's like the first day of summer or coming fully alive.

The god of life towers over me, easily seven feet tall, and he's bulky. Pure muscle he doesn't bother to cover. Gold tattoos shimmer across his bare chest and arms. They appear to be moving, shifting beneath his skin, but it could be a trick of light. His hair falls in blonde waves to his shoulders, and he wears a gold crown above it. I can tell he enjoys his power, and it radiates off of him like rays off the sun.

"Hello, mortal," Haile greets, his clovered-honey eyes fixed on me, and I can't help but wither beneath the sheer intensity of his focus. Nothing could have prepared me for how small I feel standing before the king of the gods.

"Am I supposed to bow? Curtsy? I'm not sure of your customs here," I admit, sliding my sweaty palms down the length of my smooth dress.

Haile continues his intense stare. I try not to fidget or shy away, but it becomes increasingly more difficult as knots twist in my belly. "Kneeling with your head down is preferable. If your eyes find mine, they will burn you from the inside out."

I shoot a look at Erebus who wears his annoyance like a cloak as he shakes his head.

Haile bursts into laughter that rattles the entire palace. "We do not concern ourselves with such formality. When you have lived an eternity, you learn what is and is not worth the fight. So tell me, mortal, how is it you plan on helping my dear Astoria?"

"I—ugh—I'm not sure to be honest."

Haile's relaxed face hardens, and he shifts towards Erebus. "Explain, trickster. You said she was here of her own accord. I assumed it meant you came to some understanding *before* bringing her to our realm."

Erebus shrugs. "The details of her arrival are a tad murky. She knows not who she is yet."

"Who *I am*?" I ask and turn my attention fully on Erebus. "What do you mean? Who *am* I?"

"The Utikalo." He answers while keep his eyes on Haile.

My face scrunches into one I know is unflattering as I look at Erebus. His ability to lie so smoothly, without even a hint of deception, is truly worrisome. He doesn't have any kind of tell to give him away, which will make deciphering his words that much harder.

"You do not know this already?" The veins in Haile's neck protrude and pulse with such force they might as well be snakes preparing to strike. "You are of no further use to me."

Okay, that hurts a little. Straight spine, Aislinn. Don't let your mask slip. Just like the highborns.

I fix my posture and attempt to look unaffected by Haile's words even as they reopen a wound I thought I'd closed off—my complete uselessness.

"The Utikalo must have taken its own memories. Not to worry, we shall have all returned and be on our woven path in no time," Erebus assures.

Haile glares at Erebus with suspicion and then turns to me. The furrow in his brow smooths out, and he nods once. "You should return to the Shadows. Agnar will soon realize, and this is the first gathering in some time where we haven't had a violent outburst."

Erebus tuts and says in a low voice, "I fear he may suspect her already."

Haile looks around, finding Agnar stealing subtle glances in our direction. "She doesn't leave the Shadows. Not until you fix Astoria and figure out that other problem. Make it your priority."

My laughter is met with confused stares from both gods, and I quickly compose myself. "This is a joke, right? I'm *not* the

Utikalo...I'm mortal. Born to a mortal mother and far descendant of a demi-god."

"You know nothing of what or who you are, pet, but I do." He pulls on the marks—making me shiver from the cold, and I can only guess he's reminding me to '*behave*' in front of Haile.

"Go, now, before it draws too many eyes," the king of gods says without so much as a second glance in my direction.

He doesn't have to repeat himself. Erebus takes me behind the curtain separating the throne from a small room behind, and in seconds, we are again surrounded by his shadows. When they dissipate—taking their cool caress with them—we are back in my lavish prison.

"How do you lie so easily?" I dip out of his grip.

"Well, they do call me the god of trickery. You will have to be more specific," he says while drawing my drapes closed, a pointless gesture when all that lays beyond them is eternal darkness.

Folding my arms, I lean against the bedpost. "About me being the Utikalo?"

"Who said it was a lie?"

"It's not possible." I laugh in disbelief. This is completely ridiculous.

"You honestly know nothing about yourself. It's unfortunate and rather inconvenient. Haven't you ever questioned your differences?"

"Well, of course, I have. But I am a seer, an *untrained* seer. My whole life I was taught my visions made me weak and less than, so I never embraced them as I should have."

He chuckles, the sound taunting. "An *ordinary* Isoot? Aislinn, you may be mortal, but you are not an idiot. Do not play one."

"I don't understand."

"Of course not. What a toxic existence you have lived." He rubs his brow bone. "Being taught to hide your differences instead of relishing in them. Tell me, pet, have you ever felt physical effects from your *visions*? Have you been able to break barriers and cross realms? Have you been able to touch an item and relive its memory?"

Yes. The answer is yes to all his questions. But he doesn't let me answer. He keeps speaking in an eerily calm voice while I feel the ground beneath me spinning out of control. He stalks toward me, every bit of him menacing, and only stops when he's inches in front of me.

"You, Aislinn, are the Utikalo reincarnated. On the rare occasion a god dies, our shadows do not join the rest in the Afterlands or endure eons of torture in the Abyss. No, they are reborn, usually in the same bloodline. The Utikalo bound the Forbis Stone to its shadow, knowing it would be near impossible to reach in the mortal realm without a bridge between. I have been waiting a long time for you, Aislinn, and I intend to keep you until I figure out how to get the Forbis stone from within you." He runs a finger down my sternum. "Without killing you first, of course."

I swallow, trying to absorb what he's saying. The bleeding daydreams. The odd lingering effects on my body. Being able to see the gods. Demetrius wasn't able to do that, and he's far more skilled than most seers.

"Why without killing me? Wouldn't that be easier? Quicker?" Not that I'm in a hurry to die...I'm just trying to understand my opponent's rationale, gain insight that will help me outmaneuver him.

"No. I killed the last reincarnation I found. The stone disappeared along with its shadow. I had to wait many decades until you were born, and my patience wears thin. I do not wish to hunt down the one that comes after you." Erebus pauses as he captures my chin and pulls my gaze to his. His voice lowers as if sharing a secret with a lover. "Which is why I have decided to make you immortal."

I open my mouth to ask what the Haile he means by "*make me immortal*," but he silences me with a band of shadow around my mouth and disappears without another word.

He is eternally infuriating.

I flop into my obscenely comfortable bed, the smooth sheets irritating me almost as much as the soft mattress that forms to my body like a snug little cocoon of luxury. I fold my arms and stare at the door, half dreading Erebus's return, half wishing for it.

I'm still reeling when my eyes grow heavy and threaten to close. And I know I'm dreaming when I see him.

DeLuca.

Electrifying blue eyes glow in dimly lit palace. Scaled wallpaper peels around us, and there's an odd golden glow scattering light through a large window. Warm hands trail along my skin, causing me to shiver. The feel of his mouth over mine is so real that as his tongue slides against mine, I can taste smoke. He pulls back to look at me, so much emotion swimming in his gaze. Just when I think he's going to kiss me again, the sound of crying floods my ears.

I'm torn. To stay...or find the source.

I miss this.

I miss him.

It feels as though a hole has been carved out of me, and my body is searching for its missing piece. But I can't ignore the crying. The soft whimpers of a frightened child. DeLuca doesn't speak but bows his head in understanding as he disappears into nothing more than stardust.

The strange sun casts a pink and purple light, accentuating the fluffy clouds above. A trail appears and shimmers with an iridescent sheen. When I look ahead, I see where it leads...utter darkness. I really don't want to go there.

I wonder if I turn back if DeLuca will appear again.

We can go back to making out, and whatever nightmare is waiting for me will just have to come back another day.

The sobs grow louder as if begging me to come save them.

With a sigh and a low curse under my breath, I follow the shimmering trail. Stomping through a happy ethereal meadow, past Millena's palace in the middle of the gods realm, and entering into the Imorti Woods.

Everything here is dead. Even the little animals skittering away seem to be nothing more than the bones of their past. There is a gnawing feeling in my gut that's telling me to hurry just as the sobs turn to desperate screams, and I quicken the pace.

"Where are you?" I yell. No answer, just more screaming.

Shit.

I break into a run.

Then I find it.

A creature so fearsome "nightmare" doesn't even come close to describing it. Dragon is the closest resemblance, but even that isn't quite right. The translucent skin shows the skeletal structure of the beast before me. His large teeth are on display as he snarls out cold smoke. Its claws are outstretched—reaching for a small girl with brown curls cowering in the carcass of a large tree.

Hadleigh.

"Wake up! Hadleigh, wake up. It can't get you. It's not real!"

"Aislinn?" she whimpers. "I can't. I'm lost."

I charge forward, stepping around the beast as best as I can. Its large frame gives me the advantage of being able to sneak around it. This may only be a dream, but I've learned anything is possible, and I don't want to risk it seeing me before I get to Hadleigh.

I squeeze into her hiding place while the beast snarls at us. Hadleigh wraps into me. She feels so real. Her body is shaking uncontrollably and hot tears soak through my silk nightshirt.

"Leave, beast! Return to wherever you came from. There are no dead for you to claim here," I shout at the creature.

"No dead—yet. I am not 'beast.' I am Dureias. Do not insult me again, pretender." The words push into my head while the beast's reptilian ice blue eyes glow brighter, but oddly enough, it obeys, leaving us.

Dream.

It's because this is a dream.

I turn all of my attention to Hadleigh. "What are you doing here? How did you break through the barrier?" I ask, grabbing her shoulders and looking her over for injury.

"I-I-I was looking for you." She quivers.

My heart hurts. I pull her into me. "I love that you came looking, Hadleigh. It was so brave of you. But please don't try to find me again. It's too dangerous."

"Sometimes I see your dreams without meaning to," she admits. "I was trying to follow the silver line...I wanted to see if I could save you."

I kiss her head. Sweet girl. "No one can save me."

"DeLuca will. He's coming for you."

My heart swells. I try not to get my hopes up, but it's hard. I knew it. I just knew it. I know DeLuca. If he's determined enough, he will find a way against the odds, and I don't doubt his determination to find me.

Hadleigh looks up at me, pulling away. "Have you found Heidon?" she asks.

"No." I see tears threaten to return to her eyes, and gods, I'd do anything to see her smile right now. "But I know Erebus has his shadow. He is using it to ensure I behave. If there is a way to release him, I will do it...trust me."

"I trust you, Aislinn. I wish you were home...I hate the visions. They're scary, and I think Mama and Grandpapa don't remember...but I know you do. I know you see scary things too...and

wouldn't make me hide them, right? You'd talk to me about them,
right, Aislinn?"

Oh gods.

My eyes burn, and my chest cleaves apart. I wish I could be there
for her. Be the stone I so desperately needed when I was her age. I rub
a finger along her forehead, brushing her hair behind her ear.

"I do remember. And I remember how alone I felt when they first
started. I didn't sleep. I lost a lot of the happiness. I forgot how to
be a kid...don't do that. Don't forget how to be a kid. Ask Sylvie for
Rutide. It will help keep the visions away if you don't want them."

"Granpapa says I need to learn to live with them and use them."

"Eventually...maybe...but right now, you just need to be happy.
Don't worry about Grandpapa. I'll deal with him when I come
back." *She smiles at that.*

"I won't be able to see you anymore."

I hug her a little tighter. "I won't be gone much longer. You said it
yourself. DeLuca is coming for me. Now go. Wake up. I'm not sure
how visions work here, but I don't want any of the gods to find you. I
miss you, Hadleigh. Be well."

"Are they nice to you? The gods?" *she asks with her head buried*
against my shoulder.

"Some of them are."

She nods as if that's enough, and I hold her until she feels
weightless, eventually turning to nothing but light and air. When
I'm sure she's gone, I curl around myself in her hiding place, hoping
I wasn't lying to her when I said I'd be home soon.

EIGHT
ALL WANTED
Rett

I'VE BEEN PACING IN our sorry excuse for a dining room for an hour. Sure, it seems ungrateful considering the alternative was a cave somewhere in the woods, but I don't know how anyone can live like this long-term. It's so cramped.

It's hard to believe my life would've been spent in conditions far worse than this if I hadn't been swapped for a dead heir as an infant. Lately, I have found myself wondering about my birth mother. It feels like an insult to the mother who raised me to even consider an alternative. She was the best mom anyone could ask for...but she wasn't meant to be mine. And neither was this life.

Iris is standing barefoot in the kitchen, finishing up another Roussian dinner. Iris is the best. She can cook. She's kind and funny. Crazy smart. Hot as all Haile.

Yeah.

She is everything.

"If you don't stop pacing, you're going to wear a path into the floor," she says as she sets our plates down on to the table.

Each time I look at her, I can't help but smile. She is wearing a little white apron around her waist, accentuating her growing belly.

Our child.

My daughter.

Despite all that's happened, I thank Haile for that little blessing. So desperately, I needed something *good*. Our little ember of happiness. It did come as a shock when she told me after we'd just lost our families. I had to work through a string of emotions, but the one most prevalent was thankful. I'm so damn thankful to Iris for this gift.

I grab her from behind, one hand caressing our growing child. One hand cupping her soft breasts that have grown impossibly larger in the last few weeks. She leans back into my touch, and I kiss her cheek.

"I'm sorry, beautiful, I'm just worried about my sister. I didn't mean to scuff your floors." My lips move down to her neck.

Iris turns into me, standing on her tip-toes so she can wrap her hands around my neck. "*Our* floors..." She smiles. "This is *our* home. Mine and yours."

Her soft lips mark mine as their own. Her kiss is intoxicating. Addicting. It's never enough for me. But I can't shake her words..."*mine and yours.*" They pull at a memory of another girl fighting to the surface of my mind. Of when I was just a boy and said similar things to Ailie.

Oh gods, how I fucking *loved* Ailie. When we were kids, when Mom sat me down and told me Ailie was intended to be my wife, I don't think I stopped smiling for weeks.

I was six.

She was my best friend. So wild and carefree. She always did just as she pleased, regardless of what anyone said. I loved that about her—still love that about her—but it's what got her sent away. To be forgotten, and somewhere in that stretch of time, the love I had for her changed, and all I can see now are faded memories of what once was. I held on to her for as long as I could.

After I got back from Fort Vicanti, I had planned on going to visit her, but I wasn't all there in my head. Seeing some of the ways we keep our people in line really messed with me.

The unfaltering guilt that came with all I had witnessed kept me from getting out of bed each day. It was agonizing and lonely to be so trapped within my own mind.

Then Iris was there. She patiently helped me gain control of my emotions again, and she had blossomed into this fucking goddess in the time I was gone. Pretty soon, she was all I could think about. All I dreamt about. All I wanted.

Still want.

"What's on your mind?" Iris runs her long nail along my cheek.

I shake my head, clearing thoughts of Ailie and my guilt with it. "Us." I answer as simply as I can. Iris has a keen ability to tell when I'm lying, and Aislinn is a touchy subject between us.

She smiles, but the smile doesn't quite reach her eyes. "Come, sit, eat. I'll fix your favorite tea."

She's really too good too me.

Dinner was, of course, incredible as always. Iris is finishing cleaning up while I sit and try not to stew over thoughts of my sister and DeLuca. How I should be with them, helping them find Ailie. I have to remind myself multiple times that Iris needs me here.

I look over at Iris.

She's bent over, putting a dish away, giving me a view of her perfect ass.

Fuck, how did I get so lucky?

Iris stands and turns, smirking as she catches me staring. "Something you want?" Her lashes flutter. She knows exactly what she's doing.

My voice catches in my throat. The only word I can muster is a gruff, "Yes."

She licks her lips, and I watch the motion intently. "Say it, then. Tell me what you want."

"You. I want you, beautiful."

Iris removes her apron in slow measured movements. "You want me to do what?" she prods.

I know by the gleam in her eyes she enjoys watching me struggle. She's breathing harder, and her cleavage is straining against the tight material of her dress.

"First, I want you to take off that dress. Then, I want you to put that adorable godsdamn apron back on." My voice has thickened as my desire for her grows stronger, almost unbearable while it strains uncomfortably against my pants. The need to touch her consumes me like a fire consumes coal. It covers me, leaving nothing but the ache for her.

She does as I ask, tying the little apron around her waist but leaving the top down. She is glowing. Every inch of her. I'm addicted to the way she smells, the way she breathes. The way she moves is like Haile himself fills her with life's essence.

My eyes almost roll back when she comes to straddle my lap. Lowering so our centers are lined up, her heat seeps through the fabric between us.

Leaning down, she licks the side of my face, then sticks her tongue in my ear, sending the best chill down my body. "Now what do you want, bear?" she whispers.

"Now." My thumb runs up the side of her neck until my lips reach just below her ear. "I want you to say it."

"You," her voice is low and sensual. "Are *nothing*. You are the lord of *nothing*. You will always be *nothing*. You do not deserve the life you stole. You do not deserve this happiness."

I groan and tip my head back as she sticks her hand between us, releasing my erection from my pants and teasing the tip of me with her finger.

"Do you think you deserve to enter my body? Do you think you deserve pleasure?" she asks as her thumb strokes over the little bead of liquid gathered at the head. Circling it in maddening strokes.

"Gods, no. I don't deserve any of it. I deserve nothing."

Iris tips my head back and squeezes my jaw open before spitting in my mouth. Once I've swallowed, she releases my jaw and slaps me with a savage grin. "No, you don't." She takes my hands and places one on her peaked breast. The other she slides to that part of her I'm desperately aching for. "You don't deserve to put your disgusting hands on my skin, but I'm greedy, and I want your touch, so you better fucking earn it."

It's an effort to keep from plunging into her when I can feel the warmth from her seeping over my lap. The throb of my dick is borderline painful, but she's right; I haven't earned it yet.

Iris arches her back to give me better access. I start rubbing her, using my thumb to circle above her entrance. Applying just enough pressure to coax a moan from her. When her body starts to tighten, I push a finger into her. Groaning with how wet she is.

"Fuck, babe. I want to be buried inside you."

"Earn it." She pants as my fingers continue to tease her.

I increase my pace, in and out, until her muscles clamp my fingers and she lets out a scream of pleasure. I don't remove my fingers until she's ridden her pleasure out and her breathing begins to even.

"Did I earn it?" I ask against her neck.

Her breath comes out heavily as if she's riding the anticipation just as much as I am, but she smirks before giving a single nod. "Fill me," she demands.

Iris doesn't give me the chance to move as she pulls my pants lower and slides down on me until I'm fully sheathed within her.

Both of us let out a string of curses at the sheer fucking relief of our bodies connecting. The feel of her swollen around me brings me close to the edge too quickly. She rips off my shirt and licks the tattoo over my heart. The Urson crest. The one I used to be so proud of that only increases my shame now.

I go to grab her hips, but she slaps me again. "Do not touch me. You have not earned it."

She rocks on my lap faster. I capture her nipple between my teeth as it bounces near my mouth. She lets out a gasp of pleasure as I begin to suck on it, rolling my tongue over in the way she likes. Then I bring my mouth to the other side giving it equal attention.

I know she's getting close to release again by the change in her breathing. I love how she takes her pleasure from me. Uses my body however she likes. I love when she takes charge and quiets my brain. There is only us, and this feeling of total ecstasy. I'm not a future lord. I'm not some kidnapped child from Ashe. I'm not a horrible excuse for a human being whose family is responsible for ruining so many lives. I'm not a failed protector. I'm not the man who betrayed his future wife by taking another woman to bed.

I am nothing.

"Do. It. Now." She pants out the words between heavy breaths.

I use one hand to hold her hip and drive into her harder. My thumb circles over that sensitive place between her legs. My pace quickens as her movements become more erratic. Desperate.

"Fuck the fucking gods!" she cries out. Her legs begin shaking, and she pulls my face into her chest. Nails dig into the flesh behind my shoulders. I'm suffocating in the soft skin between her cleavage, and just before I pass out, I spill into her. She moans as she slowly moves up and down, squeezing every last ounce while riding her own climax.

"I'm fucking obsessed with you, Iris," I say when she finally releases me and I can breathe again.

She smirks. "That's the whole point."

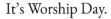

It's Worship Day.

If someone told me a year ago that I'd regularly be attending worship, I'd say they have a few screws loose. The notion is absolutely ridiculous. Sure, I knew of the gods; their stories are embedded into the foundation of Katova. But like most people in Stellera, to us, they were nothing more than wonderfully detailed children's fables. We mocked our neighbor nations to the north for their beliefs. It's ironic, really, that we thought ourselves so smart. That we were above gods. Now look at what has become of Stellera—the godless nation has fallen to chaos.

After the last four months, I'm done trying to predict what the Weavers have in store for me. I'm just riding each day as it comes. Today we are worshiping some air god. Aria, I think her name is. Thanking her for the clean air we breathe. If Aria is listening, I do not think she'd accept worship from me. Not after what my family was responsible for in Ashe.

No.

I think I'll spend this worship day silently apologizing.

Even if it's too late for forgiveness.

Priestess Alis finishes her sermon and then gestures for one of the elders to approach the podium centered in the circular silver temple. The elder is female, dressed in rich purple robes with suns stitched along the collar. I recognize her as the one who brought my sister back from Sutton. She shakes out her short brown hair, streaked gray from age.

"I now give the floor to Wrenna who would like to speak on behalf of the Elders," Priestess Alis says before sitting beside Alec and Sylvie.

"Hello, Children," she begins. "What a splendid day it is. Thanks to our gods, and a special thanks to Soren for the days of rain that have finally subsided for the glorious sun to shine down upon us."

The Children murmur their agreement and thanks, and I'm half inclined to join them because I was beginning to think we'd drown if the rain kept on as it was.

"I have some unfortunate news I must share with you all. Our resident god, DeLuca, has decided he no longer wishes to be a part of our community."

The room fills with gasps and chatter. Some of the attendees are even crying out for him, fucking sobbing like their mother died in front of them. They really take this him-being-a-god business seriously. The only thing godly about that man is his crazy powers. His attitude generally sucks, and he can't protect someone who depends on him. What kind of god can't protect *one* person?

No, I will not feel his loss.

Not. One. Bit.

I only wish he hadn't dragged my sister into his theatrics.

There was a chance of us being friends. I admit he was competent when we went to the Capital to scope out the situation with the Liberators. He knew how to blend and gave good direction. His intuition was spot on, and I could see the fires burning in his eyes when he saw the treatment of the highborns and the Children captured by Pierce. In those moments, my cause was his cause. We were perfectly aligned and understood one another.

Then...I left them at the Islands of the Sons.

I left Lysette and I left Aislinn.

I left them in DeLuca's care.

And he lost one.

He lost Ailie.

My Ailie.

She's gone because he wasn't enough to save her despite all his claims. She's gone because I chose Iris over her. She's gone...because of me.

I could have been more.

Should have been more.

But I chose Iris.

NINE
GONE
Lysette

MY BOOTS MAKE A squelching sound as they sink in the mud. It rubs my nerves the wrong way. That, along with the damp air makes me shiver in my wet clothes. It might not be so bad if my boots weren't already soaked through. It wasn't as noticeable when DeLuca was beside me, using his heat to keep us warm, but now, he's setting up a camp for the night, and I'm off searching for the ennis root to color my hair.

Even though it's wet, I'm thankful for the cold. It gives me something to focus on other than the inward spiral I go down thinking about how I will no longer look like Linnea and by changing my appearance. I feel as if I am partially erasing her.

She was always the stronger twin, born first, always thriving physically while I fell a bit short. Now I have to be the strong one. I know it's ridiculous given everything that has come to pass over the last few months. We are more than our appearance, but with the scar, the white eye, and now my hair...I hardly resemble her at all. Sometimes, in the first weeks, I would look in the mirror and pretend my reflection was my twin. I'd talk to her for hours to stave off the misery of having a part of myself gone forever.

I allow a lone tear to fall before I push it away and continue moving through the dense underbrush of the Thickett Woods. I can't dwell on it. I can't continue to think about the loss. I will overcome this, just as I have everything else. Linnea is gone. My parents are gone. My little brother is gone. But I am *not* gone, and I will push on for them. I *will* honor their memory and not waste my life. I refuse to sit on my ass doing nothing in Caeliss. No looking back. I *won't* look back.

A cliff looms ahead. My guess is it's a part of the Obsidian mountain range. If my memory is correct—and it usually is—the ennis plant likes a dark and moist environment, so this would be the ideal place for it to thrive.

I continue to follow the curve of the rock wall until I come upon it. Right along the seam where the cliff meets dirt is a shrub with clusters of tiny red berries. The berries, etaloka, are extremely toxic and can kill a large man within seconds of ingestion. The roots, however, are used in most red dyes and are harmless.

The roots of the shrub easily follow my command as I beckon them to the surface. As they rise, the ground shakes.

Wet dirt flies everywhere as the stalky roots burst into the open. I grab a handful and stick them in my rucksack before placing my hand over the disturbed ground—helping new life grow quickly to take the place of the ones I stole before the shrub wilts.

The stronger my ability gets, the harder it is to take from the plants like this. I feel their life force. Feel their pain and injury. How the flowers scream when their petals are plucked. Everytime I take,

I also try to give. I show my respect and thanks to them and try to retain a balance. But still, they scream.

There is a family of Bottinials in Caeliss, distant cousins, I suppose. I've gotten fairly close to two of them—Harlow and Davina. They helped me in the beginning, but I started to surpass their talent. My power is twice as potent as theirs, no doubt thanks to absorbing both mine and my twins gifts while I held her dying body. It became more prudent to practice on my own. Reading and researching and going to the meadows. Now my power feels like another limb, an extension of myself, and it's a wonder I ever survived without it.

The camp DeLuca set up has a huge roaring fire. The orange and red dance in hypnotic swirls—casting shadows among the trees like some kind of ritual. He took the liberty to put together two make-shift beds with quilts Maegora made us and crumpled clothing as pillows. I notice he's miraculously dry...as is the area around our little camp, including the ground that is so damp everywhere else.

"How did you manage all of this?" I ask.

"What good is controlling all the elements if you can't make a comfortable camp?" His tone is entirely too cocky for his own good.

"But *how* did you do it? And why didn't you while we were hiking through the muck?"

He shrugs. "I had time to mess around while you were gone and figured I'd try something new. I held onto my Siphon Stone and pulled the water out of my clothes, then the ground, before depositing it back into the stream. Then I kind of combined my fire with my air to warm myself and the area. It took a few tries. I kept accidentally making miniature fire tornadoes, but eventually I got it."

A shiver shoots up my spine and I repeat, "*Miniature fire tornadoes?*" with a raised brow.

He nods and I look around the camp. There is indeed evidence of uncontrolled scorching on the trees in this small clearing. He could have burned down the whole Thickett if it weren't wet...but he didn't...and what he did *is* quite impressive.

I half laugh before I can hold it back. "That's really incredible, Lucy. I would have never thought to use your gifts in such a way."

His pride deflates slightly back into his usual broody scowl. "I told you not to call me *Lucy*."

I smile—willing light to reach my eyes and break through his icy exterior. "And I told you *I don't care*. Now are you going to let me die of hypothermia, or are you going to dry me off too?"

DeLuca shakes his head as if he's exasperated but then grabs his stone from the pocket of his pants, and the moisture begins to pull from my clothes. All the water gathers into a sphere in front of me, growing with every drop taken from my decreasingly wet clothes until I don't feel even a hint of the moisture. He guides the ball of water to the stream just beside our camp and drops in. Then a gust of warm wind blows around me. My head drops back as I soak in the warmth. It's so soothing, like standing in the sun in summer. It reminds me of my mother.

"Better?" he asks.

"Much better."

He nods, looking satisfied with my answer. "Let's get some rest. I want to make it to the manor tomorrow so we're waking up at sunrise."

"I agree. I'll mix up the ennis in the morning. Then we can be on our way."

He nods again, then gestures to the sleep space nearest the fire. I climb into my blankets. It's surprisingly comfortable despite being on the ground. If I look hard enough, I can almost make out the twinkle of far-off stars through the treetops. There's a soothing noise of the combined flowing stream and rippling wind through the branches. It's peaceful. The very essence of true calm.

"Goodnight," I say with a yawn, pulling the quilt high up to my shoulder.

"Night, Lys." DeLuca puts a hand out, and the fire dies, leaving no trace of light except from the few remaining embers. Even without the flames, the warmth remains and I find myself exceedingly grateful for the god of vengeance's affinity for fire. Even if it means I have to be careful not to get burned, I'll take my chance with him.

TEN
My Fault
DeLuca

"Hold still. I'm almost done."

"Six months ago, did you think you'd be helping me dye my hair?" Lysette chuckles as she brushes a wet strand away from her face. She examines her finger, now coated with a ruddy red goop and breathes in through her teeth. "Oh, I forgot to tell you to be careful not to get it on my skin. It stains."

I groan as I look at my palms. They're completely covered with the substance Lysette whipped together from the odd roots she found in the woods.

"You could have told me before I started. I have this shit all over me."

"*Language*, Lucy, you're in the presence of a lady!"

"Vristra is more of a lady than you'll ever be."

Lysette gasps with a hand to her chest. "I'm wounded. Truly."

"Sure you are." I put the makeshift bowl down. "It's done. I'm going to wash this gunk off."

"Better hurry; the longer it sits the darker it gets."

I blow out an agitated exhale. "Of course it does."

She smiles innocently at me, but I see right through it. She knew exactly what she was doing.

We've set up near the stream we stopped at when first camping in the Thickett Woods with Alec. Watching the reddened water swirl around my hands reminds me of that night—though it wasn't dye I was washing off in these cool waters. Lysette wasn't kidding. This stuff is potent. It was on me for less than ten minutes, and it looks as though I stuck my hands in boiling water.

Once I've thoroughly scrubbed all I can, I run the water from the stream over my face and hair. When I'm done, I clench the Siphon Stone that and try to part the stream. It obeys, but it's a struggle. Like the command is fighting through a veil. I want all the practice I can get with this thing.

If only I could force it back beneath my skin and feel its soothing ripples once again.

"Go away, I'm ready to rinse," Lysette orders while beginning to shimmy out of her top.

I hold up a hand to stop her. "I have a better idea. Lay your head back against that boulder." I gesture to a large rock hanging over the lip of the stream.

For once, she listens. With the stone clenched, I pull water from the stream and guide it over her hair, careful to not get her face. She helps guide the goop out by massaging her scalp under the steady flow of water waiting for it to run clear as instructed. I continue to use the stone to draw the water out of her hair until it is completely dry.

"Finished." There's a tug of pride in my chest that I am still able to work with the water with the same fluidity I had before it was taken from me.

"Well?" she asks while looking up at me, her eyes head cocked to the side in question.

I stare waiting for her to finish the question, but nothing follows.

"Well, what?"

Lysette shakes out her hair. "How does it look?"

How does it look? How am I supposed to know? It doesn't look bad. It's different and will take some getting used to. I like the way it highlights her freckles; they remind me of Aislinn's, only a few shades lighter.

"It looks fine," I finally say after I see a splice of fear creep into her features at my long pause.

"Just *fine*?" Her eyes widen.

I sigh. "It looks good, Lys. Now let's cut it and go. We're wasting too much daylight, and that hole is gonna be harder than Haile to find in the dark."

"Right... Have you cut hair before?" she asks nervously, taking me off guard. Lysette has hardened so much after everything that I forget these things used to matter to her. I force a gentleness back into my features.

"Yes. I used to cut my sisters' hair when they were little." She exhales and nods before sitting cross-legged in front of me. I get to work with my trusted folding knife. Not too sharp, but it will do in a pinch. I begin to chop layer by layer with as much careful precision as possible.

"You don't talk about them much," Lysette says, breaking our silence.

"Who?"

"Your sisters...or family in general, I guess."

I slice another tendril of hair off—contemplating—trying not to go too deep into those feelings I have deeply buried and locked away.

"It hurts too much to think about them. When I hurt, I lose control."

"I've noticed." Lysette smirks, and I tug her hair a little extra hard for it. She yelps and swats at me.

"Be careful, in case you forgot, I have a blade near your neck." I laugh while cutting more hair off then sigh. "There were ten of us...twelve including my parents. And now there's just me. Sure, some of them left to find a better life...but when they did, they didn't turn back. Val was the only one who stuck around. We looked out for each other. She was married, but her husband and unborn child died, so it was really just us for years."

"And then Ailie killed her." Lysette's voice fills with sympathy.

"And then I *let* Ailie kill her. I had to choose. Val or Ailie. I chose Ailie, and I would again." I push back the memory before the pain seeps past the dam I've built and finish the last section of hair. "It's done. And before you ask, it looks good. This length suits you."

It's not a lie. Her once radiant gold hair that flowed to the small of her back now is now shoulder length and frames her face. It dulls the severity of her scar, and the color looks really nice with her good eye.

She's feeling the ends. The way her fingers search for the longer strands and shake slightly. This probably isn't an easy adjustment for her, but she's faking it well.

"Alright, let's get going then."

It took us until nightfall to get to the general area of the cavern. Exactly what I didn't want to happen, and as expected, the search has become extremely arduous. I remember the hole looking like nothing more than an animal burrow. It was so small from the outside it didn't look possible to fit an entire person through it.

I may have overestimated our ability to remember its location. I was really hoping we'd make it before sunset so we at least had the advantage of sunlight. We've been walking in circles for over an hour. I'm starting to lose my temper. I feel it building, and I'm clenching my fists so hard that my nails are creating little crescent moon incisions in my palms.

"If we find the tree, I think I could find it again..." Lysette pops up behind me.

"What tree?"

"Remember? There was a tree with a "U" carved in the trunk. I thought it was to show the direction to Caeliss, but maybe it was to mark where the opening was? It was only a few feet away."

"To be honest, most of that night is a blur. I was just focused on Aislinn's safety...I didn't care about anything else. Especially after I walked in on her about to be—" I can't finish the sentence, not if I want the Thickett Woods to remain intact.

That entire night brings out the worst of my rage, but the villager who I found on top of Aislinn makes me nearly blind with white-hot anger. I was seconds away from being too late, and *that* would have been my fault too.

"About to be what?" Lysette prods, ignoring my reluctance. But when she sees the severity in my features, horror flashes through her eyes, and she mercifully drops the subject. "Can you maybe do something about the dark? Like an orb of fire?"

How did I not consider that? I must be the worst god that has ever existed. I don't even think I should be able to be called one.

"Yeah, I think I can manage that." I'm about to try to shape the orb, but Lysette holds out a hand to stop me.

"Without burning down the Thickett." She raises her brows.

I give her a mocking head shake and create the orb, focusing on keeping it safely locked within a shield of air. "To your standards, Miss Urson?" I bow in front of her like I did when I was a serv in her house.

"Please don't do that." Her teasing tone is gone. She's become far more serious...and sad.

"I didn't mean to—"

"It's fine. Just drop it...please."

I nod my understanding, and we continue to search for the tree using my orb of light. It's kind of beautiful watching the chaos of the fire held prisoner in the invisible cage. Absolute destruction so close to being unleashed if not for that thin barrier. There's probably a euphemism in there, but that's more Lysette's thing, not mine.

Thanks to the fire orb, it only takes another few minutes for us to find the carved "U" in the tree. A few steps over and we find the hole. Even with its small size, it is deceptively easy for us to squeeze through.

The air smells of wet clay. Crates are still thrown askew throughout the cavern from when we were fleeing the Liberators. There isn't a pod waiting for us, not that I expected there to be after those men had used it to track us.

Thankfully, I am one of the servs who was trusted with the inner workings of the transport system, kind of ironic considering I was one of the servs plotting against them. I go to the panel stuck into the dirt walls and pull the lever that will call back the pod.

"And now we wait." Lysette hums while we listen to the groan of magnets shifting above us. I think she's trying to cover her nervousness. It's very rare to see her anything but level-headed. Logical to a fault.

"I wish we knew what we were walking into." I lose a breath. "I don't like not being prepared."

She makes a 'mmm' noise in her throat that sounds like a borderline laugh. "I've noticed."

"What's that supposed to mean?"

"You're kind of a control freak." She shrugs.

"Control freak?" I quirk a brow, and she just shrugs innocently. "I don't think wanting to be prepared makes me a control freak."

Like she's one to talk; she craves structure just as much as I do. She can deny it all she wants, but I have lived with her the last three months. I know her well enough to see the way her mind works.

"Whatever you say, Lucy, whatever you say."

Before I can retort, the pod arrives, and with it, a sharp pinch of anxiety that coats my nerves in tiny embers and raises the hair on the back of my neck.

"I want you to stay behind me at all times."

"I was planning on it, sir." She salutes teasingly as she takes a seat in the back of the pod. It's the same place Sylvie sat and tended to our wounds after the Obsidian Manor massacre.

I have to take a deep inhale to shake the image of Aislinn laying there, broken and bleeding, after I had failed to protect her. I keep failing to protect her. If I was better, she wouldn't have been taken. If I was better, I would have been able to stop the massacre before it even happened. She'd still be safe and a lady of Stellera. Even if that means she'd be married to someone else.

Gods, I can't imagine her being married to Rett while Iris is pregnant with his fucking bastard. It makes me sick.

"Whatever you're thinking about, stop. You're going to melt through the control box and then we will be stranded under the mountains." Lysette pulls me out of my thoughts and I realize little flames have started to lick over my shoulders and down my arms. I shake them off and try to keep them at bay.

"This is all my fault. Everything. It all started with me." My admission doesn't come easy, but it feels necessary.

"It's not. It's Erebus's fault. *Literally* everything has started with him. The reason for the Children, Pierce's ability to coax the masses into rebellion, and especially for Aislinn being taken. You can't blame yourself. It won't do any good other than unhinging your emotions...which, if you haven't noticed, doesn't work out too well for anyone."

"I hear what you're saying, Lys, I do. But it *feels* like my fault. I need you to understand that. Even if *logically* I know I am not the one responsible, I *feel* responsible. In my core. In my body. It feels like my fault."

Lysette looks as though she wants to argue, but her shoulders drop with acceptance. "I can't argue with feelings. They may be irrational, they may have a mind of their own, but we are all entitled to our feelings, whatever they may be. Sometimes, you just have to feel it in order to move forward."

Our gazes lock, a silent understanding passing between us. The pain the summer brought. The pain we are in daily. It dances like a cataclysmic event waiting to annihilate us at the slightest slip of our restraint.

The gears groan to a stop above us.

"Ready?" I ask as I mentally prepare for whatever may be waiting for us.

"Right behind you." She gives a thumbs up and tries to hide the small tremble in her voice.

I stand to the side of the door as it opens and slowly look around the corner. The tunnel is surprisingly clear and intact, not even one brick out of place. I nod to Lysette, and she follows me out.

We don't speak and keep our footsteps light. Little flames dance between my fingers of my left hand, while I use my right to push the series of buttons required to call the lift to us. When the lift door opens, it's surprisingly clear. Lysette lets loose an audible breath of relief.

"Don't get too comfortable yet. If there are any intruders left, I'm sure they will be holed up in the security room," I warn as I work the levers in the lift I've become so familiar with. "Fifth floor; the higher, the better. We always want the high ground."

The flames between my fingers dance steadily as we ascend through the manor. I can't help but feel relieved that the lift is even in workable condition. I wasn't sure what we would be greeted with on our return, but a mountain of rubble was my first thought. Especially with all the plans I'd heard Pierce laying out for his followers.

It is nothing short of a miracle that we have gotten this far. Maybe the Weavers are actually on my side for once. My breathing stills as the whine of the gears comes to an uneasy silence and the doors glide open.

"Well, well, who do we have here?"

Fuck.

ELEVEN

STARLIGHT

Aislinn

"Well, pet, you sure are full of surprises." Erebus towers over me while my eyes adjust to our surroundings. I'm leaning against the carcass of a tree in the same dead forest as I was when I found Hadleigh—in my vision. It was a vision wasn't it?

"How did I get here?" I ask, feeling the shadow cuff around my wrist biting into my skin with its abhorrent cold.

"That is the question, isn't it? You shouldn't have been able to leave your room, not without a portal. It appears our timeline is speeding up. I'm going to have to figure out a way to put you back together quicker than anticipated."

"I don't understand."

"Your mortal mind wouldn't."

"Then explain to me what is going on!" I'm so tired of Erebus and his vague explanations. The way he just expects me to go along with whatever he says, like he's trustworthy?! What did he think would happen when he brought me here?

Erebus tenses and sneers. "It seems, pet, that you have awoken the Utikalo within yourself. Perhaps just being present in our realm is what has done it. I'm not sure. The Utikalo possessed a unique ability. It was able to rip the stitching of realms and create its own portals, through current time or otherwise."

"Current time...or...otherwise." I mull over the words. He couldn't possibly mean—" Do you mean *time travel*?"

Erebus's eyes twinkle with something I can't pinpoint, and he nods.

"I can create my own portals?" I whisper more to myself than anything.

"Don't get any ideas." He grabs my wrist and holds it up. "I've linked us. There is no place you can go without me finding you."

"Why would I *ever* want to leave you, oh dashing prince of shadow?" I bat my lashes and rip my arm back. "Besides, I don't even know how I did it."

"You don't know *yet*, but when we unlock your subconscious, I'm sure you will figure it out. I can be *very* patient. When that day is upon us, I don't want you getting any ideas about where you shall go until our business is concluded."

"Unlock my subconscious?" I grab hold of the skeletal tree, as if it could help me find my grounding.

Erebus's eyes roll so hard they may get stuck in the back of his head. If I'm lucky, they will. "Yes, I need you to remember some things from your former life. Things that will help bring my dear wife back to her former self...among other things."

"Right, your wife that you *broke*. Where is she? Where is Astoria? Do you have her locked in a tower like a fairytale princess?" Erebus flinches slightly with my words.

He smirks. "Why, she is at home, of course. Comfortable as ever. Would you like to meet her?"

I'm utterly shocked by the open invitation. So shocked, all I can do to answer is nod.

"Come, pet, time to uncover the purpose for your otherwise meaningless existence."

Before I have the chance to prepare, swirls of shadow whisk us away. We move quickly away from the skeletal forest, and everything blurs. I can't make out anything distinguishable until I fall to my hands and knees.

Panic swells in my chest until it becomes painful. I'm not moving as far as I can tell but below me is endless sky. My breathing is coming too quickly as my body flies into survival mode. The feeling of falling hasn't left, and despite looking at a wide open night sky...I somehow feel solid ground beneath me.

Erebus scoffs. "Before you completely deprive yourself of oxygen, *mortal*, the floor is solid. My Astoria likes the view."

I gulp and sprawl my shaking hands and feet around, feeling the hard floor for reassurance. The illusion makes me dizzy while my vision struggles to catch up to my head. "As much as I enjoy stars, I don't like this," I say, rising cautiously.

"You say that as if I *care* what you like." Erebus leans down so that our noses are almost touching. "I have no interest in you whatsoever—other than the value you pose to fixing my wife. Any kindness you have thus far received from me has been an outstretch of the love I have for her."

"*Kindness.*" I almost laugh. "You do not possess such a trait."

"Not so. I just reserve what little I have for beings that matter. There isn't a thing in this realm I wouldn't give to Astoria."

"Except children." A tight smile creeps across my features. I know it's stupid to chide Erebus, but it's hard not to when he's being such a pompous self righteous ass.

His eyes blacken and shadows gather around him like dark tentacles of pure evil. I brace for the strike but it doesn't come. Our spat is interrupted by another.

"Dark. Dark. Dark. Dark. So dark. Where have all my stars gone?" a gentle voice says from behind us.

Erebus instantly cools, shadows disappearing all together. "Hello, Starlight." He greets the woman approaching with a kiss to her temple.

She visibly retracts from his touch. Silver hair tumbles in unruly waves around her. She has on a white dress made of wrapped fabric that hangs loosely off her frail body. The silver paint coating her dark skin almost reminds me of galaxies lost to the deep night. Despite the intense blue color and flecks of starlight in her eyes, they look empty. It's as if someone has snuffed out all the life, and all that's left is this vessel.

"Astoria?" I whisper. My legs are shaking, still unable to fully accept the solid floor beneath them.

"Pretty little silver bird, won't you fly? Be free, little bird. Spread your wings away from the light. All little birds must die. All die. Death is the price of balance." Astoria rambles.

"Wh—"

Erebus interrupts me. "She knows not what she says. Her mind is scrambled, and she talks in these incessant riddles."

A solid square of tile appears below my feet, and the shaking in my legs instantly stops—bringing my breath to a normal rhythm. I chance a quick look towards Erebus, but his eyes are locked on Astoria.

"For how long?" I ask.

He shrugs. "A long time. It used to come in waves, sporadic at best. Then the lucid days became few and far in between. Not even Cintamarri could break through the walls of her corrupted mind."

"Cintamarri? Lust?" My throat fills with bile. "You tried to take advantage of her depravity by forcing yourself upon her? You're disgusting, Erebus." He opens his mouth, but I don't let him speak. "*You* broke her. You're the reason she's like this. Then you have the audacity to kidnap me and put her well-being in my hands?"

I'm seething. Shaking.

To imagine how he'd take advantage of a woman not in her right mind. It's an evil only Erebus could be capable of.

"How dare you? How *dare* you imply that I would take my wife against her will?" He shouts, and Astoria shudders. Erebus closes his eyes and regains his composure before adopting a softer tone. "Yes, Cintamarri is the god of lust. He is also the god of desire. Which isn't always the same. He can pull even the smallest thread of desire and have it over take your mind completely."

I not-so-patiently tap my foot and stare at him, waiting for an elaboration.

Erebus sighs. "His ability helped Astoria hold on to her lucidity. Her desires, the things she wanted to accomplish. Eventually, it was no longer enough. I know the part I played in corrupting her mind. I *know* it, Aislinn. I know taking our children from her played the largest role. The alternative was to let the prophecy come true—to let our child destroy the Shadows. Do you know what would happen then, pet? Chaos. The end of realms, ours and yours. They would implode and fold into themselves until they were nothing more than a speck of stardust."

"Then why conceive at all? Haven't you heard of abstinence?"

"The first one..." Erebus swallows, and I think I see sadness briefly take hold in his expression, but it's impossible to tell with someone so cruel. "The first one was on purpose. Despite whatever stories you have heard, Astoria and I loved each other. I still love her. We *wanted* children. A lot of them. I went to the Utikalo after we conceived. I wanted to know what kind of life was ahead for our child. That is when it told of the prophecy. Whatever semblance of a heart I had shattered that day. I became cruel, so Astoria didn't have to."

"You got rid of your children...so she didn't have to." I glance between the two of them.

He nods and Astoria starts rocking back and forth on her feet with an empty look in her eye, cradling an invisible bundle. "Just one. Just one. Just one," she mumbles.

"I thought we could still be together without conceiving. She and I took tonics that should have prevented it. Those damned Weavers had other plans though. Each and every time I laid with my wife resulted in a pregnancy. They must have thought it to be some kind of game. They don't like when we try to defy their plans."

Astoria continues rocking her invisible bundle and my heart cracks. I shift my gaze back to Erebus and my face turns into a snarl. "And you couldn't just stay away from her? How incredibly selfish."

"I *am* incredibly selfish, pet. I couldn't stay away from Astoria if we were trapped in opposite folds of time. If I could guarantee we would survive the end of realms and still be able to be together, I'd happily sacrifice everything for her, living and dead. It is only her."

"Dead. Dark and dead. Surrounded in shadow. Death to life," Astoria adds with the same blank expression.

"If you were decent, you would have let her go once you learned of the prophecy." My words are dripping with poison. I want them to. He should break just as much as she has.

Erebus looks at me with an amused smirk playing at his lips. "I have *never* claimed to be decent."

"Astoria could have never loved you." I practically spit. Erebus grinds his teeth so hard I hear the crack in his jaw and a terrifying calm washes over him.

"Starlight, I will visit with you later. I'm afraid our guest is feeling a bit unruly at the moment." Erebus plants a soft kiss on her hand.

"Too late. Late. Late. Dark covers light, endless night," Astoria whispers as I am yet again whisked away by endless shadows.

Erebus is rigid when we land. His shadows don't retreat as we arrive back in my prison of a room. My vision is shrouded by darkness, and that cold empty feeling returns to every place Erebus has touched me.

I may have pushed him too far this time. Icy fear freezes the rivers in my veins. It's been a while since I was truly afraid of him, since I remembered who he is. The ruthless ruler of the Shadows. Son of the cruelest god in existence. An extension of Death.

"How dare you speak of what you know nothing of?" Erebus's voice splinters the air around us. "You know *nothing* of love, of *real* unconditional love. Astoria is the only one who has ever loved me, who has ever tried to. Who do you think you are to question it? A worthless girl who doesn't even know who she is? What she is capable of?"

My chest rises and falls rapidly as I feel his anger pulsating through the very ground we stand on. The emotion is a living thing, out of control and ready to implode. My ears pop with the dramatic change in the atmosphere, and just as I am about to lose any dignity and get on my knees to grovel, a gust of wind pushes through the tension, and a voice cuts mine off.

"As entertaining as your outbursts can be, brother, you have company coming." The shadows retract but still simmer around Erebus. With the sudden clarity and light filtering into my room, Helena is now visible—sitting on my bed. She looks most at home with her large white wings spread out over the entirety of my bed, leaning back with both arms behind her head as if she's been waiting for hours.

"Company?" Erebus sneers.

"Mhmm. Agnar is on his way." She smoothes out her dark hair. "Fair warning, he's pissed."

"Why would Agnar come here?" I question them both.

"I knew it was only a matter of time before he did. I was hoping I would have longer before having to endure his presence." Erebus rubs his temples.

"So you're a fan then?"

Helena snorts without rising from the bed. "Hardly. I'm not sure there are two gods that hate each other more than Agnar and Erebus."

Information to pack away. "Why?"

"It's not any business of yours. Best behavior, pet. You will only speak with permission. If allowed to speak at all."

I scowl and Helena is nearly howling. Her laughter fills the entire room.

"Something to add, Helena?" Erebus asks.

"No, no, I'm sure Agnar will be very pleased with your dominance over his—"

"I see you have been listening to conversations that do not concern you," Erebus interrupts. "Yet again."

"His what?" I ask.

"You'll find out soon enough." Helena smoothes out the feathers on her wings as she sits up. "It's about to get interesting around here. Thank Kato."

"*Shadow god!*" a voice thunders from somewhere in the palace. The walls shake around us and the chandelier above drops a few crystals to the floor.

Erebus sighs. "Come, pet, he is here for you."

"Me?" I look at Helena with shock. She's still grinning as if this is the most entertainment she's had in decades.

"Where is she?" The booming voice that I suspect belongs to Agnar rattles the palace.

Shadows envelop me in an embrace that is becoming all too familiar and we materialize in the grand entry before the shouting god.

He stands well above Erebus, and he's almost twice as wide. His eyes are the color of the sky just before a storm, and his intense red hair adds to the unhinged energy he carries.

This god was clearly built for war. I bet he could tear Erebus's head clear off his shoulders without even breaking a sweat. The thought makes me grin, especially with the hatred in his stare as he gazes down at the shadow god.

"Welcome, Agnar. To what do I owe this immense pleasure?" Erebus says with a bored expression.

Agnar comes within a few inches of Erebus. "Don't play games with me, *trickster.*" His voice is a threat in itself.

Helena flies up next to me and leans on the banister lining the exquisite marble staircase. She gestures for me to join her, but I'm frozen in place, watching the two gods go back and forth.

"Me? Play games with you? *Never.* I respect you *far* too much." Erebus's words slither, and something about the tone makes my stomach turn. "Tell me what it is you want so you may be on your way."

"I want to see *her.*" Agnar's eyes harden and his fists clench.

I swallow, trying to steady the tremble in my bones. If Erebus is frightening, Agnar is downright terrifying. I don't want to ever find myself on his bad side.

"Well, here she is, I am not hiding her—but I remind you that Aislinn is here as *my* formal guest and is to remain in *my* palace. Haile's orders." The sharp look Erebus wears could compete with my nightmares.

Agnar's gaze finally drops to me as if he hadn't realized I'd been here the whole time. I hold my breath, waiting for the worst. Wondering which of them I should be more wary of.

To my surprise, Agnar's body softens. He looks younger, less intense with just that subtle change. Dropping to a knee, he reaches out and cups my face in his large hands. Something like sadness replaces the hatred as he stares into my eyes. The whole thing is making me more than a little uncomfortable.

"Uhm. Hello, I'm Aislinn," I say with a side glance to Erebus as I try to figure out what's happening.

"Aislinn." Agnar breathes my name like an answered prayer and pulls me into a hug. "I've been waiting for you for centuries, my child."

TWELVE
Any Less a Villain
Aislinn

Blinking slowly as my mind tries to catch up to my surroundings, I stare up at the huge god. "Waiting for me?"

"Yes, you told me you'd come back. I've been waiting," Agnar says while still on his knees. This guy is out of his damned mind.

"Apologies...but we've never met."

Erebus snickers beside me, his gaze as cold as his presence. Agnar snarls at him with a flash of the god he was when he first appeared.

"You told me you wouldn't remember. Before you left. Before you became mortal after this one—" he nods to Erebus "—chased you from our realm. Trying to force you to alter past and future, as if *you* had the power to go against the Weavers."

"That's enough, Agnar. You forget who's domain you are in. In fact, I could, perhaps, take this intrusion as an act of war."

"I forget nothing, Erebus. Nothing."

Erebus's smile sharpens. "As per Haile's instruction, if you'd like to have a visit with my guest, you must ask permission. She is my property. Your presence is quite the disruption."

"You can't keep me from my child."

"She isn't your child anymore. She's hardly more than a mortal. Grieve and move on. Those are your words aren't they, Agnar? Grieve. And. Move. On."

"Excuse me, don't I get a say in any of this?" I ask as Agnar puffs his chest out, looking positively enraged.

"No," Erebus responds.

Agnar gets off his knees and into Erebus's face. "This will not end well for you, *trickster*. Do you want to test me?"

"What are you going to do? Kill my children? Oh...forgive me, I must have forgotten...you've already done that."

I gasp. "What do you mean he's killed your children?" There is no match to the fury alight in Agnar's eyes. He's shaking like a volcano moments away from erupting.

"*Don't*," he warns.

Erebus looks at me with madness twisting his grin. "Our god of the *hunt* here has made it his life's purpose the last few hundred years to hunt *my* children and kill them before they became too powerful."

My eyes widen. "Why—" I place my hand over my chest as I struggle to catch my breath. "Why would you do such a thing?"

Agnar looks down, his anger turning to something akin to shame—if gods are capable of feeling such things. "To stop the prophecy. The end of the Shadows would be the end of everything."

"But that's not the whole truth is it, Agnar?"

The gods stare at each other, waiting to see who breaks first. Agnar is the epitome of a loose cannon, and Erebus stares with his usual icy demeanor. The tension hanging around us is smothering. They're both too damn stubborn to allow even a modicum of give. We're going to stand here for years until one of them breaks.

"Gods, someone just say something!" I scream. No one moves and no one speaks. They stare at me with blank expressions. The stale silence stretches around us with its crushing weight.

"Your *father* has taken it upon himself to punish me for your previous self leaving," Erebus says. He's been killing my innocent children because *you* left us."

"Under order!" Agnar says with a deep rumble. The cool marble beneath my feet vibrates with his voice.

"An order you could have easily maneuvered a way out of if you'd only desired to do so." Erebus straightens the cuff of his suit jacket. He catches his reflection in the mirror above the entry table. His vanity truly knows no bounds.

"Sure. Make me the villain in this story. I've never had to use Cintamarri to seduce my *own* wife."

Shadows creep along the floor and the lights go out around us. We're surrounded by unbearable cold. Erebus appears to grow five feet. "Ah, you have not, true. But I've kept my wife *alive*."

"*Barely.*" Agnar crosses his arms and doesn't seem the least bit alarmed by Erebus's show of power.

"Helena!" Erebus roars, and she's on her feet in an instant.

"You require my assistance, brother?"

"Take Aislinn. Do not get into trouble. Agnar has overstayed his welcome."

"Got it," she responds, wholly unaffected by her brother's shadows slipping down the damask-clad walls as she wraps me in a tight embrace. "Time to go, friend."

"Go whe—" Before the full word is out, we're zipping through the front door and skyward faster than I've ever traveled before. Helena is even faster than the transports below Obsidian.

The Shadow Palace quakes behind us. There is a loud explosion, followed by the air rippling with power, and I glance back to see the entire front wall of the palace has blown off. Stones rain from sky, and I swear I see a limb or two falling with them.

"Oh, shit" slips from my lips as I watch black encompass the ruins and more of the walls begin to tremble.

We're flying too fast for me to make out any details of the land below us and my eyes water from the wind slapping against me. Even with my blurred vision, I find the Shadows are much more than a gray barren wasteland that I always assumed it to be. A distant mountain range appears to drip magma into the lake and the line dividing Kaoket is even more stark from above.

Finally, we slow and Helena lands in a palace covered in dead vines and surrounded by trees...if you can even call them that. They're sad remnants of a life that once was and will never be again.

"Home sweet home," she says, practically singing.

"This is your house?"

"More or less. It's my father's, but he's been imprisoned for a few hundred years, so I watch over it." She shrugs.

Wrought iron handles curve into the shape of a skull. Helena waves a hand, and the doors push open. Then she pulls me into Death's dwelling.

"What. The. Haile?" My jaw goes slack.

The entire inside of the palace is…pink. Different shades of pink and so many textures my head spins and taking it in is almost an assault to my senses. Pink feathers trimming the curtains. A rug that looks like splatters of pink paint. Pink furnishing. Pink tile. The winding staircase is covered in pink glitter. Everything, absolutely *everything*, is pink. How could someone live in this and keep hold of their sanity?

Helena bites on a smile. "Pretty great, huh?"

I sit in one of the oversized plush chairs, sinking in as the cushion forms around my body. "It's uhm…it's a lot brighter than I would have expected."

Helena plops into the matching chair beside mine and kicks her feet up on the side table. "No one ever comes here. Too depressing for them, I guess. So I did what I wanted with it. Erebus has taken the initiative of father's duties, but he prefers to run everything from his place."

Sounds lonely. I can relate.

"Do you think Agnar and Erebus are going to destroy the whole palace?"

"Most likely, until Haile comes and breaks it up. Then they will get punished like the children they are."

I shift, trying to get more comfortable. "Punished how?"

"Depends on Haile's mood. House arrest, missing limbs, blasts of pure light, a walk through Oblivion."

"Do I want to know what Oblivion is?"

She shivers. "No. You absolutely do not."

"Missing limbs?" There's no way they'd be so barbaric.

"Mhmm." She makes a chopping motion over her arm. "They grow back. Still hurts like fuck though."

"Gods are crazy." I look out the large window to my left, fixating on the field of shriveled flowers. There's a feeling of violation looming over the land here—it's like the more the Olvi shines, the more desiccated the Shadows become.

"You're not wrong. Just wait 'til you meet Revetta." She tips her head back and laughs with a darkness emanating from her voice. "Or Oonaugh. Oonaugh is a riot. She's kind of an odd one, but entertaining."

"I know of Oonaugh, goddess of the seas. But who is Revetta? I've never heard her mentioned in our stories."

"Ravetta is the goddess of chaos. She thrives off discord. She is Haile's spymaster. It doesn't surprise me that you don't know of her. She's slippery, stays hidden. Haile has worked hard to make it so."

"Why would a god need a spymaster?"

Helena flares her wings out, then drapes them so they hang behind her in the seat. "The same reasons mortals do. To squash rebellions before they begin."

These gods are so different than what I had expected. I can't believe how wrong we have it in the mortal realm. They're just like us, but instead of political power, they have *real* power.

"That doesn't make sense. If she thrives off chaos, wouldn't she encourage rebellions? Not squash them?"

"That's exactly why she was given the position. It's her punishment for the war she started."

"What war?"

"The last one. The one where Egon was going to take Haile's place as king. Ravetta was whispering sweet nothings to my poor father, putting ideas in his head while doing the same to Haile. She kidnapped Edwissa's muses...only to let them go at just the right moment...the moment Father struck through his wife, Kaleil, with a blade of aietal. It was a gigantic mess."

"Huh, we heard that story a bit differently."

Helena looks out the window. There's a glisten in her violet eyes that turns them a dark blue. "Yeah, that sounds right... Are you hungry? Want some tea or something?"

I shake my head no and she shrugs, pulling a biscuit out of a hidden pocket of her wrapped dress and taking a bite.

"And Oonaugh? Why is she so entertaining?" I ask, watching her pull a second biscuit out once she has devoured the first.

Helena licks her fingers and asks with a mouth still slightly full, "Haven't you heard her story?"

I think back to what we were told by the mistresses at the academy. Oonaugh is one of the more villainous gods with an insatiable temper. "That she fell in love with a mortal man who chose a mortal woman over her?"

"More or less."

"What's the more?"

"So she did fall in love with a mortal. But the mortal was already engaged to be married, to a beautiful woman. Out of a fit of jealousy, Oonaugh turned the mortal woman into a beast and bound her to a vile bog for eternity. Vristra has been sentenced to a life of solitude merely for being born beautiful. Or...so is the story that Isela told."

I try to suppress my laugh at the memory of my encounter with Vristra. She wasn't warm in any kind of way, but she did throw a boot at Iris. It was almost worth inhaling the vile fumes. "I've met Vristra. She's a bit, uhm, cranky."

"Wouldn't you be? Quite sad, really. No one remembers her or her name, only how she was scorned by a lover. Oonaugh now collects women, turning them into her minions. The creatures are truly terrifying. Top half mortal women with incomparable beauty. Bottom half fish. They don't show their razor-sharp teeth until they're tearing at your throat with incisors the size of a finger. We call them *isvitoks*... but if memory serves, the mortals call them '*sirens*.'"

"Why would she do that? Turn the women?"

"Why else? To build her own army. Something you should always remember with gods—they *all* have an agenda."

My shoulders roll with the chill creeping up my spine. "And you? What is your agenda, Helena?"

Helena just taps her nose and smiles. Before I can further prod her, the front doors burst open, and a freezing gust blows through with it.

Helena rolls her eyes. "So dramatic." She starts picking at her nails. "That was quicker than I thought it would be."

I don't have to turn to see him. The sudden harrowing darkness tells me all I need to know about who has just burst into the pink palace of death.

Erebus breathes heavily as he comes stomping through the doorway. His hair is disheveled, and his suit torn as if some beast crawled out of his skin. "Time to go, pet."

"You could have at least cleaned yourself before coming. What will the gods say when they see you so disheveled?" Helena chides with a shake of her wings.

He stands straighter but winces so slightly I almost miss it. "I did not trust you ladies to not get into some kind of trouble. Especially you." He gives a knowing look to Helena.

"I know how to behave." She pouts.

"You know how, yet you often choose not to. It's no wonder you've taken a liking to Aislinn. Cut from the same cloth. Like calls to like, as they say."

I shouldn't smile, but I can't help it. Neither can Helena. We both start giggling, and gods, I forgot what it felt like to laugh. Or smile. It's been so long.

"I'm glad you both find insubordination so humorous. Now, pet, it has been a long day." He holds an arm out as if he expects me to grab it. He's lost his damned mind if he thinks I'm going to willingly touch him.

"But we were just getting to know each other," Helena says, almost begging.

Erebus brings his outstretched hand in and rubs the bridge of his nose. "I'd rather you didn't."

"But if I have a friend, I won't always have to come hang around with you." She cocks her head to the side—an obviously fake smile sitting crooked on her face.

He looks between us and loudly exhales though his nose. "You are permitted to visit once every other day, so long as you two *behave*."

Helena jumps up and down with a gleeful squeal. Erebus rolls out his shoulders and, without asking, lifts me from the chair—cradling me close to his chest. I push against him and flail, trying to get on my feet again, but, too quickly, we are surrounded by shadows and pulled through a twisting void.

"I don't appreciate being carried like an infant," I snap when we arrive in my room. I'm not the least bit surprised. Why wouldn't he return me to my cell?

"Then you should have taken my arm like an adult when it was offered to you," he says. His normally condescending tone is much softer. It's as if the words took too much energy to add feeling to them.

As soon as I open my mouth to dig into him, I shut it. His back is facing me, and through the torn remnants of clothing, I see what looks like constellations inked into his skin...well, constellations *and* fresh burns tearing them apart.

"You're hurt," I say quietly.

"It's nothing I haven't felt before."

Something about seeing the savagery inflicted upon him twists my stomach uncomfortably. I shouldn't care...but I can't help it. I've never seen such hideous wounds.

"That looks really painful. Did Agnar do that?"

"No, pet, this was a gift from the king himself. This is the effect a solar blast has on a god. Again, nothing I nor any of the other gods haven't felt before."

"He shouldn't be allowed to punish you like that. Someone should stop him."

Erebus's hands are over my mouth before I process his movement. "Do not speak such things, Aislinn. Those who do have a tendency to disappear." He whispers so low his icy breath tickles my ear, and I shiver in response.

"Is there something I can do to help with the burns?" I ask when he releases my mouth.

"You...would help me?" His brows raise.

"I may hate you, but I'm not a monster."

"Not like me, you mean?"

Of course, he wouldn't make this easy. "Do you want my help or not?"

Erebus appears to have some kind of inner battle, but then relaxes his shoulders and nods almost reluctantly. "I have a healing salve. If you want to be useful, you can help me apply it to the areas I can't reach on my back."

"I can do that. Take your shirt off."

I sit on the edge of my bed as he stalks towards me. His shirt disappears—leaving his bare chest exposed and looking more godly than I have ever seen him.

It shouldn't surprise me to see the deep cuts of his muscle, but I am. It takes a second to regain my train of thought as I get lost in the constellations marking his body. From the base of his neck down is completely covered in a beautiful rendition of the night sky. Even his arms are full of the swirling designs. I've never seen him in anything but a suit, I never would have guessed what was beneath it...not that I ever gave it any thought.

A jar appears in a swirl of shadows on my bedside table. I open it and dip my fingers through the cream that looks as though it's been made from crushed diamonds. The muscles in his back tense at my touch. Despite how he is, I can't help but feel pity. No one deserves this.

He looks as though he's bathed in fire. The flesh is singed and peeling away from the muscle, disfiguring the art decorating his body. I swallow the sick feeling I get and try not to cringe as I continue to apply his salve.

"Thank you. For doing this." His voice is quiet and sincere, to my surprise.

"You don't have to thank me. I'm just doing what anyone decent would do."

"I haven't met many individuals I would consider *decent*," he admits.

Being the presiding ruler over death, I don't doubt the truth to those words. I'm starting to see more sides of Erebus despite what he chooses to show me. And there is one thought I haven't been able to shake since our meeting with Agnar. If I'm right...it may change things, or it may not. But either way, I have to know.

"Can I ask you something, while you're in a good enough mood?" I take another huge glob of the ointment and slather it onto a particularly deep gash, taking absolute care to smooth out the thickest parts evenly.

"You can ask. I do not promise an answer."

Typical Erebus response. It's an inner battle not to roll my eyes.

"When you were trying to destroy DeLuca...destroying his family and getting into his mother's mind...did you do it to break him so he wouldn't become powerful enough for Agnar to find?"

I finish applying his ointment, but he doesn't move. It seems as if his shadows have also stilled, awaiting his response.

"Tell me, pet, would that make me any less a villain to you?"

"That's not an answer."

He stands, turning to face me. His skin is gleaming with the addition of the healing salve. Paired with the ethereal glow coming off the stars gracing his skin, it creates a dazzling effect. No one would question his power seeing him as he is now.

"Yes, Aislinn. The answer is *yes*."

"How could you do that to him?" A burn coats the back of my throat, and tears build behind my eyes as I think of all the pain

DeLuca has been through at the hands of this god, but also the reality he could've been killed if he'd been spared the pain.

The stilled shadows begin to swirl again. More gather around us and Erebus waves them off as if they're insects.

"Someone *has* to be the bad guy. Why not me? Born in shadow, made from death and fury, feared the moment I entered the realm."

"That doesn't answer my question, Erebus. How can you become that horrific monster who does nothing but take and destroy?"

"Because it's what they expect of me!" Erebus shouts. He then lowers his voice. "It's what they have *all* expected of me. Except her. Except my Astoria. She is the only one who ever attempted to look beneath the darkness."

I study Erebus. *Really* study him. The tattoos on his skin. His demeanor. His words. Maybe he's not the monster I think he is. Maybe he's just become what was expected of him—exactly as I would have by marrying Rett. Something in that realization breaks through my resolve and a splinter of pity and understanding punctures through the cracks.

"You truly loved her, didn't you?"

"*Love*. Aislinn. I love her. And I will do anything to restore her mind. Even if I have to crumble this realm to stardust. I don't care what mortal lives I have to take or what else I have to tear apart."

So, maybe he is still a bit of a monster.

I fidget with the blanket covering my bed, struggling with my own conscience, but I can't deny it, that feeling of what is *right*.

"I don't think that's true. I think there is goodness somewhere in you. Buried deeply, sure, but it's there. Astoria saw it. She didn't create it."

"Maybe, but it's buried too deeply for me to care."

I can't believe I actually feel bad for the god of shadows, but I do. And my inner compass is pointing me towards him. Telling, no, begging me to fix what's been broken.

"Erebus?"

"Yes, pet?"

"I'll help you."

THIRTEEN
GOOD THINGS DIE
Erebus

THAT INFURIATING CREATURE.

My shadows have not stopped their ramblings since we left her room. They are called to her like no other. Her past is not what draws them,it is her. They want *Aislinn*. She lures them and lulls them like a pied piper. If she only knew how my shadows cling to her. How much power she could wield if she were to unlock her truest form.

If only she knew the power she holds over me. How drawn to her I am even still. Her darkness calls to mine. Kindred.

Yet, she has no idea what this thread tying us together really is. I have to know what it means. What all of this means. What path we have taken. If my actions in bringing her here have unraveled all I've done to protect the Shadows.

If she is the key to our realm's downfall.

I am standing on the threshold of Astoria's sky room, watching her sleep from a distance. My beautiful starlight. So broken. So damaged. Because of me. Because this is the cost of my love. Suffocation. Dying. Losing your light.

Madness.

Astoria's light was the brightest I had ever seen. It was euphoric. Any who gazed upon her knew what it was to love. And she *chose* to love *me*. She could have had anyone. Any god.

She chose *me*.

And I took everything from her.

My thoughts run rampant while my shadows continue to hiss excitedly from the kindness Aislinn showed us.

True kindness without expectation.

It is not something we are accustomed to. Especially not since my darling Astoria has been unwell.

It would be a lie to say it didn't feel good. But my shadows need to remember who she is, what she is. Her purpose in being here.

And that soon—her light shall fade too, just as Astoria's did.

"Queen of damned, shadows sing within cracked skin, beginnings start at ends," Astoria rambles in her sleep.

I'm at her side in an instant, smoothing the glowing hair off her face. "Shhh, starlight. Rest."

"Seasons end. Blood rain and chaos cover the sun. All good things die."

"Yes, all good things die."

The words pull at a cord of emotion I thought long gone. All I can do is hold her against me and try to calm her. My shadows wail as if they sense my heavy burden and loathe me for it. As they should. I am their god, their ruler. I determine their fate—if they're deserving of the Afterlands or eternal torture. I am cruel.

I am the killer of good things.

And this brings me peace.

Once I leave the sky room, I find I have a new sort of clarity. One in which I realize having Aislinn as an ally may be more beneficial than trying to force her into anything...and to do that, I'm going to have to do something I'm not entirely sure how to do. I'm going to have to play nice. The shadows who stay by my side seem to hiss in a kind of mockery.

"If you do not stop that indecent noise you're all making, I am going to send you all into Oblivion."

Silence.

Finally.

They know not to test me, I am true to my word.

I crack my neck to the side and roll my shoulders out, trying to relieve some of the tension held there from the brawl with Agnar. Admittedly, starting a fight with the god of war was not one of my better judgments. But watching him tangled in my web of shadows, and the anger that almost had his ridiculously large head exploding was worth the arm he tore clean out of the socket...even when he threw it across the realm for who knows what kind of monster to snack on.

The nub is almost grown back to my wrist. The illusion I cast makes it look as if nothing is missing at all. I did not want pity, so when Helena eyed it with suspicion I had to make a show of lifting my pet with ease to show her I was fine. Nothing amiss, even if it is a lie. But is that not what this realm is built from? Well told lies?

I may have overestimated my ability to *play nice*.

Days have gone by and I haven't been able to bring myself near the girl. Each time I reach her door, I am bombarded by the memory of her fingers roaming my skin—the reaction I had to it—and immediately walk the other way. The emotion she brings is one I am not familiar with and it clouds my thoughts. Anything other than a sharp mind is a dangerous thing in our realm. It is as good as a white flag begging the other gods to take what's mine.

Of course, I always have one of my subjects with her. The shadow stays hidden and does its job well, reporting through the ether of her movements, which usually consist of looking out her window, eating two bites of the food I send, or sleeping during all waking hours. The first day, she got up and dressed on her own, sat on the pale gray chaise under her large window. It was reported she looked at her door every few minutes...as if waiting for someone. She did this for three days before she stopped bothering to get dressed. Now she does not get up at all.

Shadows skitter along the walls, following me through the immaculately decorated halls of my home. They are restless, and their chaotic moods cause my skin to itch—like the shadows that live within me are trying to seep out my pores and join their brethren on their venture to drive me mad.

I exhale deeply, channeling my annoyance into the breath. "If you want to see her so badly, go see her. I have yet to find a way to speed her progress, and I am in no mood to entertain the bombardment of questions she will surely spew."

As one, the shadows make a noise that sounds suspiciously like a booing, but they abandon me, leaving my head blissfully quiet for the time being.

Perhaps I should be more bothered by my shadow's antics and where their loyalty lies, but my problems are toppling one atop the other, and the shadows' draw to my pet is somewhere toward the bottom of my priority list.

The top, as always, is Astoria.

Just below her, the realm and getting new shadows through the barrier.

It is unfortunate both priorities require the girl to regain at least a small part of her old self, a thing I am beginning to doubt is a possibility. Those three menaces must have put some kind of block on their shadows. Aislinn's bleak mood is certainly not helping any. I need to find some kind of way to lift her energy before we can make any progress.

I still my steps at the same time a metallic gleam catches the corner of my eye. It's like a call from my thread of destiny, being pulled by the Weavers. Usually, I ignore such things, considering what they have already put me through, but looking over at my imperialite basin, I realize that I know *exactly* what to do next.

FOURTEEN
REFUGE
DeLuca

THE MAN STANDING BEFORE us isn't in much of a condition to fight. He has his arm in a makeshift sling and is coated in a thick layer of grease. I'd say in his fifties maybe, but it's hard to tell what lines are from age and what are from a hard life. His wiry hair is standing on end as if he'd been struck by lightning. The rest of his appearance reeks of desperation. His dark eyes hold kindness, but desperate people surprise you. Just because he doesn't appear dangerous doesn't mean for one second that he isn't.

"We are looking for refuge," Lysette says from behind me before I have a chance to answer. Her hands are up and her voice is soft.

"Refuge, huh?" The man scratches the back of his neck. "I'm sure we still gots some room in this big ol' palace. You'll have to talk to the man in charge about that. He looks over all us here."

"Who's us?" I ask with my hand hidden behind my back, concealing the small flame.

"Eh, there's a bunch of us. We've come from all over. Some from Ashe, some the surrounding villages. We even have quite a few from the Capital, if you can believe it. Where did you say yous two came from?"

"Castona," Lysette answers quickly.

"Oh, you should find some friends here then. Come on, I'll take you to the big man. He will decide what to do with you."

I share a glance with Lysette as we silently debate our options. We could cut and run, but considering this man was all the way on the fifth level, it's safe to assume there are people scattered throughout the floors, and we don't know their intentions or affiliations. Our best chance is to try and blend in until we can locate the archive. Lysette seems to agree and taps my arm lightly, silently telling me to smother the flame.

We follow the stranger down the maze-like halls until we find ourselves in front of the office Lord Magnus once occupied. The one beside the room I found Aislinn in just moments before that disgusting pig was able to violate her.

Nope. Don't think about it, DeLuca. You will only burn this place down.

"New arrivals, sir!" our guide says with a light rap to the open door frame.

"Send them in, Tank," a voice grunts from behind the door.

The man in charge has a stack of papers in front of his face when we walk in. Tank shuts the door behind us before heading off to do whatever it is he does around here.

Lysette and I sit in the two oversized chairs facing the large uncut obsidian desk. After a few moments of waiting for him to put down his papers, I clear my throat.

"Apologies. Reports on the anarchy and chaos throughout Stellera. I was sucked in." He sets down the paper and Lysette gasps.

"Evander?" she asks on an exhale.

He squints and looks at her harder. The moment realization washes over him, his eyes widen to saucers. "Lysette?" She nods and jumps over the desk to tackle the man she called *Evander* to the ground.

"You were dead! You were dead! I saw you fucking die!" She's pounding on his chest, and tears are falling off her face and onto his shirt.

"I thought *you* were dead!" he counters, squeezing her tight, pinning her arms to his chest so that she can no longer hit him.

"What the Haile is happening?" I ask. Clearly, she knows this guy. He looks vaguely familiar, but I can't quite place him. I'm not sure if I should intervene or not.

"Oh, right, yes." Lys stands to her feet, the man following her to his as well. "This is Evander. He was Rett's friend and was one of our officers. Evander, this is DeLuca."

Evander looks between me and Lysette before asking, "Is he your—"

"Absolutely not!" The blush in Lysette's cheeks creeps down her neck. "DeLuca is with Aislinn."

"Aislinn's here? What about Rett? Did anyone else make it?" Evander asks, standing straight and looking at the door.

"Well...it's just us. But Rett is safe. He's with Iris in...a camp. Aislinn made it out during the attack but has since been...uhm...taken."

"Taken? By who? Pierce is dead. There hasn't been anyone to rise up and claim his place as leader. Who would want to take her?"

"Erebus." I say the name like a curse.

Evander starts laughing. The sound rubs me the wrong way, and I stare down at him with narrowed eyes.

He notes that he is the only one laughing. "Wait, are you serious?"

I could explain everything in detail. All we've been through and learned over the last few months. But I am out of patience, and it's much easier to show him. I call to my fire, and it swirls in an orb hovering over my palm. I let him absorb the image for a second before giving him a very short explanation. "All the stories about the gods are true, and we seem to have found ourselves mixed up with them."

Evander keeps his eyes on my flames and steps in front of Lysette, as if I'd hurt her. "Yeah, I'm going to need more information than that because it sounds impossible."

Lys steps out from behind Evander and puts her hand in his. "Improbable, yes, but I assure you it is not impossible. I will explain it all, I promise, but later...It's a lot."

Evander stares at her for a minute. I see a million questions race in his eyes, but then he closes them and nods. "Later then, I trust your judgment."

She tucks a strand of red hair behind her ear and tries to hide a smile. "Later. Meanwhile, there's a room here. It was a secret. It's why we came back. We are hoping it has information or anything that will help us get Aislinn back."

Evander's brow furrows below his overgrown dark brown hair. "Yeah, of course, anything. It's *your* house, Lysie."

Lysette smiles, but there's pain hidden beneath it. "Not anymore."

"How did you survive the attack? And what have you even been doing here?" I ask. Even though Lysette seems to trust him, I do not. I don't trust anyone but especially not those who take power.

"I don't know, to be honest. I was pretty messed up after the explosion. I took a lot of shrapnel, but my skin seemed to force it out. One of my arms was broken. The bone was sticking out. It was...it wasn't right. It looked almost like it was made of volcorium. Green and metallic. Just as hard too. Once I got it into a makeshift splint, it took a few days, but the break healed completely." He holds out his arm for emphasis. You'd never know it had been mangled.

"And then?" Lysette encourages.

"I laid low, blended in with the Liberators who'd stuck around until they eventually headed to join the others at the Capital. The ones that remain have taken residence in the palace there. Well, between there and Fort Vicanti, but by all my intel it would seem they're not organizing under a new leader, just kind of lying in wait. Ever since they left, I've kept the doors open to refugees. Anyone who needed a safe place to stay. We've been working together as a small community of sorts. We mostly have women and children here, older folks. We make do with what we have to work with. It was smart to try to conceal your identity. A lot of them still blame the highborns for this mess."

"Shit," I say on an exhale. "This *is* a fucking mess."

"It's not ideal, but could definitely be worse," Lysette agrees. "But you've done a good thing, Ev. I'm glad you were able to use this place to do something worthwhile." She squeezes his arm.

They stare at each other and seem to forget there surroundings. I clear my throat to remind them and Evander blinks and looks between us. "It's the middle of the night. You two must be exhausted. We can finish this tomorrow. We still have a lot of spare space left. Most of the rooms on the fourth floor are occupied. Your room is open, Lysette. It didn't feel right putting someone else in there. It's still yours if you want it."

"No," she says too quickly and then clears her throat. "No, I'll stay in the east wing. Is Aislinn's room open? I'm sure DeLuca would be most comfortable there, and I could take the room across?"

"I believe it is, yeah. That should work. After we get you settled, I'd love to hear the story behind this." Evander trails his finger along Lysette's scar. A sound similar to a growl erupts from my throat, surprising even myself. Evander doesn't seem bothered and leads us out of the office with an amused smirk. Why do I suddenly feel an urge to punch him?

"You're no better than Rett," Lysette whispers aggressively as she passes me.

This is a dream I've had many times...waking up in this canopied bed stitched to look like the night sky. My girl beside me, her hair a mess and sleep still hanging heavily in her eyes. I've wanted it for so long. Wanted her for so long. She once told me that she's been dreaming about me her whole life...but the truth is, I think I've been dreaming about her too.

Being in this bed without her hurts as it reminds me of all the things that aren't and all the things that could have been. The furniture remains mostly intact. The bedding is gone—likely looted along with the other valuables—but I've slept in worse conditions.

It feels strange to be in this room without her. It reminds me of the first time I brought her coffee. She wasn't on my rounds that morning, but I wanted any excuse to come see her again.

Her eyes. Fuck. I've never seen a green quite that pure. So full of life, despite the purple lining them from so many sleepless nights. I was captivated from the first moment our hands touched.

After she tended to my wound, I knew I was a goner. She had me completely. Even if it seemed like too much for such a small cut. It took every ounce of self control not to kiss her in that moment.

The way she looked at me as if she wanted me just as much...

And she did...she wanted me.

"Are you wallowing in self pity again?" Lysette leans against my doorway with mockery in her tone.

"I don't wallow."

"Sure, Lucy. Whatever you say. Keep moving forward, that's what I say."

I get out of bed and grab a shirt from the chair beside it. "Seems like you were certainly moving forward with that reunion last night."

"Evander is the reason I'm alive. When the Liberators blasted through our front door, we were right there. My dad, Evander"— She closes her eyes and inhales deeply—"Linnea. He was trying to get us to the tunnels. I think he saw the blast coming. I was closest to the door, and he threw me forward and shielded my body with his."

I'm an asshole. "Gods, Lysette. I'm sorry. I didn't—" She puts her hands up and stops me.

"I don't want to talk about it. Move forward, right?"

"Right...but if you ever do, uh, want to talk about it, you can talk to me."

"Okay. I probably won't, but thanks. Now let's go. There are three places I think we can find the entrance in."

"Lead the way, Lady Urson." I keep my eyes low as I would if I were still a serv.

"Gross. If any good comes from any of this, it's that I will never have to be a lady."

"You would have been a good one though, you know?"

"A good what?"

"Lady, leader, governor, whatever. You would have been great."

The sparkle leaves her eyes which doesn't align with the smile she tries to maintain. "No use looking back."

We try the servs quarters first. Nothing but old memories and forgotten lives. Half of the west wing is in ruin. Anything that was near the front doors also is completely obliterated, and it causes a chill to waft through the manor. It looks and feels as if it's aged thousands of years, filled with the dead who couldn't pass to the Shadows. I can almost feel their energy around us.

So far, the search has lasted all day, and we've come up short each time. Lysette showed me the room with the mirror. "The watching room" she called it—as if that makes it less creepy.

We have, obviously, avoided the rooms she already checked with Aislinn and Linnea at the beginning of the summer. In my opinion, we should be focusing on the fifth floor, but for some reason I can't even fathom, Lys wants to try everywhere else first.

Her parents's room is last on our list before we head upstairs. She drags her steps the whole way—hesitating before opening the doors, and when she does, she has to take several more breaths before stepping through the threshold.

It's bare, like the others, aside from the furnishing. Aislinn's room is huge, bigger than my old house in Ashe, but the Lord Magnus and Lady Lyrica's room could eat three of her rooms and still have walking space. It's like a whole separate house, and I can't help but groan thinking about how long it is going to take us to search through it all.

FIFTEEN
DON'T LOOK BACK
DeLuca

A LONG DAMN TIME.

It took a long damn time, but we're finally in the last section of it. The bare furniture is now scattered all over the room. It looks as if they'd been robbed blind. I move the bedside dresser into the pile of furniture we've thrown into a pile.

"I don't see anything that looks like a switch, Lysette."

"Yeah, it was kind of a longshot for the access point to be in here. It would make more sense for it to be in the office or conference room, but I figured we might as well try since we were closer."

I try not to show my irritation, considering I suggested both those places hours ago. I have to remember this is hard for her. My monsters were her loved ones, and she still grieves for them.

"Let's go see if they have anything to eat then head up. If we can't find it, we can always try and melt the glass in the watching room." I wiggle a small flame around my fingers.

"That's not funny," she deadpans.

"Who's joking?"

"DeLuca, you can't! What if you burn the books!"

"Oh no, not the precious books! Let's hope we find the entrance then." I give her my best smile.

"Don't make that face. It looks like you're about to be sick."

I follow her out with my head shaking—fighting back laughter.

We make our way through the familiar, yet unrecognizable, halls. Lysette has put on a brave face, but I sense the shift in her. At the bottom of the stairwell—on the ground floor—we run into people. Literally. Right into the back of a kid standing in some kind of line.

"Oh, sorry about that. What's this line for?" I ask.

"Evening gruel." A small girl smiles weakly, and I notice the younger boy beside her is missing his arms.

"Your parents work in the factories?"

"Yes." She bites her thumbnail, and the line moves forward—gently nudging the small boy's back.

I don't let the pity show on my face. "What's your name?"

"Winnie. And this is my brother, Castiel."

I kneel down in front of the little boy. "Castiel, is it? That's a very strong name. I bet you're very good at taking care of your sister, aren't you?"

"We take care of each other now," he says proudly.

"And where's your family?"

"All gone. Just me and Winnie now."

As I suspected. I find myself overcome with a grief I'm sure can be traced back to my own childhood if I felt the need to look inward. My hand lands on the boy's shoulder, and I squeeze it. "Always stay together. You'll be okay, kid."

"I've been taking care of us. We don't need anyone else," the young girl—Winnie—says. Her tone is far stronger than I would've guessed judging off of her appearance.

"I'm sure you have been. You look like you're getting on very well."

"Leave the poor kids alone; they don't want to talk to boring adults." Lysette lightly kicks the bottom of my shoe while fiddling with her eye patch to make sure it's straight.

"Good thing I don't see any boring adults around here." I wink at Castiel who giggles. His sister grabs two bowls of gruel for them both. All I want to do in this moment is follow her and make sure they're okay, but I don't. I stay and try to push out the flood of memories.

Lysette's brows pinch. "You okay?"

"That was me. Me and Val. That girl even has her personality. Right down to the walk." I notice my breathing deepen as my chest begins to constrict. My hands ball into fists at my side.

Block it out, DeLuca.

Block it out.

"DeLuca. I know it's hard. But we can't get involved. Not now. Keep your eye on the bigger picture." We grab our bowls and go sit outside in the courtyard with a fountain and exotic potted plants that all appear to be on the brink of death.

"That's always been the problem with highborns. You forget about the little people while looking at the *big picture*."

Lysette dips a finger into the soil of one of the potted plants and twirls it. The drooping ends fill with life and are restored to their succulent texture. She smirks to herself before turning towards me. "Fine. Stay. Adopt them." She shrugs. "We can leave Aislinn to find her own way back to us. I'm sure she will be thrilled to find out you've started a family without her."

"That's low, Lysette."

"I'm being realistic, DeLuca."

I shovel the tasteless gruel into my mouth. In three large spoonfuls, my bowl is completely empty. I look down at it, then around at the other refugees eating.

"They're rationing...I wonder how they're doing on supplies." I continue to look around at the sunken eyes and sallow cheeks around us. The people of Ashe weren't in great condition before everything went to shit. It's hard to know which ailments are remnant of that life and which were made from trying to survive this new one. "How bad off do you think Stellera is?"

"Bad. Without any kind of leadership, I'm sure trade has stopped. Who knows how many high houses are still intact to communicate needs to each other. It's not like the Liberators were very organized...just very angry."

"I never thought about the after," I admit. "When I was helping them...I never thought about the trade or anything like that. I just figured...I don't know, that people more organized than I am would figure it out."

"Yeah, well, what do we say, Lucy? Don't look back." She finishes her bowl and sighs at it, discarding it to her side.

I'm still sucked into thoughts of my mistakes. "It's hard when I feel like my past is trying to swallow me whole."

Lysette claps in my face. "Snap out of it. We have things to do today. Come on, let's go upstairs."

I nudge her with a shoulder as we pass through the hall, and she gives me an almost convincing death glare. "One of these days you're going to have to think about it, Lys, and when you do, I'll be here."

Under her breath, she mutters, "Unless you won't." Then she turns to me with a cocked smile. "If we never stop moving, the past can't catch us."

"That sounds logical." I tease. "Beside the fact that you're not a fast runner—"

She gasps and places her hands on her hips. "Hey!"

I put my hands up for her to let me finish. "Beside that fact, the events of our past leave scars, both seen and unseen. You can try to leave them behind, but they are a part of you and will always be there."

Lysette trails her fingers over her scarred cheek. I let the silence hang between us, my words sinking in further with each step. I'm a hypocrite. I'm running from my past just as fast as she is. Each day that I've gained enough distance to feel like I can breathe, something rips me back, hurtling me toward a cliff there is no coming back from.

Evander is behind the Obsidian desk looking over more papers when we make it to the study. He's more than amenable when we request to dig around and immediately begins helping us look through drawers and shelves, even going as far as to pull up a few loose floorboards.

"I honest-to-gods thought it would be in my father's office...It would make sense because Lady Soleil's was." Lysette says after our search reveals nothing.

Melting the window is starting to look more and more appealing. "Yeah. I thought it would be too. So...conference room?"

"Conference room." Lysette nods. "Thanks for letting us disrupt your day and poke around, Evander."

"I already told you, it's your house," he says, running a hand through his deep brown hair.

"Ev...really. It's not. You're doing more here than I ever would have." She places her hands over his.

There's something going on with those two and I don't want to watch any more of it.

"I'm gonna go next door," I say awkwardly, stepping around them. They're completely transfixed on each other and don't seem to notice me leave.

It seems like a good idea until I put my hand on the doorknob with the 'U' engraving. Now all I can see are flashes of that pathetic excuse for a man on top of Aislinn. What he almost did to her, if I hadn't happened upon them by pure dumb luck.

Breathe, DeLuca.

You're going to burn the place down.

When I've calmed myself down enough that I'm certain I won't catch fire, I enter the room that has haunted so many of my nightmares.

The ones where I don't save her.

I'm under the table feeling for any groove or loose planks.

Nothing.

Bookshelves, nothing.

Pictures, nothing.

Nothing.

Nothing.

Nothing.

Lysette isn't having any luck either as she crawls around inspecting the baseboards. I'm going to lose my mind if we don't find this room soon. Every minute is another minute Aislinn is exposed to gods-know-what.

I slide against the wall and place my hands on the back of my neck, trying to breathe through the stress and disappointment. I'm spiraling, I feel it, like a current trying to burst through a dam. My head smashes back against the wall a few times, an attempt to focus on anything other than the buzzing beneath my skin.

"Lucy!"

"I can't find anything, Lys. This is useless."

"You foolish man-god." She runs up and kisses my head.

"What?" Her burst of excitement provides the right amount of distraction from the ticking time bomb that is held captive within my very bones.

"Don't you hear it? When you were banging your head against the wall?" She knocks on the place where my head was hitting for emphasis. It takes a few seconds to click, but fuck me I feel a weight lifting the second I realize what she's showing me.

"Hollow," I say as our gazes clash, and a smile spreads across my face that mirrors hers.

"Hollow." She nods.

"So it *is* up here. We just have to look harder. The other side of this room is the office. Meaning there's dead space between. We could have missed it in the other room," I say.

"Maybe...But I've always found it weird this room is the only one in the whole house that has an engraved door knob. My intuition tells me it's in here."

"Mmm, I can't argue with intuition." I laugh, and she nudges me. "Okay, okay. Well, it's not in any place obvious."

"Well...yeah...it would defeat the point."

"Alright, smart ass, where would you hide a secret button?"

"Hmm. I'd put it somewhere it didn't look out of place...but was still clearly marked."

"Right. Well. Your father's not here anymore. Let's turn the place upside down."

"Let's do it," Lysette agrees, almost too eagerly and with a mischievous little grin.

We feel along the moulding at the top and bottom of the wall and look over each detail in the room—pushing on anything and everything. Lysette is on her knees examining the underside of the shelves. I don't bother to point our that a lord wouldn't get on his knees for anything, and the chances of her finding it somewhere down there is slim. I'm on a chair examining the tops of them. Nothing up here but a bunch of dust.

"Anything?" Lysette asks from under the table.

"No, you?"

"Not yet. I'm going to try the paintings next."

"Sounds good." I hop down from the chair and run my finger along the shelves, pulling each book out as I do.

Still nothing.

By the time we start pushing the furniture around, we've looked at every crevice at least three times, and the small spark of hope I allowed myself to feel begins to fade again.

It's not until I'm leaning against the wall in yet another breath of frustration that I notice it. Squinting a little harder to be sure of what I'm seeing, I huff out a laugh. A tiny "U" at the bottom of a sconce. Identical to the one carved into the door.

"Lysette." I point to my finding with a smile, because I know, I *know* this is it.

"No way. It's too perfect," she says, hopping to her feet before pushing the tiny "U". It sinks beneath her finger, and the room begins to shake while the wall between the study and the conference room lowers into the floor, revealing a staircase.

"We found it," Lysette whispers, disbelief draping her features. A light creeps into her widened eyes and she exhales. "We found it!" she shouts and then proceeds to sob loudly with large tears rolling quickly down her reddened cheeks.

Not the reaction I was expecting. "Lys?"

"I'm fine. I—I'm fine. It's just Linnea, Aislinn, and I spent weeks trying to find this room. We were supposed to find it together. It was right here. The whole time it was right here, and I'm the only one who will see it."

I place a gentle hand to her shoulder. "You'll have to savor this moment for the three of you, then."

"Yeah." She presses the heels of her palms into her eyes—knocking off her eye patch. "Yeah, I will. I'm sorry. I didn't mean to cry."

I pick up the patch and hand it back. Her fist clenches around it a bit too tightly and her knuckles turn white.

"It's okay to cry, Lys. Especially after the last few months we've had. Let it out and let it go. We don't look back, remember?"

She nods and then swiftly punches me in the arm. It might as well have been a flower petal thrown at me, but it still takes me off guard and I pause dead in my tracks.

"Why did you do that?"

"It made me feel better to hit something." She shrugs.

I laugh. "If you need a punching bag, we could always go back for your brother."

She swats my arm and sticks her tongue out at me before pushing me out of the way to get to the opening.

I nudge her with an elbow. "Such violence from such a fickle houseplant."

I wouldn't even be surprised if we were below ground. It's hard to say. There's a dim purple light. Oxidous energy, no doubt. The stairs lead down at least five flights and curve almost like we're in a tower. I've never seen any kind of tower in Obsidian Manor, so it's hard for me to know exactly where we are. When we finally make it to the room, it's surprisingly similar to the one in Sutton, though this one is quite a bit larger, and one of the walls is made entirely of a mirror. You'd never know if someone was on the other side watching. I wonder if those who used this room knew.

"Where should we start?" I ask. "This is your area of expertise."

"Well, considering there aren't any labels or indications of any kind just like in Lady Soleil's archive, your guess is as good as mine," Lysette says while already pulling three large leather bound books off the shelves. They release bursts of dust as they hit the table. "Just skim for the words 'Erebus' or 'portals' for now." She immediately goes to work and cracks open all three books.

"Got it." I look at a shelf, trying to decide what to grab first. I pause at a tiny box. Curiosity gets the better of me, and I open it. "There's no way."

"What did you find?" Lysette looks up from her book expectantly.

"You're not going to believe this."

"Well, show me then!"

I bring over the little box to her, opening it to reveal a cylindrical stone with purple light striking against the interior. "It's the Siphon Stone the Guardians used. This is the Kaillen girl's lightning."

SIXTEEN

MEMORIES

Aislinn

"WHEN I TOLD YOU I'd help you, I didn't expect to be left in my room to rot." I huff while fiddling with the locket around my neck. Erebus has finally come for me after days of leaving me alone with nothing but shadows for company. I had felt like something shifted between us when we last saw each other, but apparently, I was wrong.

"I was healing," he says plainly.

My arms fold in front of me as a reflex to his blatant lie. "It took you nearly two weeks to heal?"

"If you are not in the mood to play nice, I can leave *before* I give you your gifts."

My back straightens. "Gifts?"

A slow knowing smile pulls at the corners of his lips, making his wrong eyes light up with a look that sends ice through my blood. "Yes. Gifts. Well, I suppose not—considering they were always yours to begin with."

His finger does a slow circle, and at first I think it's because he's calling his shadows to produce the "gifts," but then I realize that by the way he's impatiently staring, he wants me to turn around.

I do so with a sigh of irritation. My foot begins tapping, and my eyes roll to the ceiling as the seconds tick by.

"Is this your way of—" My words freeze in my throat as a cold hand wraps around it.

"Be. Patient," Erebus says with his mouth beside my ear.

It takes a lot of self control not to swallow—partially because I don't want him to feel it beneath his icy touch, partially because I don't want to admit the effect his touch has on me. The way the call of his shadows speaks directly to mine. My eyes remain fixed on the large window in front of me, desperate for a distraction.

Though I can not see his face, I feel his smile, as if he knows exactly how stunned I am. There's a cool caress around my upper thigh, like it's being circled with an icicle. The sensation causes my entire body to shiver despite my attempt to hold it back. It's an odd sensation between nausea and a connection I won't let myself admit to.

My voice shakes. "Erebus?" And I don't even know what I'm asking because I am completely caught off guard. So utterly in shock from the cold continuing to envelope me that I can't think straight.

"Look down, pet," Erebus says, backing away. The ice holding me in place immediately begins to thaw with his retreat.

With a pinch between my brows, I do as he says and look down. A different kind of shockwave replaces the first. This one is full of heat and anger.

"The Child Blade?" I ask.

The familiar dagger is strapped to my thigh by the same leather garter DeLuca had given to me before meeting with Erebus—the same dagger I killed my best friend with—and tied to it is a ruddy brown scrap of lace. The last memento of the life I was meant to live.

"Why would you give these to me?"

"What ever could be wrong, pet? Do you not like being reminded of the darkness that dwells beneath your own skin?" he asks tauntingly, as if he knows exactly what I'm thinking about.

The veins in my neck pulse with the restraint it takes to not stab him with the very dagger he has returned to me. I ask again, "Why, Erebus?"

He sighs. "Because, dear pet, I am trying something new. It is called trust. I have just given you back the very thing you need to protect yourself against me."

I scoff. "Trust?" Though he is right...he has just handed me what just might be the only thing in all the realms that can kill him. When I first arrived, I would have done so without hesitation. His death was what I clung to in those days of anger and grief. But now? I shake my head subtly and clear whatever thoughts tried to break through.

"Yes. I will require a bit of your trust for what comes next."

The snappy comeback is on the tip of my tongue, but I can see the sincerity in the depths of his disturbingly gray eyes...not to mention how difficult this appears to be for him. No way in Haile I'm going to trust him...but I can play my part as all the highborn training has prepared me for.

I run my finger over the lace on my thigh. "What comes next?"

"A lesson."

He begins to walk out the door, and when I don't follow, I feel a tug on the shadow marks covering my skin, as if I am being led by a chain.

Pet, indeed.

I'm pulled into the unfurnished room with the uncut stone basin used for enhancing visions. The same one he used to show me an image of Lysette and DeLuca being *extremely* friendly with one another. His attempt at provoking jealousy from me almost worked. His game is emotional warfare and I've seen it done countless times.

"What are we doing here?" I ask, rubbing the burning cold spot around my wrist that felt the strongest pull from his shadow chains.

"I'm accepting your previous offer to help me."

It says something about my patience that I'm able to keep a straight face. I was locked up for days after I had offered him help. *Days.* I was beginning to lose my damn mind. Time works differently here. The hours ebb and wane like a tide led by the changing moon.

"You didn't have to give me gifts if you wanted help. I offered it freely."

"As previously stated, the gifts were to establish a line of trust, though I will caution about bringing the dagger outside of the Shadows. It is a considerable offense to have such a weapon here."

I step around him and rub a finger along the lip of the basin. It hums beneath my touch. "And you are going to *trust* me and show me something in this strange portal-thing that can help you?"

He shakes his head and exhales heavily. "I am fighting against my nature and trying to indulge your eagerness, but you must stop with all the questions. I will provide the answers you seek if only you wait."

"I wouldn't have so many if you would just speak plainly." I place my hands on my hips and cock my head to the side with just the right amount of attitude to stoke his agitation.

"We are retrieving this." He conjures a few vials, filling them with the pearly liquid from the basin. I stare and wait for him to explain. He notices my attention, and after releasing a sharp breath through his nose, he continues. "This fluid is called oktalei. It is an elixir made from ground imperialite that helps enhance certain abilities...like visions."

So, essentially a performance enhancer. We have similar things for soldiers...or had is more accurate. Too many of the soldiers lost their minds, and it has since been outlawed. Oh gods, what if this 'oktalei' causes me to lose my mind? What if it has contributed to Astoria losing hers? My stomach clenches. "And I'm supposed to drink it?"

"Eventually. Of course, we must have another piece in place for it to do us any good.."

I wait expectantly, but he doesn't offer any more information while examining the vial in his hands.

"If you don't tell me what that means, I'm just going to ask."

Is he trying not to smile...? Oh, he definitely is. The corner of Erebus's lip twitches, and it takes him a moment to answer with a straight face. "We need to reunite all of your stones. I have the Opari. You have the Forbis and I need *you* to find the Viitor. The original Utikalo tethered its shadow to the Forbis Stone. You, essentially, *are* the stone."

"I am the stone?"

"Obviously, I just said that." His eyes drag over my body and end with a quirked brow. "But that little tricky creature hid the Viitor stone somewhere in the time to come. It is constantly moving. Once you are whole, we can restore my wife's mind...as well as do something about the barrier—if only to herd the new shadows through."

"I'm not sure how much help I can be." Considering I'm not following his trail of thoughts whatsoever. How am I supposed to find the Viitor stone if it's always in the future? That makes absolutely no sense.

"Yes, well, I'm hoping by reuniting two-thirds of the stone—and with the help of this elixir—we may be able to unlock some memories. Or skills, at the very least." A swirl of shadows produces the familiar stone swirling with gold mist into Erebus's hand, and he says more to himself than to me, "Useful skills would be wondrous."

"The Opari Stone?" I put my hand out, expecting him to give it to me. "Do I just hold it like you do?"

"Oh no, pet." His cruel smile has my nerves buzzing in anticipation as he says, "This is going to hurt."

Shadows gather from the corner of the room and scratch along the walls. I can almost hear them, almost. They're no more than the flap of a butterfly wing...almost nonexistent, but there.

He takes my outstretched arm into his icy hand, squeezing so tightly it sends a shock of cold straight to my bones.

"Wh—" I'm cut off by my own screams. The pain is sudden and sharp—shooting acid up my veins. My vision goes black. Then the tears come—silent and steady. My vision returns only for it to be darkened by the swarmed shadows around us.

Erebus has shoved the stone in its entirety into the flesh of my forearm. It's throbbing and radiating a power that feels foreign yet comforting at the same time. It takes my breath away and fills it with its own beautiful and tantalizing air. The pain is hardly there as the euphoric raw power tangles itself into my blood and dances with what was already there, like long-lost friends reuniting at last.

Shadows dance around the wound, dulling the pain with a numbing cold. When they're gone, the skin around the stone is healed. Only drying blood and a small bump in my arm remain.

"That was unforgivable." I breathe heavily as I try to adjust to the new feeling of my own body.

"It was necessary. I thought it better the pain be a surprise to lessen the nerves." He shrugs. "Do you feel any different?"

I swallow while taking stock of my body which feels infinitely lighter. The stone still juts out of my arm as if it's trying to break free, but my body holds it like a prison of flesh.

The words that come out of my mouth next surprise me...because they're a lie. "No. I feel the same."

He mumbles, "mmm," then hands me a vial. "Drink this, and think of something you want to see."

Gods, please, please don't turn my mind inside out. I bring the cool vial to my lips, and before I can over think it, I tip my head back and pour. The thick elixir slides down my throat. The oktalei is much sweeter than I anticipated. It has a similar taste to a floral tea filled with too many sugar cubes.

I close my eyes and picture the only person I want to see, DeLuca. I fixate on him completely. Let myself remember his scent; smoke and stone. His bright blue eyes. The feel of his lips on mine. His warmth, so drastically different than the cold I've grown accustomed to with Erebus. I think of how desperately I crave to be near him again. I continue this until my feet go numb from standing still for so long.

"This isn't working." I peek one eye open and gasp—finding myself in some kind of archive. I'll be damned. It actually worked.

The room is familiar. I have never been here, yet somehow I know it. There is a large mirror taking up the majority of one wall and shelves upon shelves of old books lining the others. Even through the vision I can smell the dust coating every inch of this place. DeLuca's smiling as he spins Lysette around. He has a true, honest to gods smile that warms my chest and fills it with the same love I felt when I last saw him. He's devastatingly beautiful at any given time, but when he smiles...it's like everything else melts away and he is the sun and stars. I watch the two of them twirl with a lightness in my chest at his happiness...but then he sets her down...and DeLuca's lips press against Lysette's soft cheek, just beside her scar.

The lightness in my chest turns leaden.

It's like I'm falling, then crashing into reality.

My chin quivers.

I try to block out the image.

I try to remember his words.

I try to remember his love for me.

But who knows how long it's been for him. Maybe he really has moved on. I keep my eyes shut tight—wanting to be anywhere else but here.

My ears are ringing as my consciousness drifts back to my present. Erebus must sense the shift in me because he asks, "Did it work?"

I nod, swallowing the burn in my throat.

His gaze is intense as it fixes wholly on me. "What did you see?" He wipes away a tear I let escape with his thumb.

"You were right. He's moving on."

"Hmm. Mortals are impatient. He seems to have molded himself to fit his surroundings." Erebus clicks his tongue, not needing clarification about whom I'm talking about.

Biting my cheek, I add, "I think I know what can help provoke memories."

"Are you going to make me ask?" His voice is teasing, as if it's a joke between the two of us.

"Sometimes when I touch something, I can see a memory attached to it. Maybe if I go to where the Utikalo lived before, I can find something that will help."

Erebus goes rigid, and his gray eyes turn black. "No."

"Why? Isn't it worth trying?"

"I said no, Aislinn. We will continue this course and work to stregthen your visions *here* in the Shadows."

"But *why*?"

"Because to do what you ask, you would have to go back to Kaoket. To Millena's palace...to Agnar."

Not that I am itching to see Agnar again, but some invisible pull tells me I'm supposed to go there. Something awaits me in Kaoket. It calls to the stone in arm. "I think it's my best chance."

"I said *no.*" His shadows flare.

"Well, what do *you* suggest, Erebus?" The shadows shrink and some rally around me like they're choosing a side. I try not to let the smugness show on my face, but it warms my chest with a sense of victory.

He opens his mouth, then closes it as if another thought has come to him. The glint in his eyes is full of menacing promise. "Tell me, pet, have you ever been able to jump into someone else's memory?"

My brows knit. "I don't think so. It only works with objects."

"Would you oppose trying with me?"

"You want me inside your mind?"

"I want you to learn control over your power. I can start with a simple memory. This is where our new line of trust comes in."

Yeah, I'm not about to trust him. Though, I am surprised by his offer to let me glimpse in his head. To see through his eyes, it's intriguing. Erebus doesn't strike me as someone who gives freely without ulterior motive...but the temptation is overwhelming.

"The last time our minds connected, you ripped my cousin's shadow from his body."

Erebus glares at me. "Are you no longer interested in learning control?"

I want it, the control. He knows I do. I stare at him until his glare softens into what I can only assume is his attempt at sincerity? I roll my eyes, not fully believing I'm about to do this. "What do I need to do?"

He straightens his suit, looking far too pleased with himself. "Remove all of your clothing."

A huff of air leaves my throat, suffocating the unamused laugh and choice words sticking there. But I do as he says and begin unbuttoning the back of my dress.

Erebus's eyes widen, and he sends bursts of shadows to my hands, stopping their movements. "Stop!"

I pause, hands still holding a button, and look at him in question.

The shadows retreat and he starts laughing. His face brightens with mirth. "Were you really about to undress before me?"

"You said—"

"Humor truly is lost on mortals. Don't be so serious all the time, pet."

"You're a pervert."

"A *pervert* would not have *stopped* you from undressing." He has his shadows buttoning my dress back up. They are a cold caress against my spine. The sensation has me leaning into them and rolling my shoulders back.

"Oh yes, your chivalry is endless."

"Come now, pet, I have just the memory for you. Do not be frightened; you might enjoy this particular history." Erebus is practically bouncing on his toes. "Place your hands on top of mine." He holds his hands out, palms down, and I place mine above his as instructed.

"Now what?"

"Clear your mind, should not be too hard since there is not much in there anyway." I scowl and he smirks. "Now, focus on me. Focus on the feel of your hands above mine. Close your eyes, Aislinn, feel my mind. Reach down our shadow bond. Follow it to me."

I do as he says. His voice is less slithery and more soothing, hypnotic even. There's a burst of shadow and light before I find myself in a familiar meadow in Caeliss.

I'm looking at Audrina. But I'm not me; I'm much too tall. She's crying. Actually, she's sobbing. I can feel her desperation. There's a dark aura surrounding her. The moon is clouded in shadows. Beside Audrina is an altar of sorts. I can't see exactly what is placed upon it, but somehow, I know whatever it is was used to summon a god. This god, me. Erebus.

"Mortal?" His voice passes through my lips.

"Yes. Not fully. I am a Whisperer," Audrina says with a shaking voice that sounds so unlike the version of her I remember. Where is the cunning girl who could bring men to their knees with a simple look?

"I know you...Whisperer...you keep company I am rather interested in. Why have you tried to summon me this night?"

"I-I'm sorry I don't actually know who you are, I found this ritual in a book, but it wasn't fully translated... I don't know what to call you, all-mighty—?"

My brow quirks of its own volition. "You are brave enough to perform a summoning ritual, yet, you are not smart enough to use intention?"

"I do have an intention...I intend to go home, to the Islands of the Sons."

With her words, I feel a shift in the body I'm inhabiting. It feels like the islands hold some kind of meaning for him.

"Ahh. You want something. How typical." I turn and stiffen as I take in the village before me. Caeliss. It looks beautiful beneath the slivers of light from the shadowed moon. It glints off the stone building like stars winking in and out of existence.

"Please don't go!" Audrina falls to her knees and begs. "I need to get back to Sutton, to my mother, to my people. If you help me, I swear to do my duties to them. I swear I'll be a lady that deserves the title and will be better for them. They will never feel the desperation the Stellerans do."

"None of that has any worth to me. What do I get in exchange for this favor you ask?"

Her tears stop. She takes few breaths, then sits up straighter, pulling the sleeve of her dress down suggestively. "Whatever you want." Did her voice just drop? Oh gods, Audrina, you didn't just try to seduce a god into making a deal, did you?

Erebus's laugh bellows out of me. "What would I want of you, mortal? Ridiculous."

She pulls her sleeve back up quickly, a rosy flush spreading across her cheeks. Anyone else would think it embarrassment, but recognize it for what it is, frustration. "Ask it then. Anything within my power I will give to you."

"Anything?" He drawls.

"Yes! Yes! Anything. For my return to my island and for the island's protection."

"Oh, asking for even more, are we? You are either brave...or greedy."

"I—"

"Stop speaking! I will accept a favor for a favor."

"Anything! I swear it."

A sharp smile spread across my face that feels so wrong, so...dirty. "Good."

She swallows. "What is the favor?"

Erebus wanders to a nearby tree and examines its leaves, rubbing his thumb along the underside of it before snatching it off the branch. He tsks as it instantly shrivels and turns to ash in his fingers.

"I have interest in someone you call a friend. She is known as Aislinn to you."

"Aislinn?" Her face contorts. "Why?"

"I have my reasons. I would like your assistance in meeting with her."

"With Aislinn? You're not going to hurt her, are you?"

"It is not my intention to inflict any physical harm upon her."

"You just want to...meet?" she asks.

"Indeed, and it just so happens my meeting place is exactly where you want to go."

Audrina frowns as her eyes shift back and forth between Caeliss and me...or Erebus. "The Islands?" Audrina looks at her feet, eyes searching for an answer that won't appear. "You swear she won't get hurt?"

"I swear no physical pain will befall the seer."

"Deal." She holds out her hand to shake.

"Wait." A finger that is too long to belong to me is held up in front of Audrina's lips. "You asked for two favors: To return to your island and to protect it. In return, I require two favors as well."

She blows out a breath and looks up at the sky, cursing. "What is the other?"

"To be determined, Whisperer. You shall owe me a favor of my choosing in the future."

Her face changes into one of determination. "Done."

I put my hand out. "Deal."

She takes my hand. The second our palms meet, shadows twist around our clasped hands and a strong wind seems to encircle us, blowing Audrina's hair around rapidly. Her amber eyes widen while looking around with realization.

"Are you—"

"*Monsterously handsome? I do think so.*"

"*What?*" *She shakes her head.* "*No. Are you...him?*"

"*Yes, foolish girl.*"

She exhales. "*God of the shadows.*"

"*And trickery. Everyone forgets that part.*" *The wind and shadows halt.*

"*Are you tricking me now?*" *she asks.*

"*No, mortal, you have really just sold your friend to the Shadows.*"

"*I take it back!*"

"*You made a deal. It is bonded to your shadow now. If you do not complete it, your shadow becomes a part of my collection, to use as I please, while your mortal body rots and your mother mourns your pathetic end.*"

"*So, if I break the deal...I die?*"

I sigh. "*Yes, your mortal body will die as your shadow is painfully ripped from it, and you become bound to me, to serve me for eternity.*"

"*No.*" *She clutches her chest.*

"*Oh, yes. Well, it has been an interesting evening, but I'm afraid I am running out of time and must be on my way. See you soon, traitor.*"

Audrina drops to her knees, head falling into her hands, and a painful tearing begins to consume me from the inside out before the memory sputters out all together.

When I open my eyes, we are in the exact same position. Erebus's hands still remain beneath mine. His eyes are closed, and the longer I look at his pompous arrogant face, the angrier I get.

I rip my hands back from his, then push against his chest with all my might. "You played her!"

"We made a deal. It was entirely fair." Erebus is unphased by my anger, though it thrashes inside me with the need for release.

"Fair?! She didn't even know who you were!"

"She shouldn't have asked help from the gods without being specific. She could have summoned anyone. She could've gotten someone much worse."

"You manipulative bastard! And what was the second favor? Was that her betrayal of DeLuca?!"

Erebus shrugs. "Seems you already know the answer to that."

"She was my *best* friend, Erebus. The person I trusted most in this world. She was the closest thing I had to family for six years!"

"It isn't my fault you put your trust in the wrong person. If she knew loyalty, she would have turned me down the second I asked. I told her I wanted you before she made the deal. She accepted. Those are the facts and they can not be changed, no matter how much you try to make me fully responsible."

A tear of anger slides down my cheek.

I can't argue with him. He's not wrong. I would have said no if the roles were reversed. I never would have even entertained the deal, not for a second. If the choice was Vallae or Audrina, I'd choose Audrina without hesitation. But I *felt* the desperation in her, the sadness and grief. She was afraid and I was blind to it.

So maybe...maybe I deserved her betrayal. If I had been a better friend... If I helped her leave like she wanted...Maybe she never would have gotten so desperate. I never gave her a chance to explain.

I didn't want to hear it.

All I felt was the pain of a friend turning on me. Fear for the first person I ever truly loved as I watched him floating unconscious. I let that rage consume my rationale completely. There wasn't a rational thought in my mind. It was like being possessed by something else completely, and as the life slid from her in ribbons of red and the light left her eyes... I was glad of it because I thought it was justice.

But, what if it wasn't?

What if she was only trying to survive, just like the rest of us?

Does that make me a villain?

SEVENTEEN
VOLCORIUM
DeLuca

IT'S BEEN FOUR DAYS of reading through stacks upon stacks
of books. We found journals passed down from generations of
Ursons that Lysette is rifling through, though I think it's more
to connect with her family than anything. She's made it through
three of them. According to one of the journals, her father was the
leader of the Guardians, and the role has always been given to the
Ursons as they are the oldest recorded bloodline.

Equally as interesting, before the gods stopped traveling freely
between realms, the Guardians had a very close relationship with
quite a few gods. Most surprisingly—Agnar. There are many
references to some gift he gave the Ursons, but she hasn't yet
figured out what the gift is.

I'm currently reading through a passage about Isela, goddess
of seasons and wife to Haile. Apparently, they had dozens of sons
but only one daughter, Astoria. Isela grew quite jealous of the
attention their daughter received from Haile and wouldn't allow
him any more children. Not quite helpful...but I can't help being
a little curious about my birth mother's parents. My lineage seems
like a real piece of work, if what these old books say has any merit.

Trying to read all these dusty old books by the dim purple light is driving me close to insanity. Especially since I am trying to make anything out of the ones written in Old Daeil. I close the book with an exaggerated sigh and put it back on the shelf carefully even though what I really want to do is throw it across the room. In fact, I'd love nothing more than to knock all these shelves over and light them on fire. Maybe break that creepy mirror that seems as if it's mocking me. My fingers brush against each of the leather book spines, hoping one with something useful will call out to me.

"Holy Haile," Lysette says loudly, shaking me from my thoughts of igniting the book beneath my fingertip.

"What is it?" I leave the bookshelf and slide into the chair beside her.

"You're not going to believe this." She looks up at me as if she were just given the moon straight from the sky.

"Believe what?"

She taps the page excitedly. "I found out what the gift was."

I try to peek, but she closes it before I can see. "Well? What was it?"

"The Obsidian Mountains." She smiles slyly.

"Interesting?" A whole mountain range is a pretty big gift, I guess. Maybe that's why the Ursons wouldn't let anyone else build on them...because they were literally gifted from a god.

"Ask me what they're filled with." She shakes my shoulder. "Go on, ask."

"I already know. Veins of oxidous, steel, volcorium, the usual gems."

Lysette is practically shaking. "Ask me what volcorium is when melted down in the correct conditions." She buzzes.

"Just tell me, Lysette!"

"It's aietal." She pauses for dramatic effect, then holds her hands out as if to say "ta-da." "Obsidian is a mountain of aietal."

"No fucking way." My jaw goes slack as she passes me her ancestor's journal that I quickly scan over. "Why would a god supply mortals with a mountain full of the only thing guaranteed to kill them?"

"My best guess? Probably Millena's influence. Being the goddess of balance, she probably wanted mortals to have a fair chance if we were to ever war with them."

"I suppose that makes sense."

"That's not the best part." She takes the journal back and flips to a different page.

"What's the best part?"

"Each family in the Guardians was given some kind of gift. Like the Siphon Stones were given to the Soleils."

"What are the other gifts?"

"It doesn't say...but DeLuca, if a war breaks out because of what we are doing, maybe we should hunt down the remaining families and tell them to start preparing."

A war? A war with the gods on mortal soil? That would be insane...wouldn't it? Such a thing could destroy everything. "Why would you think war is coming?"

"Because, you're either going to break into the gods' realm and die, or you're going to be successful. If you're successful, that will mean you've stolen from a god. I don't expect him to take that well, and if gods are anything like man, they will follow their own."

"You think he'd start a full war over Aislinn?" I would. In a heartbeat. But she means something to me. To him, she's likely no more than a trophy.

Lys closes the book and grabs another journal, dropping it in front of me and another for herself. "I think most wars are started from hurt egos."

I chuckle a little, unable to find a flaw in her logic. At least with her on our side, we'd have some semblance of a chance at reuniting the high houses. "I just realized something."

"What's that?"

"You're the last Urson."

She pales, but I can tell she is trying not to let her face drop. "Yes."

"And your mother was a guardian as well...which means you would have likely taken both their places on the council...or perhaps, they intended for you and Linnea to."

"Maybe." She exhales. "What are you getting at?"

"Well, if your father was the leader, and the role has always been filled by an Urson, wouldn't that make you the new leader of the Guardians?"

"I guess. But the only Guardian I know is Lady Soleil... I mean I've met ambassadors for the other families, but I don't know them too well."

"You could call a meeting." I look into her eyes. "You can get them started again. Maybe figure out a way to piece Stellera back together. At the very least, the Guardians are all a part of what remains of the leadership for this nation."

"I suppose...maybe. I'll have to figure out how to get into contact with them all, or if they're even still in their provinces. It will take time."

"Well, keep doing what you do best—read. I'm sure there's something in there. Whatever guardians are left. We can't just do nothing."

"It's a nice idea...but I'm not sure we can do much of anything, the nation might be beyond us."

I wouldn't know. I have never been much of a leader. I couldn't guess the first place to begin trying to put back what was broken...though it shouldn't go back. Not necessarily.

"Just think on it." I squeeze her shoulder. "Have they been creating weapons from the aietal or just collecting it?"

"If he had been making weapons, there would probably be record of it in his journal—or maybe even in his office. Though, if we did have a stock of god killing weapons, I'm positive my father would've had it heavily guarded."

I nod. "Yeah. I'm sure he would've too. Your father was a lot of things, but an idiot isn't one of them."

We continue searching in silence for another few hours. The air down here is just as musty as the air in Lady Soleil's archive, and sitting still for so long has my skin crawling as if thousands of tiny mites are burrowing homes into my pores.

I'm just getting ready to call it a day when I'm flipping through pages and a map falls out. With gentle fingers, I unfold the old parchment and lay it flat on the table. Of course, it would be in Old Daeil. It's similar to the one hung on the wall in Sutton, but the labels seem different, and I recognize some of the gods' names all over the continent.

"Hey, Lys, do you want to look at this and see if you recognize any of the words?"

"Honestly, DeLuca." She huffs out a breath and shakes her head. "If you're going to call yourself a god, you might as well learn their language." She gives a slight shove to my shoulder, moving me out of her light, then laughs softly. "They should call *you* the god of luck instead of Felix."

"What's it say?"

"Pouais Guiseiolis."

I look at her expectantly, feeling my patience wearing thin. "And what is that?"

"Gods' portals. You just found yourself a map of all the portals in the continent."

For a second, I am too stunned to react. To speak. Exactly what we have been searching for for months, and it literally just fell into my hands. I could scream. I could burn everything. Haile, I could even pass out from lack of oxygen because I've forgotten how to breathe. I don't know what to do, so I settle on lifting Lysette and spinning her in a circle, kissing her cheek as I set her back to her feet.

She instantly wipes my kiss off, her scar discoloring as she rubs it out. "Okay, we found the portals, but you have to remember, if you're not the god they belong to, it will tear you to shreds."

"Right, unless we trick the portal somehow."

"Right."

"Just let me have this moment, Lysette. After months of searching, we have finally found something."

"Have your moment. Then put your nose back in that book." She points at a shelf we haven't touched yet, then sits back in her seat.

"Yes, Lady Urson, queen of the Guardians. I'm feeling lucky now. Something tells me today will be our last day spent down here."

"I like your energy and pray to the god of knowledge you're right."

"Is there a god of knowledge?"

"No. But honestly, there should be."

"Hmm. If there was, I doubt anyone would listen to her anyway."

She cracks a smile. "Her?"

"A god of knowledge would definitely be female. Every woman I have met has been infinitely smarter than I am."

"And why wouldn't anyone listen to her?"

"Because the men in charge will always think themselves the gods of knowledge, despite history proving them wrong time and time again."

"I can't say I disagree." She smirks. "I think I may have an idea of how to get you through a portal."

"What is it?" I rub my hand through the scruff growing along my cheeks.

"Okay, fair warning, you're not going to like it."

"Lys, I haven't *liked* any of this."

"Fair. Okay. Hear me out...we use your Siphon Stone and try to slip you into the god's realm through Oonaugh's portal off the coast of Rilyse. Her portal is located just here. See all these jagged rocks? That's the Levithan's cavern. There's a small lagoon there; that's where it will be." She points on the map, demonstrating.

"That doesn't seem so bad."

She lets out a little nervous giggle. "Well. It's guarded."

"By who?"

"It's more of a by *what*...a lot of whats...Oonaugh's monsters, the isvitoks, creatures half-woman and half-fish with sharp teeth and an unmatched bloodlust. Also called sirens." Her eyes are shifty. She's leaving something out.

"And?"

"And they notoriously hate men."

I exhale. "Of course they do."

EIGHTEEN
ENDEARED
Aislinn

EVER SINCE EREBUS STUCK me with the Opari Stone, he's been visiting my room more often, acting almost...concerned. It's completely irritating considering he is the last person I want to see right now. I've only interacted with him when absolutely necessary. I don't know who I am more angry with, him or me. I keep circling back to what I could have done differently with Audrina. If I had only been there with her, what would that have changed? Would I be here, in the shadows? Or would I be with DeLuca, in our little cottage house somewhere near Astoria?

Am I the reason everything has gone straight to Haile?

He's here again. Leaning against my door frame, talking at me about who knows what nonsense now. I don't bother to listen to what he's saying. I'm in bed with my back facing him while I rub my thumb across the ridge now permanently embedded into the skin of my forearm. The protruding stone hums to me, like the ringing in my ear. It's like being called home.

I've been practicing with it. I'm able to conjure small visions from across the barrier, but they're muffled. It's hard to get a clear picture without the oktalei, and I don't dare ask Erebus. I am still unsure of his true intentions, and I definitely don't trust him enough to let him know I've been attempting to strengthen my visions on my own.

Better to pretend to be weak and let him underestimate me.

"Are you listening, pet?"

I roll over and blink at Erebus. Clearly, I was *not* listening and have no idea what he just said. "No," I answer plainly, my voice expressionless.

Erebus sighs, but his demeanor is suspiciously soft while his eyes search me as if...maybe as if he's worried? But that can't be the right emotion.

"I said, I'd like to take you for a tour of the palace. If you can *behave,* that is."

"If I behave like your *kept pet,* you mean."

Erebus rubs his temples and his shadows wrap around me, pulling me out of bed and altering my appearance in one swish of his hand.

"What if I wanted to remain in my pajamas today?" I ask while scowling at the black fitted dress he's put me in. It hugs my figure but breathes in a way that shouldn't be possible for a dress so tight. My hair is swept up off my neck with a few loose strands hanging around my face. Always so godsdamn formal.

"It's been days. Your time to sulk is over now. You *will* get dressed each morning and accompany me for breakfast in the parlor, where you *will* eat. During the days, you will train to use your Utikalo gifts. I am not your parent. I shouldn't have to tell you how to take care of yourself."

I shrug my shoulders. "Fine."

Erebus looks like a muscle is going to pop in his neck. "Fine?"

"What do you want me to say?" I'm tired, so incredibly tired of these antics, and my fight is holding on by frayed threads. I'm afraid that if I push any harder, they will snap, leaving me to fall for eternity.

"You usually have a bit more snap in your speech." He looks as if he is about to say more when a gust of wind blows my hair back, and in a flash of white, Helena is standing by my side. Her violet eyes are full of fury as she fixes them on Erebus.

"You said every other day. It's been over two weeks! I'm not taking no for an answer this time!" Her voice disrupts the very air we breathe as it pulses with the manifestation of her anger.

"She was unwell, sister. You know how mortals are with their lack of immunities," Erebus says.

Helena turns, her lashes almost touch as she squints to assess me. "She seems fine."

"I *am* fine," I say.

Helena's posture softens to its usual carefree appearance. "Good, because I want to have some girl time...the kind that doesn't involve getting naked." She pauses, then adds, "Well, actually, I'd be good with that kind too if you're up for it."

I smirk, and when I do, Erebus turns his attention to me so quickly it would have made any mortal dizzy. He looks as if he's assessing and that he likes whatever it is he's thought of.

"Why don't you join us for a tour of the Shadow Palace, Helena?" he asks, earning a side glance from both me and Helena.

"You're actually inviting me?" Helena asks with narrowed eyes.

"You're the one demanding time with my pet. I had plans for the day. If you must collect on my offer now, then you will just have to accompany us."

"Of course, I'm collecting. This is the first opportunity you've given me!" She claps excitedly and then she wraps her arm around mine and pulls me in like we've known each other our entire lives.

"Why do we have to walk?" Helena whines. Her wings mimic her shoulders as they sag and drag behind us while we walk through the palace.

This *tour* has been dull and predictable. Especially because Erebus doesn't actually show me through each room, just gestures to the general direction and says, "You are not allowed here. Nor there. And *definitely* not there."

Apparently, we have one more stop before he will be satisfied. I suppose I should be grateful to get out of my one room. I was beginning to talk to the shadows on my wall and questioning my sanity.

Erebus makes an exasperating sound as he answers Helena. "Because I want my pet to know her way around. If I shadow her in, she will get lost when wandering on her own."

"You could just give her wings." Helena huffs, unimpressed by the long corridor stretching before us. Erebus smirks at her in a taunting manner. At least it isn't just me he likes to torment.

Wait, he said... I couldn't have heard that right.

"I can wander on my own?" I ask.

"Do you not listen to a word I say? We are here," he says while opening a large double door with incredible engravings along the rounded trim.

It's like something out of a fairytale. Even the smell of the wood feels as if I've been transported to another time. The engravings continue from the doorway along the walls like the roots below ground. They look strangely familiar, but I can't quite place it.

I'm unable to hide my awe at the enormity. The room looks endless. Filled with shelves upon shelves of books in either direction.

"A library?" I ask.

"My personal collection." Erebus straightens the cuff of his sleeve and Helena rolls her eyes.

There are more shadows gathered here than I've seen anywhere else in the palace. They don't seem quite as menacing and cold—but seem to shimmer and circle above us—giving the illusion of infinity. The magic is thick enough to dance along my skin and awaken something in my core. Where there should be a wall, there is instead a misty waterfall that flows down from a sky swirling with dusky lavender-tinged clouds.

Odd, seems like anyone—or thing—could gain access to the Shadow Palace from there.

"Why is there no back wall?"

"Oh, pet, you should know by now that nothing is as it seems. It is yet another illusion. Beyond that wall lies the very heart of the Abyss. Would you like to see it?"

"No," Helena says quickly with her arms crossed.

"Yes," I say quietly under a breath. Morbid curiosity overtaking anything else I had felt before stepping into this enchanted room.

Erebus nods with a look of victory and waves his hand. The illusion shatters like broken glass spider-webbing into ruin. When it finally falls apart, there is nothing more than an infinite dark. If I strain my eyes enough, I can make out movement of the shadows trapped beyond in their eternal torment. I walk closer, past the books and rows of shelves, until I am right against the invisible wall separating us from them.

Condensed puffs of air come out with each jagged breath. With my hand upon the icy barrier, I feel an indescribable calling. It's like the shadows of the Abyss are singing to me. Begging me to join them. A frigid hand presses against my lower back and I shiver beneath it, but I still feel that tug from the other side, almost like a trance.

I lick my lips before speaking with an uneven voice. "Why does it feel like that?" I ask Erebus, whose hand still rests on my back.

"Feel like what, pet?" he asks quietly.

"Yeah? Feel like what?!" Helena shouts from the other side of the Library. She hasn't dared step a foot closer.

"I—nevermind. My friend, Lysette, would love this place. In fact...if I didn't know it was yours, I'd say this was her version of the Afterlands."

"Hmm. After the Whisperer's betrayal, I thought you'd have the sense to realize you can't trust anyone enough to be considered *friends*," Erebus says.

"I *don't* trust anyone." I step out from his grasp. "What's in all these books, anyway?"

"Words, mostly." He shrugs. "At times, pictures as well."

"Obviously. I meant a little more specifically."

Erebus looks at me with a devious expression. "This is a copy of every book from the mortal realm... I sometimes like to assist in the knowledge provided in them."

"Assist? You can't mean you change our histories?!"

"Can't I? I like to consider it dabbling in storytelling."

"You're corrupting our knowledge!" *That's why we couldn't find anything written about Erebus in the archives.* "You're erasing yourself." It doesn't make sense why a god would want to be erased from our realm. What could he possibly gain from that?

"Oh, who cares? It's just a bunch of gibberish anyway," Helena says. "It's almost always wrong to begin with. Can we go? This is too close to Oblivion for my comfort."

"You never had to be here, Lena, this tour was for my guest," Erebus says.

"What is Oblivion?" The name alone is enough to send a strike of fear to my belly, but for Helena to fear it so drastically, it must be really bad.

"Oblivion is a path between the Abyss and the Afterlands that shreds your shadow. If you're worthy, the core of your essence will remain. If you're not, then you will become nothing more than tattered filth, floating in Oblivion forevermore, completely aware, yet with nothing to grasp to. It's quite painful."

"What is Oblivion used for?"

"I just told you, to find the worthy."

Helena adds, "The worthy get to pass through to the Afterlands."

"We haven't used Oblivion in years though. Mainly, Haile uses it as punishment for those who cross him. Our shadows repair themselves, but it's excruciating, and we have to live out every worst deed we've ever committed."

"He keeps—"

Erebus interrupts her. "Enough, Helena." Then he recasts the illusion to make the Abyss look like a beautiful dusky sky again.

Nineteen
A Million Paths
Rett

IRIS IS ASSISTING WITH a birth tonight. Are babies born to Children different from mortal-born babies? Maybe they come out with some indication of their inheritance...like the twins and their scars up their legs and torsos. I was so young when they were born, but I can clearly remember being upset by it, wondering what was wrong with them. My mother told me it was a blessing from the gods to bear such a mark. Then she looked at my legs, unscathed, and my smooth skin, with a strange, pinched expression. Aislinn had told Lysette my mother never knew what he'd done. Switching their dead babies for healthy ones from Ashe, but that moment has been stuck in my mind for a long time. I think she knew. She had to have known I was an imposter to the child she bore.

With that thought, I throw back another shot of honeyed whiskey. This has become my usual dinner when Iris is working late. Partially because I don't know how to cook. Partially because I feel like shit when she's gone. Physically, it feels like a withdrawal, and mentally...well, my thoughts take a million paths—all of which lead back to me being a shit-bag.

Therefore, whiskey.

And now the bottle is gone. Splendid.

I bet Alec has more. It might be rude to go knocking in the middle of the night, but considering his wife is currently with Iris, I'm sure he's not too busy to spare a drink for a neighbor. Probably just has his dick in a book or something. I laugh while letting myself out of the house, immediately tripping over the raised step in front of the door.

Who put that fucking thing there?

Probably DeLuca. He's always messing with me. I just know it. Such an asshole.

What does Aislinn even see in him?

Well, aside from the obvious. I'm not blind. I see what he looks like.

What was I doing again?

Shit.

Where am I?

It would appear as though I've gotten myself turned around. All these damned roads look the same. I know I'm not on my row, and I'm not on Alec's. I have no fucking idea where I am.

I turn in circles, looking at each identical house and cursing whoever designed this insanity. If I were the lord of Caeliss, the first thing I would do is paint each row of houses a different color, so it isn't so godsdamn confusing. This row would be green, yeah, green row. My row would obviously be black like Obsidian. A rainbow of streets, no, the Rainbow Rows! Yes! We will rename Caeliss once the painting has commenced!

I wonder how Lysette is? Maybe I will go after them. I probably should have gone with them to begin with. What kind of brother am I?

Oh right, Iris. Always Iris.

The gurgle of stomach acid burns the back of my throat. Maybe I shouldn't have more whiskey. But I will.

"Rett?" A small voice dripping in sorrow and salvation rings around me. I whip my head around so fast it knocks me off balance, and the next thing I know I'm on my ass and looking up at a beautiful girl with big doe eyes and a halo of gold. No, wait...that's just her hair.

"Oh, he-e-e-y, Cass," I say, and gods damn it, I'm proud of how unintoxicated I sound.

"Are you drunk?" she asks with her nose crinkled.

Maybe I sound a *little* intoxicated. "Not nearly drunk enough."

"Mmm. I can relate."

My brows shoot up. "You wanna get drunk with me?"

"Can't. Hadleigh is waiting for me to tuck her in. I've been doing it every night since we got back. Heidon...he, well, he used to do it, and Aunt Maeg hasn't been fully herself since, well, everything."

I nod. "It's been a shit-show, hasn't it?"

"The shittiest. Can I help you up?"

"Nah, I'm good. Military man, remember? They used to get us wasted and then run maneuvers and scenarios so we were never caught off guard."

Her brows raise. "You're still on the ground though."

"It's where I want to be." I flash a smile.

She shakes her head and offers me a hand. I take it, and she squeaks as I pull her down so she is laying on the cobblestone beside me, and we're both looking up at the sky.

"See, this is where I want to be," I say and point up at the stars.

"I used to do this," she says, quietly. There's a hint of sadness to it.

A cool breeze ruffles my hair and its kiss has a sobering effect. "When you were a kid?"

She makes a sad noise in her throat. "Growing up all the way until a few months ago. I used to love the gods and talk to the stars as if they could deliver messages to them. Then, Heidon was taken by one of them."

Taken by the same god who stole away Aislinn while I was here playing fucking house with Iris. My teeth grind together and there's a pulsating throb in my temple. I'm becoming thoroughly ticked off now that my buzz is wearing off.

I turn and face Cass, leaning my head into my hand and propping myself up with my elbow. "Everyone knows Erebus isn't like the rest of the gods. He and his father are the founders of evil."

"Even so, the other gods just sit by while all these horrors take place and they do nothing. They do not care for us." She pauses as if internally wrestling with her thoughts, then blows out a heavy breath. "Can I say something without you judging me or telling the Elders?" she asks.

"Yeah, of course." I roll to my side and try to give her my attention, which is actually way harder than it ought to be.

"I'm not so sure they're worthy of our blind devotion as the council says. Even in our recorded histories, they've done countless horrors and have stood by and watched civilizations burn to the ground when they could've easily stepped in to prevent it. Tell me, does that sound like an entity worthy of our love and faith?"

"Not to me."

"Not to me either." She sighs. "The air whispers to me, you know? Not words but feelings. There is something unsettling about the breeze lately. Something big is coming for us."

"Like what?"

"Change."

Cass laid with me in silence for a few minutes before getting up to go say goodnight to Aislinn's new little cousin. She told me how to get back to my house on the newly named—by me—*black row* but refused to tell me how to get to Alec's—stating that I absolutely did *not* need more whiskey. She's wrong, of course, but

I'm in no mood to play minotaur in this labyrinth of a city, so home I go.

My shoulders tense and I freeze when I open the door and see Iris sitting at the dining table in a chair facing me. A dim glow from the candle on the table illuminates the pinched features of her beautiful face.

"Where were you?" she asks.

"I went for a walk."

"Oh yeah?" She taps her long fingernails on the table. "Where to?"

"I started out looking for Alec and somehow ended on green row."

"There isn't a place in Caeliss called green row." She folds her arms over her protruding belly.

"There wasn't, but there is now."

Iris stands and walks toward me with exaggerated steps until her chest is a fingertip from my stomach. She has to tilt her head back to look up at me, but instead of cute, it's almost menacing. "And *who* were you with?"

This interrogation is one I've grown accustomed to whenever I do anything without her. I swallow—knowing she won't like the answer. "Cass."

"Ohhh, I see. *Cass.*" She laughs. "Did you fuck her?"

"No, of course not!" My heart thrums and twists painfully. Her accusation makes me feel physically sick.

"Of course not? You think I believe that?"

"Iris, there's no one else but you. You know that. I would never."

"Yeah, here's the thing, you said the same thing about Aislinn, yet *I* was in your bed every night."

My skin begins to itch with the agitation coursing through my body. "That's not fair. I *loved* you!"

Iris steps back, suddenly looking at me with wide eyes. She's not afraid of me, right? I'd never hurt her. She *has* to know I'd never hurt her!

"Loved?" she asks.

I stare at her with a blank expression. *Loved? I did say that. Love, I love Iris. Right? Of course you do, you stupid fuck. It's just the whiskey messing with your head.*

"I'm sorry, bear," she says. "I don't mean to get insecure. I just can't lose you. I've already lost everyone." Her shoulders begin to shake, and tears fall from her eyes as she wraps her arms around me.

"You're not losing me. I'd never leave you. I can't—I don't think my heart could bear it." The salted kiss that follows has us melting into each other. Usually, her touch is all I need to forget the world around us, but for some reason, there's still a tug of unease at my back. Change is coming.

TWENTY
COMPANION
Aislinn

"TRY HARDER!"

"I'm trying as hard as I can! You can't just force the visions!"

"We absolutely can!" Erebus pinches either side of my cheeks between his hand and pours a vial of oktalei in my mouth—my third in this session alone. He grabs my hands and pushes another memory on me. It's nauseating, and my veins buzz with power. Too much power.

The smell of body odor and dirt is as strong as the blazing sun beating down on me. Droves of people gather around a rickety stage. His voice sends a shiver down my spine...but that voice...it's coming from me. The crowd hangs on every word as if enchanted by it. They salivate for more and he delivers. When the speech is concluded, their cheers turn to chants.

"Liberation! Liberation! Liberation!"

The scene shifts and I'm in a tent. Sitting in a broken chair in front of a desk made from scrapped pieces of wood. It's full of carvings. I recognize them as Old Daeil. I'm holding an onyx totem. My thumb runs over the head and I'm whispering to it. There's a panic swelling in my chest. The whispers grow frantic and tumble over each other. The only word I can make out clearly is "Erebus."

The flaps to the tent open. My hands—Pierce Decatur's hands—tremble slightly as he hides the totem in his lap.

"Pierce!"

It can't be. Erebus would not be so kind as to show him to me, and yet, there he stands in all his glory—hair mussed and a wild look in his electric eyes.

A coarse male voice passes through my lips. "Ahh, what can I do for you, DeLuca?"

"Call it off, Pierce. Innocents will be in attendance too. There are good people who will become casualties."

I feel my brows pinch. "Good highborns? Mmmm. Tell me, DeLuca, where were these good highborns to protect our innocents? Where were they when my wife was taken from our bed in the dead of night and thrown into the stables? When she was mauled by that beast for sport?" There is no anger to the voice, but the tone is so much more sinister.

"I can't speak for them. I only report what I have seen, and I have seen the good in the future Lady of Obsidian. I am only here because of her dedication to protecting one of the servs...and by default, me."

There's a pause. DeLuca's determination seeps off of him like the cinders off a fire.

The voice that comes from me is cool and measured. "You'd want to undermine everything we have worked for because of one woman?"

"No, not everything. Only the slaughter of innocents. I ask you to reconsider this plan."

"*Hmm.*" *My hands clasp in front of me.* "*But you want this as much as we do.*" *The emphasis lands on the word* "*want*" *and there is a chill rolling through the tent with it despite being midsummer. My ears ring and a cold bile freezes in my throat.*

DeLuca doesn't seem to notice the drop in temperature. "*Wanted. I have since reconsidered my stance.*"

Pierce recoils. "*Oh? Very well.*" *There's a pause while Pierce assesses DeLuca. His rigid stance and the fire within him. My throat bobs, and I shake my head, trading the deep frown for a smile.* "*I shall think on your words. Perhaps a delay is in order to further assess.*"

DeLuca nods and his posture softens. Valera comes in the tent behind him, placing a hand on his shoulder as he leaves.

She stares at me for a moment. My stomach twists at the sight of her. My own memory flashes and collides with Pierce's, and for several blinks, we transport between the tent and King Carrigan's bedroom. Blood coating us. I see myself through Pierce's eyes. I look small, yet there is something I don't recognize beneath my hardened gaze. My vision stabilizes back in the tent. The wind blows the canvas flaps in and out.

Valera is running her hands through my hair. "*Are you actually going to postpone the attack because of some snobby highborn girl?*"

A laugh sticks in my throat. "*Of course not.*"

When we come out, I am breathless and have a sheen of sweat along my hairline. "What the Haile, Erebus?"

He's smirking, completely ignoring my irritation. Shadows dance in his eyes and they appear to glow. I'd love for someone to smack that look off his face. "That was different."

With my breath returning to normal, I ask, "What was?"

"You started dragging me into your own memory. It was almost powerful enough to take over."

The blood. Valera's blood. Pierce's blood. When my eyes close, I still see it. Way too much power. "The flickering?"

"Mmm." He nods. "Progress. Small progress, yet, progress still." With his pointer finger, he swipes some of the hair from my face with a sigh. "You're leaking. Come, you must eat."

I'm much further along than he thinks I am. It's hard to dull the visions he walks me through, but I don't trust him enough to let him know the true extent of my gifts. I wouldn't say I have *control* by any means...just that I am perhaps less reliant on him and the oktalei as I appear. In exchange for my *good behavior*, I've been allowed to roam the Shadow Palace. Each time I want to push his limits or spite him, I remember what it's like to be stuck in a room day after day and bite my tongue.

The first few days of working with him were tense as I still am angry about how he coerced Audrina into betraying me. Seeing the deal first hand was excruciating, witnessing something as if I were there but completely unable to change any of it. It's a pain I wouldn't wish upon anyone.

I keep thinking about her face, the desperation that radiated off of her like rays from the sun. I missed it. How could I have missed the pain there? We were living together and I didn't even have the slightest suspicion.

Reminding myself of my goal is the only way I freeze out the rage. I've never been described as patient, but I am a quick learner and plan to use the time I'm here to my advantage.

We've been having breakfast together in the sunroom. It's not a true sunroom because the room faces the Abyss, so instead of natural light greeting our mornings, we gaze into endless darkness and despair—which is more fitting.

I need to visit Kaoket if he wants me to unlock my true potential. I can't quite figure out the reasoning, but it's a thread that continuously tugs at me, beckoning me toward it. If after everything I've experienced lately, when those threads tug, there is no option other than to follow them.

"Listen, I realize there's bad blood between you two, but we're not getting anywhere here. You want my help, right? You're getting your own way. You and your issues with Agnar." I shove another bite of toast in my mouth after adding a hefty heap of jam to it and stare at him with accusation.

"I did not know gods were able to get headaches until I met you," Erebus says while rubbing his temples.

I stick my tongue out at him. Childish as it may be, it was either that or gesture with my middle finger. He goes back to glaring near the window—I suspect the glare is to actually hide at least a *mild* amusement. Getting under the shadow god's skin may be my newest hobby.

With a smirk and a bit of attitude added to my voice, I say, "I'm glad I could teach you *something*. Anyway, I don't condone his actions anymore than you do. He may have answers I need."

"Or he might kill you to spite me."

"You think he'd kill me? Doesn't he believe I'm his child?"

"You'd be surprised how many gods have killed their own children," he says.

I gulp the bit I had just taken and push my plate away, no longer having an appetite. The dish disappears in a swirl of shadow that I have grown very accustomed to in my days living in the Shadow Palace.

"Well, if you want my help, we're going to have to go eventually," I tell him, even though I'm sure he already knows and is delaying the inevitable.

He chuckles. "I have faith you will be able to find a solution in time...*without* the assistance of Agnar. You forget, pet, we have an eternity together."

"Yeah, so you said. Yet you never quite explained what you meant by wanting to make me immortal."

"*Want*? No, foolish girl, I've already done it."

My brow quirks and I look him up and down, waiting for an explanation.

He sighs, though I don't think he hates answering my questions as much as he would lead me to believe. "The markings I gave you."

"The ones that claim me as yours while I'm in the realm of gods or the one that tether us together so you can always find me?" I ask sweetly.

"The ones on your back and middle. When I caught you vision-walking—"

"Vision-walking?"

"When you travel through visions. Stop interrupting." He stares at me, waiting, and when I don't say anything more, he begins again. "When I caught you vision-walking, I put a tracker of sorts on you so that I could easily find you. It was easy to watch you when you were in the Obsidian Mountains, but the Safe Haven is different. It's protected by old god magic, by Astoria's magic, in fact. So I had to bind your shadow to this body so I can always find you."

I pretend to gag at the thought before registering the rest of his words. "Wait, Astoria created Caeliss?"

He looks taken aback, disgusted even with his face twisted and brow raised. "Obviously. Who else?"

I always thought Caeliss looked as if it rested in the middle of a crater. Astoria must have sent an asteroid or something to protect her children from the cruelties they'd face in the mortal realm. It makes too much sense, and I feel kind of stupid for not seeing it before.

"And the marks on my back and arms?" I hold up my arms in emphasis to show the lines running down them.

I've never seen a smile as wicked as the one Erebus has spreading across his sharp features. "That, pet, is what will make you immortal. When you die, your Shadow will stay with *this* body, as I said. *Those* marks are what will officially make you a member of my house... As a harbinger."

"A harbinger?" Ice wraps through each of the marks bestowed upon me by Erebus.

"Mhmm."

"A harbinger of what?"

"Death, Aislinn. You are a harbinger of death."

Death. I mouth the word as I take it in.

Death.

I wish I could say that I am surprised, but death has always been my companion. I also can't deny the draw I have felt to the shadows since arriving. It's like they always knew I'd someday be a part of them.

Utikalo. Forbis. Lady. Harbinger.

Of these four titles, only one feels true, and the silver threads of fate sing their praise.

Erebus smiles as if reading my thoughts. "Poetic, is it not?"

"Poetic...sure. So, again, the question is—why not kill me? Especially if I will be bound to you?"

"Because it will be you, and it will be the Utikalo. Your shadows are one in the same, however I am unsure if your abilities will transfer or die with your mortality, and it's not something I am willing to risk."

"So, I really am to spend eternity here...in this realm." I fiddle with the locket around my neck. "You're not worried about DeLuca finding me and the prophecy coming to pass?"

"Not in the slightest. He cannot travel through the portals without an escort, and the barrier prevents any new shadows, even ones still inhabiting bodies, from crossing between realms. With all the rules in place, there is no way any of the gods would be idiotic enough to bring him here. So, no, pet, it is not something I am the least bit concerned with."

"Mmm, I see," I say, not wanting to give him any reason to keep watching DeLuca.

His eyes narrow on me. "Indeed."

"Well, dark overlord, if I am bound to this realm forever, I'd like to be able to explore more, especially if my future lies here."

"Impossible."

"If I am not a prisoner, as you say, then why not?"

"Most gods are testy about who enters their region. One misstep and *you* will be the one needing the healing salve." His spine straightens and he looks mildly irritated. A few seconds later and his face is back to the impassive expression he likes to keep.

"Don't you have *any* friends?"

He scoffs. "Of course not."

"That must be lonely," I mutter and, as if queued, Helena bursts through the doors wearing a goopy face mask, robe, and fuzzy pink slippers.

Erebus exhales his annoyance, though I think he's not as bothered as he leads on. Turning slowly toward his half-sister, he asks, "What are you doing here?"

"I came for my playdate with Aislinn." She bats her lashes over her vibrant lavender eyes. "And to make sure she's in one piece."

He groans. "You're early."

"Well, I'm technically here on business." The feared *Reaper* twirls the belt of her robe around and winks at me. It's astonishing how anyone could see her and be afraid. I can't help but wonder where the rumors of her ruthlessness began.

Erebus's real agitation shows now. His jaw is flexed to the point he may pop a blood vessel. "Who?"

Helena twirls around like the lead performer in a ballet—dipping into a bow while handing Erebus a letter. "Cintamarri."

"No."

"On Haile's behalf. It's Estaleiki eu Kato Arisi." Helena grabs Erebus's mug off the table and takes a swig, then points it toward me. "Mandatory attendance for all."

"What's Estaleiki eu Kato Arisi?" I ask, looking between the two.

"'Thanks be to Kato day," Helena says. "We show our appreciation to the creator for our existence by partying our asses off. Each year, it's at a different palace, and everyone's on their best—and *worst*—behavior." She gives a sly grin.

"I'm sure Haile will forgive me," Erebus says. "I am taking care of my *guest*."

"Nuh uh. You're not getting out of this one. Haile demanded Aislinn come as well." She pretends to examine her fingers while attempting to hide a smirk, a tell Erebus clearly missed as he pales with her words.

"She cannot go to *Cintamarri's*," he says.

"Well, no, not like that." She eyes my silver pajama set with distaste. "I'll help her get ready, don't worry yourself."

Before Erebus can argue, she grabs me and flies me back to my room.

"Did Haile really demand my presence?" I ask, my brow raised in skepticism. Out of all the gods I've met so far, Haile is probably my least favorite. He reminds me of everything that was wrong with the highborns of Stellera.

"No, but I couldn't stand the idea of going to this without you! We haven't had anyone to shake things up in hundreds of years." She laughs. "Besides, sir doom and gloom will be preoccupied looking after his beloved wife to care about what you're doing. I'm sure you could use a bit of fun."

"Astoria is going?" I can't hide my surprise. In her state, I didn't think she'd go anywhere near the other gods. Not when she's so vulnerable.

"Of course. All gods are required to attend. It's to honor Kato!"

"So Kato will be there? What are they like?"

"Why would Kato be there?" She cocks her head to the side. "I'm sure our creator has much better things to do than watch us make idiots of ourselves."

Helena hums a tune I don't recognize and waves her hand. In a flash, I'm wearing a matching robe with fuzzy blue slippers with some kind of pink goop that smells like the first day of summer caked onto my face.

I sigh and shake my head—just going with it. Helena is strange, but I've grown to really enjoy her company...and if I'm being honest with myself, she is filling a hole Audrina left.

"You look perfect. Just like one of us." Helena finishes pulling the last tendril of hair up in a purposeful mess adorned with tiny gemstones.

She could have snapped her fingers and we would have both been ready in an instant, but she said she wanted to experience this like *mortals*, that it would be more fun that way. I can't say she's wrong. It was fun getting ready together. For the first time in a long time, I wasn't solely focused on what I lost or what could be. I'm actually kind of excited to go to a party thrown by gods.

"I hardly recognize myself," I admit while standing before the mirror with dark smokey makeup that would have been considered risque in Stellera.

I'm dressed similar to the way goddesses are depicted in the old records. A length of silver fabric twists around to form a dress of sorts. My hips and back remain mostly uncovered. The dress falls mid-thigh and gives view to the sandals crossing up my calves. Helena wrapped the makeshift dress beautifully, holding it together with a pin engraved with three stars.

Helena's hand rests on my shoulders and she triumphantly smiles at our reflections. Her outfit is similar, but the sheer fabric is white with pink ends and far shorter than mine. Helena places a little tiara with a golden skull centered on top of her dark hair.

She squeals and claps. "Our first party together!" Her face drops to a scowl. "Incoming," she whispers.

Erebus arrives in the form of a shadow. When the smoke dissipates, he is revealed, wearing black fitted suit more in line with the modern style in Stellera.

"You look nice," I say politely. Though, if I'm being honest, his attire isn't far too different than what he wears daily. The idea of him wearing anything else is almost laughable.

His mouth hardens into a flat line and his gray eyes turn the color of a moonless night. "You're going to draw far too much attention dressed like that."

"In a good way or a bad way?" I ask, looking down, feeling newly insecure about the length and trying to pull it down a little. It is short...perhaps the shortest dress I've worn publicly. The other gods dress racy. If I don't, I might stand out *more*.

Helena slaps my hand away from the hem. "You're going to undo the whole damn thing," she hisses.

"It doesn't matter if it's good or bad. I don't want you drawing attention. At all."

I frown as Erebus raises his fingers.

"Oh no, you're not ruining this for me too," Helena says and wraps me in her arms and wings protectively.

She jumps and shoots into the air. I brace for the feel of the ceiling to crash into me, but we go right through as if it doesn't exist at all. Then we're high in the sky. She's fast, faster than Erebus's shadows. Once we are out of his region, they stop following behind. She doesn't slow until we are outside a palace. The night sky reflects off of the crystalline structure, creating the illusion of dancing stars. It's only intensified by the lilac river surrounding it—filled with white flower petals and floating candles.

"How long do you think until he gets here?" I ask without turning from the awe-inspiring structure. My heart races, and the need to go into the palace chases away any anxiety. The blood in my veins thrums in tune with the thumping music—drawing me closer.

"Who knows?" She shrugs.

"Well then, we better get in there before he drags me back." I smile. She nods and links her arm in mine, leading me into the pit of Desire.

TWENTY-ONE
EDGES OF REALITY
DeLuca

EVANDER HAS A DIFFICULT time hiding the shock on his face. I have to admit, he's taking the news rather well considering gods were supposed to be nothing but myth. Better than most would have, even. Must be the military training.

"And you think that there's an armory somewhere storing all these weapons made of—aietal, was it?" Evander asks from behind the obsidian desk.

"Volcorium melted down to aietal, yes. We also believe whatever is left of the Guardians will answer Lysette's call, given that she is an Urson. If they do, we would like you at the meeting as a representative for the refugees," I say.

Evander's brows furrow and he looks up at Lys. "Why me?"

"Because we see what you've done here. The role you've been playing. You're important, Evander." Lysette smiles warmly at him and places a hand on his arm.

For a moment, he looks as if he may argue but shakes his head, then nods. "I'll go to this meeting." He rubs his hands down the scruff of his jaw. "I may know where such an armory is located as well. Along the border to Dailotta, inbetween the Capital and Fort Vicanti, there's a building always under heavy guard that only people with the highest clearance were granted access to. I'd be willing to bet that's where your secret armory is located."

"Of course," Lysette says with an exhale. "The most convenient way to move so much of the mineral undetected...the transport system below the mountains! I always thought they'd just wanted quick access to the Capital for business...but what if they'd been using the tunnels to move the volcorium to make aietal?"

Hidden in plain sight. It would be the perfect route to transport the metal in large quantities undetected. The first Ursons may have been insane, but they were also methodical, and their paranoia made them excellent strategists. "It's what I would do," I say.

Lys scrunches her nose as she thinks. "Father too, I know it."

"How are you going to gather the Guardians? Do you have a radio or something?" Evander asks.

"We were hoping you could help with that. Do you have some kind of messenger you've been using to gather your information?" My arms cross and I assess him as I would when I was still spying for the Liberators.

"I do. All I need is a list of names, a place, and a date," he says without looking my way. He's so comfortable in his position. It comes easily to him. I don't know yet if it's a good thing or not.

"The best bet is to have them meet us in Rilyse. In the home of the Kaillen's since we're headed that way anyway. Three weeks should be enough time," Lysette says thoughtfully.

"And you're going with him, Lysette?" Evander's eyes flash with sadness that disperses as quickly as it comes.

Interesting.

She gives me a cocky grin. "I don't think he'd make it far without me."

I don't want her to feel as though she has to come...but I would be lying to myself saying I don't want her to, especially if we're going to Rilyse. That is her domain, not mine. So I keep my mouth shut and shake my head in mild annoyance.

"Without leaving a trail of carnage behind you," she adds.

I shrug, not daring to argue. We both know it's probably true.

"I'd come with you...but I can't leave all of them," Evander says, moving closer to Lysette.

"I wouldn't want you to leave them. They need you far more than I do." Her hand moves up his arm to his bicep, and she's staring up at him with a flickering in her good eye that reminds me of the way Aislinn would look up at me.

There's so much tension between them, I feel it buzzing around us. Nausea consumes my senses and I have to work hard to keep my face from contorting. They're about two seconds away from realizing what I already have, and I'm not going to wait around for the moment they do.

"I'm going downstairs to—" I don't finish the sentence. I can't think of an excuse. I just know I need to get out of here. Not that I need one. They don't spare me a second glance as I slip out.

As soon as the door shuts behind me, I realize I don't actually want to be around the refugees...especially those kids. I'm holding on by a *very* frayed thread, and the memories they provoke...they're too much. So I end up going down to the archive, not looking for anything in particular. Mostly to give Lysette however much time she needs to say goodbye.

All the books we got out still lay in neat piles on the table. With a sigh, I begin placing them back on the shelves. There's no need to leave this place in disarray, even if no one else ever sees it. It would be a shame though, to let all the knowledge in these books become lost. I bet if we gave them to Caeliss, they'd be shown the appreciation they deserve—if we're ever allowed back in Caeliss.

I'm stacking the remainder of the Urson family journals when I come across the latest addition, one belonging to the most recent Lord Magnus. Lysette would probably want this. The leathery cover is smooth beneath my fingertips. Curiosity wins over what little respect I have for the dead. I flip it to the last few pages, and the last date he wrote in it was only a few weeks before his death. Surprising, considering it didn't appear anyone used this room for decades. He writes of the uprisings and Liberators, how out of control the hardships in Ashe had become. Turning back further, he writes of the birth defects plaguing the newer generations and other hardships, not a whole lot of—

Wait...what the Haile is this?

What. The. Fuck. Is. This?

I zone into the passage with the nausea returning, accompanying the repulsion igniting my blood. This entry is about the experiments he was doing on the kids with defects in Ashe. The familiar prickles of anger start rolling beneath my skin as I flip through the journal.

It's sick.

Sicker than I could have ever imagined, and it was happening right under our noses. We let it happen. Not only that, we fucking *thanked* him for it.

The mirrored window cracks beneath my knuckles. It's not enough. I'm going to explode. It's fighting to the surface. Fighting against every sane thought I have. Completely consuming. The rage blinds me. All I see are their faces. The children of Ashe. The broken-hearted families. Val's daughter who died from her deformities. Deformities that were *caused* by Lord Magnus. My jaw trembles as I take a calming breath and flip to the beginning of the journal until I find what I'm looking for.

The first.

Patient zero.

Evander Clayne.

Rage turns to disgust, heartbreak, back to rage. I'm a tsunami of emotion. They discovered him as a toddler. He'd fallen out of a window at the factory his parents worked at. He was covered in blood but had no wounds. They'd miraculously healed. Finding his bones to be indestructible—as if they'd been filled with volcorium.

Lord Magnus wanted to replicate his genetic makeup. He wanted a legion of super soldiers with his same mutation. They told his birth parents that he had died from his injuries sustained in the fall. They kept him and treated him like a gods damned experiment.

I have to hold back the vomit as I continue to read, how they'd break his limbs over and over again to watch them heal. How they'd told him his parents were dead and he grew up with a general until he was shipped off to Fort Vicanti at the age of fourteen. They injected pregnant women with different variations of a volcorium mixture, trying to recreate his "defect." They created the birth defects in all of these kids. They *created* it.

I need to get the fuck out of here before I burn the place down.

Taking three steps at a time, I rush to get out of the archive and through conference room. When I open the door to the study, Lysette jumps back—away from Evander, with swollen lips and reddened cheeks. I can't think about it right now. I just toss the journal at her.

"Your father was a fucking monster," I say and turn around. I can't stop. I can't even breathe or I'm going to lose it.

"DeLuca, wait!" she yells after me.

"Don't follow me, Lysette. I need to be alone. Read the journal."

The cold mountain air does nothing to cool the fire burning around me. I barely make it through the still blown-in front door of the manor before they engulf me. Thankfully, there isn't a whole lot to destroy that's not already severely damaged on this side of the manor. The light layer of snow hisses as it melts beneath my boot. I have to try to channel the rage into something else other than fire unless I want to take down the whole damn forest.

Wind.

Come on.

Wind.

The flames double in size.

Fuck. Fuck. Fuck.

If I try to mess with the ground, the whole mountain could collapse.

My vision blurs.

Godsdamn it. Wind. Not flames.

Wind. Please.

My entire body convulses with the restraint it takes to keep from erupting.

I clench the stone in my pocket. Water.

Water could work.

Please work.

When I can no longer contain the force that is my emotion, I erupt with a yell powerful enough to shake the snow off the treetops. A bolt of lightning shoots up from me towards the sky.

As it cracks above, it illuminates the world around us in violent purple sparks. My senses completely shut off. It doesn't stop until I feel empty—an overwhelming calm. My vision starts fading in and out. The edges of reality blurred.

My knees give out and hit the snow. I don't even feel the cold as I fall forward. Numb. Unfeeling. With an insufferable ringing in my ears. There's a blurred vision of Lysette running toward me, Evander in tow. Then my vision blackens completely.

The fight is leaving me.

My will.

Everything that makes me who I am.

I am a shell.

I don't know if I'm dreaming, but in the absence of anything, I see her. Emerald eyes glowing as if a beacon showing me the way back to life. Her hand reaches out. I try to grab on to it, but there's something blocking us, an invisible wall of sorts keeping us apart.

It hurts.

I feel as though my insides are being shredded apart.

Then she's gone, and I am again utterly empty.

TWENTY-TWO
DISTRACTION
Lysette

EVANDER HELPED ME GET DeLuca into his room. I tried to do it on my own, but the god is as heavy as he is stubborn. He's essentially a meat suit filled with stones—explains why he's such a block head sometimes. I am truly grateful for Evander's help. He's been watching me sit with DeLuca for the last hour while we awaited a healer. My knees are tucked to my chest. Each breath hurts. I can't lose him. My throat constricts. I can't. I've lost too many. So many. Everyone.

It's just me and Rett...and DeLuca.

He can't leave me too.

"Breathe, Lysie," Evander says.

I turn to him with widened eyes. "What?"

"I can see your mind ticking away with worry." He places a finger between my eyebrows and smoothes out the line delicately.

"Oh, yeah. I suppose I am."

"You care for him." It's not a question and I don't detect jealousy in his tone. It's merely an observation.

I blow out my first full breath since we found DeLuca unconscious. "Very much so. We've clung to each other a lot over the last few months. We haven't had anyone else really... Well, I have Rett, but he's been preoccupied with Iris."

Evander swallows and moves closer, brushing the back of my hand with his. "If I had known you were alive, I would have searched for you. I would not have stopped until I found you."

I try to smile. "I know. But I'm glad you didn't. You have done so much good with your time here, and you wouldn't have found me anyway."

He moves his knuckle down my cheek. "Don't be so sure about that."

We stare at each other for a long moment before the sound of a woman's throat clearing interrupts us.

"Ah, Healer Cilla, thank you for coming so swiftly."

"My patient?" the healer asks.

Evander nods to the bed.

Cilla tsks. "Over exhaustion. I shall need a few hours with him. You may go."

"I'm not leaving him," I say.

Cilla turns toward me. "I said *you may go*."

"Come on, Lysie. Let's go look at your father's journals some more." Evander nudges me.

I exhale loudly while glaring at Cilla but follow Evander anyway.

We end up back in my fath—back in Evander's office. He sits in what was once my father's chair and I sit on the desk in front of him, flipping through the journal with tears flowing down my cheeks. My eye patch doesn't sit right when I cry so I have to remove it. Evander, being the gentleman that he is, didn't even blink at the sight of my white eye.

"He *was* a monster," I say under my breath.

"We are all capable of monstrosities," Evander says, not looking up from the papers he's currently reading.

"Ev...he was *your* monster."

"In what way?" He drops the paper onto the desk to fix his attention on me. "Your father was always so kind to me. He favored me over all the other officers aside from Mikail." He reaches up and traces the side of my eye, along my scar. I lean into his touch a bit, not wanting to say this next part.

"I'm not surprised after reading this." I flip the journal over and hand it to Evander. "Promise me you won't hate me for what he's done?"

Evander's brows scrunch to the bridge of his nose. "I'm not capable of hating you, Lysie. Especially for something you had no part of."

"It's bad, Ev. It's *really* bad."

He takes the journal, and I watch him as he reads about what was done to him. His family. The cruelties inflicted upon him.

He's quiet for a while. My lip is raw from the consistent biting while waiting for him to say something. Anything. Scream at me for what my father has done. Throw something. Any reaction at all. Evander looks up and catches my gaze. He frowns slightly and uses his thumb to trace my mouth where I've been holding it between my teeth.

"Are you okay?" he asks *me.*

"Am I okay?" I laugh into borderline hysteria. "Are you okay?"

This man is more concerned about my damn lip than the years of abuse he faced at the behest of my father. He should be livid. He should want to burn villages and reap vengeance.

"Lysie, I'm fine. I feel sorry for my birth parents... but I've lived a decent life and have been none the wiser."

"None the—Evander...they *tortured* you as a toddler."

"I'm impervious to pain." He shrugs.

I half laugh in exasperation. "Well, thank the gods for that. You're taking this remarkably well."

"One of us has too, and since you've already begun spiraling, I figure I might as well remain the reasonable one."

"*Reasonable?*" I scoff and throw my hands up. "Unbelievable."

"Oh yeah, I can be very reasonable when needed." He smiles as if endeared by my flustered antics.

"You're absolutely ridiculous! How can you be so calm?"

He puts his papers on the desk beside me. "Because I learned something else from all this."

"Oh?"

"I learned how much you care for me. It's written all over you, like an open book."

My face heats. Halie, my entire body heats. I must be bright red because he starts to laugh. Then stands and holds my cheeks in his hands.

"Have I ever told you how much I love to read?"

I look down, feeling slightly abashed. "No, I didn't know that about you."

His hand is still cupped around my cheek and he uses his pinky to lift my chin. His eyes ensnare mine into his rich gaze. "Don't be embarrassed. Never be embarrassed around me. Ever since my first day at Urson Manor you have been the subject of my thoughts. You, Lysette, with your thirst for knowledge and your affinity for getting into trouble. I just never imagined you would feel the same."

"Ev, I do feel the same. I always have. But it can't be anything. It can't mean anything."

Evander brushes my hair behind my ear before lowering his mouth to it and whispering, "Why can't it?"

His hot breath has me melting into the obsidian desk I sit upon and I have to swallow before answering. "There are just too many variables right now. Too much happening. Too much I need to accomplish before I can consider being romantic with anyone."

He drops his head to the crook of my neck. "Do you want me to back away then?"

"No."

"Tell me what it is that you want, Lysie."

"I want to finish what we started earlier."

Toying with the ends of my red hear he asks, "Oh?"

Heat flares in my chest. "I want you to kiss me."

"If that is all you want from me, you shall have it. If it is the only piece of yourself you will allow me to have, I will savor it until my dying breath." His words are hot on my neck, and he pushes his hips between my thighs. My body turns molten as I allow myself to mold to him.

"Ev?" I say breathily.

His mouth is hovering over mine now. "Yes, Lysie?"

"That's not all I want," I say in a voice so low and sultry, it doesn't even sound like mine.

I feel his smile against my lips. "Then tell me what else. Name it."

"I want the hurt to go away. I want a distraction from all the pain. I need to feel something good."

He stills while processing my meaning, but it only takes seconds before he's devouring my mouth with his. His warm breath tastes so damn good. The combination mixed with the feel of him pressed between my legs... I can't help but let out a moan of satisfaction. He laughs into our kiss, dipping his tongue in my mouth.

One of his hands has me pressed against him and the other is sliding up my thigh. His fingers are agonizingly light. They're barely there but leave a trail of electricity shooting to my core. The ache between my thighs has me desperate for any kind of friction.

"Ev..." My breathing stutters between kisses. "Please."

"Please what, Lysie? Tell me what you want."

I whimper as his fingers get closer, his thumb stroking the inner line of my thigh. He's so close. So fucking close. "Please touch me."

He chuckles low in his throat. "As you command, *my lady*."

Oh, bless the merciful gods of old glory.

Any coherent thoughts are gone. His fingers begin their brutally euphoric movements through the fabric of my pants while he continues kissing me. He groans, no doubt feeling how much I want him. And *gods,* do I want him. Everything else around us seems to fade from existence, and the only thing I see is Evander.

"Holy Haile, Lysie," he whispers. "You're soaking through your pants."

"Take them off then."

He smirks. "As you command."

His mouth leaves mine and I instantly miss it. Lifting me with one arm around my waist, he successfully pulls them off with the one free hand and throws the pants across the room. Papers scatter as he knocks everything off the obsidian desk. Gently lowering me so that my back lies flush with it.

Evander has a look of hunger in his eyes before he pulls me toward him by my legs. I am practically hanging off the edge of the desk. His eyes lock on mine as he spreads my knees apart and lowers his head.

Holy shit.

If I thought his fingers were euphoric, I didn't know the meaning of the word until his tongue took their place.

Holy shit.

His movements are slow and teasing. He starts gently using his teeth. My moan encourages him, and his pace quickens.

Holy shit.

I've had a lover before. A lord's son who often visited the manor on business, but he was always so rushed, so afraid of being caught. I've never had...*this.*

"Oh gods, Ev! Ev! I'm about to—" Evander sticks a finger in and begins pumping it in time with the thrusts of his tongue. I am no longer able to form words over the screams of pleasure.

My body quakes and Evander slows his movements until my body relaxes beneath his touch.

"I love the sound of my name from your mouth as I'm making you come apart," Evander says, pulling me up so that I'm sitting on the desk. He kisses my jaw, and just like that, my body is ready to go again.

"I've never screamed someone's name in such a way," I admit.

He smiles, biting my bottom lip slightly, then kisses up the side of my neck. "Then no one has ever been serving you the way they should have."

"Thank you for the lesson. I will be sure to remember it."

"Do you want to stop?" he asks, his fingers toying with the buttons of my shirt.

All I can do is shake my head.

"Thank the fucking gods." He pulls me towards him, jerking the buttons open on my blouse so that I am completely exposed.

I grab at his shirt like a possessed animal. It rips, but I'm too lost to care while I run my fingers down the sculpted planes of his tan chest until I find his waistband. I unclasp his belt and he slides his pants the rest of the way down.

"Holy Haile," I whisper as I take in the size of him.

He laughs throatily and the sound makes butterflies dance in my belly.

"Ready?" he asks.

I swallow and nod, staring down at him as he aligns with my entrance. Evander bends one of my legs at the knee to give him better access and then he eases himself in. He's painfully slow at first. Allowing my inner walls to adjust to him, watching my face for what I assume are signs of discomfort. I show none. Never have I felt something *this* good.

I was wrong about both his fingers and his tongue.

This is euphoria.

I'm aching to take the whole of him, but it would probably tear me open if I did. Each small thrust has him just a little bit deeper. It's agonizing and incredible at once until I finally adjust to him and he's able to sheath himself completely. I gasp. Not in pain...in fact, quite the opposite. It feels like the end and the beginning of realms.

His movements have me losing my breath. He presses me tighter against him and I savor each place our skin touches. I catch his bottom lip between my teeth and he groans so loud it rattles my bones.

Oh gods, nothing has ever felt this good.

Nothing will ever feel this good again.

His large hand tenderly grips around my jaw and his breathing grows heavy as he says, "I'm going to flip you over, okay?"

I nod, unable to form words. When he pulls out, I feel empty, I could die right here on this desk. But then he's flipping me over so

I'm standing on the floor and bracing my weight against the desk. His body forms to mine as he guides himself back in. With one arm around my waist, he moves my hips meet his. His fingers rub my center as he moves, thrusting harder and harder. Hitting a place so deep inside of me I would have never thought it possible. Ev's head comes down to the dip between my shoulder and neck, and he kisses it before biting down, not hard enough to break skin, but the pressure only intensifies every sensation.

"Gods, Lysie, I just want to drown in you."

"Don't stop, Ev, please, don't ever stop."

"Never, my lady, not unless you beg me to."

Gods, I wish this really could go on forever, but I feel that familiar quaking sensation, and my legs are beginning to shake as my pleasure peaks.

"You're gripping me so tight, Lysie. Come for me."

With the next slam of his hips against my ass, I scream out his name with my release. He continues pumping and holding onto me as if I am the only thing keeping him on the ground and he'd float away if he could no longer touch me.

His pumps slow. Suddenly, he pulls out and groans out my name as I feel something warm and sticky hitting my back in streams. Our heavy breathing synchronizes as we stay secluded in our own little bubble of bliss.

Evander uses his torn shirt to wipe off the mess he's made on my back, then traces a line of kisses down my spine. We both fall to the floor. He pulls me into the crook of his arm while I try to remember what my legs are and how they work.

"Was I distracting enough?" Evander asks.

"Hmm," I say, pretending to ponder, "I think I could perhaps be a bit more distracted."

"Oh yeah?" He quirks his brow.

"Yeah, when I can feel my legs again."

He laughs, fully and wholeheartedly, which makes me laugh. Gods, it feels so good to laugh again, until we're interrupted by a knock at the door.

"Not now!" Evander shouts.

"Ah, I know yous busy boss, but that healer lady has finished with the boy and asked to discuss treatment."

Evander runs a hand through his hair and groans. "Thank you, Tank, give me a few minutes."

He looks at me apologetically, but I'm already up and putting my clothes back on. I'm anxious for news on DeLuca's well being.

Ev rolls on to his side and stares at me. "I see your legs are working again."

I try not to smile, but it breaks free as I toss his pants at his face.

The Healer Cilla is impatiently tapping her foot when we arrive.

"Sorry to keep you waiting," Evander says.

She looks at his bare chest and exhales loudly to convey her annoyance. "The patient is exhausted. He needs rest."

"That's it? He needs rest?" I ask with my hands on my hips.

"Lots of it. I have never seen someone's energies so depleted. He is empty. Hollow. By all accounts, he should be dead, but the gods must favor this boy for they are letting him cling to his life." She shrugs and packs up her kit.

By all accounts, he should be dead.

My heart sinks into a sea of panic as I look at DeLuca's paled features.

Dead. Dead. Dead.

Just like Linnea. Just like Mom. Just like Papa. Just like Orynn. Dead.

Dead. Dead. Dead. Dead

A warm hand slides into mine. "Lysie?"

I shake my head and look at Evander. "Yes?"

His brows squish together deeply and he uses his free hand to push the hair away from my scarred eye. "Don't get lost in there, okay?"

"Lost in where?"

He kisses my temple. "In this magnificently complicated mind of yours."

I lean into him and let Evander's strength be my own for a moment. "I'm so tired of people dying," I admit. "I don't think I can handle any more death."

Evander lifts my chin so that our gazes meet. "You can handle anything, Lysie, *anything*. More death will eventually come, as it does with life, and you will handle it. You are stronger than you think."

I offer him a tight smile and he kisses the corner of my mouth.

"I have to go check on our supplies. Cilla will be back tomorrow…Will you come stay with me tonight?"

I look between Evander and DeLuca and exhale deeply, shaking my head. "No, I should watch over him."

Evander doesn't let his disappointment show, but I know it's there when he nods in understanding. "Then I will come check on you later. I'll bring you food." He digs in his pocket, then hands me my eye patch. I hadn't even realized I left it. "For the record, I think you look hot without it." He winks.

My lip twitches as I try to conceal the smile. "Hey, Ev?"

"Yeah?"

"Thanks for the distraction."

"Anytime, *my lady*."

TWENTY-THREE
TWO OPTIONS
Aislinn

"HELENA." CINTAMARRI'S WORDS DRAWL once we've entered through the threshold to his palace. "Sister, come, come. I have been waiting ages for you to get here. Everyone else is just so dull." His lashes flutter as he rolls his eyes.

He's painted gold from head to toe, wearing only a cloth low on his hips, barely long enough to cover himself. His sculpted muscles glisten in every light and my mouth instantly waters. I have to swallow several times before I can stop staring at him like an idiot and fully take in my surroundings.

Gods clad in clothing ranging from very little scraps of fabric to completely covered—even their faces—are gathered in the ballroom, already drinking and dancing in slow sensual motion. Floor-to-ceiling windows cover two of the walls and open to the balcony overlooking the river surrounding the grounds. The banquet table's contents keep shifting. One moment, covered in fruits and pastries. The next, meats and grains. It doesn't stay the same for more than a minute. The other two walls of the room aren't walls at all but fountains of some kind—the water raining down to create a kind of curtain effect. Behind it, I can just make out the silhouette of nymph-like creatures moving in such a way that instantly draws the eye.

"Do you like what you see?" Cintamarri asks. There is a glimmer in his eyes as they drag up my body, leading me to believe he doesn't mean his home.

"It's...not what I expected."

"Tell me, dasi aeitli uko, what is it you expected?"

My face turns red. "*More* debauchery from the god of desire, I suppose."

"Hmm." The gold surrounding his pupils brightens. "That comes later. Though, if you're so impatient, we could sneak away for a few moments before we are missed." He uses a golden finger to trace a line from my shoulder to my collarbone, causing me to shiver and my knees to weaken.

"Careful, Cintamarri. Erebus is on his way." Helena nudges the god with her elbow.

"He does have a nasty habit of spoiling our fun, does he not, sister?"

"Too true, brother, too true." The looks shared between them tell me I'm missing something, but with centuries of time together, I'm sure there is much I'm missing.

"Well, beautiful darkling, if you should want to seek me out, I shan't be far away. Just follow this feeling down here—" He places his fingers along my low belly—"and you shall surely find me." Cintamarri air kisses with Helena before greeting some of the other gods.

Helena laughs. "Breathe, Aislinn."

I blow out my breath at her instruction. "Does he affect everyone like that?"

"Yes, but those of us who have been around for a few hundred years learned to push down the feeling. It hasn't been as fun around here since, if you ask me."

"I can't imagine."

"Well...it was like this, but everyone was naked and fucking." She sighs dramatically and tilts her head as if recounting fond memories. "Let's get you a drink before sir broody forces you back into your cell."

Helena leads me through the crowd of gods—ones I am careful not to make eye contact with—to a large fountain spitting out a plethora of different colored liquids. She waves her hand, and two goblets appear. Helena thrusts one in my hand and uses the other to catch a shimmering blue liquid that begins to smoke in her cup.

"What is it?" I ask, looking sideways at all the colors.

"The wine of gods, literally. Spirits. Different kinds. The one I have tastes like the way it feels to kiss someone for the first time."

My brows knit. "They taste like a feeling?"

"Mhmm." She nods, taking a huge gulp.

"What is this silver one?"

"How it feels to fly." Helena rustles her wings for emphasis.

"The pink?"

"To be loved." She bats her lashes.

"Green?"

"Pure happiness."

"Green it is. I forget what that feels like...or maybe I've never felt it. Either way, I could use some happiness." I fill my goblet with the green liquid. It seems to sing, calling my name. The closer I bring it to my lips, the louder the song becomes. Drums join in, thundering like a parade of horses.

One sip.

I take one damn sip and my consciousness spins.

Everything else is gone. It's me and the green song, but I am not afraid. No, I am at peace. This emptiness isn't hollow. It's enchanting.

My smile is stretched so far that the corners of my mouth hurt. I'm crying tears of joy and only vaguely aware of the bodies around me. Helena's face comes into view, but it's brighter, happier, glowing. She looks beautiful. I touch her cheek and smile as the connection between us becomes a tangible thing. My fingers spark lilac beneath her skin. Her hand claps over my wrist, and she's laughing. Her joy fills my body and causes it to vibrate.

I need...I need...I don't know what I need.

More. I need *more* of everything.

The only thing that could make this better would be...DeLuca.

My Luc. Oh gods, that would make everything perfect!

As if the god of happiness existed and was really a genie or something, my wish has been granted. The rest of the party has disappeared—everything except this glowing ball of light and the fuzzy little feeling beneath my skin. The light flutters around me before taking off. I follow it into a new fold of reality. He's here, with me, in this void. He looks panicked though...disheveled. Hair wild. Stubble growing along his jawline. No, no, that won't do!

"Don't panic. This is a good place," I say, trying to tell him, but he can't hear me. There is a veil between us. A barrier. I just need to tear it down. "I'll get you, Luc, don't worry. I've got you. I've got you."

I beat on the invisible wall, trying to get to him. The movement makes me dizzy. Cold and hollow yet again. It pulls on my back. My arms. Spirals down my belly. I'm being ripped away. No matter how hard I fight, I am no match for eternal darkness. My heart splinters and cracks as I take one last look at DeLuca before surrendering to the shadows.

Everything is dark again. I'm pretty sure my eyes are closed, and I can't remember how to open them. "What the fuck, Helena?" I hear Erebus's voice slither in an angry whisper.

"I forgot how weak mortal blood is," she answers nonchalantly.

I roll over in a soft bed, and my head is spinning.

My eyes begin to flutter open as I regain control but the assault of the light is too much.

"Vomit." I groan. "I'm going to vomit."

Shadows produce a large bowl just before I ruin the gold sheets I've been lain atop. When I finish, the bowl disappears and a glass of water appears in its stead.

"What happened?"

Erebus grinds his teeth before speaking through his still clenched jaw. "You, *a mortal*, drank something meant only for gods."

"You passed out. Crabby-cake over here blew in just before you hit the ground and swooped you up with his shadow friends. You've only been out for a few minutes."

"Where did you go?" Erebus demands. "Your body was here, but your mind was not. I felt you, then didn't. You were gone. Where did you go?"

"Is that concern I hear, brother?" Helena quips.

"Go check on Astoria, *now*," he orders. Shadows dance along the wall. Helena rolls her eyes and skips off, her wings fluttering out in a taunting motion.

"Where were you, Aislinn?"

I try to bring the place back but...it's fuzzy. My body tingles as I try to grasp the memory. "I don't know. It was empty. A void."

"Alone?"

"Mostly."

"Mostly?" The shadows dance violently around us, a sight that may have frightened me weeks ago, but I've grown so used to that I welcome them like old friends.

"DeLuca was there...I think. There was some kind of invisible barrier. I'm not sure he was there at all."

The shadows stop and retreat. Erebus' face changes to something I can't quite recognize.

"What?"

"Go to the party. Don't tell anyone about this. No one. Not even Helena. The only ones who can know are in this room. Do you understand, pet?"

"No."

His eyes harden. "Do you understand not to tell anyone about this?"

I fold my arms. "Sure, but you will explain *why*?"

"If I find what I am looking for, I will. Not here, though. Too many ears."

"So secretive." I fold my arms. "Fine. I won't say anything."

"And don't drink anything. Don't eat anything either, *and* do not speak to the other gods."

"So many rules."

"Do you want a repeat of what just happened?" My answering eye roll and silence has him cursing under his breath. "Just stay out of trouble until after the ceremony so we can leave."

I shrug my shoulders. Not a promise. But it's enough for him to let me walk out of the room. A cold feeling has me looking down to see that a shadow has wrapped around me. As it retreats, I realize several inches have been added to my dress. With a scowl, I turn around to find Erebus is no longer behind me.

Damned god complex.

The celebration, it seems, is in full swing. Indeed, the debauchery was saved for later. Helena said I'd only been out for a few minutes, but from the way things have progressed, I think it may have been longer than she let on. Gods have begun losing articles of clothing. Some are even huddled off in full view of those around them exploring each other's bodies.

It's nothing like a highborn party and *everything* you'd expect from the god of desire. I'd be lying to myself if I didn't admit to being curious. I try not to watch, but it's hard to turn away as I feel waves of pleasure in the energy filling the palace.

It creates an ache in me I haven't felt since being with DeLuca.

I don't see Helena anywhere, so I decide to find somewhere quiet to sit and nurse this pounding headache that is surely a side effect of the wine.

A hand filled with static runs down the length of my arm, instantly turning my stomach sour. "Hello, love."

I turn slowly, my movements stiff. I have to bend my head back to look upon the god who so brazenly touches me. He has a similar golden aura that Haile does, but this god has large wings. His features are sharp, and though his eyes have a jeweled glow like the rest of the gods, his are very dark, almost like a garnet, and fill me with a sense of dread...or maybe it's the way he's looking down upon me as if he can't wait to bite into my flesh.

"I noticed you all alone over here. Where did your shadow guard go?"

I swallow. "My...shadow guard?"

"Is captor a more accurate title?" he asks, placing a hand above my head on the pillar he has backed me into.

My hands are sweating. I don't know why this god makes me so nervous. The energy he gives off is suffocating, and for the first time since entering the gods' realm, I'm afraid.

He tsks. "Hmm. That one has a way with theatrics. My name is Soren. You have no doubt heard of me, god of skies—" he runs his fingers along my arm and electricity follows. "—and storms."

I try to remember how to breathe normally again, but I can't seem to get a handle on it and the breath comes out too quickly. "Aislinn. My name is Aislinn." My voice is quiet. I hate how weak it sounds. I'm shaking. I have no reason to be, other than my intuition telling me Soren has nothing but malevolent intentions.

It seems to amuse him. He smiles and sunlight dances in his stormy eyes. He grazes his fingers down my side, and I think I let out a whimper, but it's hard to be sure when the bells in my head are ringing in alarm.

Soren leans down near my ear. The tip of his tongue darting out along the shell in a move that makes the bile burn the back of my throat. "This dress leaves very little to the imagination. Though, I'd be lying if I said I was imaginative...you see, I'm much more visual." His fingers dust the strap on my shoulder until it falls.

I jump when a deep, sultry voice interrupts his next words. "Soren! There you are! The nymphs have been looking for you. They said you promised them three orgasms each, and you know how impatient they are."

Just behind Soren, Cintamarri stands in all his beautiful glory. I don't think I have ever been more grateful to see a god's face before. The desire to run has been magnified tenfold, and with Soren's attention divided, I adhere to it. It's only when I've gotten across the room that I turn back to Cintamarri and mouth "thank you." He blinks with a subtle nod in acknowledgement.

It takes a few breaths, but I am able to shake off the encounter and search for Helena. I realize without her or even Erebus that I feel much smaller in this sea of gods. As eyes follow me and conversations halt, I am acutely aware of just how out of place I am here. Thanks to Soren, I also know just how vulnerable I am.

It's just like any other highborn party. You can do this. You've done it countless times. You pretended to be a lady. Now pretend to be someone worthy of being in the presence of gods.

With my little pep talk, I square my shoulders. If I let them see me as anything but deserving, they will peg me as prey. If I am to survive, I have to adapt. I can do this. I am capabl—

"So, you are what the fuss has been about," a voice dripping with venom says once I've entered the next room.

I whip my head around and find no one. So much for not becoming prey. I'm being hunted.

The voice laughs; it's wicked and cruel. "So, the seer cannot see? Pathetic." She emerges near a shadowed pillar. The woman has dark brown hair that is fastened back with two combs in the shape of serpents. She wears a tight green dress that might as well not be there at all with the way it hugs to every line in her curves, yet she moves in it with grace and effortless agility.

"I don't know you," I say—trying to place the goddess but coming up short.

"No, you wouldn't." She scoffs. "Ravetta. Surely, you have heard the name, at the very least?"

"Goddess of chaos and Haile's spy?"

"The very one." Her sharp smile only reaches half her face. "I've been watching you, *mortal*. There is nothing that makes you special. *So* I wonder, why? Why have Erebus, Haile, and Agnar taken to you?"

"You're not a very good spy if you can not find the answer yourself." I sink into an oversized chair, not letting her rile me.

There's a slight twitch below her left eye, but she smiles coldly and bends down so that our gazes are level. "You're nothing more than an annoying girl who didn't have the common sense to see your prophetic dreams for what they were." She straightens and taps a long sharpened fingernail on the armrest beside me. "Now, Lysette, she would've been a prize. What raw talent she has. Audrina...she was my favorite, of course. She and I could've had so much fun together. Even *Iris* would have been more interesting, but *you*? It's laughable."

I lose my bearings at the mention of my friends or former friends. "How do you know about us...them?"

"It's my entire purpose to know these things. What I would like to know is how you have turned Erebus's head when no one else has been able to for hundreds of years." The yellow-green of her eyes flares and darkens, almost turning black.

That was the only slip I needed to figure out how to play this. We are pieces on a chessboard, just as I had been in Stellera, and while I may not have always been the *best* player, it is a game I know well.

I smile. "Oh, oh, I see what this is. Did you try to get with Erebus? Did he turn you down?" I make a sympathetic pout. "Did his high-and-mighty lord of darkness and shadow not find you appealing in the way you had desired?"

"You know nothing, mortal bitch." She spits with her words.

"Revetta—" a booming voice interrupts us "—you're needed elsewhere. Now."

I know before turning who stands before me. Revetta snarls at me but sulks away, disappearing into a crowd that has chosen to ignore the disturbance. Haile comes to sit beside me in the open seat.

"She's a little bit testy *but* effective." He winks.

I murmur, "mhmm," not really knowing how to behave in the presence of the king of gods and overcome with a ringing in my ears That tugs of desire, the one I had telling me to leave Soren, has returned. Beyond Haile's shoulder I catch a glimpse of Cintamarri talking to a beautiful goddess, yet, it would seem, he's keeping one eye on me.

"Are you nervous?" he asks, eyeing my bouncing knee.

"Yes." The word comes easily.

He smiles. "Good. You should always be on your guard in our realm. How is your progress?"

"With what?"

"Helping my daughter?"

Progress helping Astoria...have I even made progress? Not with portals. I suppose being able to use my visions more accurately is progress but most definitely not enough, and I have this odd urge to please Haile, so telling him how little I've come is painful, yet I can't seem to lie.

"It is...stunted. I believe if I could go back to Millena's palace, I could maybe find something to help me unlock more of the Utikalo's memories. Perhaps that could give me some insight as to what to do with Astoria."

He clasps his *very* large hands beneath his chin and his eyes narrow. "And you have yet to do this? Why?"

I try to hold the words back, remembering the burns on Erebus's back, but can't control it as they spill from my lips. "Erebus won't let me near Agnar."

The air around us buzzes and light ripples beneath Haile's skin as though gathering for release, though he schools his features into neutrality. "I had also hoped to keep you from Agnar. He can become quite emotional and I had wanted to spare us all from it."

"Why?"

"A story for another day, perhaps." Haile's smile widens in a way that seems painful as a beautiful woman strolls towards us. Her gown is a sheer iridescent which gives her black hair a blueish hue. She wears a dainty crown, the band just a thin weaving of metal. Her presence is almost as cold as Erebus's. "Aislinn, this is my wife, Isela."

"It's an honor to meet you, Isela." I bow slightly.

"*Your majesty.*" Her sapphire eyes glow.

"Your majesty, I apologize."

Isela takes a sharp inhale, and her nostrils flare as she offers me her hand. I bow lower and take it into mine, pressing my lips against her smooth knuckle. A vision flashes through my mind.

A memory.

Not mine.

Hers.

One that has me sweating and clearing my throat. I try to keep my features as they were, to not give away what I've seen.

The queen of gods takes a quick side glance at her husband who has turned to talk to someone else. Her smile drops and her eyes harden. She leans in close as if to tell me a secret.

"I know what you saw," she whispers. "I know you know my secret."

"I didn't see anything."

Liar.

"Do not fake ignorance here, Isoot. Some of us can taste lies. Some of us can see into your mind."

My fingers begin to fidget as I look around for Helena...I'd even take Agnar at this point, anyone other than this ice queen of nightmares.

"We have two options. One, the safest choice for me, I have you killed. Or two, you leave the gods' realm for eternity and never mention a word to anyone about what I did to Astoria.

TWENTY-FOUR
FEEL EVERYTHING
DeLuca

HOLLOW.

Utterly empty.

A shell. That's all I was. All I am.

Floating in a void of our realm.

But her face. Those bright emerald eyes.

A beacon, helping me find my way back.

Aislinn.

I'm awoken by sunlight reflecting off the snow outside, magnifying the brightness to a near blinding level. My will is being tested. All I want is to keep my eyes closed and try to find Aislinn again...even if she was only a dream. But sensibility wins, and I force my eyes open—taking in the dark blue drapes hanging above me with the silver threads woven to resemble stars. My head might as well be pounded by a mallet, it would likely hurt less. Lysette stirs from the oversized chair placed in the corner of the room—flipping through some old book.

My throat is raw and the words come out hoarse. "How long was I out for?"

Her entire body flexes and then relaxes with relief. "Days. It's been three *days*." She closes the book and gives her attention to me. Far more serious than I've ever seen. "DeLuca. You can't..." She sighs. "You have to learn control...not suppression. We don't know the limits of your assumed immortality and I'd rather not test it. You must allow yourself to *feel* without erupting."

We're going right for the hard conversations then. I guess being out cold doesn't give me any sympathy points. "I can't, Lysette. I don't know how. I don't know how to feel anything without feeling *everything*."

"Then feel everything."

"Until we have Aislinn back, I can't."

She crosses her arms. "Can't or won't?"

"Both. If I let it in. If I accept the weight of the loss. The grief. The heartache. The godsdamn anger. The guilt..." My voice cracks. "I'll break, and I'll break the realm with me."

"You might do that anyway."

I smile at her, it's soft and doesn't reach my eyes. "I might."

A silent conversation passes between us, one in which I see how afraid she has been and I allow her to see how lost I am. As the lines between her brows smooth out, I decide I've given her enough to placate her worries. But she's right. The power inside of me grows each day. I have to adapt to the new reality that I *am* a god. Not a mutant like I thought. Not even a *Child* like the others. A full-blooded god. I'm not sure what that means for my future, but it's time for me to embrace it.

"Well, we shouldn't waste any more time sleeping the days away. We could have already been in Rilyse if someone didn't need Katova's longest nap," Lysette says with a bit of playfulness that pulls my thoughts from their path.

I chuckle and sit up in the bed. My head feels empty yet filled with stones at the same time and I grunt with the effort. "What happened to the Lightning Stone?"

"I'm letting Evander hold on to it for safekeeping. Eventually, I will bring it back to Caeliss and give it to Alec."

"Wouldn't it be safer to keep it with us?" I ask.

Lysette says nothing with her voice but everything with her eyes. They're hard and accusatory. As if I *meant* to use the stone.

"Fine. Whatever you think is best. I trust your judgment." I don't add that it was *her* stressing how dangerous the stones could be in the wrong hands, but I'm not in the mood to argue. "What time of day is it?" I sit up and realize I'm shirtless. My hands go to cover the scars on my arms instinctively.

"Midday."

Fuck, midday? We've wasted so much time already. "We should go then?"

She nods. "If you're feeling well enough, then yes, we should go. Evander has already sent the letters we asked him to and we are on a clock to get to Rilyse now."

I get out of bed. My legs shake as if I've been at sea for months. Lysette is up and by my side quickly, offering an arm for support. I shake my head in refusal. I'm determined to get going as quickly as possible, and that means getting my body functional again.

"My shirt?" I ask.

"In shreds. I hung what I could find in Aislinn's wardrobe. I need to wrap up a few things and then I can meet you at the lift."

"With Evander, you mean?" My brow cocks and, to her credit, she doesn't blush like I expect her to.

"Not that it matters, but yes, with Evander." Lysette sticks her book in a rucksack and marches down the hall.

I have the desire to go after her and threaten Evander. Give him the good old "*if you do something to hurt her*" speech. I don't trust men. The things they say when they think they're in the company of like-minded barbarians is disgusting, especially when it comes to talking about women. But I'm fairly certain it would be futile considering Lysette with probably chew him up and spit him back out again. In fact...maybe I should go comfort *him*. She's probably breaking his heart right now.

He seems fine enough. I admire how he organized the refugees and the way he offered help and accepted a story *I* would have deemed utter lunacy if the positions were reversed. Gods know he's been through more than I have. I can't imagine what it was like growing up as an experiment.

"Do you trust him?" I ask after we board the Capital transport. I drop our bags in the front and sit across from Lysette. This transport makes the other two look like relics of an ancient world. It's sleek, and the leather seats are pristine. We can even look out the windows and see the veins of minerals within the mountain as we speed past. I can't watch for long...it brings back memories I wish would disappear completely.

"As much as I trust anyone that isn't blood or family," Lysette says, while propping her feet up on the seat in front of her. My brows raise and I give her a pointed look. She sighs. "*You* are family."

"Am I?"

"Yes. You're Ailie's family, which makes you *my* family."

"I see." Her answer scratches at a lifelong wound, the one dug deeper with each disappearing sibling. They never embraced me the way Val had. "So after all this, after training our minds and bodies, and living together, and researching, and everything else, it's only our shared love of Aislinn that binds us?"

Her face scrunches, intensifying the scar slashed across her white eye. "That's not what I meant, DeLuca. We are bonded by something stronger than fate—*tragedy*. Each moment since we've entered each other's lives has been a constant wheel of traumatic experiences. I'm not even sure I'd like you at all if we hadn't been forced into this life."

I half laugh. "You probably wouldn't have cared for me one way or another."

"Can you not say the same?"

"I always liked you, Lysette. You and Linnea were my favorite Ursons, and now that I've seen what you're capable of...how great you could have been if you were given the role as a leader of Stellera, my admiration has only grown."

"You didn't like us enough to try and save our lives...not like Aislinn."

Shame fills every molecule in my body. She's not wrong. I was half tempted to leave her when we found her in the aftermath of that explosion. But I knew Aislinn would want me to get her...so I did.

I try to shove it away. Try not to feel it, that eternal guilt. If I hadn't met Aislinn, I would've let them all burn.

Fuck. I'm just as monstrous as the rest of them.

"Stop, DeLuca. Stop pushing it away. Feel it. Talk to me about it."

With a shaky breath, I unclench my fist. Tiny flames flick across my palms like candles at an altar. "My part..." I have to swallow to continue, the words stick in my throat like thorns on a bush. "My part in the Liberator's rebellion is something I will regret until the end of time."

She nods, her gaze warm and understanding. "I know."

"Do you forgive me?"

"No." She drops her gaze. "I will never forgive the slaughter of my family. Of my friends. The loss of my home. It's why I can't look back. Because despite your role, I don't *want* to hold it against you, but when I look back, it's harder."

All this time, I thought she couldn't look back because of the pain of losing her family. She didn't want to remember what *I'd* done that led to it... Gods, it must be unbearable to be around me. I run my hands down my face and clasp them behind my neck. "Lys—"

She holds up her hands. "Don't, please. We don't need to talk about my feelings."

"So I have to stop holding my emotions in, but the same doesn't apply to you?" I give her a pointed look.

She shrugs and leans back in her seat. "I'm not a risk to the entire realm when I lose my shit."

I fold my arms and quirk a brow. She is gravely underestimating herself. "I don't know about that. I was there when you impaled that guy in the woods."

"Feels like a lifetime ago." She half-heartedly smiles.

"It *was* a lifetime ago. We were all reborn that day."

The ride lasted a few uncomfortable hours. Considerably fast for the distance. It would have taken five times as long in any regular transport, or gods forbid if we had to hop from shuttle to shuttle. That would have taken days.

We are let out in a cave, much nicer than the ones in Ashe or the Thickett Woods. Instead of compacted dirt, the walls are made of concrete and create a tunnel. The sound of our boots echoe throughout the otherwise empty walkway. There is only one direction to go, and it leads to the large circular metal door.

Beside me, little clouds of breath make me realize that it must be below freezing in here. I know Lysette won't accept my jacket, so instead, I focus on raising my temperature. Bringing the fire just to the surface of my skin but not above. The air around us warms, and though she doesn't acknowledge the heat, she moves an inch closer to me.

"We should be somewhere along the border. The track follows the mountains until they end, which is only a few miles from the Capital."

"I can't imagine your father walking so far."

Lysette scowls. "He didn't. He usually arranged for a transport to pick him up here."

"That sounds more likely."

"Let's not discuss my father, okay?"

I throw my hands up in surrender. "That's fine with me."

"Do we even know where we are going?'

"We need somewhere to sleep for the night. It's too cold to camp, and honestly, I don't want to be caught out in the open with so many unknowns."

"The palace?" she suggests.

I smile. "Not the palace, but I know a place."

"You're not a spy anymore. You could give a straightforward answer." She twists the wheel on the large metal door when we reach the end of the tunnel.

My eyes are on her with a retort readied on my tongue, but the second she gets the door open, a large body rushes in—taking me off guard—and pushes me to the ground with a hard thud.

"DeLuca!" Lysette's voice fills my ears, but I can't see her as my assailant blocks my view. His elbow digs into my shoulder while trying to keep me pinned, but his angle is all wrong and I push him off easily—sending him flying into the wall beside us.

A dozen more file in. All wearing the King's Army uniform but with Liberation circles pinned to the collar. One of them has an arm around Lysette to keep her in place against his chest. He uses the other hand to run his fingers through her red hair and I see a dozen thoughts race across his mind while he smiles to himself.

"Touch a single hair on her head again, and you will find yourself without hands." I level him with a glare, one filled with the promise of violence.

One of the men steps in front of the others. His eyes are wide while surveying his friend's unconscious body on the other side of the tunnel wall.

"There is no need for fighting. We only wish to inquire about your intentions," he says, walking slowly as if approaching a rabid animal.

"Your friend other there sure has a way with words." I nod in the direction of the unconscious man. "Lysette?"

"Yeah?" she asks with heavy breaths, giving me her full attention.

"You good?" I ask.

"She's fine. Now, state your business," the man who'd stepped forwards says.

Ignoring the man, I let the flames surface along my skin, and I ask her again, "Are. You. Good?"

Whispers from the false soldiers start.

"*Abomination.*"

"*Freak.*"

"*Get him while his eyes are on her.*"

Lysette's gaze stays fixed on mine, silently communicating a plan. "I'm good," she says with a smile.

I nod at her, and the soldiers close in on us.

"Squad leader asked you a question, *abomination*," the man holding onto Lysette says.

"Okay," I say. "Here's what we're not going to do. We're not going to pretend you have any intentions other than capturing us. Right?" They look between each other with sheepish expressions. "Right. Now, I will give you all to the count of three to run. You will lose your dignity, but you will keep your life."

"There's twelve of us!" Lysette's captor laughs. "How are you going to take on twelve of us by yourself?"

"*One.*" I begin my countdown, and a grin slowly spreads across my face. There's a hesitancy in some of the soldiers, but a few stand firm and reach for their weapons.

Lysette throws her head back into her captor's nose and jabs an elbow into his side. Another man tries to grab her, but she knees him in the groin. I'm not sure I have ever felt more pride in my life.

"Bitch!" The captor pinches his bleeding nose while the other guy doubles over, wailing in agony.

There are no plants in this tunnel, but there's a vibration below my feet, which means she's calling the roots beneath us. She has a wild look in her eye, one I haven't seen since she killed that guy in the woods. She comes to stand beside me. "He's not by himself."

"*Two.*" My flames grow. There's a clattering of weaponry on the ground as three of the soldiers take off running.

Lysette sighs. "And then there were nine. Lucy, this would be an excellent time to release all that pent up rage you've been suppressing."

"*Three.*"

The nine charge at us. Their yells echo off the tunnel walls and their weapons are raised. We both stand still—waiting. Blood still pours from her captor's nose. I'd rip his fucking arms off for touching her, but I'll let Lysette take care of herself. I have a suspicion she has just as much aggression to let out as I do.

I wink at Lysette and crack the ground just enough for the roots to push through. She uses them to trip the soldiers while I create arrows of fire and have a little target practice. First shot went into the arm that had held Lys against her will.

The soldiers recover quickly from their fall...except the guy who impaled himself on his own axe. He's not going anywhere. The squad leader starts shouting at his men. They scramble and I watch with amusement. Something stings my shoulder. I whip around, quick on my feet, and find the man I knocked out earlier smirking at me.

His smirk drops the second before my fist collides with it. I don't stop there. I pursue him as he stumbles back. The man tries to swing, but I catch his arm and smash my forehead into his.

"DeLuca! Behind you!" Lysette warns. There's another sharp pain as a blade slices through the skin below my ribs. Blood drips to the floor. With my hand on the first guy's throat, I do the same to his friend behind me—heating my hands until I melt through the flesh of their throats, and there's a sick bubbling noise popping from their mouth. When I pull my hands free, the men collapse and I use their deep purple uniforms to wipe my hands clean.

Lysette has three of the men tied up in the roots and her captor strung upside down. The squad leader is trying to sneak up on her with some kind of syringe, but I throw a disk of air just in time to stop the needle from puncturing her skin. The squad leader looks up at me in shock with the same syringe protruding out of his cheek. I pull a dagger off one of the bodies beside me and throw it at the squad leader's head—hitting him dead center between the eyes. He falls back, landing with a sick crack as his skull smacks into the concrete.

"Hey, Lys, have you had enough yet?" I ask as I shoot a fire ball at another soldier. He drops to the ground with an agonized scream.

"Just about!" Lysette encourages a root to rise around her captor and hold him in place. "Stay there, would you?" she asks, then grabs his sword out of its sheath and swings at his arm. Blood spurts with each hack. The guy screams hysterically. There's glistening of sweat above her brow despite the low temperature. When she finally rids the weasel of his limb, she slaps him in the face...with his own hand...then throws it to the side. "You really shouldn't touch a lady without their permission." She tuts. "Okay, I'm done now, Lucy." Blood coats her clothes and there is a sated look in her eye. I hardly recognize her.

"You're not going to kill him?" I ask.

The screaming must be getting to her because in seconds a root is clamping his mouth shut. "I already took his sword arm. Isn't that worse?"

A man charges at my side, and with the lift of my hand, he's incinerated. "That bastard would have done much worse to you."

The last soldier runs out of the tunnel, and the ones Lysette has tied up squirm against the roots securing them in place.

"I know, but I don't want to be like them. If I mindlessly kill them all, how would that make me any better?" she asks, walking over the wriggling soldiers to where we dropped our packs.

I grab two knives and clean them on my pants, then hand one to Lysette. "You're better because you wouldn't slaughter innocents just for being on the wrong side."

"I'm *not* killing them. There's already so much death. Too much."

Looking around at the carnage, the familiar twinge of guilt flares. I just killed four people with ease. Sure, they were coming after us, but was it really necessary? Lysette has me second-guessing myself. What if they were just soldiers following orders?

"Nasty freak bitch!" The captor's roots have loosened enough for him to speak. "When I get free, I'm going to take out your eye and have it made into a pendant. Then I'll send it to your pretty little abomination friend, along with your red hair and a note entailing all the times I fuc—." The captor is silenced by my knife stabbing through the side of his neck.

"He deserved it." I look at Lysette and wait for her to argue.

She doesn't. She shrugs and finds a new knife upon the wreckage, handing it to me hilt first. "Are you going to pull that star from your shoulder, or is it a momento of our time together?"

Star? What fucking star? Oh shit, I forgot that guy had stabbed me with something. I pull the throwing star out, wipe my blood off, and hand it to Lysette. "Your momento, miss."

She rolls her eyes and takes it, examining the metal, then sucks in a breath. "I think Ev was right."

"About?"

"The armory must be nearby. This star is aietal."

TWENTY-FIVE
ACT DECENTLY
Aislinn

I NEVER THOUGHT I'D be happy to see Erebus. Never thought I'd find comfort in his darkness. But as soon as I catch that flash of shadow, every bone in my body relaxes to the point it almost brings me to tears. His eyes snap to mine and he's inches from me within seconds. His hand is beneath my chin, turning my head in either direction—searching.

"What happened?" Shadows flicker out from him, his eyes a shade darker and a scowl upon his face.

"Nothing." I swallow. "I just sat and talked to Haile. I met Ravetta and Isela...and Soren." The tremble in my voice gives away my unease, but I'm not really sure what to do with the information I have. "It was...it was just a lot to take on my own."

"Did Soren touch you?"

I raise my gaze to his and let him see the swirl of emotion in them. "Cintamarri intervened before it got too far."

Erebus's jaw tightens and goes eerily still. It's as if even taking a breath will cause him to combust. The cool air wraps around us in a vortex of ice, providing a small amount of privacy while he gathers his emotion. "Later, pet, you *will* tell me what happened," he whispers with his forehead centimeters from mine.

I nod and he drops the dark veil around us. "Where did you go?" I ask.

"To check something."

"And will you be telling *me* later?"

"It wouldn't matter if I did. The journey proved a waste."

Emotional exhaustion stops me from prying further. I have never felt this drained before. The adrenaline of the night has long since worn off and we haven't even gotten to the main event. "I haven't seen Astoria or Helena since you left."

"Haile doesn't like for Astoria to be around the others, does not trust them. Helena was looking after her for me."

"Then why bring her at all?"

"I believe he hopes Kato will fix her, though none of us have seen or heard from Kato in almost a millenia."

"Sounds like the people in Rousse and Dailotta...praying to all of you for miracles that go unanswered."

His brow cocks as if this truly surprises him. "They *still* pray?"

"Not in Stellera. But yes, Rousse and Dailotta are still very much devout... You don't hear them?"

"No, we do not hear them, not unless they do a summoning ritual. Not since the barrier between realms went up. We stopped visiting long before that. After the Gods' War, nothing was quite the same for any of us."

"When was that?"

"It's been a long time." The muscle in his cheek twitches, and he gives me a look that says "later." "Come, it's almost time for another of Haile's self-indulgent speeches about thankfulness and being all together under one roof."

"Now?" I look around at the inebriated and semi-nude gods.

"He likes to wait until the spirits have taken effect. Less chance of someone starting a fight. The first few thousand years of Estaleiki eu Kato Arisi ended in bloodshed. It was far more entertaining back then."

Ravetta wedges herself between us. "Hello, darling, I was looking for you."

Erebus barely acknowledges her. "*Chaos.*"

"I hear you've been getting into fights again—stirring up trouble." She flashes her pointed teeth. "Just like old times—do you remember? How much trouble we made?"

He steps around her. "I do not recall."

She frowns. "Don't lie for your mortal pet's sake. Before it was you and Astoria, it was you and me." Revetta catches his gaze and tilts her head. "How *is* our dear goddess of night?"

A shadow whips out and slashes across Revetta's cheek, drawing a line of deep blue. "Do not dare to speak of her! Go crawl back to the depths of Haile's ass you prefer to dwell within."

I can't help but laugh as Erebus wraps us both in shadows and we appear in the next room. I'm still smiling when the shadows disperse, and Erebus is looking at me as if I've grown horns.

"What?" I ask, suddenly self-conscious.

"I have never heard your true laugh."

"So?"

"It is different. It makes your shadow sing." I stare at him in confusion until he shakes his head. "Never mind. Come, sit. You will be by my side, Astoria on the other."

"Whatever you say." I shrug and sit in the seat he's pulled out for me at one of the many large circular tables. The room is grand, larger than the first. Lavender silks hang from the ceiling with weavings of colorful floral garland. The vases centered at each table are ridiculously tall, making it impossible to see across from me to where the throne is.

Good, the less Haile the better.

Erebus leans in and whispers from behind me. "Stay, pet. I am going to fetch Astoria." The tiny hairs along my neck rise to meet his breath. The second he's gone, the chair beside me is pulled out, and an unfamiliar god places himself in it.

"A new face. Thanks be to Kato." He relaxes into the seat and crosses one knee over the other. "It's been so dull around here since the barrier went up. I am called Raza. Dreams and nightmares are my territory, something I have heard that you may struggle with?"

"Heard from who?"

He shrugs a shoulder and flashes a dazzling smile. Why do all gods have to look like this? It's kind of ridiculous how good-looking they all are.

"I have struggled with nightmares in the past, yes," I admit. Not sure whether or not to reveal that said nightmares are actually visions.

"Well, if you find yourself struggling, I am a uldoaka to mortals." He winks.

Before I have the chance to ask him anything more, a blast of shadow passes beside me and Erebus appears. He gently helps Astoria in to her seat and kisses her temple. She is smiling blindly, looking at a spot that is neither ceiling nor wall, as though she sees something we don't.

Helena arrives moments later and huffs at Raza while taking the seat beside him. "I wanted to sit next to *my* friend."

"And I wanted to get to know the first mortal to enter our realm in hundreds of years."

"She is not an attraction for your amusement." Erebus's tone sends a chill up my spine.

"I am my own person and can speak for myself," I tell all three of them, but my gaze is pinned on Erebus.

He has a less than amused smile as he says, "You forget *who* you are. Do I need to remind you, *pet*?" That hollow chill wraps around my core and tightens until I can't breathe.

"Can't you act decently for Kato today?" Helena throws a grape across the table, hitting Erebus in the shoulder.

To all of our surprise, Astoria laughs. The sound is like a chime in the wind on a starry night. For a second, her eyes look clear. Only a second, and then she's back to looking at that spot between the wall and ceiling, muttering about being surrounded by darkness.

The speech lasted so long it was an effort to keep my eyes open. It didn't help that I couldn't understand any of it. Haile spoke entirely in Old Daeil, and Helena was too interested in flirting with Raza to translate. The two of them were continuously whispering to one another throughout the entire speech. The look in Helena's eyes is one that I recognize from the many outings with Audrina where she'd set her sights on the next conquest.

Once Haile finishes, Erebus immediately whisks Astoria away, only to appear a few moments later. "Are you ready to go home, pet?"

"Do I have the choice?"

"You do. If you wish to dwell in the company of these pillocks, you may, but their behavior only worsens after the speeches."

I try to hide my shock and am tempted to see how much truth his words hold, but my eyes are heavy as well as my body. I'm more than ready to leave, especially after the encounters with so many gods. I could go the rest of my life without seeing three of them again.

"I'm ready to go home."

He smiles. Erebus *smiles*. Not his usual predatory grin. Not a smirk. A *smile*. His grey eyes shine, giving them a silver glow. And I realize what I've said.

I referred to the Shadows as *home*.

Riverstone was never home. Obsidian was never home. Caeliss was never home. The Academy came close. But the Shadows...this realm...

"Let's go *home*, pet." Erebus takes my arm and we're gone before I can blink.

When we arrive in my room, I'm already wearing my night clothes, thin, gray, and unbelievably soft.

"Thanks," I murmur.

"Aislinn—" He turns away as I crawl into bed.

"Yeah?" I yawn.

He stares for a few seconds and then shakes his head. "It can wait until after you've slept."

"Okay." My eyes start to flutter closed. "Erebus?"

"Yes, pet?"

"How do you plan to help her? Astoria? How am I supposed to help?"

He sighs and there's a long pause. It's an effort to hold on to my consciousness. I'm not even sure he is still in the room.

Then he finally says, "I'm going to go back in time and erase myself from her life."

The blankets creep up to my chin, and I know it's the shadows pulling them. "You're not the villain you pretend to be," is what I try to say, but I'm pretty sure I'm asleep before I finish the words.

I awaken with a jolt, sitting up so fast that my head spins. It is not morning yet. Something is off. Something is terribly wrong. The very air feels like it's dancing on the edge of a blade. I sense a presence. Someone hiding in the shadows of my room. It's too quiet. I can't even hear my own breathing. It's as if someone has stolen the sound—suffocated it. I go to reach for my mark, to call Erebus, to scream, but two yellow-green eyes appear above me and black powder is blown into my face. It takes all of one breath for everything else to fade out of existence.

TWENTY-SIX
SUFFOCATING
Erebus

WRONG.

Wrong.

Wrong.

The shadows hiss and swarm as they do when they sense a disturbance. I have only just calmed myself from the events that had unfolded at the Estaleiki eu Kato Arisi celebration, how close Aislinn was to becoming Soren's next prey. I left her unprotected and alone against our realms. All for nothing. The barrier is still firmly in place and all the new shadows are still stuck on the wrong side.

And now this?

The moment sleep claimed my consciousness, we felt it. Someone who does not belong to my portion of this realm has entered without invitation. My shadows hiss violently—carrying me faster than ever before. To her bedroom. *My* pet.

I do not even need to look inside to know. I feel her absence.

Aislinn is gone. Taken.

It had to have been seconds ago.

A sliver of their shadows remain, Aislinn's—midnight blue with a sparkling silver mist. The other—dark green, flecked with amber—a shadow I'd recognize in a sea of millions.

Ravetta.

My palace shudders under the rage reverberating from my core.

They could be hidden anywhere in this realm with Ravetta's ability to jump through the folds of reality.

She wouldn't be stupid enough to risk my wrath as well as Haile's.

Which can only mean one thing…she was under order.

It takes me less time to exhale than it does for my shadows to carry me to the front of Haile's palace.

Pristine.

Gold.

Always lit.

It is the only place my shadows recoil.

They hate this false light.

It is suffocating.

I do not bother knocking as I blow through the dramatically oversized front doors. Past the fountain. Block out the sweet serenade that plays on a constant loop meant to ease all who enter.

Straight to Haile.

Sitting on his godsdamned throne as if he's expecting me.

His pious, self-righteous smirk tells me all I need to know.

"Why?" My voice is deep and carrying the promise of violence.

Haile looks down at me with one brow cocked. "You take too long to produce results."

"She was making progress."

"Not enough... and—" he drawls with a yawn, "—she told me herself that she could have been making more progress in Kaoket."

"We agreed. We agreed to keep Agnar out of it. He is far too possessive and we may very well find ourselves in the same position as last time."

"I made a deal with Agnar."

The ice beneath my skin radiates a chill so strong I am sure even Haile can feel it. "*What deal?*"

"Deliverance of the mortal, and in exchange, he will coerce her to do what needs to be done, for Astoria *and* the barrier."

"You will not keep her from m—the Shadows. She belongs there. I have claimed her. Marked her. She is *mine*." I bare my teeth in a snarl.

Haile is before me in the flash of a blinding light. "Remember *your* place, trickster. Remember your oath and allegiance. You will *obey*. You *will* leave the mortal in Kaoket until she makes progress! I tire of waiting."

Even with my shadows recoiling, I stand firm and keep my teeth bared. "And what of *your* oaths and allegiances?" My eyes drift to the throne beside his, the one that has remained empty since Isela fulfilled her duty and gave Haile his daughter.

"Enough!" His voice is that of a king—or tyrant. His light blasts me all the way back to the Shadows.

The ground beneath me shakes with every step. Ignoring the sting of my burnt skin, I head for the Abyss, the only place I won't do any damage in a mood like this. Only the damned reside there, eternally doomed to be wholly aware of the emptiness that surrounds them.

Here is where I can find release. Here is where I can fully let go. It is like watching a supernova. The intense calm, followed by the explosion of chaos.

Until all that is left is a black hole.

I have always been a black hole, sucking in everything around me until nothing remains. Even the stars fall in my presence.

I'm as deep into the Abyss as it gets before I fully let go. The shadows scatter away to avoid the explosion that begins within me and spreads like a tsunami of pure death. The white light spreads and blocks my vision. Although harmless here, if I were to release this anywhere else, it would level it to create a barren dark field forever to be void of life. This is how the Abyss came to exist.

Once I have calmed enough to see straight, I feel her—tugging against the shadow chains I placed on her wrist when I first brought her to Kaoket. She's afraid. I taste it. Feel it.

With all the focus I can muster, I send her a message down the connection. "*Do not fight them, pet. Play their game. I will have you home soon.*"

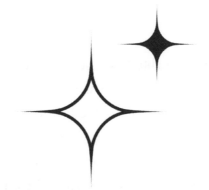

Part Two
PIECES

TWENTY-SEVEN
UNDERGROUND
Lysette

WE'RE DEEP IN THE Capital's heart now. After our altercation, we washed up in the river and changed into some cleaner clothes. I bandaged DeLuca's shoulder. When I went to do the same to his side, it had already healed. I'm not sure I will ever get used to that.

Staring at what was once a great city, I can't help but feel a tug of sadness. King Carrigan and his family...the king may have been corrupt, but his children were innocent. I feel like we were just here. Only then, we were all together. Now, it's just me and DeLuca. And he's grating on my nerves.

I hate surprises. *Hate* them. He knows this, yet, he refuses to tell me where we're going. I'm on edge after our ambush. My fingers tingle with my abilities stirring, ready to attack if I have the need.

The top of the castle is visible over the dozens of buildings sprawled before us. Getting nicer and more well-kept the closer their proximity to the once mighty palace. Empty now. Those buildings that once housed great families of influence, some that I have known all my life, are likely now empty or taken. There are still people in the streets. The temperament is, well, bleak. Their faces are dirty and bodies are too thin and frail with not enough layers to protect from the cold. Thank Isela, the snow hasn't fallen here yet.

We travel away from them, away from the people who desperately need someone to take charge. I search deep in my memory to bring forth images from maps and passages I've read regarding this part of Stellera. There's nothing past the farmlands beyond the borders for hundreds of miles. It would take weeks on foot. Perhaps we can find an abandoned transport. We could take the river to Vallae...if we had a boat. It would be the easiest route to Rilyse...taking one of the famed Vallae rivers and—

"You're thinking so loudly I can hear it." The note of amusement in his voice really tests my already thin patience.

"Why won't you just tell me where we are going?"

"It would ruin the surprise."

"I hate surprises."

"I know." He grins. DeLuca then turns a corner and lifts a large cloth from a clothesline, beckoning me to follow underneath. "You're going to like this one though, I promise."

My shoulders drop with my exaggerated exhale as I duck under the cloth.

The slums. He's led us to the slums. I should have guessed based on the direction we were heading.

"It's more than it seems." He gestures to a grate in the ground.

He can't actually expect me to go down to the sewage tunnels. "We're not..."

"Oh, but we are." DeLuca easily pulls the top off the grate and begins the descent down a ladder built into the stone street. I follow behind him, grumbling to myself about how I'll make him suffer. Perhaps I will bind his legs with tiny vines the next time we find ourselves on a lengthy walk. I smirk to myself at the thought.

We drop on solid ground below. Surprisingly, dry. Rows and rows of cells line the walls. All open and filled with various belongings and beds. But cells nonetheless. Though, the way the hinges are rusted over indicates that they have not been closed for some time.

"What is this place?"

"Some sort of prison, old. Older than any building in the capital. A part of a forgotten history...*and* home of the Underground."

"What is the Underground?"

"A place where status and politics don't matter. A people on their own. Started during the Trinity War for refugees. Kept for those who don't fit above. Everyone here can be trusted because they are all hiding in one way or another."

"What people?" The cells certainly appear lived in, yet there is not a sign of life.

"Come on." He nods toward a tunnel.

This tunnel is dark and made of stone. It's foreboding and makes my stomach tighten. This incomprehensible sense of dread that makes me nauseous. I've always felt uneasy in dark places like this, but the feeling I have now is so strong that I can hardly convince my leaden feet to push forward.

We finally reach a metal door at the end of the tunnel, and to my surprise, a woman is sitting beside it. She looks weak and dirty, as if she's been lost down here for years. Her glassy blue eyes look up at us, and her grease-stained forehead crinkles.

DeLuca smiles at her and nods. "Keeper."

"I only know a life shrouded in dark," the woman says to him.

"And I have come to bring you light," DeLuca replies.

The woman smiles and rises to her feet, clasping DeLuca on the forearm as he does the same to her, and then they say, "Forever free" in unison. My brow scrunches as I watch the woman procure a large key from beneath her filthy poncho and turn it in the metal door. With a click, it opens wide to reveal another dark corridor.

This is significantly worse than crawling through tunnels at Obsidian Manor.

I give DeLuca a side eye, but he breezes past me and the other woman into the corridor without a single qualm. Thankfully, this walk in the dark is much shorter than the last before we come upon a railing and a spacious cavern. There's a faint glow on the ceiling, perhaps from gems below?

I reach the rusted railing and have to grab it to keep from falling to my knees from the shock. On the far side of this corridor is a long set of stairs carved into the stone wall, but below that, far below, are people. Hundreds...maybe thousands. A village all its own. There's people bustling through the bazaar. Tents. Homes carved into the walls going on as far as I can see. It isn't until we pass through the rails that I can hear them. Chatter, laughter, and...music. And that glow? Not crystals at all but orbs of light. Bright colors and plentiful. It's breathtaking.

"H-how?" The only word I can manage.

"A long-held secret. No one knows how they're able to block the sound out. With the knowledge we now possess, I suspect there is a Child here that has the answers. Maybe a family that has dwelled here from the beginning."

"A ruler?"

"There are no rulers in the Underground—it's a community. A place of second chances. They take care of each other because it's the right thing to do."

A warmth blooms in my chest. The more I watch the people below, the more in spreads. It's something I have long given up on...something I didn't think was obtainable, a newfound hope for my people. "It's beautiful."

Nearly an hour. That's how long it took to climb down the steps to the Underground. My legs ache in places I didn't know possible. The light is provided by little orbs filled with a glowing substance. A multitude of colors. It's gorgeous. Yet, the lack of natural light has me withering inside and more exhausted than I have ever felt.

Every face we pass has been kind. Happy. Content. They smile and nod in the way of greeting. The children run freely through the paved walkways. Their laughter nearly brings me to tears. I have never heard such free joy filling the streets of Ashe. Never knew what it could feel like.

As if DeLuca senses how close I am to losing it, he squeezes my shoulder. "Not much further, Lys."

I still don't have words. Not for this brilliant...village doesn't feel right...sanctuary, maybe? It's a glimpse of what Stellera could be.

We finally arrive at one of the homes carved into the wall. DeLuca knocks once...twice... Before the third knock, the magenta door flies open. This time I can't stop the tears. I'm on my knees sobbing. It's like all my air has been stolen from my chest. Or maybe I've just forgotten how to breathe.

Kind hands etched with the creases of time trace the band around my eye patch before the familiar face sinks to her knees in front of me. She cups my chin in her gentle hands.

"Well, is that any way to greet an old friend?"

My answering laugh rattles my chest. Remembering how to take in air at the same moment I'm upon her. My arms crash around her old yet sturdy body into my chest—holding on as if any second she might be taken again.

"Good gods, child, you reek. When was the last time you had a bath?"

I still can't speak. Can't remember words. Except one, her name. The women who had cared for me and my siblings like we were her own. Who taught us to read. Who'd bandaged us when we hurt ourselves. Who loved us, despite having every reason not to.

I laugh as I say it, the only word I remember. "Elinor."

TWENTY-EIGHT
FULLY ALIVE
Rett

THERE'S A CHILL IN the air. I heard some talk in the village that the snows have started on the mountains. Obsidian winters were always my favorite. I love the crisp smell of the forest in winters and nights by warm fires. Not to mention, the first snow usually signaled the Delphia's annual visit. When Ailie came.

My chest seizes as I think of her and what this first snow was supposed to be for us.

Our wedding.

It was always supposed to be the first snow after her twentieth birthday. There are a series of ticks carved into the wood of my closet where I counted down the winters. No one knew about it, of course. I was afraid if they knew how much I wanted it, they'd take it away.

My parents were not cruel, but hers were.

I begged my parents so many times to keep her. To raise her with us. My father was blinded to Phillipe Delphia's cruelty and didn't care about Sescily one way or another.

Mother just told me to be patient.

Apparently it doesn't snow in Caeliss. The Children work together to keep it out and ensure the crops and animals thrive in any season. Maybe they will let me out to see the snow. It seems we've been pushing their rule of no one being able to leave. Considering it's happened so often since our arrival. I understand the need for secrecy, but Katova is changing, and maybe Caeliss needs to change along with it. They can't stay hidden forever.

Iris grabs hold of my hand and smiles up at me. I pull our enclosed fingers to my lips and kiss her knuckles.

"You think too much, bear."

"I was just thinking about Obsidian winters. I'm going to miss the snow."

Iris nods and pouts sympathetically. "They were pretty, however, I much prefer watching them from indoors."

"I'm sad Emberlin won't ever get to experience the first snow. The celebrations were always my favorite growing up . Even more so than my birthday."

Iris stops walking. "Oh gods, your birthday is in a few weeks. I almost forgot!"

"It's not like it matters anyway. Our attempt to celebrate Lysette's birthday was depressing and I'm no better than an outcast here. My only family is gone."

"I'm here," she places our hands on her belly, "and so is Em. Maybe Lysette will be back in time. I can make a cake, and we can celebrate, just us."

"Well, if Lysette is back, that will hopefully mean Ailie is back, which means she will come and bring her—DeLuca."

Iris drops my hand and there's a muscle twitch in her jaw. "Maybe."

I kiss Iris on the cheek and watch her walk into the healing center to resume her training. Sylvie waves from the window, causing me to shiver. Her not being able to see, yet always knowing exactly where everything is, really makes me uneasy. I guess a lot of the gifts make me uneasy if I think about it. Maybe it's jealousy....maybe something else. Probably jealousy. And these headaches are not improving my mood.

Now back to my daily routine of nothing.

My entire existence now is hanging out with Iris and waiting for her to get done at the Healing Center. I work out, I read, and I wait.

This stagnant life is almost unbearable, and I'm tempted to go try to hunt Lysette and DeLuca down just to give me something to do.

But I can't leave Iris alone, especially not while she carries my child.

"Hey Rett!" I turn on the cobblestone path and find Dover waving me over.

"Oh hey, Dover, what's up?"

"I was about to meet up with some of the guys. We get together every few days and blow off some steam. You in?"

I'm about to decline—Iris would rather me hang out with her—*but* Iris is at her training and won't be home for hours. "Sure, why not?" I shrug and join him in the direction he is heading.

Dover smiles. "Nice. We need some new blood."

"New blood? What kind of steam are we blowing off?"

He smirks. "You'll just have to see when we get there."

There is a dirt clearing near the edge of Caeliss, far away from the village. It's large and circular with a strange metal rope enclosing it. There are already three others here sitting on boulders and laughing. Leighra, I recognize, but I'm not sure I've ever seen the other two. They stand when they spot us.

"Bout time Dover! Rett," Leighra says, arms crossed and eyes assessing the both of us.

"I got held up." Dover gestures to me. "Rett, this is Oyrik, Skinshifter." The shirtless man covered in tattoos with subtle Roussian features extends his hand. As our hands clasp, I notice his tattoos are constantly moving beneath his skin.

"Skinshifter, is that what it sounds like?" I ask him.

Oyrik smiles, and before my very eyes, his skin begins to ripple and roll until I am no longer looking at Oyrik—but at myself.

"Sure is," he says, and damn, even his voice sounds like mine. He steps back and shakes out his body until it resembles his own again.

"That's creepy as fuck," I say with a laugh.

Dover shrugs. "You get used to it."

The other guy, a redhead who is as tall as my father was and made of pure muscle is next to introduce himself. "I'm Mase." His grip is crushing as we shake hands.

"Let me guess, your superpower is being strong as fuck?" I ask.

"No, I'm a Gale. Why would you think that?" Mase asks with a confused expression.

I stare at his arms which are quite literally bigger in circumference than my head. "I— ugh—."

"He's messing with you." Leighra rolls her eyes.

"Mase is a Isetuko, basically just a little stronger than the rest of us," Oyrik says.

"A little?" Mase says, picking up a boulder the size of a baby cow and tossing it clear across the open field as if it were a child's sports ball.

I'm not even trying to hide how impressed I am. "Damn."

"So these are the guys," Dover says.

Leighra clears her throat and the other three groan.

"The guys and Leighra." Dover corrects himself.

"I still like the Fist Club...or Club Eat Dirt...or the Fight Frights," Mase says while counting the names off his fingers.

"Those names are shit," Oyrik says.

"We aren't naming ourselves." Dover shakes his head.

"What is it the Fight Frights do, exactly?" I ask

"Please don't indulge him," Leighra says.

Dover smiles and claps me on the back. "We fight."

"You train your abilities then?" I ask, trying not to show the let down in my face.

"No. We fight as mortals. You see this ring here?" Dover asks, pointing to the metal rope around the clearing. "This is a rope made from aietal. It blocks our abilities, leaving us just as mortal as you."

"Why would you do that?" I ask. If I had any kind of power, I'd use it to the fullest extent.

"Because this exists." Leighra points to the metal. "Weapons against gods and Children. We want to be prepared in case we find ourselves without our abilities."

"And because it's fun to kick the shit out of each other," Mase adds.

"So, you in?" Dover asks.

I look at the four with a brow lifted. "You all are crazy. Of course I'm fucking in. Let's do this." Before anyone can answer, I'm already pulling off my shirt and stepping into the ring.

I'm bouncing on the balls of my feet, waiting for Iris to come downstairs. It's been nearly two weeks since I started joining the guys to "blow off steam," and fuck if it's not the best part of my day. Iris was a little concerned when I started coming home covered in blood and bruises, but I think she's used to it now. Honestly, I think she might like it a little because she has been practically ripping my clothes off as soon as she lays eyes on me.

The tea she makes is a little stronger today, but the burn of the hot liquid paired with the frigid air outside is amazing. Life is good. I couldn't ask for anything more in this moment. I have the girl of my dreams. A baby on the way. A good group of friends that like to kick the shit out of each other. Though, sometimes I feel like I'm missing something or someone...but I can't quite figure out where the hole is coming from.

"How is the tea today, bear?" Iris asks while she rounds the corner.

"It's great, babe. A little stronger, but, as you know, I like a little bite." I pull her in by the waist and kiss her. "You're incredible, you know that?"

Her hands wrap around my neck, deepening the kiss, and I set the mug on the counter behind me so that I can give my girl all of my attention. My hands grab her ass and I pull her over the hardened line in my pants so she can feel exactly what she does to me.

A little flutter against my lower abdomen pulls my attention away, and I look down at Iris's rounded belly. "What was that?"

"Our girl is a fighter, just like her daddy. She's been kicking nonstop this morning."

I drop to my knees and rest my hands over Iris's belly, over our child. "Hello, little Em. This is your daddy. You are very loved. I hope you always know how special you are. How much light you have brought to my life."

A thump pushes against my hands and my eyes widen as I look up at Iris with a stupid grin on my face. I rise to my feet and kiss her with so much emotion I feel I could burst from it. "You incredible woman."

She giggles. "You're going to make me late!"

"Oh, we wouldn't want that, would we?" I grin.

"Rett! I'm serious! I'm learning how to flip babies today!" She swats me away.

I twirl her around like we're dancing, then tap her ass toward the door. "Alright, alright. My smart, beautiful, ambitious, wonderful babe, let's go flip some babies!"

She shakes her head, but I can tell by her smile she still finds me charming to some degree. I'm finally beginning to see a future.

Rik's fist collides with the underside of my jaw, and I fly back into the sand. Even without their godsgiven abilities, all four of them are crazy strong and good fighters. I never had my ass handed to me so many times in my life, even in the King's Army.

Leighra cheers while Dover yells at me to get up. I rise, cracking my neck to the side, and charge for Rik at full force. I catch him by the waist and bring him down to the sand pinned beneath me. It only lasts a second before he swoops his leg around my chest and thrusts me back so that he can get on top of me, pinning my right arm to the ground with the weight of his leg.

Damn, this dude is flexible.

The position has him off balance though, so I throw my weight into him and he rolls sideways. I come up behind him and get my legs around his waist. Before I can get him into an arm bar, his elbow collides with my nose and blood gushes out.

I smile at him, reveling in the feeling of blood running down my mouth and chin.

"Tap out!" Dover yells.

"Nah, man, you know Beast doesn't tap," Mase says with admiration in his voice.

"If you keep calling him endearing pet names, I'm going to think you like him," Leighra teases.

I'm distracted watching them when Rik comes out of fucking nowhere and slams his foot into my head, knocking me clear out of the circle.

I lost.

But damn, it was a good fight.

And I feel fully alive.

Everyone's burnt out. We're sitting around the ring on boulders drinking from a flask of whiskey when I notice the sun going down.

Shit. Iris is going to kill me.

"I gotta head home, guys. Iris is probably already there waiting."

Leighra rolls her eyes, and the guys share a look.

"What?" I ask.

"Man, that girl has you straight by the balls," Mase says when no one else speaks up.

"You're just a little different around her," Dover says.

"She's giving me everything," I say. "A family. A home. And, of course, I'm different around her! I can't go around calling her an asshole and punching her in the face like I do with you shitheads."

"It's not our business," Rik says. "If she makes you happy, fuck everyone else."

"Yeah, fuck everyone else. I'll see you guys tomorrow." I hand him the flask and nod to them. The crew murmurs their goodbyes, but I'm left with an uneasy feeling pinching the back of my neck.

The sound of dishes crashing into the sink and the smell of whatever Iris has been cooking greet me when I walk through the front door. I enter the kitchen and she doesn't even turn around to look at me. She continues to scrub a dish as if it has personally offended her and she's trying to smite it.

Oh, yeah, she's pissed.

"I waited for over an hour at the healing center. *Where were you?*" She grinds out.

I wrap my arms around her middle and lean my chin down to the crook of her neck. "Sorry, baby, I lost track of time. I was with the guys."

She turns to look at me, eyeing my battle wounds. Her nose scrunches with disgust. "I see that...and smell it. You guys were drinking?"

"A little," I admit.

She sighs and nods. "Go upstairs."

I pull back. "What about dinner?"

"I already finished eating. Now, go upstairs and wait for me. I won't ask again," she says, and I catch the flash in her eye. A look I know will end in a punishment, and gods, does it get me hard as fuck.

I race upstairs, pulling my clothes off as I go and get into our bed—waiting for her to give me whatever punishment I deserve. She doesn't keep me waiting long. My beautiful goddess has a mean look in her eye as she pulls a length of ribbon from behind her back. I realize quickly she's torn it off of my favorite apron that she wears.

"Stay still," she says as she binds my wrist with the fabric and then secures it to our bed frame.

"Yes ma'am," I say with a grin.

"Don't speak. I'm very angry with you. You have disappointed me...but I wonder if it's actually me who has disappointed you in a way? I thought I could be everything you needed... Maybe I was wrong?" She straddles me and pulls her clothes off.

"Fuck, babe," I say, appreciating her beauty.

"I said *don't speak*. I guess I'll just have to shut you up myself." *Oh gods yes, please do.*

Iris lowers herself onto my face and begins to ride it. I'm pretty sure my nose is broken because of the crippling pain each time she passes over it, but I don't give a damn. I open my mouth and fuck her with my tongue until she's dripping into my mouth. I really wish I had use of my hands right now so I could hold her in place and make sure not a drop gets wasted, but if I escape my binds, Iris won't be happy. What I want more than anything is Iris to be happy. I continue moving my mouth the way I know she likes until her movements become jerky with her release.

She falls over and grabs the bed frame to steady herself while panting. "You did good."

"Come on, babe, I might die if I can't touch you. Actually die." I plead with her, and she sits up straighter.

"Oh no, Rett, you will not be touching me tonight. It is your punishment." She smiles deviously, then slides back until I'm inside her.

"Shit." I groan, and my eyes roll back at the same time she begins to roll her hips.

Smack!

I pop my head up in alarm at the pain in my cheek, processing what just happened. "Did you hit me?"

"What? Don't you like it?" She slaps me again, harder this time.

And godsdamn it, I know how messed up this is, but I *do* like it. She picks up her pace.

"Iris, slow down, I'm going to come."

"Do it. Give yourself to me completely. I want *all* of you." She punctuates with another slap.

"Oh shit!" I can't hold back. I spill into her, and her breathing quickens just as I finish. She grinds until she finds her release, then folds on top of me before rolling over and cuddling against my chest.

"I can be everything you need," she says, as if she's trying to convince herself.

"I never doubted it for a second." I kiss her head. "Now untie me so I can hold you."

"No. I told you, you don't get to touch me tonight. It's your punishment."

TWENTY-NINE
TWISTED WORDS
Aislinn

My MOUTH IS COATED in ashes. Throat raw. Eyes crusted over. It takes too long for the panic to register. I quickly sit up, and my head betrays me for it. The room spins. I try to blink in my surroundings, and, through the foggy slit in my vision, I make out an unfamiliar bedroom. My fingers run along my wrists...no chains. None noticeable, at least. But when they slide over that cold place on my wrist where the shadow chain remains, his voice slithers through my mind.

"Do not fight them, pet. Play their game. I will have you home soon." The voice is calm, but the vibrations through each of my marks is anything but.

No, Erebus is not calm. Erebus is furious.

It is that thought that allows my own breath to steady, my heart to calm. I wipe the gunk from my eyes and figure out where I am. A window. There's a window concealed by silver drapes. I pull them away and curse. Oh, Erebus is more than furious.

I've been brought to Kaoket.

I must be somewhere in the middle of the palace because I have a perfect view of where the skeletal trees of the Imorti Woods melt into the lush gardens surrounding the Vivutus Forest. The strange sun resting where it always does in this part of the realm, exclusively on the side that bares life. But my attention stays on the skeletal trees and beyond to where I know the Shadows lay, however far away.

"You're awake." I do not have to turn to know who stands behind me. Agnar.

"You're observant."

"Are you angry, child?"

Am I angry? Maybe not so observant then.

"It's only... the last time I was taken by a god, it was more pleasant, sealed with a kiss and everything."

When I turn, I find Agnar's skin glowing and his face in a deep scowl. When he speaks again, his voice is hard. "Erebus took you, or you chose to come?"

You must want to come. That's what Erebus told me, multiple times on the island—I had to *want* it. I school my features into boredom as I've seen the god of trickery do many times. "I chose to come. *Taken* was a manner of speaking." I pause and with a vicious smile add, "As in, he took my mouth to pass through the portal." Agnar looks as though he may be sick. "Are you going to tell me what you want, or can I go home now?"

"This is your home, Forbis."

"I'm not Forbis. I am not your child, not in this life."

"Oh, but you are. You have the same energy. The same shadow. Surely, that's how Erebus found you—the shadows sing for him."

"I have no memory of you and do not take kindly to being kidnapped...Wait, if he couldn't take me against my will, how is it okay for you to do so?"

"I didn't, Haile sent someone to rescue you."

"I did not *want* to be rescued."

"He'd argue that you were not allowed freedom, that you had wanted to come here to connect with your past self."

Twisted. Haile had twisted my words in order to scheme. To what end? What do they get from this?

"Why am I here?"

"I want to help you remember...yourself. My children had told me of this day long ago. That it was vital when you returned and I be able to help guide you, teach you."

"Am I free to come and go as I will?" Agnar's silence is all the answer I need. "So I am a prisoner, then."

"I choose not to see it so. You're free to roam Kaoket, anywhere in Kaoket. Our lands are vast. You will not feel caged."

I snap. "How would you know what it is to be caged?"

A flurry of emotion passes over his features. "I'm going to give you some space. I'll send for you when it is time to eat."

He slams the door like a child throwing a tantrum. I do not need to try the handle to know that it is locked, but this strange room feels oddly familiar. The large four-post bed is covered in pillows—too many pillows. There's sturdy black furniture all engraved with detailed swirls and patterns. Everywhere I look—silver. It feels as though I've seen it before, in a dream.

He had no right. They had no right to bring me here. Not the way they did. It is true I wanted to explore Kaoket to see if it unlocked a vision. But the way they did. Taken in my sleep. It's violating in the deepest of ways.

I cannot conceal my yell of frustration as I kick the bed post nearest to me. My ears ring so loudly I fear they may bleed and I drop to my knees while covering them. It's there, right beneath the post I kicked, that I see it—the corner of a folded piece of parchment. The closer my fingers get to reaching it, the quieter the ringing becomes until all that is left is my wild heartbeat. But then my heart is stunned to silence when I read the name scrolled on top in beautiful calligraphy.

Aislinn Theadora Delphia.

Mine.

This letter is *mine*.

With trembling fingers, I unfold the paper. Miraculously, the parchment is still crisp as though it was just written yesterday.

FOR OUR PART, WE APOLOGIZE. FOR OUR SECRECY, WE APOLOGIZE. FOR WHAT IS TO COME, WE APOLOGIZE. YOU, AISLINN THEADORA DELPHIA, WILL PLAY A VITAL ROLE IN THE SHIFT IN REALMS, AN OCCURRENCE WE HAVE BEEN HURTLING TOWARD SINCE THE BEGINNING. SOON, EVERYTHING WILL CHANGE. WE, THE UTIKALO, HAVE BIDED ENOUGH TIME AS POSSIBLE. THERE ARE FORCES AT WORK, FORCES IN THE REALM OF GODS THAT WOULD ENSLAVE THE MORTALS.

TAKE BOTH REALMS.

THE TREATIES WERE OUR DOING. THE TRINITY WAR
AND THE GODS' WAR, ALSO PUT INTO MOTION BY US.
NECESSARY FOR YOU TO BE HERE TODAY. WE MADE IT AS
DIFFICULT AS WE COULD TO STOP THE TRAVEL BETWEEN
REALMS. THE GODS NEVER SHOULD HAVE MERGED THE
TWO. THE BARRIER WAS NOT US, BUT THE BARRIER MUST
STAY. THERE IS A PROPHECY, ONE WE DO NOT DARE TO
WRITE DOWN, THAT TELLS OF THE END TIMES AND THE
CHILDREN THAT INCITE IT. YOU ARE NOT THE UTIKALO.
YOU ARE NOT US. YOU ARE A FRACTION OF WHAT WE ONCE
WERE. WE MUST NEVER BE WHOLE. <u>NEVER</u>. DO NOT TRY
TO JOIN TOGETHER THE THREE STONES.

SOME THINGS ARE BEST LEFT AS THEY ARE.

WE HAVE LEFT AS MANY CLUES AS WE DARE RISK. IT IS NOT
MUCH, AND WE HAVE ERASED MANY MORE. BE WARNED,
AISLINN, DO NOT FIGHT FATE. EMBRACE IT, BECOME IT.
SEEK THE WEAVERS. ONLY WE CAN. ONLY SOMEONE WITH
THE SIGHT MAY SEE. THEY LIVE IN A FOLD OF THIS REALM,
THE ENTRANCE IS IN KAOKET, YET MOVES. DO NOT SEARCH
IT OUT. IT WILL FIND YOU.

TRUST NOTHING BUT BALANCE. TOGETHER, YOU WILL
BRING SALVATION, BUT IF YOU DEVIATE FROM YOUR
CHOSEN PATH, YOU WILL NOT BECOME THE SAVIORS BUT
INSTEAD THE DESTROYERS.

NEVER SAVED. BETRAYED TWICE. ONE MUST DIE TO SAVE
THE NIGHT. SMOTHER IT—DARK OVER LIGHT. HE'LL TAKE

MORE, BUT HE'S TAKEN TOO MUCH. WHAT IS BEAUTIFUL WILL BE DUST.

-V.O.F.

What the Haile?

What am I supposed to do with this nonsense? Go find the Weavers, but don't look for them? None of this makes sense. How long has this note with my name on it been here? How many hundreds of years before I was even born? No one should be able to see so far into the future, to know the fates of all, or to have such influence yet hold so many secrets.

I wish I did have my past life memories back. Not for the benefit of others, for *my* benefit. I'm tired of being helpless. Useless. Unworthy of the positions I've been given.

What I know is that my future includes him. I'm not going to sit on my ass and do nothing this time. I'll train my mind and body. Learn my power. Hone it. I will play my part. It is time that I accept my place, my role.

It's time to meet the Weavers.

THIRTY
GRIM TOPICS
DeLuca

SITTING HERE IN THESE mismatched chairs at this rickety old table while Lysette and Elinor catch up brings me back to the days at the manor. Where I was nothing more than a shadow on the walls. Observing, listening, back when my only goal was to obtain information. The Liberators should have recruited Elinor instead. She is much better at getting information. Just in the few hours we've been here, she has managed to coax the entire story from Lysette, even about Caeliss. Lysette didn't mention the location, not that Elinor asked. She mostly wanted news of Rett and Aislinn—and, of course, Orynn and Linnea—but Elinor saw the solemn look in Lysette's eye at the mention of her deceased siblings and understood well enough.

"I'm glad you are well." Elinor gently squeezes my arm after Lysette leaves to wash up. "I owe you a great deal, bringing me to this place."

"You owe me nothing. It was Aislinn who warned you."

"Yes, but it was you, DeLuca, who brought me to the wonderful place. Somewhere truly safe. A safe haven, like yours, but for us mere mortals."

"Caeliss is not mine, and the Underground is far better. Less rules...and I wouldn't be so sure there are just mortals dwelling here. Those of us with gods' blood are very good at masking who we are."

"And what does your *gods' blood* allow you to do? You told me of the Ursons—I feel like a fool for not noticing after all those years—but what about you?"

"Terrible things, Elinor, things too dangerous for the mortal realm."

"They can't be so terrible if they're a part of you. I know your heart, and your heart, DeLuca, is as good as they get." Her hands wrap around mine. I never had a grandmother...hardly had a mother...but if I had had either, I would have hoped for them to be like Elinor. Her very presence is comforting enough that I feel my shoulders relax for the first time in months.

She runs her thumb on along the side of my head. How can such a simple gesture bring so much comfort? "Relax, dear boy. Rest. I'll fix us something to eat. I only have one bed. You and Lysette could share it?"

I open my mouth to object, but Lysette beats me to it, rounding the corner in clean clothes and wet hair, most of the red now washed out, giving it a pink hue. "That won't be necessary. The floor will be fine with us, Elinor. Thank you for your hospitality."

"If you insist." Elinor shakes her head as she goes to the little kitchenette and starts clattering pots around.

The homes in the underground are all fairly small. Providing only what is necessary. Elinor's home is about half the size of the one we'd had in Caeliss. The metal door opens into a common area with only two wingback chairs—no sofa. To the right of that is the dining table we currently sit at. There's an archway leading to that small kitchenette as well as the single washroom and bedroom. Elinor has added her own touches. Even though she came without any belongings, she has done quite well to make it feel like a home.

"Still don't like surprises, or do I get a pass for this one?" I smirk at Lysette. She does her best to look like she's still pissed, but there's a flicker of light in her eye that wasn't there before.

"As long as you promise me you won't surprise me again, I suppose you can have a pass."

"I make no such promises." Her answering glare has me biting the inside of my cheek to keep from laughing. "I do, however, promise that whenever I surprise you, it will be a good surprise."

"I don't agree to that."

I shrug. "I wasn't asking you to."

Lysette shoves me. "How did you even find this place?"

There it is, the question I have been dreading since deciding the Underground would be the safest place.

"My brothers are here. The two oldest ones, Dunst and Kierne. They abandoned their duty station along the wall and followed some of the scavengers down the tunnels. They took one look and never went back. We thought they were dead for years."

I have to pause and swallow, breathing evenly to keep the emotional dam I've built over the years intact. "It was years until they found us and told us about this place. Two of my sisters, Briella and Isrie, went back with them. Val...she was already married and with child. Her husband's family was too large and relied on the help they got from Val. She wouldn't leave them, and I wouldn't leave her."

Lysette's features soften with understanding. "Are they still here? Your brothers and sisters?"

"Yes." The word burns my throat. "They're who I sought when I promised Aislinn to get Elinor to safety. They helped her get settled and then begged me to stay...I almost did. Almost. Even before I left, I often thought about asking Aislinn to come here with me. If I hadn't seen her kissing Rett that day, I probably would have."

"Wait. *When* did Rett and Ailie kiss?"

"Really? *That's* what you're concerned about?" My eyebrow raises.

"It just seems so—unnatural." Lysette's face turns sour.

"Well, thankfully, they seemed to think so too, but I didn't know that until it was too late."

"Well. I'm thankful for that too. If you had whisked her away before the attack, then you wouldn't have dragged me off Linnea's body. You wouldn't have saved me too."

"Haven't you two had enough with the grim topics?" Elinor huffs out while setting two bowls of stew in front of us. The steam hits my nose and my stomach gurgles in answer. We haven't eaten a hearty meal since leaving Caeliss. I think Lysette is just as starved because she immediately digs into her bowl, barely coming up for air between bites.

Elinor gave us her only pillows and insisted we take the warmest quilt from her bed before retiring for the night, leaving Lysette and me back to back on the carpet by the wingback chairs.

We're giving each other as much space as we possibly can while sharing a blanket. Despite being on the floor, I'm relaxed. Far more relaxed than I felt in the manor. These conditions, they feel like home. Remind me of a time when my family was together.

"What happened to the baby?" Lysette asks on a yawn.

"She died. She was born deformed. The deformities were fatal. The baby had an odd shaped head and got stuck in the birth canal. By the time they got her out, the damage was done. Val would never be able to have kids after that. Her husband died just months later, in the mines."

"No wonder she hated us," Lysette whispers.

"She wasn't always so cold." That familiar scratch catches in my throat—and with it, the burn behind my eyes. It's hard for me to think of before. When it was just Val and me. How she took care of me as a child, took on way more responsibility than any teenager should.

"DeLuca?"

"Yes?"

"I'm sorry."

"For what?"

"All of it. For what your family endured. For what you had to do. For what my family did."

I roll on my back and stare at the ceiling. "I used to blame you. All of you. The same way Val did."

"Used to? What changed?"

"I saw that you were not all the same. That some of you were capable of empathy and compassion. Some of you were good and uncorrupted and, given the chance, maybe would have been able to bring the change our nation so desperately needed."

"Aislinn was the best of us," Lysette agrees.

"You have a good heart too, you and Linnea...but yes, Aislinn *is* the best of all of us."

Lysette rolls on her back as well and pulls the quilt up to her chin. "We will get her back."

"We will."

"Will I meet your siblings?"

I blow out a breath. "You have to, they're how we're going to get to Rilyse."

"How do you mean?"

"We're going to ask my brothers for help."

"Will they? Help us, I mean?"

"I don't see why they wouldn't, as long as they get to stay in the safety of the Underground. As long as they don't have to get their hands dirty."

"What about your sisters?"

"I'm sure we will see them too."

"Despite how it happened, I am looking forward to meeting your family—see if the brooding is in your blood or from circumstance of upbringing," Lysette teases.

My chest aches as I try to form the words that make me feel like a coward. "Most likely both...Lys, I need to ask something of you."

"What is it?"

"I need you to not mention Val...or what happened to her."

"I would never. It's not my place."

My shoulders relax at the lack of judgment in her voice and I allow my eyes to close. "Thank you."

THIRTY-ONE
HOSTILITY
Aislinn

I'VE BEEN GIVEN A full day to *adjust* to my new lodgings. Mostly I've been confined to this room, with the exception of last night's awkwardly silent dinner with Agnar. I've used the time to practice my Opari gifts. It feels like an invasion of privacy each time I try to find DeLuca. It's like I'm spying on him, so I don't do it nearly as often as I'd like to, just enough to make sure he's okay. Sharing a blanket with Lysette on a floor I've never seen before probably means he's okay. I try not to dwell on the image, I really do have the worst timing.

Twisting the doorknob, I find it is still locked. I haven't taken to trashing the room...yet. I suppose I should be used to this treatment by now. Being taken in such a way, I can't refuse and then stuffed away until someone is ready to deal with me. At least the pattern is familiar. Soon, I'm sure Agnar will try to find common ground and tell me what he wants. Then, with time, I will be given more freedom.

And so the cycle continues.

My door flies open with a loud clang, causing me to nearly jump out of my skin.

"Master of the house requests your presence for dinner." Standing in the threshold is a small creature covered in black and white fur. His eyes are dark and sunken. Lips small and drawn in a tight line. With large pointed ears and claws on its tiny pink hands. He—at least I think it is a he—wears a white vest with a matching bowtie. He...it...is adorable.

"What are you?" I ask with a smile flirting its way to my lips despite my sour mood.

"Master of the house awaits." The small creature ignores my question and gestures for me to follow him. I admit my curiosity beats my stubborn nature, and I follow the strange thing, holding back a laugh as it waddles down the halls.

He leads me to a smaller dining room. Different from the formal one we sat in yesterday. It's almost cozy. Smaller than Lady Soleil's parlor but larger than the entire downstairs of my house in Caeliss. At the head of the rectangular table big enough for eight is where Agnar sits, sharpening a ornately carved throwing knife.

"That will be all, Chimmy." Agnar dismisses the creature without looking up from the opalescent blade. "It's good of you to join me again for dinner, Forbis. Are you ready to talk or will you again be glaring at me through the meal?"

"I am *not* Forbis, and I'm not sure I had another choice, did I?"

Agnar looks up and smiles, light reaching his eyes. "Not if you'd like to be fed. And you *are* Forbis, despite your lapse in memory."

I force a sweet smile. "Shall I call you *father* then?"

"If you wish it."

I have to hold my fists to keep from cringing.

The creature, Chimmy, and four others that look to be the same species waddle in carrying trays of food. They raise them over their heads and place the dishes in front of Agnar and me before scurrying off again.

"What are they?" I ask, watching the last one leave the room.

"Creatures that dwell in Kaoket. We call them by their names, though the one who fetched you is called Chimmy. His family has worked in our house for over a thousand years. Not everyone has *shadows* to do all their bidding."

"But what are they? What kind of creature?"

"We aren't as obsessed with naming each species we come across in our realm. The creatures tell us their names. What if I decided to call you an ostrich because I didn't know your species? You probably wouldn't be too fond of that."

"I suppose not. Though, it seems odd to have entire groups of species without a name."

"Like I said, they have names, the names they wish to be called. Mortals like to be in control of everything. They play at being gods when they don't even know what it is to be one."

"I've never thought of it like that." I look down at my food. It appears to be glowing. "Is this safe for mortals?" I'm a little skeptical after my experience with their wine.

"You're not mortal. But yes, it is safe. It glows because of the enchantment on the gardens. Keeps everything growing as it should."

"I *am* mortal." I take a tentative bite and involuntarily moan as the flavors burst on my tongue.

"I had them whip up your favorites."

"I don't even know what this is, but it is the best thing I have ever eaten."

"See, I know you, Forbis. I hope your hostility toward me will come to an end."

"You think you can win my trust by feeding me?"

"Is it working?"

"It's not *not* working." I take another bite. Agnar seems perfectly content to watch me stuff my face. "It's not poisoned, right?"

"No...no...I only... It has been a long time since I have shared a meal with anyone in this room. The Utikalo, my children, left hundreds of years ago." He fidgets with his knife once again with sadness in his eyes, just before stabbing it into the large portion of meat in front of him. "Their mother, my beautiful and fair Millena, was killed prior. I hadn't realized how much I had longed for another to sit at this table. I've been patiently waiting for you. Just as Viitor had foretold."

This isn't getting weird at all. I try to remain impassive and polite. If I have learned anything from the life I was thrown to, it's that the more amicable you are, the further you will go. Just because I seem docile doesn't mean I won't squeeze every bit of information that I can from Agnar.

"Viitor saw the future, right?" I ask.

"Yes." He maims his meat. "I always chuckled at the depictions of my children in your mortal texts. A three-headed creature. How absurd for a god to be born with three heads!" Agnar lets out a laugh that shakes the walls and I have to place my hand on my cup to keep it from spilling. "Forbis, Opari, and Viitor were not some three-headed beast! They were triplets. Though, their abilities worked best when they were joined together. Perhaps that is where the silly notion comes from."

"They were triplets? Why hasn't anyone thought to tell me that if I'm supposed to be a reincarnation of them?"

"You bear the shadow of my Forbis. Somewhere in your realm, other's bear the shadows of Opari and Viitor. If you were to join, you would be Utikalo once more. *God* once more."

Something the original Utikalo did not want happening.

"Is that what you want? What Haile wants?"

"Haile wants to break down the barrier between realms. He believes you are able to do so with your ability to create portals."

My brows furrow. "Did he ever want to restore Astoria's mind, or was it all a ploy for me to open a portal?"

"Perhaps a bit of both. Haile truly cares for his daughter, favors her over all his sons. Perhaps largely due to the prophecy."

"Which prophecy?"

"The one stating the birth of Haile's daughter will signal the greatest reign since the beginning of time. Greater than Kato's."

"And he believes that daughter to be Astoria?"

"She is his only daughter in a sea of hundreds of sons."

"Who comes up with all these prophecies?"

Agnar looks completely amused and props a fist under his chin. "You do, my dear."

My cheeks flare with the heat of embarrassment. "Seems the past version of myself may have given Ravetta quite the challenge as a chaos creator."

Another deep bellied laugh from Agnar that has me holding my cup to the table. "Indeed. My children were quite troublesome!"

Despite my best attempt to remain cold and impassive, I crack a small smile. "I'd love to hear more about them."

"I hope by bringing you here that you will regain your memories."

"Speaking of memories, do you know where I can find the Weavers?"

"The Weavers—nasty things. They're always moving their portal. Opari was able to find them. No one else has had such luck. You're welcome to try, but I warn you, the Weavers are temperamental and vicious. Fate is a game to them. You know Ravetta is one of theirs? They created her to enact their chaos on the realms when the gods started fighting against their weavings. Kato punished them for it by banishing them to their own little pocket of time. You will be able to get in and out, but they are stuck for eternity."

"They can create gods?"

"They can create anything. They thrive in discord and tangled threads."

Interesting. "Am I confined to the palace, or may I explore the grounds after we eat?"

"I've already told you, you are free to roam Kaoket as you will."

"Yes, you said, and then proceeded to lock me in my room."

Agnar's sheepish expression is completely at odds with his hard presence. "I had to be certain you didn't call upon Erebus, or that he didn't try anything."

"Do you think a locked door would stop him?" I quirk a brow in amusement.

"It would have bought me time, perhaps."

"For what?"

"For Haile to get here and blast that piece of shit back to the Shadows where he belongs."

"Did you really hunt down all his children in the mortal realm?"

"Yes."

"Then it seems to me, *Father,* that *you* are the piece of shit."

THIRTY-TWO

PURE

Aislinn

KAOKET IS CONFUSING AND ever changing. Even the ground seems to shift beneath my feet as if it can't decide which form it wants to take. Oddly enough, the side of the Vivatus is more uncomfortable than the Imorti. Flowers bloom constantly and the strange glow combined with the constant ringing in my ears thumps in tune with the dull throb in my head. I wish I had the Child Blade strapped around my thigh, though I suspect I may be protected by three of the most powerful gods in the realm...until they get what they want from me, that is.

There are many strange creatures that roam this land. They mostly keep to themselves, but as I sit here on a crumbling vine-covered bench near the edge of the Imorti Woods, I hear an unsettled rustling through the skeletal branches. Something large is storming the grounds, and it's enough to make me find a new location to spend my afternoon.

In the three days I've been bound to Kaoket, I haven't found the Weavers or even a trace of them. I avoid Agnar as much as possible. Which isn't all that hard, considering he spends most of the days with Haile in the Auric Mountains with the rest of Haile's soldiers.

Why? I have no idea, nor do I care to ask. I'll leave the gods' politics to them. I have too much on my plate as it is. Chimmy and the creatures like Chimmy check in on me every so often, likely to inform the war god of my movements.

I'm not sure I will ever get used to how strange this realm is. The lake that sits between the Olvi and the Shadows is a shade of purple, and even though the air around me is still, the water ripples as if it were breathing. It's peaceful here in the inbetween.

Leaning back on the brightly colored pebbles with my eyes closed, I let the tranquility and quiet wash over me. Inhaling the salty—*What the Haile was that?*

A child's laughter disrupts my little moment I carved for myself. I sit up and look around frantically.

What's wrong? Erebus says down the line of shadows connecting us. With his words comes the whisper of ice that causes my shoulders to shiver.

Are there children here? I ask down the same line, hoping he can hear me.

There have not been children in our realm for hundreds of years. That makes the hairs on my neck stand.

I heard a child's laughter.

A child's laughter? Are you near the lake?

Yes.

Erebus chuckles down the line. *It is likely Fabron. He stays near the cave opening on the border of the Imorti.*

Why?

Because that is the home of the innocents. The shadows lost too soon.
Fabron is the god of youth, but he is also the guardian of the pure.

The pure...you mean...

Children who died before their time.

Oh gods.

Indeed.

"Hello," a small voice says, causing me to jump back into the rocks.

My hand flies to my chest as I stare at...Orynn. My breath comes out ragged, and my entire body begins to quake.

"Orynn?" There's a raw edge in my throat and tears burning my eyes. "Oh Gods, Orynn! How are you...here?"

Whatever you think it is that you see is a lie. Fabron appears as a familiar to keep from frightening the young ones whilst gathering them.

Even with Erebus's words, I can't shake the shock while staring into the face of the nine-year-old boy I used to spend the afternoons playing chess with. The same boy I knew as an infant. The one lost much too soon.

"Fabron?" I ask.

Orynn—I mean Fabron—smiles. "Hello, Forbis." Even his voice sounds like Orynn's.

"I'm not—"

"Yes, I know, dark one."

I nod. "Uhm. Dark one?"

Fabron tilts his head and his likeness to Orynn sends a painful jab into my chest. "You cannot see your fate?"

"No, I can't see what is to come."

"That is not what I asked."

Thoughts scramble with the feeling that I am forgetting something important, yet not having the faintest clue as to what it could be. "Oh."

"May I hold your hand, dark one?"

I swallow and nod, offering my hand out to the child-god who looks like Orynn.

"I'm going to show you something. Something that must remain a secret."

"Why show me? You don't even know me."

"I knew you before, and what I'm going to show you only exists because of that version." Fabron leads me around the lake and to a cave that is snuggled into the mountains lining the northern edge of the Shadows.

The cave has a bounty of clear crystals protruding from it like jagged teeth and there's a strange yanking feeling from beneath my skin as we pass them, like something is trying to escape from my body. The air vibrates in front of us. It's like a standing body of water, and it feels as if it's calling out to me.

"What is that?" I ask him. We stop in front of the invisible waves that act as a wall—keeping us from going any farther.

Fabron rubs his hand along cave wall. "The portal you made me." He stares at me then scrunches his nose. "The *other* you."

It tickles my skin as I push a hand through and pull it back again. "Does this go to the mortal realm?" I ask with hope.

He sighs. "No, Aislinn. This portal is something different. Something special created for just us and the Pure Ones. We wanted to protect them from the fate of the other Shadows that pass through, so we created a paradise for them."

Something...good. Finally, something good my past life was responsible for. I hadn't known I needed to hear this. With every scheme uncovered and each god I meet, I was beginning to wonder if there was a monster in me too.

My heart cracks and a lone tear falls down my cheek. "*We* created this?"

"We did." He nods. "I have been the only one granted access since you left. No one else knows how, and even if they did, they cannot breach your portal without one of us. This was the greatest deed you have ever done for the realm."

"And you've looked after them all on your own?" I ask the small boy in front of me. I know he's a god, millions of years old, but he looks so young while wearing Orynn's face.

"I have. But now, you're back, and I need your help...well, I *need* your oath."

"What can I possibly offer you?"

"I want you to protect them at all cost. No matter what allies you must betray or what else may be at risk. We protect their right to live in their eternal peace."

"Of course."

Fabron smiles. His face is youthful, but there's a knowing glint in his eyes that is so much older. He clasps his forearm around mine. "Swear it to me, dark one."

"I swear I will always protect the Pure Ones and their eternal resting place." A swirl of silver and white light dances up our arms and binds them together momentarily before winking out of existence.

He looks up at me, placing his small hands on my arm where the light had been. "You will be excruciatingly shredded apart if you break your oath to me."

Maybe I should feel tricked, but this is one of the few times I don't mind. I will happily protect the innocents. "I won't break it."

"Good, because they're in danger, and I fear I won't be enough to save them."

THIRTY-THREE
TALOG DAO
Erebus

WE'RE ONLY ON THE fourth night of Aislinn being gone and I don't know if the shadows will make it much longer. They're literally crawling out of my skin, hissing at me nonstop. It has me so on edge that I haven't been able to leave my palace since my visit to see Haile. I haven't even dared visit Astoria in fear of disrupting her peace. Tonight, that changes. I crave the other half of my heart like I crave a life source.

"Hello, starlight." My voice is a whisper of breath as I sit beside Astoria while she sleeps. I hate to admit it, but its easier like this. Easier not to have to look into her eyes and see a hollow shell of what she once was. I did this. Ruined the only person who ever saw me as more. I stole her light and, eventually, her mind. Her moon white hair is draped across her face, and I take great care to be gentle as I push it behind her ear. She doesn't so much as stir.

"I miss you. I miss the *real* you every day. I hate myself for what has happened to you. I should have known, should have known better than to try to keep you. I should have known better than to think I could have anything good and bright...something so alive." I have to swallow. My throat burns, and the Shadows are at an unease which tears at my insides.

"They took her. Your father and Agnar schemed behind my back, and they took my only hope of making it right. I've lost and I'm failing you."

The skin on her temple is ice cold beneath my lips. When I break the kiss and make to move away, a midnight hand wraps around my wrist. My shadows skitter, ready to defend if I call upon them, but after a heartbeat, I realize it's just Astoria. Likely, no more than a reflex. I slowly pry her fingers from around my wrist. Her grasp is surprisingly firm, but I am able to remove it easily. As I go to place her hand beside by her side, I notice the movement. Her pointer finger is tracing something. Her eyes are still shut, but her lips are moving, and I lean down to listen. There's noise coming from her throat, so soft that I wouldn't be able to hear it if I didn't have my ear to her lips.

"Is-isolvie... isolvie."

"Split?" I ask. She taps my palm once with her finger.

"Peit—"

"Ban?" She taps twice and tries again.

"Peittviot."

I lose a breath. "Barrier... the barrier?" One tap.

One tap, yes. Two taps, no. I lift my head to check her eyes. She's still asleep.

"Split and barrier? What are you trying to tell me, darling?"

"Y'taluolo kue."

"Not whole, the barrier's not whole?" two taps—no. No, it's not whole? Or no, that's not what she means?

"Is—" She starts and gasps. Her soft voice becomes frantic. "Dao! Talog dao! Talog dao! Talog dao!" She repeats the same two words over and over again.

I can't stop the break in my voice. "I'm trying. Starlight, I'm trying."

She goes still. Her fingers stop tapping. There is no longer a faint murmur under her steady breathing. She is yet again in a deep and peaceful slumber. What remains of my withered heart shatters, and my urgency has increased tenfold. Astoria needs me.

I'll never get it out of my head.

"Talog dao"...*help me.*"

THIRTY-FOUR
CIVILIZED
DeLuca

MY NERVES ARE GETTING the best of me. Little flames lick the back of my neck. I shouldn't be nervous. This is my family. I may have had some choice words when they first came back to Ashe, but we have made our peace about it. They will be glad to see me, and I them, but I know. I know they will ask me about Val. I will have to lie. How can I tell them I'm responsible for the death of our sister? How can I admit I chose a highborn daughter of Stellera over *our* sister? I can't. I will go to my grave with this secret...if I ever go to my grave. Another thing I don't know how to tell them, my blood. My parents.

"You're overthinking it." Lysette nudges me with her elbow.

"I can't help it."

"Do you think they will like me?"

"No." Lysette stops in place and stares at me, so I sigh and elaborate. "My family has no love for highborns."

"Oh."

"Keep your eyepatch on. It will earn sympathy from Isrie at least."

"I'm not sure I want nor deserve their sympathy." She tucks her now strawberry blonde hair behind the ear near her eyepatch. "My family has caused a lot of harm, and your family has suffered greatly for it."

"None of it was your doing."

"I still feel responsible." If this conversation was happening months ago, I would have agreed with her, but now that I know Lysette, I know she shouldn't shoulder the blame for her parent's mistakes. In fact, I fully believe that, given the chance, she would have righted a lot of the wrongs and made Ashe—and all other towns under the Obsidian province—better.

"You shouldn't," I say, gently squeezing her arm.

She gives me a sad smile. "I can't help it."

We walk the rest of the way in silence, though the Underground is anything but quiet. It is midmorning and all the vendors have set up for the day. The inhabitants of the Underground are going around trading goods while children play. There's music at every turn, a different street performer in each section. I think the thing that impresses me most of all is the expressions of each of the Underground people. Utter happiness. They speak to each other with smiles—real ones, not the forced sharp grins I've seen used by all the highborns. Each person has a lightness to them—freedom. This is what free people look like.

"Ready?" I ask Lysette. We get to the familiar door with painted yellow flowers running along the side—Isrie's doing, of course. She's always been artistic. She used coal from the mines to draw the most amazing sketches. If she had been born in the Capital or anywhere in Dailotta, I'm sure she could have made a living off her art. Isrie is the closest in age to me, two years older, but I have felt a need to protect her more than the others. She's always been good, kind. Her spirit is unaffected by the hardship of life.

"I'm ready," Lysette answers with a tight smile.

"Here we go." I rap my knuckles a few times on the door before we hear a baby crying. The flames prickling my neck extinguish. A woman with long red hair and soft brown eyes holding a tightly swaddled infant answers the door.

"May I help you?" Her accent isn't from here...but I can't quite place it.

"Oh, apologies. My family used to live here. They must have moved," I say, ready to turn around and head back to Elinor's to revise our plan. It wouldn't be the first time my family packed up and left without a trace.

"Are you Rainier?" She smiles, beaming...practically glowing.

I hesitate. "I am."

"Well, it's about damn time!" She pulls me into a hug, completely taking me off guard, and I look at Lysette, who shares the same "*what the fuck*" expression.

"Who is it, Kira?" I hear my brother's voice from somewhere in the back of their house.

"Come on and see for yourself yuh lazy-bones!" the redheaded woman yells back.

She opens the door a bit wider, and Dunst comes from behind her. His dark eyes widen when he sees me, and he practically runs the rest of the way. It isn't until he swoops me into a tight hug that

I notice the wooden brace circling his thigh and calf with a long rod attaching the two pieces.

"What happened to you?" I grunt out as he continues to squeeze me so tight that he may actually be attempting to break some ribs.

"They sent those fucking hounds on us the last time we did a supply run. Tried to take a piece of me with 'em, but they didn't realize how stubborn I am—knocked that creature of the Shadows tumbling off the border wall!"

"Yeah, and he went tumbling with him!" the redhead adds.

I can't help but smile. Dunst has always been a brute and clearly has not changed his ways. Lysette clears her throat, drawing my attention. "Oh, right, Dunst, this is Lysette. Lysette, my eldest brother, Dunst."

"It's very nice to meet you." Lysette smiles warmly, and I cringe at the formality in her voice. Knowing it's a dead giveaway.

Dunst eyes squint with suspicion. "Highborn?"

Lysette doesn't miss a beat and offers a tight smile. "Not anymore."

The redhead knocks the back of Dunst's head with her free hand. "I'm Kira. Intended wife to this knucklehead, also, mother to your nephew, Cohl." She holds the tiny bundled babe out so I can have a better look. Red hair, but Dunst's dark eyes.

"My nephew?" I repeat and blink between the two of them.

"Seems we all have some catching up to do. Why don't you both come inside for tea?" Kira gestures for us to come inside.

"Tea? Going civilized, are we? Let's break out the good stuff. I have a feeling we're going to need it." Dunst laughs, clapping me on the back as I walk in. Kira outstretches her arm to Lysette who takes it graciously and follows behind us.

⟩

"So let me get this straight." Dunst folds his hands below his chin and his eyes are narrowed. "You grow plants, and you make fire?" he asks after we give him a rundown of the last few months.

"If that's what you choose to take away from all that, then sure, yeah." His oversimplification has me shaking my head.

"Hmm," he murmurs. "Go ahead and show them, honey." Dunst nods to Kira who hands the baby to my brother and begins shrugging off her long sweeping robe. I avert my gaze instantly to a spot on the wall in the other direction.

"You're going to want to watch this, Raini," Dunst says with a knowing grin.

Kira stands before us in her undershorts and shirt. She holds her arms out as if she is a bird about to take flight and begins to glow. Not figuratively. She doesn't have a glow about her, she is actually fucking glowing. Her skin burns as bright as a small sun. It is almost painful to look at.

"I think it is now your turn, brother, to fill us in on what's been going on in your life." I'm still staring while Kira shrugs back on her robe and dims back to a subtle, hardly there, glow.

"Well, I heard the girls tried when you stopped in a few months ago, but you were in too much of a hurry to listen to 'em!" Dunst says.

"Your brother saved my life about a year ago." Kira beams at him.

"Ah, she's just saying that. Kira can take care of herself. You should see her fight. I've never seen anyone move like she can. I just helped her get out of a bad situation in the palace."

"What kind of bad situation?" Lysette asks.

"The kind where she was held in the dungeons for stealing," Dunst says while looking down at Cohl and using a baby voice. "On a supply run, we were using the tunnels below the palace, and I saw this glow. My gut told me to follow it, though Kierne called me an idiot, as well as a few other choice words. Found this beautiful woman, beaten and in rags, and the rest is history."

"Sounds like a fairytale." Lysette half smiles.

Kira forces a smile that doesn't fit quite right. "Just like one, especially the part where my people were starving while the king was throwing away enough food to feed the entire Capital daily."

Lysette swallows and sinks back into her chair.

"Anyway. I tried to help Kira get back to her people in the mountain range that lies between Azelean and Baymob. The Lightbringers, that's what they call their clan. Mountain folk. Always moving. We couldn't find any sign of them, and one thing led to another. Soon enough, Kira's belly was swollen with my child, and here she is, about to become my wife."

"I thought the Mountain Folk were a myth," Lysette says quietly.

"And I thought gods were a myth. Looks like we're all learning something today," Dunst replies with a cocky smile.

The door slams open against the inner wall and the clattering of boots fills the hall.

"We're back!" Briella shouts in her usual sing-song voice.

"Get in here. We have company!" Dunst shouts, causing baby Cohl to stir and make a rather upset face.

"Raini rainstorm? What in the Haile are you doing here?" Kierne shouts and tackles me to the ground. He puts me in a headlock and I let him think he's winning. Once he lets out a victorious laugh, I maneuver my body out from under his. In a split second, I have him pinned to the ground with my knee in his back and his arms pinned together.

"Stop it, you two. This sitting room is not large enough for all that! You're going to break something!" Briella shrieks.

"You've been practicing, Raini," Kierne says with pride.

"I'm sure it's a requirement of becoming a spy." Dunst pulls out a large bottle of whiskey and gestures for Kierne to sit down. "Here, you're going to need this, Kierne." Briella sits beside Kira, and Isrie comes and gives me a tight hug before joining them. Briella glares at her, then me, then notices Lysette for the first time. Kierne follows her gaze and he rubs his jaw.

"Gods, is she pregnant?" he asks.

The desire to punch my brother has never been stronger than it is at this moment. Especially with the way Lysette's visible eye widens in horror.

"Be nice." Isrie swats him. Her nail beds are caked in paint which makes me smile.

"You're gonna want to drink that now." Dunst points to the whiskey he had handed Kierne. "Go ahead, Raini, tell him what you told me."

I tell them all about my time with the Liberators, Obsidian Manor, Aislinn, the Safe Haven, Sutton, and the refugees. I tell them about gods and the Children. I tell them as much as I can. Only leaving out our part in the assassination of Pierce and, by default, Val.

"A fucking god? How the fuck did we live with an actual fucking god and not know?" Kierne takes a large gulp from his whiskey.

"And how did you have abilities without us knowing?" Briella asks.

"You guys had your own stuff going on...until you left. But honestly, I thought it was a mutation from the blast. I was afraid to tell anyone. I didn't want word getting back to—" I pause and look at Lysette, feeling guilty for my next words—"the Ursons."

Isrie nods. "None of us were the same after the blast...I'm sorry you didn't feel like you could tell us."

Everyone is quiet, somber. The pain of losing our brothers like a wound reopened.

"So what do you need from us?" Kierne asks. His face is straightened, without a hint of the menace I know him to be.

"We need to get to Rilyse as quickly as possible. I know you have ways around Stellera—you have to in order to have accomplished all of this."

My siblings share a knowing smile. "The Underground may or may not have a transport you can borrow."

"Well, which is it? May or may not?"

"Let's go for a walk." Kierne smiles.

We leave Dunst, Kira, Cohl, and my sisters at the house to make dinner. Kierne takes Lysette and me down a series of narrow alleyways and hidden stairwells. In the faint light given off by the orbs floating throughout the Underground, I notice Lysette's coloring is off. She is sluggish and dragging.

"Are you okay?" I ask her quietly so that Kierne doesn't overhear.

She breathes out a little too hard. "I'm fine...I'm just feeling a little claustrophobic."

"Claustrophobic? But it's only wide open. Do you feel sick?"

"Just a little." She tries and fails to give me an assuring smile.

I stop and give her my full attention. "Can you make it another night?"

"I'll be fine. Don't worry so much, *Raini*." She knows exactly how much the name annoys me. I can tell by her smile.

"No, never. Never that. Anything but Raini," I say, eyeing her.

"I quite like *Lucy Rain*."

"Lysette if you—"

"We're here!" Kierne says excitedly a few feet ahead of us. "Welcome to the Underground Depot."

"Holy gods!" Lysette exclaims with her visible eye-widening.

"Fucking Haile!" I say, running a hand through my hair. Hundreds of transports. They have *hundreds*. And crates of gods know what. Weapons. A surplus of grains. A stockpile that would make an entire nation envious.

"What is all of this?" I ask.

Kierne shrugs. "The Depot."

"But why so much?" Lysette asks.

"For the Underground army."

THIRTY-FIVE
IMPOSTER
Aislinn

SEEING THE PORTAL TO the Pure Ones yesterday has made me realize I may have a greater purpose in being here in the gods' realm than I had previously allowed myself to believe. It has become clear as of late that my being here has been no chance of fate, but rather a carefully woven path...and *that's* why I haven't felt the need to resist as I should.

Fabron's words about protecting the innocent shadows has stuck to my mind like sap on a tree, but if a god isn't enough to protect them, what good will I be? I still can't control my visions. Though, I will admit, it is easier to pull visions of the past and searching the present isn't as strenuous as it was when Erebus first impaled my arm with the Opari Stone. Anything to do with the future is still murky—the same muddled visions I've always gotten.

Chimmy is escorting me to the gardens. Apparently, there is a place where the Utikalo spent the majority of their time and may point to where to find the Weavers. He waddles in front of me, only coming to my knees. He seems to take his job very seriously and hardly speaks to me at all, not for my lack of trying.

"So, Chimmy, Agnar says your whole family serves in Kaoket. How do you like it?"

"We are very pleased to serve Kaoket. Balance is important to every realm. Balance is the *most* important."

"Even more important than the king?"

"You say it, not Chimmy." He continues waddling, saying a little more quietly, "Be careful whom you speak of and how you speak of them. Spies everywhere. Even the trees speak."

A chill runs along my spine. The warning is eerily similar to the one DeLuca had given me in Obsidian. "Yes, I've had a run-in with the king's spymaster already and would prefer not to repeat the experience."

"Nasty, nasty goddess she is."

"I've noticed."

Chimmy leads me to the divide between lively colorful blooming plants of the Vivatus and the skeletal Imorti on the other side. When we were here before, I hadn't noticed that the plants had a faint glow to them, similar to the food we'd had at dinner. I pluck a leaf from a branch to examine it more closely.

"What enchants them? And why? If they're on the side of life, shouldn't they just grow?" I ask, rolling a shimmering gold leaf between my fingers.

"The side of life is fading. Has been for some time. The realm has been fighting to restore balance ever since."

Balance. It always seems to come back to balance. Without Millena's influence, each sector of the realm has been hindered in some way or another. "Why not just appoint a new god to bring balance?"

Chimmy laughs. The sound is similar to the honking of a goose, and I have to bite my lip to keep from joining in. "We do not *appoint* gods—they are *made*."

"Okayyyy," I drawl. "Then why not *make* a new god of balance?"

Chimmy honks again as if this is the most hilarious conversation he's had in his entire life. His little ears twitching with his mirth. "We do not choose what they come out as! They simply *are*."

"So Agnar was just born with weapons in hand?"

Apparently, Chimmy no longer finds me amusing as his face instantly puckers and his eyes dull. "Master Agnar was born with the temperament of a warrior and the skill to push his emotion onto others. He takes orders and fights well." He motions for me to come closer, and when I do, he whispers, "If it were up to Chimmy, someone a bit more *balanced* would rule *balance,* but it is not up to Chimmy. So, we have Master Agnar."

I straighten and contemplate his words. I believe I just may have found a real ally in this realm. "Mmm. I see."

Chimmy pauses, his pointed ear twitching again. "This is where Chimmy leave you. Good luck finding *Fate*, Master Mortal," he says before waddling back to the palace behind us.

Silly little creature.

Okay, Weavers. Weavers. Weavers. If I were a secret portal prison, where would I be?

"You're not looking in the right place." I whirl around to find Helena leaning against a tree.

"Can you be here?" I ask, remembering Erebus's words about gods and their territories.

She places a hand to her chest and pretends to be offended. "I'm a messenger god. *I* can go wherever I wish."

I can't hide my smirk. "Well thank Kato for that."

"I'm here on business, but I had planned on dropping in anyway to see if you wanted me to break you out."

"A tempting offer, one in which I will have to decline." Despite the crude way I was brought to Kaoket, I do need to be here. I feel it, the calling in my blood. "What's the business?"

"Lord grumpy darkness wished for me to check on you." She shrugs a shoulder. "He's pissed. I think he may have opened another wormhole. He hasn't done that in ages. I knew it had to be bad before I even reached him." She tries to keep her tone even, but I detect a slight change in octave.

"I'm fine, annoyed, but fine. Tell him I'm going to get answers and then I will come home."

Helena's eyebrow raises until it's hidden beneath her straight black bangs. "Home?"

My cheeks heat. "The Shadows. You know what I mean."

She narrows her eyes. "Indeed."

"What do you mean, I'm looking in the wrong place?"

"The Weavers portal. They prefer the Imorti. *My* domain." She flashes a sharp smile.

"I thought they were always moving."

"They are, but no one likes this fake bullshit." Helena gestures to the enchanted garden. "The constant use of magic has an annoying buzzing sound that drives most of us to the point of insanity."

I can't help but let out a half laugh. "I thought I was the only one who had a ringing in my ears all the time."

"Oh no, we all hear it. If you listen closely, and if you're skilled enough, you can even hear a different ring for each god's magic."

"Huh, how interesting. It all sounds the same to me like a far-off bell being rung over and over." I try for a second to focus on the ringing, going as far as bending down to feel the brush of the leaves on my ear, but it makes me dizzy, and I decide that particular skill may not be worth pursuing. "How long would it take me to comb through until the edge of Kaoket?"

"Days. But you shouldn't need that long. You have a map."

"A map?"

Helena doesn't answer, just stares at my forearm where the Opari Stone is implanted with raised brows.

Of course, only Opari could find it.

"Well, I must be off to deliver the words of the day. Call me if you need me dah-ling," Helena says with a fake accent. "I'll be sure to give his royal gloominess your best."

Before I can even say goodbye, she takes off, her massive wings blowing a wind large enough to nearly topple me over.

She's an odd one too. This whole place is odd.

My fingers brush over the bump in my forearm.

Okay, think. Weavers. Calm breath. Just picture them. Well, that would be easier if I knew what I was picturing...five creatures, let's say spinsters. I picture them as five ladies with soft-sagging skin sitting in a knitting circle.

Nothing.

Okay.

Weavers.

Where are you?

I start walking deeper into the skeletal forest. Cursing and muttering under my breath with each step.

"Aislinn."

The hairs on the back of my neck rise. My name is nothing more than a whisper on the wind. I could be imagining it, but I stop and strain my ears to listen for it again.

"Aislinn."

I shiver. Undeniable. It is my name. Someone—*something* is calling me.

Well, shit.

I suppose following an eerie voice into a dark forest is as good a plan as any.

"That's it. Come to us, Aislinn."

"Hurry."

"Hurry."

"Hurry."

"Hurry."

"Hurry."

"That's not at all terrifying," I say to the echoing voice that is neither male nor female yet both at the same time.

Maybe I should ask Erebus to...no, I can do this on my own. The Weavers have been assisting the Utikalo since, what, the beginning of time? It will be fine.

A burning sensation starts from the stone beneath my skin and begins pulling me to the left. It's more like being yanked than pulled. Its urgency has my full attention.

"The creature of the Imorti is stalking you," the eerie voice says.

There's a rustling somewhere behind me that sets a fire beneath my feet. I'm running. Following that invisible pull and trusting my gut to take me to where I need to go. It isn't until I have already been running for a few minutes and my chest burns that I hear the thundering stomp of large feet behind me. I'm not sure what it is, but it sounds like something I don't want to ever come into contact with. The rustling grows nearer. My heart is thundering in my chest. Just as I feel the ice coat around my wrist, a sign Erebus is reaching down the shadow chain, I trip.

I'm falling with my eyes closed. It isn't until I realize I haven't hit the ground that I peep an eye open and start flailing violently. I'm suspended in midair but all around me is black. An empty void. There's no sign of life, no sign of anything.

"Hello, old friend," a voice says from all around me.

"Uhm. Hello?"

"We've been waiting for you—you're late."

Unease coils and tightens around my belly. "Who are you?"

For a disorienting second, the space around me shifts until I am sitting in a dark meadow of sorts, surrounded by trees dripping in a stringy substance glowing of all colors. There is a large murky pond beside me and five hooded figures gliding my way.

"Had you not been seeking us, imposter?"

"The Weavers," I say under my breath.

The one who spoke lifts her head and flashes her razor-sharp teeth into a smile. "Yes." She hisses. Her hood falls, revealing a circular tattoo on her forehead. It looks like some of the symbols I have seen on ruins in Stellera.

"It is not right," a male beside her says.

"Yes. Not whole," another male says

"Wrong." A female sniffs in distaste.

"Where is Viitor?" the last female says.

"You called me here. I'm only looking for answers." I put my hands up defensively.

"We can not reveal what is to come without Viitor." One of the females crosses her arms.

"I'm looking for information about the original Utikalo and opening portals. Why did they leave? Why don't they want to be joined together again?"

The one in the middle with the tattooed forehead smirks, "Because, imposter, they tried to beat us. Tried to outwit us. Outrun Fate."

"Do you know what you are?" asks another of the females, one with three dots on her forehead.

This feels like a trick question, but I answer anyway. "Aislinn Delphia...the Utikalo...Forbis? Any of those?"

"Yes...and no...dark one... *harbinger...so much more wasted in this mortal form*," she says with a vicious smile.

"Oh right. Harbinger of death." I roll my eyes, forgetting the newest title bestowed on me by Erebus.

"And destruction." A light shimmers in one of the males' eyes. His tattoo is a series of swirls that takes up the majority of his forehead.

"Child of light and dark. Of moon and shadow. Child of balance," the third female with a straight band tattooed around her forehead says.

"You will free us," the last male with five lines tattooed down his face says.

What the Haile is wrong with the immortals of this realm? Between the gods, the ambiguous creatures, and these damn Weavers, I'd almost make a deal with a god just to get a straight answer!

"I'm loving this conversation, but I hate to break it to you that I am unable to free anyone at this moment. I have no idea what is going on."

"Would you like your memories back?" the one with the circle on her forehead asks.

I hesitate...I'm not really sure I do, but it is what I came here for, right? I need to know...it's not about Erebus or Haile or Agnar. I need this for me. I need to know who I am.

I'm not given the chance to answer.

"Take them, Forbis. Remember who you are," the one with the three dots says before kicking me into the pond.

Something takes hold of my feet and pulls me to the bottom. The water is warm...and not water. I'm not sure what it is. It's light like air but thick enough I could swim through it. The Weavers stand above, their figures rippling through waves. They throw some of the glowing strings in and join hands as they begin chanting in Old Daeil.

My head becomes bombarded with visions. They're coming too quickly. Overtaking my sense of time and reality. They're moving through me like parasites. Painful, head-splitting parasites. I can't scream. All sound is muffled. All I know are the visions. My life as Aislinn clashes with the memories of Forbis...then Opari. Three lives, three sets of memories. I can't make out the clear line defining them. I can't remember who is who.

And then nothing but pain. Only realm-breaking pain.

I'm not sure how long I have been in the pond.
Somewhere between a few minutes and forever.
But when the burn subsides, I remember.

THIRTY-SIX
MORTAL COMBAT
Rett

THINGS HAVE BEEN OFF between Iris and me since I started hanging with the boys. Mase's newest term for our group is *Mortal Combat*, but I doubt that will stick any better than the *Eat Dirt or Die Crew.*

Even though it's causing a strain on my relationship, I don't know if I have ever been happier than when I am in the ring with them. They have become my brothers in a short amount of time. Well, I suppose brothers *and* Leighra. I'd never tell her, but she is growing on me.

I wish Iris would just be happy for me finding a small place where I'm something more than a failed lord bastard, something that is mine without being a part of a false legacy. I was happy for her when she started down the path of midwifery—just like her mother.

We probably need space from one another...more than just a few hours a day, but I can't seem to get myself to suggest it. It's like the words dissolve from my mind before my tongue catches up to speak them. Our attachment to each other can't be healthy. My skin itches whenever we're apart. I become irritable. When she is near, she can't be near enough. I'd carve a hole in my center to have her inside of me, and even that wouldn't be close enough. My love for her is bordering on an obsession and a dangerous one. It's insatiable. *I'm* insatiable.

Today, I'm sharing my weapons training with the guys...and Leighra. They're incredible at hand to hand, but when it comes to swords and knives, I have them beat by miles thanks to my time in the King's Army. We invited two Bottinials, Harlow and Davina, to come watch...mainly so we could convince them to make us practice weapons using their gifts, but it's honestly been nice expanding our little group.

We even let a Wolfshifter in who goes by the name Bones. I suspect that isn't his real name, but it's badass and I'm a little jealous. Though, Mase has taken to calling me "beast" which I suppose is just as cool.

Leighra is surprisingly good at throwing the little makeshift daggers. She has hit the target drawn on the tree dead center with each throw. They don't stick, of course, given that they are made of dull wood, but you can see the little dents from each hit. Rik is showing Harlow how to hold the sword and swing it while Davina makes a crown of flowers and places it atop Mase's head. I'm fairly certain she's only here because her younger sister dragged her, but she's incredibly skilled at creating with her gift. She was the one who helped with the majority of Lysette's Bottinial training.

I make my way to where Bones and Dover are facing off in the ring with their wooden swords and daggers strapped to various places of their body. Bones has good reflexes and excellent footwork, but Dover moves with a fluidity that can't be outmatched. He's a natural. I'm pretty sure if he'd been born in Stellera, he would have ended up head of security somewhere. I've gotten to know Dover over the last few weeks, and he's swiftly becoming the best friend I've ever had—only matched by Evander.

I fucking miss that guy.

"Nice pivot, Bones!" I yell out encouragingly as he dodges another advance of Dover's wooden sword. Dust kicks up around them as he sweeps low and attempts to catch Dover from behind, but Dover is quick to spin, grabbing Bones by the arm and holding a fake blade to his throat. Training like this brings me back to the days in the army, something I didn't realize I missed—or maybe forgot I missed with all the chaos of being a future lord.

"Ugh!" a female's voice cries out, followed by a thud on the compacted ground. I turn and see Harlow pinned by Rik. The guy's a savage. In hindsight, I probably should have paired her up with Leighra. It was stupid of me to expect Rik to go easy on her.

"Get off of me, you oversized snake!" Harlow says from beneath him while trying to shove at his shoulders.

Rik smiles. "Do you yield, yet, little rose?"

"Absolutely not."

"I'm staying right here then." There's a challenge in his gaze. Their practice swords are discarded a few feet away, and he is nestled between her hips. I don't have to get any closer to see that he's using his entire weight to keep her pinned and she looks as if she's struggling to breathe.

"Ayo, Rik, make it fair," I shout the command in a voice that is remnant of my time in the army.

Rik's skin ripples and changes until it no longer resembles his, but Davina's. He smiles cockily while wearing the petite young Bottinial's face and shaking out her long red hair. I'll never get used to his shifts.

"Better?" he asks in Davina's voice.

"I can't fight you like that!" Harlow shouts from beneath him and, in the same moment, hooks her leg around his and rolls so that she's on top.

"Okay, what about this?" Rik asks as he sheds her sister's skin in favor of her own. The red locks shorten and turn strawberry blonde. I run a hand over my jaw, trying to decide if I should be frustrated while simultaneously trying not to laugh at the pure rage on the *real* Harlow's face. That girl is feisty. With training, I'm sure she will be just as good as any of us.

"Okay, you two, you're done. Pick up your swords and start again," I instruct.

The rest of the training went well. I have far fewer cuts and bruises than I usually do, so Iris shouldn't be too upset with me. I'm headed down the path to pick her up when I hear Davina calling after me, so I stop just ten feet from the healing center.

"What's up, Davina?" I ask. Her arms wrap around me in a tender and genuine hug. She's two years older than me but only comes up to my chest. Her sister is even shorter, tiny but mighty.

"Thank you. For what you're doing and for including my sister," she says as she pulls back. "Harlow has had a really hard time lately, and I feel like this is exactly what she needs...so, you know, thank you."

"Oh, yeah." I reach an arm behind my head and scratch absent-mindedly. "Of course. She has a lot of promise. I'm happy to have you both, though it isn't up to me. I'm just your friendly village weapons master." I laugh.

"Rett?" Iris asks while walking down the path toward us.

"Hey babe! Davina was hanging out with us today." Davina smiles broadly at the future mother of my child. They've met before but haven't interacted much.

Iris's eyes do this narrowing motion that tells me she is assessing the girl before she blows out a gust of air and forces a smile. "Nice to see you, but I'm tired and ready to go home."

"Oh, of course!" Davina's gaze drops to the large swell of Iris's belly. "I'll see you tomorrow. Rett, thanks again for everything!" She waves, and I wave back with a smile.

"And what was she doing? I take it by her flowy, spotless dress she wasn't fighting?" Iris asks.

"No, she and her sister were there helping create practice weapons and then her sister ended up sparring a bit. Davina mostly made flower crowns." I laugh.

Iris makes a little noise in her throat that sounds less than impressed and trudges on towards our little home.

"What?"

"So just anyone can join now? I thought it was a boys' club?"

"Well, Leighra was always there so..."

"She doesn't count."

"Ahh, okay, I see. Do you feel like one of those Bottinial girls will turn my head away from the woman giving me the single greatest gift anyone could ever give?" I ask with my hand grazing her belly.

She just pouts instead of answering.

"Because I assure you, there is no one capable of turning my head from you. Not in this lifetime. Not even a witch with all their fucking interferences. I'm so obsessed with you that sometimes it's physically painful to be away from your side for even a moment." I kiss the top of her head. "You never have to worry about me leaving you, beautiful."

She scoffs. "I'm sure if a witch wanted you bad enough, she'd find a way to sway you."

"You don't know how stubborn I am, babe. One track mind, and that track is all you." I believe the words I say down to my very bones, yet there is some pulling sensation telling me something is off. I don't know if it's me or her or both of us, but something has shifted with us. It makes my stomach turn and my skin crawl. It's probably nothing. I didn't drink much water today, so maybe this dizzying feeling is just dehydration. It wouldn't be the first time, and I'm positive it won't be the last.

THIRTY-SEVEN
DANGER TO US ALL
DeLuca

MY GUT IS TWISTED with unease as we head back to my siblings' house. I haven't mentioned it, but Lysette is looking worse and worse by the minute, and I am starting to worry. I promised Aislinn I'd watch out for her, and I would hate to fail her again. Lys keeps her head up and a tight smile, but the light in her eye is fading, and there is a shift in her energy.

"I can't believe this has been here all along. Can you imagine if Pierce had found out?" Lysette asks between labored breaths.

"We keep our army well trained and well supplied to defend the Underground. We want no part in the schemes above. Liberators *or* kings, someone always wants the control. We just want to remain free, and we will fight for that freedom," Kierne says.

"Won't you be in some kind of trouble for showing us?" I ask, keeping my eye on Lysette. She has begun to sweat, and her skin has gone practically translucent.

"Yeah, anyone else would get into loads of trouble. Fuck, probably end up in the cells for a few months," Kierne answers with a cocky chuckle.

"But not you?" Lysette asks.

"Nah."

"Why not?" I ask.

"Because I run this shit."

My mouth hangs slightly agape. "You?"

"Yeah, General Kierne, at your service." He salutes with a cocky grin.

I'm lost in a memory of young Kierne, probably no older than fifteen, stumbling home after a run in with the Obsidian guards. He'd stolen three days worth of food from a transport headed up the mountain. When he got away and had the exact same grin on his face. Now he's a general? The tug of pride surprises me, but I feel it all the same.

"Th—" Lysette gasps and stumbles.

I'm there in an instant before she can hit the concrete ground.

"Lys? Lysette?!" I try, shaking her. No response. I run my free hand through my hair. "Fuck!"

"What's wrong with her?" Kierne asks while placing two fingers on her wrist below her thumb.

"I have no idea. I noticed she was pale. Fuck, I should have listened to my instincts! She said she was fine."

"Well, obviously not. Her pulse is there, but it's slow. We need to get her to Kira."

"Kira?"

"Yeah." Kierne scratches at his thin beard. "She's got some kind of healing power."

"I thought she glowed?"

"She radiates light, a light that also heals. I don't know how all the hooey works, but she can help your friend."

"Can everyone in her tribe heal people?"

"So she says."

"Useful," I say, cradling Lysette in my arms and following my brother back to his house.

"It is. It is also why they are so coveted. Why they move their camp so often."

They could eradicate unnecessary death... Who would run from that kind of gift? "They hide to keep from healing those in need?"

"They hide to keep from challenging Fate. They once healed all those who asked, but it came at a price. The balance was off. Those who should have died lived...so those who should have lived...died."

"What do you mean?"

"Children...her tribe's children and the villages surrounding them for hundreds of miles. Fate took what had been denied."

"Fate? You believe in that?"

"At some point, with all the shit I've seen, I had to believe in something," he says. "That's why they've spent the last four generations in the mountains. They're tender-hearted and have a hard time refusing someone in need...but they learned to not mess with the balance."

Always balance.

Maybe I'm tired of balance. Maybe I want righteousness and the end of suffering for innocents. What the fuck kind of good is balance if it means the good suffer?

Carrying Lysette the rest of the way isn't hard. She's tall but still weighs so little I fear I may hold her too tight and break her. I should have made sure she was eating more—given her my rations at the manor. I'm not even sure I *need* to eat. I do get hungry but not nearly as often as I should. Maybe we will get lucky in one of these old archives and find a book that explains how gods work—our powers, strengths, limitations...the limit to our immortality.

When we finally get to my siblings' house, Kira takes one look at Lysette—her pale skin, her nail beds that have begun to brown...as well as the ends of her hair—and instructs me to lay her on the dining table as she pushes everything off it.

"Can you help?" I ask, while gently laying Lysette down—a feat considering how fast my heart is beating.

"Yes." Kira hands baby Cohl to Briella and starts rubbing her hands together and rolling out her shoulders.

I stand off to stay out of the way. "Do you know what's wrong with her?"

Kira's accent thickens as her glow begins to radiate. "I'm fairly certain... You said her gift is flora, correct? Plants and such?"

"Yes."

"I do wonder if her genetic makeup is similar to that of a plant, and going too long without daylight will cause her to wilt away into nothing."

Wilt away...but we've hardly been down here for two days. "I'm sure she's been indoors longer than we have been down here."

"Yes, but even in passing windows, she would be exposed to the rays of life given from the sun. Here, she is completely shut out—essentially buried beneath the ground." Kira holds Lysette's hand. "Look at the nails. They turn brittle and darken as does a dying plant."

"So she needs sunlight?"

"Yes."

"Is your light conne—"

Kira cuts me off. "Yes." And then she begins to glow. She hovers her hands over Lysette, who immediately starts to pinken.

Relief washes over me at the sight. Even her nails go back to normal...though the tips of her hair still seem to remain brown. She's going to hate that. Her eyes blink open, and I have never been so fucking happy to see her scowling at me.

"I told you I was fine, Lucy Rain. You didn't need to make such a big fuss," Lysette says weakly as she takes in Kira's glow and her current position on the dining table.

"She needs water," Isrie says from behind me, already filling a glass. She takes the water to Lysette, who gulps the entire thing so quickly Isrie is already filling another.

"My gift will help...but it's synthetic. She needs the real thing and soon..." Kira says while feeling Lysette's forehead.

"That's her nice way of saying to get the Haile out of here," Dunst says with a smile while leaning a broad shoulder against the door frame.

"Leave? But you just got here," Isrie pouts as she hands Lysette more water.

"I'm sorry, Isrie. We were never staying long anyway. We have to save Aislinn."

"Right. The *highborn* you traded your own for," Briella says.

I knew this was coming. "She is not just *some highborn*, Brie. I love her. She is my entire heart, my home."

She huffs. "Right, your *home*. A home we apparently never were."

Her words feel like a punch to the gut. "I didn't say that."

Briella bounces baby Cohl who has begun to fuss. "You didn't have to. You've always resented us for leaving!"

"No, I haven't." The lie doesn't roll off the tongue as I'd like it to. I have held resentment towards the four of them for leaving, it's true. It's something I have been carrying for years. Each time I think I have moved past it, the pain sears just a little bit deeper.

She rolls her eyes. "Then why did you stay away? Admit it, Rainier."

The heat starts flickering below my skin. "Someone had to stay with Val as her life shattered!"

Briella hands the baby off to Dunst and comes within an inch of my face. "Right, but you abandoned her for your highborn, and now she's dead. Her death might as well be on your hands. I don't know how you can stand there so high and mighty when you did the same thing we did! Only when we left, neither of you died!"

"Briella!" Isrie's eyes are huge, and she looks at our sister as if she's never met her before.

Lysette sits up with a newfound strength, the table wobbling beneath her as she shifts. Her voice is raspy but better than it was moments ago. "I wouldn't bring up Val." She says in warning.

"She was my sister, I'll talk about her as much as I'd like. I wouldn't expect you to know anything about loyalty."

Anger prickles my neck and I know I'm seconds away from igniting. "One...two..."

"Are you counting?" Briella asks. "Gods, you're pathetic. You can't even have a conversation like a normal person... Oh right, you're not a normal person." She huffs a laugh. "Some *god* you are."

"Briella!" Isrie's round cheeks redden with anger.

"Shit," I hear Lysette mutter.

But it's too late, the damage is done. I'm trying to rein it in. The fire. The air. The ground beneath us. They're rumbling, shaking as I do.

"DeLuca, stop!" Lysette's voice is a cry. "Look at the baby. He will get hurt. Your nephew, your family. You have to control it. Don't suppress it, control it. *Feel* it."

"*I killed Val.*" The admission comes out on its own. "I killed her."

Every eye in the room is on me. The rumblings lesson as I feel a weight lifted and control a little easier to hold onto. Kira grabs the baby back from Dunst, whose face changes from white to violet to a red brighter than Kira's hair. As soon as his hands are free, he stalks towards me and grabs me by the collar of my shirt.

Kierne is lunging at me now. Briella steps in his path to me with her hands on her hips.

"Not in the house, Kierne," she says sternly and points him to the other room.

He stares at me, breathing heavily through his nose for a few seconds, then turns with an agitated yell. My sister gives me a look of pure hatred before following him out.

This is a fucking disaster.

Dunst jerks my collar and sneers. "What do you mean 'you killed Val?'" Anyone else would already be on the floor, but this is my brother, and I have enough control to realize that would only make things worse.

I exhale shakily through my nose—fighting against my nature and not hurting him, I allow him to think he's in charge. "What I mean, brother, is exactly that, I *killed* her."

Lysette comes to my defense. "No, you didn't, DeLuca. Aislinn did. It was to protect yourselves."

"Because of me! I might as well have killed her. I was there. Briella is right. I left her. I chose Aislinn. I will always *choose* Aislinn. Over any of you, over the entire realm. I choose her."

Dunst is now the one shaking, I realize I no longer am. The admission gave way to some kind of release in its own way.

My oldest brother's eyes reflect a mixture of pain and anger as he stares into mine. "DeLuca...one time. I give you this one time to leave. If I ever see you again, I will kill you. God or no, I'll find a way."

"He's still our brother," Isrie says in a small voice.

Dunst releases his grip on my shirt. "Our brother... a traitor to his own, therefore a danger to us all." He looks between me and Lysette and sighs, his shoulders drooping. "You have two minutes to get the fuck out of my house."

My mouth opens to say something...but what? What can I possibly say? He has every right to throw us out. He has every right to be angry. They all do. I nod my agreement and help Lysette down from the table. She squeezes my arm, and the small gesture was exactly what I needed. Kira smiles sadly at the both of us then walks Dunst into another room.

Isrie's dried paint-covered hand slides into mine. "I love you, Raini," she says with a tear sliding down her round cheek.

Why did that hurt more than anything else my siblings have said? I kiss the top of her head. "I love you, too, Isrie."

Of course, we made a stop by Elinor's to say a quick goodbye. She must have anticipated our departure because she had already packed us a basket full of food. We're now in the boxy military-looking transport Kierne offered to us earlier, before he hated me.

There's a map in the little compartment located under the seat and a full carton of that sickly purple fuel in the back. I'm not completely sure it will be enough to get to Rilyse, but I hope it will be. I'm not in the mood for another run-in like the one we had in the tunnel.

I follow the tunnel out the way Kierne had instructed, and after some long minutes, we can see the faint sunlight peaking at the end.

"How are you?" Lysette asks, breaking the silence.

I keep my eyes on the light. "I'm fine."

She puts a hand on my forearm and looks at me with pleading eyes. "DeLuca."

"Fine, I'm not fine. I hate that my family hates me. I hate that Val is gone and that I had to choose the way I did. I hate that Aislinn is gone. I hate all of this and I'm barely holding it together." I grasp the steering wheel harder. "Fuck, Lysette. I really don't know what the fuck I'm doing. I'm going off instinct alone."

She looks at me with...pride? "Thank you."

My brow raises. "Thank you?"

"For being honest with me...and yourself."

I shrug, not really sure what to say. It didn't feel awful to open up...and I didn't explode. "How are you? I ask.

"I'm okay...still feel a little weak."

"We can take the top off when we make it out of the tunnel, so you can soak in as much of the sun as possible."

"Okay," she says with a small voice. "Linnea...she—" Lysette swallows a few times, fighting some internal battle.

"You don't have to talk about it."

She shakes her head. "I should though. I should keep her alive...even if it's just a memory. Before the wedding, Linnea, Aislinn, and I were searching for the way into my family's archive...though we did not know what it was at the time. To us, it was a silly mystery to pass the time. Anyway, we were talking about how Linnea and I both got a little cranky when we were indoors for too long...Linnea admitted to eating dirt."

I burst into laughter. I know I shouldn't, but it's too bizarre and not at all where I thought this story was heading. "Dirt? Really?"

"She said she needed the minerals." Lysette is laughing along with me.

We are still laughing when we make it out of the tunnel and into an open plain somewhere between Azelean and Thalia. I pull over so we can remove the top of the transport and hook it to the back. The sun blazes overhead, but it's still bitterly cold with the promise of an incoming winter.

Wind whips Lysette's multi-colored hair behind her, and she tilts her head up, soaking in every ounce of the sun's rays. When she finally drops her head again, I notice her eyes are watery and slightly red.

"Are you crying?"

"It's just...I missed all the signs. About what we were, and I wonder if Linnea knew? If her ability had shown itself. She had been distant towards the end, secretive—her and my mother. What if they knew, and were still hiding it? My gift didn't appear until she died...what if I stole it from her?"

"How would that even be possible?"

"How is it possible that my blue eye turned white when she died? How is any of this possible?" She flails her hands around us as if there's magic everywhere around us.

"Good point. Well, from what I know of Linnea and of the two of you, if your ability did come from her somehow, it wasn't stolen. She would have given it to you."

"You think?"

"I do. Honestly, it's probably why you're so strong."

Lysette wraps her arms around her legs. "Maybe."

"Definitely." I nod. "Are you cold?"

"Yes."

I raise my body temperature and her grip around her legs loosens a bit. She scoots a little closer to me on the bench seat—soaking in my warmth. She's quiet for a while, and for a minute, I think she's sleeping while I continue to drive on the empty dirt road until her voice breaks through the hum of the engine.

"I tried to stop it."

"Stop what?" I ask her, completely puzzled.

"This bond. I thought if we didn't get close, it wouldn't hurt so much when you leave...I can't feel another loss, DeLuca, I just can't."

I pause, contemplating her words, then smooth back her hair in a soothing pattern like my mom did to me when I was really little. "Loss is a part of this realm, Lys, but the memories made will live on forever. You're keeping all of them alive just by keeping them in your heart...I'm not good at friendships. I've always kind of stuck to myself other than with family, but knowing you has been one Haile of an honor. If I don't make it out of this, I don't want you to mourn for me. Celebrate the fact that you were my first best friend."

She sniffles and tries to hide the crack in her voice when she says, "You're my best friend too, Lucy Rain."

The name doesn't even bother me this time as I continue to rub her hair back. It isn't long before she's snoring with her head in my lap and her legs curled on the bench seat. I continue driving toward the sunset, towards Rilyse, and another step closer to Aislinn.

THIRTY-EIGHT
DESTRUCTION AND CHAOS
Lysette

I'VE ALWAYS WANTED TO travel across Stellera, but almost three full days on the road is too much. I feel disgusting. We have stopped to rest every night, but there hasn't been any opportunity to bathe. DeLuca hasn't spoken much, which isn't unusual for him, but I can tell he's hurting about what happened with his family in the Underground. To his credit, the temperature around him has remained surprisingly neutral, and I think he's improving with regulating his emotions and power.

Finally, the large white wall that stretches around Rilyse comes into view on the horizon. We do not know what to expect with the state of the province...but considering the destruction and chaos everywhere else, we do not expect much. A bed to sleep in and a bath, that's all I want. I don't care about anything else. Then after a full night's rest, we will venture to the Leviathan's cavern and find the portal. We are so close to this being done. *So* close, I feel the tension in the air coiling, ready to snap with release once this is over.

We approach the iron gate. It appears unmanned but begins creaking up as soon as we are close to it. A man comes running to us from underneath.

"Are you well enough to call your gifts if you need to?" DeLuca asks, his voice low and on edge.

I close my eyes and inhale, feeling for the stirring beneath my skin that calls to the growth below ground. There is a tiny rumble of vines as they slither, waiting for me to call upon them.

"Yes. I am fully recharged."

"Good. I'm not going to sit here and tell you to get behind me or anything like that. Gods know you wouldn't anyway. So just stay alert. We have no idea what awaits us."

The man approaches our transport. It's hard to tell his station or position by his plain beige clothing—pretty typical garb for this side of Stellera. It could go either way.

"What business do you have in Rilyse?" he asks.

I'm not sure how to play it—to tell him of my parentage or to hide it under the ruse of being common born. So I decide to ask a question of my own. "Do the Kaillens still govern here?"

"They do, Lady Petra Kaillen and her husband, Lord Craven Earh-Kaillen, have shielded Rilyse from the chaos erupting across the nation. Have you come for refuge?" The man accesses our dirty clothes and faces, causing me to internally cringe.

DeLuca gives me a look that says he's not sure what to make of the man and the situation, but I'm too damn tired to care. Either he's telling the truth, or he's not. If he's not, then we have an immense supply of power between the two of us, and I am not afraid to use it.

"I am Lysette Urson. Our families have been friends and allies for generations. My travel companion, DeLuca, and I need their help."

His eyes narrow and my heart slams against my ribcage. "An Urson?" There's a long stretch of silence while he looks between us. His face is unreadable. The air around DeLuca warms, and I know he is starting to get anxious. I start breathing a little harder.

Finally, the man cracks a smile. "We thought you were all dead. The Kaillens will be most pleased. I am Dominic Avier. You may call me Dom. I am from one of the high houses of Rilyse." He waves to someone we can not see beyond the wall. "Please, follow this road to Luppitier House. I will radio ahead so that Lady Kaillen will be prepared for your arrival."

My entire body relaxes as I smile in thanks to Dom. I have heard of the Aviers, loyal to the Kaillens for years and one of the most influential high house families in Stellera.

"Do you trust him?" DeLuca asks as we drive along the road that winds through the vineyards Rilyse is so famous for.

"I think so. If he's lying, we can always fight our way out and run straight to the Leviathan's cavern...though I pray to the gods that's not the case because I'm exhausted."

"We haven't discussed what you will do while I am in the gods' realm... Will you stay here and wait for me?"

"Well, I have to wait for the Guardian meeting."

"What if I take longer than that?"

"Do you plan to?"

"No, but I also don't know what to expect. It's a whole other realm, Lys. Anything is possible."

I pause and think about that. He's right, what will I do? Go back to Caeliss? Obsidian? I don't hate the idea of helping Evander restore some kind of system to help the common born...but how long do I wait for DeLuca and Ailie? I sigh. "Let's just take it one day at a time. See how welcoming the Kaillens are."

DeLuca nods. We drive past the villas where most of the people reside. They get larger and larger the closer we get to Luppitier House. All of them are so well kept. I have been to very few other provinces other than the ones in Obsidian's territory. Ashe was the largest but the least well-kept, but none I've been to have been as beautiful as Rilyse. Most of the villas are made up of vine covered white walls with a terracotta type roof. The vegetation is beautifully kept, and there is a sea breeze that compliments the bright sun shining bright above us.

"No wonder they didn't have a problem with the Liberators. Look at this place, it's a dream," DeLuca says.

"It is." I feel a sharp pinch of guilt while watching a family with small children playing outside one of the homes and wishing we could have changed things before it was too late. This is what Obsidian could have been if my father had only given two shits about his people—f any of my ancestors had. How much could have been avoided?

"Obsidian seems almost savage in comparison," I say.

○

Lady Kaillen, a beautiful woman with dark golden skin and endless brown eyes, gasps when we are introduced in her study. "By the gods...a living Urson."

"So you've heard of what happened at Obsidian Manor then?"

"There isn't a soul in Stellera who hasn't."

"This is DeLuca...he's...ugh..." I look at DeLuca, wondering how much to disclose.

He saves me by answering himself. "I am a first generation Child. I don't want to beat around the bush. We know of your familys history in the Guardians. Lady Soleil filled us in on much of it."

Lady Kaillen's eyes widen. "First generation?" she whispers. "So that makes you a—"

I finish for her. "God. Indeed, but don't let it get to his head more than it has."

She sinks into the giant wingback chair perched near the fireplace. "By all the stars in the sky. What can I do for the two of you?"

DeLuca and I take a seat on the green sofa placed opposite of her. "Well, we could use a place to stay...and to hold a Guardians meeting," I reply.

"I won't be staying long...but I do want to ensure I am leaving Lysette in capable hands. I have business to attend to nearby."

"Of course, of course. Lysette will absolutely be safe here. She is one of our own," Lady Kaillen assures him.

"Good. Because if I were to come back and find some harm has befallen her...well...let's just say I've earned my nickname as god of vengeance." Even though DeLuca's threat is not aimed at me, the tone of his voice sends a chill racing down my spine. If Lady Kaillen is at all affected, she doesn't show a glimmer of it. She just sits straight with a smile plastered across her face.

"God of vengeance, is it? I swear on my house that Lysette will be well taken care of while I am in charge here."

As if on cue, a serv carrying a tray of refreshments comes strolling into the office. She sets the tray on the table in front of us, and with her head down, gives a little curtsy before leaving again.

My brows raise. "You still have servs?"

"Why wouldn't I?"

The air grows a little warmer and I place a hand on DeLuca's thigh to try to silently calm him.

"Well, a great deal of servs turned on their governing families and murdered them." I give her a pointed look. Red tinges her cheeks, the only sign she is affected by my words.

"Well, we have always taken good care of our servs. I like to believe they're happy here."

DeLuca scoffs but thankfully doesn't say any more. We sip on the tea brought to us, and I devour six of the little finger sandwiches before the serv girl comes back and tells us that rooms have been prepared for us.

"Thank the gods," I mutter with relief.

"Lysette, you will be in my sister's room. DeLuca, you will be in my childhood room. They're the nicest in the house aside from my own." Lady Kaillen smiles broadly at us.

"Your sister, Sorena?" I ask.

Lady Kaillen's gaze darkens a little, and her presence becomes heavier, but she keeps a smile. "Yes. My sister, Sorena."

"So she no longer lives here?"

"She does. She just has a special room in the west wing. It is more suited to her needs." Lady Kaillen's eyes travel to the serv, and she gives us a look that says "we can speak about it later," and I nod my understanding.

We follow the serv girl. She's young...maybe a few years older than I am. She does indeed look well taken care of—plump with glossy brown hair and bright eyes. She introduced herself as "Hannah" in a cheery voice. I am probably not the best judge of her happiness though. I thought the Obsidian servs were happy too...at least I think I did...I'm not sure I ever paid much attention to them, actually.

"Here we are! Mr. DeLuca, you first." Hannah opens a large white door to reveal a spacious suite that could rival the one I had back at Obsidian Manor. It has a maroon and cream color palette that matches the aesthetic of the village below. It's also very bright with large windows that have a view of vineyards that stretch for miles.

"Thank you, Hannah." He smiles warmly, and I almost laugh at how out of place it looks on his hardened face. Hannah blushes in return and nods before leading me two doors down to my room. She shows me the fully stocked closet and pulls a fresh towel out before leaving me alone.

I immediately go to the powder room and start the tub, ready to wash the week's journey off of me for good. My skin itches in anticipation as I watch the large clawfoot tub fill. My clothes hit the floor, and in the same breath, I am dunking under the water, instantly feeling relief. I feel more alive than I have in a while and my skin sings. Thank the gods. I rest my head behind me and stare at the clouds painted on the ceiling, relishing in every second of this calm.

The sun has been set for a while now. We had been served dinner in our rooms, which I was immensely grateful for as I was engrossed in one of my father's journals already dressed in a night set with my hair thrown up. Thankfully, this last wash got the rest of that ruddy red out, and my hair has returned to its honey shade—other than the browned tips that I am tempted to just cut off. The further I read my father's journals, the more I realize how much I do not know about my own family. It's impossible to think this was the same man who had made our home sing with warmth and love my entire childhood. How could he have been such a monster to everyone else? It's hard to swallow the fact that, to many people, he's the villain.

There's a bright glow of moonlight shining through the window. It catches on the purple accents of the room, making them look as if they are glowing. It must be after midnight when I hear a soft rap on the door. I jump back, falling off the bed with a small yelp.

DeLuca barges through the door with slightly wet hair and a freshly shaven face. A look of worry contorts his features as he rushes to where I still lay upside down. "Are you okay?" he asks as he lifts me back to standing.

"I'm fine!" I laugh. "You just scared me is all. I wasn't expecting any visitors."

"I—ugh—I'm sorry."

"Did you need something?" I ask as I sit back in my bed.

DeLuca goes to the other side and slides in beside me, his hands folded behind his head as he blows out a breath. "Remember when you said I need to talk things out instead of letting them fester?"

"Yes."

"Well. I'm burning hot right now. Really hot. I took a shower, and it helped a little, but there's an itch beneath my skin, and it wants to break free."

"Why?"

"What do you mean why?"

"I mean, what were you thinking about? Why did the power rise to the surface?"

"Oh. I was thinking about tomorrow. About the portal...that if we succeed, I could see her tomorrow. After all these months, I could see her *tomorrow.* Then I started thinking about what she's been going through in the gods' realm. What Erebus is putting her through. What if he forced her to..." DeLuca shakes his head, unable to even finish the thought, but a shudder rolls through my shoulders as I imagine what he is considering. He's burning so hot that his wet hair is steaming.

I put my arm out. "Come here."

"I don't want to burn you."

"Then don't burn me."

He snorts and smiles. "Like it's that easy?"

"I believe in you, oh powerful god."

"I don't know how to not hurt you." His voice is barely a whisper.

"Try." I move my fingers in a beckoning gesture. DeLuca hesitates but breathes deeply and moves into the crook of my arm. His skin is hot on mine, but not unbearable, more like a fever.

"See, Lucy Rain? You can do anything you set your mind to." I begin to stoke his hair, and his temperature decreases. We lay like this for a while, I keep stroking his hair until he becomes utterly still and his breathing steadies—I'm so proud of the progress he's made controlling his power and emotions. I lean my head against his and close my eyes, trying my best to rest despite the anxious pit growing in my belly with what tomorrow will bring.

THIRTY-NINE
UNRELIABLE
Erebus

THE TUG OF SHADOW chains pulls me away from my morning rounds. Aislinn is afraid. Not just afraid, terrified. Or was. Now the bond has gone still, as if she's gone. So here I am, appearing through the Imorti Woods, trying to catch a hint of her shadow. I know I risk the wrath of both Haile and Agnar by being here, but let them fucking come at me. She would have been safe if they'd just left her with me. We were making progress. I could have gotten it done. Anything could happen to her here, especially in these woods. Terrible beasts roam these lands. Winged skeletal creatures, whose very breath blows so cold it could freeze the sun. Creatures that have no masters and whose only purpose is to watch over the Imorti and keep out those who do not belong.

My shadows slither along the ground, searching for any trace of Aislinn. A crunch behind me has me sending out whips of them and a grumbled choking noise sounds from behind a tree, followed by a large crash. I go to investigate my newest captive.

"Oh, it's you."

"Get...your damn...shadows...off of...me." Agnar struggles to say the words with the shadow tightening around his neck.

"Why would I do that when you're exactly where you should be?" I grin. "Below me."

"Because...Haile...will be...pissed."

I shrug. "That isn't a reason to let you go."

"What...would...Aislinn...think?"

My shadows erupt. "I don't know. What *would* she think? I wish I could ask her, but it would seem that *you* lost her!"

"What do you mean he *lost* her?" Haile's voice booms from behind me, shaking the very ground we stand on.

I don't give him the satisfaction of turning around. "I felt her fear and then I felt nothing. I can't pull on her shadow chain at all. I can't feel her in this realm."

"Explain, Agnar!"

Agnar makes a noise similar to a donkey braying as he tries to speak through the constricting shadows around his neck. Haile rolls his eyes and snaps his fingers. A light ignites at the tail of the shadow and it evaporates before our eyes. Agnar rubs at his now-freed neck, swallows a few times, then speaks. "She's fine. She went looking for the Weavers. If you don't feel her, it is likely that she found them."

I ensure my tone is low and threatening as I say, "Or was eaten by one of those winged beasts that roam free in these woods."

"Wouldn't that be a good thing for you? Then you get to keep your *pet* forever as her harbinger shift would be complete," Agnar says.

"We need her to open the barrier first," Haile says plainly.

"And to help Astoria," I add, glaring at him.

"Do you even want that anymore? I'm not the only one who has noticed your little obsession with my child," Agnar says. I know he's baiting me—he wants me to lose it in front of Haile.

"Watch it, Agnar. Lest you forget, Astoria is *my* child," Haile says. I can't hide my smirk.

"Oh, I don't forget. I'm sure it's the only reason you allow this one to live as he does."

"He allows me to live because the universe would implode without me. Especially after your last shit show of a war. Do you want this place crawling with the corrupt shadows? Do you want the end of all realms?" I get into his face until our noses are almost touching. "You need me."

"Enough, you two," Haile says. "I swear, it's like having toddlers trying to wrangle you two in."

"You won't find any toddlers here, Agnar made sure of that."

Agnar crosses his arms. "I do what I must for the realm. You know the prophecies as well as I do."

"The prophecies are all bullshit! Astoria being born was supposed to strengthen Haile's reign but look around. The gods' realm has never been weaker. The rot leaks into the side of the living. The lands of the dead no longer glow under the moon. New shadows haven't emerged since the barrier went up. It's all bullshit, probably designed by the Weavers to fuck with us."

"The prophecies came from Viitor. Are you insulting my child now?"

"Viitor, Forbis, and Opari were all known to give us half truths. They were unreliable and a menace upon the gods."

"Say that again." Agnar's fist curls.

A slow smile spreads across my face. "Your children were unreliable menaces, and the best thing they ever did was leave."

Crack.

Agnar's fist makes contact with my jaw and I go flying back, breaking several trees in the process. I stand, shadows splayed around like dark tentacles. The light around us snuffs out until it's pitch black. I pull my fist back and slam it into Agnar's smug face. He flies back several feet, and before he lands, I wrap him in a cocoon of shadow.

"You may be stronger, Agnar, but I am more powerful. I think it's time for a reminder." I turn the cocoon of shadows so that Agnar is head down, and I spit in his face before sending him flying to the other side of the woods.

"Is that necessary?" Haile asks while rubbing out the lines between his brows.

I shrug. "Maybe not, but it was a good outlet for my frustrations."

"I'll let it pass this once, but that was the end of it. You two need to work together towards our common goal. We are all on the same side here."

I doubt that.

"Look I—" I start but am overcome with an intense tug on a familiar chain.

Pet.

In a burst of shadow, I follow the pull. She's okay. She's calm. She's alive.

I appear to find her at the base of the Efren Mountains, a range that serves as a border for Kaoket.

Aislinn's back is to me so I use the opportunity to sneak up behind her. I lean in close to her ear. "So far from home, little pet."

She turns and gapes at me with wide eyes, but they're not hers. They're not the most brilliant emeralds to have graced this realm. No, they're swirling with silver and a pearlescent color. Her face is utterly blank.

"Pet?"

No response.

My jaw tightens, and I mutter to myself, "Fucking *Weavers*."

I scoop Aislinn into my arms. She's limp and her head falls back. I could have my shadows carry her, but there's something about this, about her not fighting me that makes me want to hold her closer. The shadows in me usually beg to be near her, and for once, they're quiet.

I'm tempted to just go home to the Shadows but decide at the last second to take her back to Kaoket, just in case she is somehow still tethered to the Weavers. I barge through the front doors and am met with a red-faced Agnar. He's pissed. I can't help but smile. Haile comes up behind him and my smile fades.

"So you found her," Haile says.

"Yes, at the base of the Efren Mountains."

"What's wrong with her?" Agnar asks, his face a little less red now.

"No clue. My guess is it has something to do with the Weavers."

Agnar eyes Aislinn in my hands and his face twists. "We should lie her in bed and call upon Sana to heal her."

"No," Haile and I say in unison.

"The less people who know about her, the better," Haile adds. "We don't want anyone to know what she is, and the moment Sana lays her hands upon her, she will know this to be Forbis."

"So, you're just going to leave her like this?" Agnar's face begins to redden again with his rising temper, and I feel my own temper rise with it.

Haile goes to place a hand on her head, and I instinctively hold her tighter, stepping back out of his reach.

"I am just looking into her consciousness," Haile says.

I hesitate but then nod him over. In his hands, she appears tiny and frail, like he could crush her easily if only he were to squeeze.

"Why are you looking at her like that?" Agnar practically spits the words.

"I'm not looking at her like anything. I was just trying not to laugh at how comically large Haile's hand looks next to her head."

"Stop talking, the both of you. I'm concentrating." Haile's composure snaps.

We glare at each other in silence while we wait for Haile's assessment.

"I believe her memories are coming back," he finally says.

"You believe?" I ask.

"It's hard to say. Her mind is a mess. One of the most tangled webs I've ever looked in on. It's as though she has three lifetimes in there, but that can't be right... She should only have her mortal life and Forbis."

"Fucking Weavers," I mutter. Their eyes snap at me. I let out a sigh. "The Opari Stone is embedded in her arm."

"Is that going to be a problem?" Agnar asks.

"Aside from a wicked headache, she should be fine," Haile answers.

"*Should* be?" I ask.

"What do you want me to say? None of this has been done before, and we lost the only one of us who could tell the future," Haile says in that usual condescending voice of his.

"I'm not leaving her until she wakes up," I say firmly.

Haile raises a brow. "You need to watch over the Shadows."

"Helena can do it. I am *not* leaving her until she wakes up."

Haile rolls his eyes. "Fine. Send for me immediately when she awakens. I have questions for the little beast." Haile evaporates in a sprinkling of speckled light.

"So, her room?" I ask.

Agnar growls at me like the primitive Neanderthal he is. "Chimmy!"

One of the odd little creatures that serve Kaoket waddles in. "Yesss," it drawls.

"Take the trickster to Forbis's room."

"Right away, sir." The creature bows.

I'm not entirely sure what is happening to me, but I can't lay Aislinn down. Her bed looks comfortable enough...but her face looks so peaceful now that her eyes are closed, and she's nestled against my chest.

"Fucking Weavers," I say under my breath as I crawl into her bed and hold her. I have no intention of moving. I am a patient man. If it takes her a decade of mortal years to wake up, then I will still be here in this position. It's not like I have any new shadows to tend to anyway, and Helena knows what to do to the ones that are there. My grip tightens around Aislinn as I shift her closer. Her head is in the perfect spot for me to rest my chin on it. Her scent assaults my senses. She smells of lunalilies and fresh water. My eyes close as I inhale her deeper. It's such a calming scent and not unlike my Astoria who smells of lilies and starlight. We stay like this for hours. The false sun has long set.

I finally look down and find her large emerald eyes staring back up at me.

"Erebus?" Her voice is raspy and broken.

"Yes, pet?"

"You lied to me."

FORTY
CHILDREN OF BALANCE
Aislinn

I DON'T KNOW WHERE I am.

I can't tell what's real.

I don't know who I am.

I'm no longer in the Weavers' fold, but as the memories continue to race across my mind, I can't tell which ones belong to me. They all feel like mine. Some have been tampered with. The memories are still there, but it's as if the sounds have been snuffed out. Some are nothing but sound. Each memory has a glowing orb that I race to, and each time I reach it, I am transported to another...as if it is some sort of magical door—or portal.

Shadows skitter along the floor and I follow them. We enter a chamber I am familiar with. It is the room where the gods' court in Kaoket takes place. Each chair is filled. Astoria is in the seat with a moon engraving rather than Erebus. She looks beyond healthy and is glowing as the moon does on the darkest nights. She is happy and her belly is round. Erebus takes a seat beside Helena in the crowd with the other gods.

Soren sits to Haile's left, and beside him sits Agnar. They all look relaxed as they make idle conversation. Twins glide past me and stand on a raised platform facing the council. The pair wear long robes that shimmer in different metallic colors depending on the light. Tightly pressed to their necks are jeweled necklaces with a large star at the hollow of their throats. They have similar features—dark eyes, pointed chins, dark hair, and perfectly sloped noses.

Upon closer inspection, I see that their dark eyes are lined in different colors, one with gold the other with an iridescent purplish color. My feet move of their own volition and join the two. I look down and notice a robe the same as theirs is hugging my body as well.

"Now, Utikalo, what have the Weavers foretold of the next generation of gods?" Haile asks the twins...triplets...with an ease in his features. He looks happy. They *all* seem happy or content at the very least.

"We spoke with them as requested," the one with gold around the irises says.

"You will not like what they had to say, and once it is said, it can not be unsaid." My lips move, but the voice is not my own.

"I tire of waiting, Utikalo, out with it," Haile says.

"Very well," the one with iridescent around the irises says. "The Weavers have chosen. They've tied the fates of all the ones to come, of all the children. God-born children will usher in a new tide of power. Stronger than before. A child of moon and shadow—dark and light—will pave the way into a new era. The shadows of past mortals will be released and run rampant among us. This realm *and* the living realm will fall to chaos and forever be changed. There will be no room for life among all the dead. This destiny can end in two ways. One, the end of all things. Two, the beginning. Nothing will remain, and the harder you pull against the threads of fate the Weavers have woven, the tighter they will pull."

The gods in the room have fallen silent. All eyes shoot to Astoria and her rounded belly. Her glow dims ever so slightly and Erebus is before her in a flash with his teeth bared and shadows flowing over them in a protective bubble.

Haile's nostrils flare, and his eyes turn to slits. "We can fix this. We can beat the Weavers at their own game. From this moment on, any child born of pure gods' blood will be executed at birth."

"Executed at birth?" a woman shouts from the crowd. "That's monstrous!"

Haile's head whips in the direction of the voice and his cruel gaze turns into something bone-chilling, despite his calm tone as he speaks. "Bring Mari forth." At Haile's order, men in golden cloaks grab the woman and bring her to the platform. The Utikalo step off to make room. "You've given me an idea, fertility goddess."

She places her hands on her hips with a scowl. "I do hope it is something better than murdering infants, *god of life.*"

Haile's smile turns up in a way that makes my insides squirm. "Oh, it is. We won't have to murder infants if they never come into existence." He doesn't give her a moment longer to question him before he slams a burst of pure light into her. Her scream curdles through the air, but he doesn't relent. Haile keeps hold of his beam of raw power until all that is left of the goddess of fertility is a pile of shimmering green dust.

"What did you do?" Edwissa whispers from her seat near the front, while every other god in the room looks at the platform in a state of shock and horror.

"What had to be done, for the good of our realm," Haile responds. "Without new gods, the prophecy can not come to pass."

I catch Astoria guarding her belly and Erebus guarding her. They are trying not to draw attention to themselves, but a flicker of the shadows catches Haile's attention, and it causes him to turn towards them. His face falls as he takes in his daughter and her round belly as if he'd forgotten. "Everyone out!" he orders.

The gods and goddesses shuffle out, all except the small council sitting on the raised platform. The small council stands and moves closer to Astoria. Erebus encases her in a cocoon of shadow but leaves himself out of it, tendrils of shadow ready for a fight all around him.

"I'm not going to hurt my only daughter," Haile says.

"*We* won't hurt her, but we do need to figure this out," Agnar says, a wave of calm pushing out from where he stands.

"Come now, trickster, drop the shadows and let's discuss this as civilized gods," Soren says.

Erebus looks at each of their faces and at Astoria who nods to him. The shadows evaporate and Astoria stands.

"We will take the baby to live amongst the mortals," she says matter-of-factly. "We will raise him there, and our child will never know of this realm." Erebus slides his arm around her and nods his agreement. They are completely united.

"No, you are needed here." Isela steps in from a curtain behind the thrones. "Send away the child. We will watch it, and if it grows too powerful, we can send Agnar to take care of the problem using the Opari Orb. I'm positive the Utikalo can spare it now that they've mastered their portals, yes?" She pats Agnar on the arm, and his eyes quickly shift to his children before he nods to Isela.

"No. We will all go or none of us will," Astoria says firmly.

"If none of you go, you will doom us all. How selfish can you possibly be, Astoria?" Isela hisses and looks at Haile who is running a hand along his jaw.

Erebus and Agnar exchange a look of silent communication. Agnar shakes his head subtly.

"We need to do what is best for both realms." Soren's voice holds no empathy for his sister.

"Y-you can't." Astoria looks with wide eyes between all the gods before her, lastly at her husband. "Erebus, they can't!"

He closes his eyes. "Haile?"

"The child may walk amongst the mortals, alone, but if it becomes powerful, we will send Agnar to take care of it. We can not risk the realm falling and the shadows being released, not for anyone." Haile turns away and marches past the curtain with heavy footsteps that match the beating of my heart.

Astoria sobs, falling to her knees, and Erebus takes her away in a burst of shadows. The other gods file out one by one. Except for Isela, who kneels down beside the powder that was once the goddess Mari and scoops up her remains. She produces a leather pouch and dumps the remains within before stalking off.

An orb of light appears and I race through it. Again two of the Utikalo are before me, but now one has silver irises instead of iridescent.

"Did we do the right thing, Viitor?" the silver one asks.

"We did what we had to. I told you what I saw, Forbis," Viitor says calmly.

"They will hate us if they find out." The words pass through my lips.

"They will, Opari." Viitor nods.

"Erebus will hunt us to the ends of the universe for denying him his happy family," Forbis says.

Viitor sighs. "Everything will happen as it should. You all know as well as I do that there is no beating the Weavers. There is nothing we can do to alter any of it. We are as much their pawns as the rest of them."

"But did we really have to say it was a child of moon and shadow? They're going to assume that any and all of Astoria's children are a threat." The words again pass through my lips, though I believe this to be a memory from Opari.

"The children of balance will be tied to a child of theirs. No matter what, they are just as a part of the prophecy as we are."

Another orb appears and I touch it. This time, I'm falling through the memories so quickly I only catch the faintest glimpses. I watch the moment Erebus realizes that there is more to the prophecy than we let on—watch him hound us to the point we knew we had to leave, never revealing the truth. My heart races as a cloud of darkness chases me and I jump for the next orb.

I watch as Astoria fell pregnant again and again and again, to Haile's surprise and dismay. He couldn't order them to part. Once the gods' shadows were bonded, they could no longer be separated without destroying them both. Not just emotionally—they would be physically torn apart. Each time she gave birth, Haile was there to ensure Erebus removed the baby immediately. There was no kindness in the king's eyes. No sympathy for his daughter. Even as her light continues to fade.

The black cloud chases me to the next orb. I pass by memory after memory after memory before getting stuck in another one. I'm back in a vision I've already seen, one where Isela is giving a tonic to Astoria. She's gently brushing back her hair, assuring her the tonic will work. That it will keep her from getting pregnant. But then the memory jumps back to Isela making the tonic. She sprinkles the shimmering green dust and stirs it while humming to herself with a sharp grin. "We will see who the favorite is now," she says to herself.

An orb appears and swallows me. The memories seem endless, and I don't know how I will find my way out. I keep following the lights and find myself deeper in the depths of my mind. The dark cloud of shadow is looming over me. Instead of choosing the orbs of light, I stop and turn toward the cloud of shadow.

"You want me? Come and take me then! I'm tired of running from the darkness. Take me!" I'm firm as steel. Not a hint of a tremor as I run full force into the cloud. It absorbs me. I'm sucked into pitch black. It's cold, and for a moment, I think I'm trapped in the Abyss.

It takes me a few breaths to realize that my eyes are closed. The room is dark with night. It takes me several blinks to adjust to it. There are cold hands wrapped around me, and my head is bobbing with the rise and fall of a chest which makes my already splitting headache so much worse. I'm in my bed in Kaoket. As if reading my mind, one of the cold hands begins stroking my hair. He looks down and his gray eyes almost look blue in this light.

"Erebus? I ask, still disoriented.

"Yes, pet?"

"You lied to me."

He is cradling me like I am something precious to him and I'm not sure I like it. "What lie do you speak of?"

"You did hunt them. You wanted their knowledge."

He relaxes a fraction. "I never said I did not, so is it truly a lie?"

I lift one shoulder in a shrug. "I'm not sure what is or isn't a lie anymore."

His face is twisted with what seems to be a deep concern, but I don't buy into his sincerity. "What do you mean by that?"

"My head is swimming with memories that don't belong to me. I can't make sense of them, and some are missing pieces, but nothing here is as it seems, that much I know."

"Did you see—"

The door flies open and Agnar walks in. "Chimmy said he heard voices and I came straight away. Are you well, my child?"

He drops beside the bed. I scoot out of Erebus's lap and sit beside him. I'm flooded with mixed emotions, some that belong to the mortal version of me, some that belong to the others sharing my body. Part of me wants to embrace this god before me as father, but part of me can not forgive him for hunting down the Children and murdering them. Or for watching Millena die and doing nothing about it, still taking all Haile's orders without question.

"You let her die." It escapes before I can hold it back, and I know the words come from a deep-seeded grudge.

Agnar looks at me with horror. "You have your memories back and think that of me? Think I would let my beloved's murder go unpunished?"

"I don't know what to think," I admit. "My head is a mess, overflowing with memories that feel like mine, yet, do not belong to me."

He nods with pursed lips. "We can work with that, give you a few days before Haile comes to question you."

Erebus and I both look at him with questioning expressions.

"You know what he wants. Now that she is more herself, he is going to come looking, but as long as her head is clouded, she can't be expected to perform," Agnar says.

"Perform what, exactly?" I ask them both.

"Haile wants you to open a new portal to the mortal realm. He wants to be able to travel freely without being summoned as he could years ago. He keeps saying his business with the mortals is *unfinished*," Erebus says.

I snort. "Well, if it's a portal to the mortal realm he wants, he's going to be in for a nasty surprise when he finds out I can't open one to the mortal realm."

Erebus looks at me with confusion. "What do you mean? The Utikalo could open a portal anywhere."

"When they were all together," I remind him. "I do not have the Viitor stone. I am not whole."

FORTY-ONE
EVILS OF MEN
DeLuca

WAKING UP IN LYSETTE's bed was not something I ever planned on. So waking up to beams of sunlight hitting my face next to a soft body snoring—yes, snoring like a damned bear—it's extremely disorienting. She looks so peaceful and unbothered by the rays of light dancing through the window, I decide to let her sleep and gently sneak out of her bed...mostly because it will be awkward as Haile if I stay.

I walk back to my room and change into some clothes left for me. The shirt is made of material that probably cost more than my entire house in Ashe. I feel like such a fraud each time we stay in one of these governing houses, each time they give me their fine clothes and rooms fit for kings. *Especially* when they treat me as an equal.

A knock raps on my door just as I finish buttoning the maroon shirt. Hannah comes in with a cart of coffee. I am instantly transported to a time when the roles were reversed and my fists tighten at the memories.

"Cream or sugar?" Hannah nods to the cart in offering.

"Black is fine. Thank you, Hannah."

"Of course. I'm happy to serve you, sir."

I smile, thinking of Aislinn and her insistence that I drop the formalities when I was serving her. "DeLuca is fine."

Hannah blushes. "I'm happy to serve you, DeLuca. Will you be dining with the Kaillens or in your room today, sir?"

"I'll join the Kaillens. I don't want to be rude when they have shown us such hospitality."

"I will let them know to expect you. Breakfast will be served in an hour." She curtsies before leaving.

A whole hour to kill.

There are many stories I've been told about the highborns that have only provoked more questions for me. Lady Soleil's story about the Guardians most of all. Something about her account of events didn't sit well with me, and I have been anxious to dig to meet another who may fill in the gaps. One such person happens to be here in this very house. I wouldn't say that I'm still gathering intelligence, but old habits die hard, and I am exceedingly curious to meet Sorena Kaillen.

The west wing is just as grand as the rest of the house. Large windows overlook the ocean and bring in natural light that gleams off the gold decor. A statue of Oonaugh stands tall, holding a shimmering trident with a purple sheen in certain light. The spiral staircase wraps around the statue. I'm pretty sure even the paint has gold leaf in it.

Insanity.

Absolute insanity.

They could feed the entire nation for months with the wealth in this one room.

It's not challenging to find Sorena. All I have to do is follow the wailing cries to the end of the corridor, and there she is. In the center of what once was a sitting room sits a clear cage, void of anything other than a woman in her midlife who looks like Lady Kaillen...perhaps a few years older. I'm careful to stick to the shadows, unsure of how my explorations will impact the mood of our hosts.

I study the unhinged woman for a few moments. Sorena Kaillen continues to wail over and over and in the tiny moments between is continuously saying something under her breath. She looks deranged. Like someone has taken a whisk to her mind and left her to fend for herself. Pity sits heavy in my gut as I watch her. Making the decision not to disrupt her fragile mind any more by asking questions about her past. I'm about to turn and leave, but some of her rambling cuts through the cries clearly enough for me to understand the words.

Her voice is hushed, pained, and frantic. "Whispers, so many whispers."

Is it the voices of her victims she hears?

Or her own mind trying to break free?

Breakfast is grand as it always is with these kinds of people. It makes me sick to my stomach looking at the bounty and knowing there are people starving all over Stellera, but I know I must eat to maximize my energy for later.

Do I even need to eat?

What would happen if I didn't? Life would be so much simpler if I never found out about my heritage. But would it really? Eventually, I'd stop aging. I'd have just as many questions about myself, and still, no one to answer them. At least now I have people to help me find answers. Maybe in the gods' realm, I'll find Astoria...maybe she will want to.

"Lysette, tell me what you hope to accomplish by getting the Guardians together," Lady Kaillen says between mouthfuls of poached egg.

Lys clears her throat. "I'm hoping that whatever is left of the Guardians can piece Stellera back together. Perhaps make a safety net plan in case the gods ever decide to come back in a hostile way given our recent contact with them. Be leaders not only for the Children but also for the nation as a whole."

Lady Kaillen folds her hands below her chin and nods as she contemplates Lysette's words. Her husband, Cravan, rolls his eyes. The disrespect for Lysette sends heat coursing through me.

"Something to add, *Earb*?" I ask him.

"They decided they didn't like how we ran things. Let them run it themselves. We are content behind these walls." Craven stirs his tea, takes a sip, then scowls and gives the cup to a serv. "We are close enough to Dailotta we can continue trade there and just let Stellera burn," he says with the arrogance of a highborn lord.

On the word "burn," my opened hand ignites and I let the fire flare in front of me. Not enough to do any damage, but enough to have him push away from the table so quickly he tips out of his chair—hitting the floor with a thud. A serv carrying a fresh cup of tea offers a shaking hand to Craven, but he rejects it with a swat.

"You don't think their treatment by the previous *leaders* had anything to do with the uprising?" I ask with a dare in my voice. Craven looks between Lysette and me with enough hatred I can feel it. My eyes narrow. "I used to be one of those low born servs Haile-bent on overturning the king and governing families. I can tell just by looking at you that if you had spent a single day waiting upon a prick like you that you'd have joined the Liberator's too."

"How dare—" Craven begins but gets cut off with Lady Kaillen places her hand out to silence him.

"Enough, Craven. These are our guests and they will be treated with the respect they deserve."

"Treated how they deserve? Did you not hear the way the freak spoke to me? If this had been my father's house, they'd have been whipped and forced into the Hunt," Craven says with a sad attempt of intimidation aimed toward me.

"Well, as luck would have it, this is *my* house, and we have never whipped a living person like they do in Nylen." Lady Kaillen raises her brows in a challenging expression. Craven doesn't rise to the bait. He simply grabs a piece of toast and walks out of the dining room with an expression that is too calculated for my liking.

"I apologize on behalf of my husband. He has not taken too well to Nylen being overthrown by the Liberators. His father and brother were both killed in an effort to defend their house."

Good. Nylen was the worst of all. Pierce had been a serv there, and his wife also, before she was taken to one of Lord Earh's games. The disgusting excuse for a lord liked to hunt. He liked to hunt what he could not have—women. He was as twisted on the outside as he was on the inside. But he was rich, and he was powerful. The very image of the evils of men.

Sick bastard.

I hope Helena dragged him straight to the Shadows and he is facing whatever version of his worst nightmare there is. If I were the one deciding, I'd make him participate in one of his own games...as the hunted. Break him over and over as he had to countless servs.

Hannah comes in and whispers something to Lady Kaillen. Lady Kaillen huffs out a breath in response but nods. "I must excuse myself. I wish you luck on your journey, DeLuca. I swear to keep Lysette out of harm's way, on my name and on my house she is safe with me." Lady Kaillen nods, and as much as I want to not trust her, my gut tells me she means what she says. Despite being married to one of the realm's worst families.

The trail of footprints left in the wet sand disappears into the distance. The Leviathan's cavern is a few miles away from the edge of Rilyse. It's a brutally cold day, especially with the wind carrying ocean mist over us. I've created a kind of shield of air to keep the elements out and have been using my body's heat to warm it.

I can't help but think of Lysette walking back alone. I'm not too worried for her safety. She can take care of herself...but I do worry about her comfort. She shouldn't suffer because of her decision to help me.

"Are you ready for this?" Lysette asks as we follow the shoreline to the cavern.

"I'm ready to get her back, so I *have* to be ready for the rest."

"Remember, the isvitoks do not take kindly to men, nor will Oonaugh if she is there...and DeLuca, if using the Water Stone doesn't work, you will cease to exist. It's possible, Haile...it's probable. You very well might not make it back from this."

"I *know* what's at risk, Lys." My voice is clipped, not to be harsh, but because I know how serious this is.

"I know you know. I just felt like I had to say it again." Her hand slides in mine and she squeezes. She goes to pull it back out, but I tighten my grip on her wrist.

"Thank you, Lys. For all the help you've given me to get her back. Anything you ever need from me...all you have to do is name it."

She smiles while pulling her hand back. "Ailie is my family too. I didn't do it for you."

We walk the rest of the way in an awkward kind of quiet, the kind where your thoughts are almost loud enough to be heard outside of the safety of your mind. It makes the time stretch on until we are finally moving around a series of jagged rocks beside a large cliff.

"Shit," I say as I take in the enormous cavern. It almost has the shape of a giant worm with giant jagged teeth.

Lysette nods.

"Are you going to stick around and watch or head back?"

She bites her lip. "I'll wait here for an hour. If you don't come back, I'll head to Rilyse."

My stomach bottoms out and my instincts tell me not to leave her, but what choice do I have? It's already been months—I can't wait any longer.

I nod. "Just whatever happens, whatever you hear, don't come in after me."

"I know," she whispers. We stand there for a second, not really sure what to do, before she groans and pulls me into a hug. "Come back, Lucy Rain. I've lost too many people as it is. Just...please come back."

"I'll do everything I can. I swear it. Be safe. Be smart." I kiss the top of her head, then shrug off the heavy leather jacket—draping it over Lysette's shoulders.

She smiles, but neither of us say anything more. There's no use prolonging the goodbye when it's already so hard. As I turn toward the cavern's mouth, my muscles clench so hard they could pop so that I maintain control of my own body to not look back.

This is it.

I'm coming, Aislinn.

The already chilled air rapidly plummets the deeper into the cave I go. I hear nothing but my own steady breathing. The sound of ocean waves has been silenced. Even the smell of salt water has faded into an overpowering stone scent that is not unlike the streets of Caeliss. Sharp rocks jab out from all angles, and I have to be very conscious of where I step. It's pitch black in here, but I've created a ball of flame to light my way. The moment I hear the sound of dripping water, I halt. My skin prickles with warning.

A warning far too late as I find eyes on me.

There's a soft song filling my ears that lulls me into an unnatural state of calm. My orb of fire is extinguished by a wave of water, and before I can call another forth, the pair of pale blue eyes glowing against the dark of the cavern stare at me.

A sharp pain stabs through the base of my spine. I drop to the floor. Fire has never hurt me, but the flame consuming my legs burns in a way I haven't felt since I was a child in that mining explosion.

Gods, the pain is unbearable! I will go mad from it!

I can't form coherent words as the warmth spreads until I lose all mobility in my body. Two metal bands snap around my hands.

Through the agony, I try to call forth my fire, but nothing comes, not even a flicker.

I try to call forth any of the elements. Anything to get free. Nothing answers.

An unseen force ties my shackled hands together and begins to pull me along the ground. I can't turn my head to get my nose out the thin layer of water coating the muddy sea cave. I try twisting my body, but I have no control over my power or body.

I have no control.

FORTY-TWO
ENDLESS SKY
Aislinn

 EREBUS LEFT TO DO his rounds in the Shadows, leaving me with the time I need to set things in motion. With my memories slowly defogging and new information surfacing, I've been trying to sort through it all. It's harder than I care to admit, but a real viable plan is taking shape.

Part of my preparations heavily rely on Chimmy and his ability to move around unnoticed...as well as his loyalty and dedication to protecting balance. He seemed grateful to be given a purpose after receiving the small package, and thanks to my newest memories, I strongly feel I can put my faith in him.

Agnar has been following me around like a stray dog all day. I think he expects some divine moment where I realize my love for him and all else is forgiven.

That's not going to happen.

I don't condone the murder of children, for any reason.

He still can prove useful. I may not be able to see the future without Viitor, at least not clearly like I can the past and present, but I do know a great war is coming. One that will involve both mortal and god. Both realms. It could be the end of all things or the beginning of a new way of life, and I don't want to be caught unprepared and useless.

I want to at the very least know how to defend myself and those close to me. Fortunately, I have just the god to help me achieve this.

"I'm glad you have finally taken an interest in strengthening your body and not just your mind," Agnar says with a proud grin as he opens the door to his training room. It's a mostly bare room with a soft red floor and weapons of every kind lining each wall.

"Are they aietal?" I ask, eyeing an intricate double-sided axe.

"No, we don't keep aietal here. There is an armory enchanted to remain locked, no god can access it."

"Then why even keep them if no one has access to them?"

He looks at me as though he's internally struggling with some kind of decision. "Aietal is made from a metal indigenous to the Fiorian Mountains, the ones that surround the Shadows, if you don't remember."

Memories flash through my mind of the liquid metal gliding through crevices of the mountain. "I remember, go on."

"The metal is created when the Fiorian lava mixes with the waters of the Lake of Eternal Life, a place of second chances." He runs his finger down the blade of the double-sided axe. "The shadows who refuse their walk through Oblivion are to swim in it. If worthy, they get a do-over at life in the mortal realm. If not, they become guardians, more animal than human, and bound to one place for the rest of eternity. This same water that grants second chances also makes the metal indestructible, even to gods."

I hadn't known that. I must have, in some lifetime. But the information is just...gone. Each time I'm close to grasping answers, they fall deeper and deeper into a fuzzy void where memories used to live and have since withered and died.

"But the lava that flows from the other side of the Fiorians—the side bordering the Afterlands—also run into the Lake of Eternal Life, creating a different mineral we call imperialite. It is aeital's counterpart. It makes us invincible. Enhancing our strength tenfold. These weapons you see here are forged from imperialite."

I take in the opalescent sheen on each of the blades and am struck with realization. In Caeliss...the houses were made of imperialite... Alec told us the ground was rich with it. Is it possible that the meteor Astoria sent to create the safe haven had been made of it too? If so...she was trying to give us a fighting chance.

Then why wouldn't she have given us aietal? Or maybe that wasn't her purpose at all...but if not to make her children stronger...then why?

"What is the metal called that crafts the aietal?" I ask.

Agnar lifts the double-sided axe off the wall and starts swinging absent mindedly as if reliving a battle of its past. "Volcorium."

My eyes widen as the pieces fall into place, and I turn towards the god of war in shock.

He places the axe back on the wall and wears a proud expression as he says, "The Obsidian Mountains were my way of trying to balance the scales."

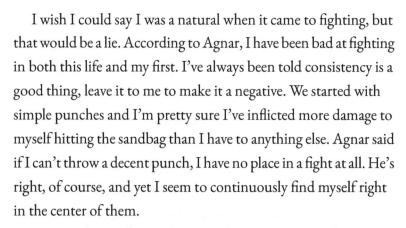

I wish I could say I was a natural when it came to fighting, but that would be a lie. According to Agnar, I have been bad at fighting in both this life and my first. I've always been told consistency is a good thing, leave it to me to make it a negative. We started with simple punches and I'm pretty sure I've inflicted more damage to myself hitting the sandbag than I have to anything else. Agnar said if I can't throw a decent punch, I have no place in a fight at all. He's right, of course, and yet I seem to continuously find myself right in the center of them.

Between the sandbag and a strength training circuit that has my muscles screaming, all I want is a hot bath and a good night of sleep, but I still have the Weavers to contend with. They have to have answers for the tampered memories, and I'm determined to get them to talk. I know how conniving they can be, especially when they face resistance against their woven fates.

Leaving without an escort was a bit of a challenge, but I reminded Agnar that he *did* give me permission to roam all of Kaoket and that I needed space to try and trigger more memories. A lie, and one that didn't help sway him in the least. What finally did it was the reminder that keeping me in the palace would be against my will, and therefore he put his own skin at risk thanks to Kato's enchantment.

An eerie quiet blankets the Imorti Woods, magnifying the crunch of dead leaves below my boots tenfold. Why do the Weavers prefer this side of Kaoket? Who wouldn't choose the bright colors and cheerful feeling of the Vivatus Forest, where the strange sun never stops shining and everything feels enchanted?

Over here, it is dark and gray and dreary. I find this atmosphere calming, but I feel most wouldn't. It reminds me of something...of home? I'm not sure which home, it's more of the feeling of home rather than a place. A large rustling of wings, followed by a gust of wind makes me stop dead in my tracks with a slight prickle of anticipation.

"I know you're here, Helena."

"Damn. I knew the wind was too much." Helena drops down from a tree and lands by my side. "I've missed you. I was so bored on Shadow duty while my brother played valiant knight." She pouts.

A laugh slips through my lips. "You act as though you were there for a century. It's only been a day."

She makes a disgusted face with one eye squinted and her tongue hanging out. "A day in the Shadows feels like a century, Aisli-kins."

I shake my head, about to make fun of her, but then I remember her reaction being close to the Abyss. There are things I don't need to know unless she wants to tell them. I change the subject. "What are you doing here?"

"I wanted to hang out with my bestie! Some friends and I were talking about you one moment and the next I was here...but why are we in the Imorti Woods? This place creeps me out." She fakes a shudder.

"You're the daughter of Death and a bunch of trees creep you out?"

"It's not the trees. It's the creatures that roam through them."

A rustling sounds behind us. She jumps and turns, smacking me with a portion of her very large wing. "Did you do that to mess with me?"

"How would I have made a sound coming from behind us?" I arch my brow and pull a white feather from my hair.

She exhales loudly. "Shit. Wherever you were going, let's hurry up and get there."

The Opari Stone pulses with power as I close my eyes and focus on the noise, searching for its creator. There's a flash through the woods and I follow it in my mind until I find what I'm looking for—a woman with midnight hair and a murderous expression.

"Isela is following us," I say under my breath.

"Better than that winged beast I guess." Helena laughs.

"I wouldn't underestimate her."

"I don't underestimate *any* of my peers. Wh—" She gets cut off when we become swarmed by large fuzzy insects with stingers...they're almost like bees, but the size of a fist.

"What in the name of all things?" I shout through the constant buzzing. "How do you have bees in this realm?"

"We don't!" Helena shouts, "Isela must have sent them! She loves these pollinating bastards!"

The buzzing intensifies as the insects swarm toward us. They're coming too fast, locked on their target, and my gut tells me I really don't want them to catch us.

"Can you fly us out of here?" I ask over the buzzing.

"I can try." She grabs hold of me and takes off for the sky.

The bees follow and easily catch up despite her speed. They multiply rapidly, obscuring our vision. All I can think about is getting out of here to safety. My veins vibrate—with fear or power, I can't tell. My eyes are shut and I picture DeLuca and getting back to him. I can't die here.

Helena screams. My ears ring and vision warps. Space and time flash around us in chaotic bursts, and all at once, everything ends.

The bees drop dead in a circle around us. If I look over the cliff we're standing on, an endless sky of swirling color looms below. As I walk closer to a bridge that seemingly leads to nowhere, my body runs into something solid. I place my hands in front of me and run them along the invisible wall blocking off the broken bridge.

"We're at the barrier..." Helena says.

"The Barrier? Why did you bring us here?" She doesn't expect me to open it, does she?

Her brows pinch and she squints. "I didn't. *You* did."

"Me? I was just thinking I wanted to be somewhere safe..."

Her violet eyes widen with realization. "You tried to go back to the mortal realm."

"I didn't! Well, I didn't mean to."

Did I? No...I wanted...I wanted DeLuca. Oh...gods...I tried to portal to him.

She places her hands on my shoulders and shakes me. Judging off her behavior, you'd never guess we were nearly attacked moments ago. "So, you *can* portal!"

Apparently. "I don't know."

"Try on the barrier! Try to get through it. You can go home!" Her eyes sparkle with hope while she gestures toward the invisible wall.

"I don't know how, Helena!"

"Just try!" She almost cries. Her voice is coated in desperation, it reminds me of Audrina's in the vision Erebus had shown me. So, with guilt pulling my strings, I put my hand up to the invisible barrier and try to move past it, to open a hole, a tear, anything. I push all my power into it the intention. My teeth chatter from the exertion, but I keep firm.

"Let. Me. In!"

I'm not sure if I voice the command or if it's in my head. The sheer overwhelming pressure coaxes a final scream of exertion before the barrier finally gives. Instead of breaking through, it consumes me. Drags me into the depths of my own mind.

No, wait, this isn't *my* mind.

There is no ground below me, only wisps of clouds darkened by the night sky that stretches on forever. Despite being suspended in midair, I am surprisingly calm. In fact, this is the most tranquil I have ever been in my life. It's like the air is made of serenity. There's a waterfall of stardust in the distance, and I swim towards it in languid strokes as easily as swimming through the rivers of Vallae.

The stardust waterfall parts as I approach, revealing a cave-like opening made of more clouds, I am greeted by a goddess whose dark skin glows beneath silver paint. Her shimmering white hair is adorned with a diamond tiara, and below it, silver-speckled blue eyes fix on me with curiosity.

"Hello." Her voice is soothing like chimes blowing in the wind. "I don't believe we have met. My name is Astoria."

FORTY-THREE
NAME OF OTHERS
Aislinn

I'M STARING. I KNOW I'm staring, but I don't know how to stop. It's just so...*so* unreal.

"Astoria...how is that possible?"

Astoria circles me, her eyes scanning in a way that is similar to one trying to solve a puzzle. "A question I share. How is it that I sense both Forbis and Opari within you, yet a third who is most definitely not Viitor and feels like a mortal barely more than a child? Who are you?"

A fair question, one that doesn't have a straightforward answer. "Forbis's shadow is bound to mine. I am a distant descendant of theirs...as for Opari..." I hold out my arm to show her where the Siphon Stone is still firmly in place. "Your husband decided to reunite two-thirds of the Utikalo using me as the vessel."

Astoria looks concerned, eyes flashing from my arm to my face. "Why would he do such a thing as this?"

"To save you."

"Save me? From what?" She gestures around her sanctuary. "I am perfectly content."

"Astoria...you're trapped in a barrier. Your mind, it seems, is well an intact here, but the version of you he has, the version

Erebus visits each night and talks to and cares for…it's nothing but a shell."

"A shell? My body remains in the Shadow Palace?"

"It does."

She scoffs. "And how, pray tell, did my husband intend to 'fix' me?"

"By erasing himself."

Astoria's eyes snap to mine. "He wouldn't dare!"

"That's what he said. He's been working with me to enhance my abilities so I can perfect my time-walking to do it."

She sits on a cloud procured from thin air. "Typical. That does sound so very like him. Always the one to sacrifice in the name of others."

"Are we talking about the same Erebus?"

She smiles and forms another cloud, gesturing for me to sit. "He has his moments, I admit, but he is the most selfless god I have ever known." I look at her skeptically, and she laughs. "Here, Forbis, allow me to feed you some memories." She reaches out her hand in offering and I hastily take it. The moment our skin touches, I'm pulled into bright white starlight and thrown into her memories, but I am no longer me.

I am Astoria.

The strange sun seems less strange. The glow coating the Vivatus has dulled to a shimmer, and the air seems to be singing. I'm following behind a goddess I recognize, one with hair both dark and light—Millena.

"Your father will be busy with the new court," Millena says in a hushed voice. "You should go while discussions are heating up. He's waiting at the base of the Fiorans."

She leads me past the Vivatus and into the Imorti which is no longer a skeletal wasteland—but covered in glowing spheres and iridescent plants. It's as if someone has painted all the remnants of previous life with a joyous new beginning. My heart swells at the complete beauty and celebration.

Millena leaves me—Astoria—near the place where I know the secret cave and portal to the Pure Ones is hidden.

"I will keep my brothers distracted and give you as much time as I can. Make it count." Millena kisses my cheeks and dissipates into specs of light floating on the wind.

I shudder while walking through the mouth of the cave as a draining sensation fills my body. Astoria's heart races with anticipation.

"I don't like the feeling of being powerless." Her voice passes through my lips.

"My darling starlight, you're never powerless," Erebus says, stepping out from beyond the darkness. He takes my hand and holds it to his cheek, looking completely vulnerable and unlike I've ever seen him. "Someday we will no longer have to hide in the shadows."

"The Shadows is exactly where I want to be, dasi istaleia." A moon-like glow flickers out around us.

Erebus rubs the hair out of my eyes, and for the first time, I see him as he is. No shadows following him. No icy air. No dark aura. Just him, and he's beautiful. Our lips crash in a tsunami of need and *pure desire. My body trembles. The need to bring our bodies closer is overwhelming. Our hands roam each over each other, and just as Erebus begins removing clothing, the memory transforms, taking us to a glowing meadow outside the Shadow Palace.*

We're looking up at the night sky. My head rests on Erebus's shoulder as we lay in the grass. Erebus has shadows dancing across the field, leaving trails of luminescence in their wake. His cold is comforting and lulls me in to relaxation.

"You did great work on these, wife," Erebus says in my ear while pointing up toward the sky.

"I'm not finished." Astoria's voice passes through my lips, and my hand—her hand—reaches for the stars.

Two new constellations appear side by side. Upon first inspection, they look like random swirls and a crescent moon, but I know them for what they are, shadows and moonlight, Erebus and Astoria. She finishes it off by adding three stars brighter than any other in the sky. One at the beginning of the swirls. One at the tip of the moon. And the third, between the two, forever connecting them.

"There, now they're done."

He runs the tip of his nose along my shoulder and kisses the top of it. "You are truly incredible, do you know that, starlight?"

I bite my lips and wait. I don't know what I'm waiting for. I'm just looking at Erebus expectantly, and his brows draw as if he's trying to figure it out as well. I point to the center star. Erebus's hand clasps over mine to trace it. Then he sits up rapidly with widened eyes.

"Astoria? Are you...are we..." He's speechless and breathing rapidly. It's as if he can't say the words in fear of being disappointed if the answer isn't what he's hoping for.

I get up and stand beside him, placing his hands on my soft belly. "Our child."

Erebus repeats in a whisper, "Our child." And when I look up, I see tears gathering in his eyes and then they blur through my own. All around us, stars begin to fall like liquid diamonds. He huffs out a laugh filled with joyous wonder and...love. So much love.

"We will be better than those before us," I say, kissing him gently.

"On my life, we will be." Erebus smiles, still holding my belly in the softest caress. "Darling, I wish to freeze this moment. Will you help me?"

Wiping away tears, I say, "of course."

Erebus removes his shirt, fingers slowly unlatching each button while keeping his eyes on mine. Astoria's body reacts in a way that feels like bursts of starlight kissing her skin. His sly grin says he knows exactly where her mind has gone as he shrugs off the shirt completely.

He nods me over, and in the same gesture, a swirl of shadows encapsulates his arms, back, and chest. I place my hand in the mix of freezing shadows. Pushing my magic within them, it looks like a little storm with flashes of light within the clouded shadows. When the flurry of our combined ability settles, Erebus stands before me, shirtless, sculpted, and covered in constellations that mirror the ones surrounding us.

"Beautiful," I say, marveling at what we can create together.

"Beautiful," he agrees, staring into my eyes in such a way that makes me feel like he's seeing into my very heart.

The memory again warps until I'm screaming in agony.

I'm laying on a chaise coated in starlight, my arms shadow-chained to the floor. My bones are breaking. Every one of them. There's a creature trying to claw its way out of my stomach.

"You can do this, Astoria. Just a little more, my darling," Erebus says from the foot of the chaise. His face is contrite with worry.

"Move aside, let the god of life bring the little one forth," Haile says from his place in the corner. He's wearing a hooded cloak and pants but no shirt, so his swirling gold tattoos are on display.

"You think I'm letting you anywhere near this child?" Erebus grits out, but the words are drowned out by another of my screams as a burning pain between my legs becomes so unbearable I'd rather die than endure another moment of it.

"As long as you stay true to your word, I have no cause to harm this new life," Haile says firmly.

"Father, please!" I scream, not even knowing what I'm begging for.

Haile's eyes soften and there's a gust of golden light, then a flash of silver between my legs. The combination is blinding.

My senses pulse in and out. Then, we hear it. The sound of little lungs screaming out for the very first time.

Desperation fills the body I'm inhabiting and panic claws at my rationale.

"Let me hold him!" Astoria says through my lips as Haile wraps the baby in a black cloak.

"No, starlight...my love, it's better this way," Erebus says, taking the baby from Haile. The baby stops wailing as it looks up at Erebus. He hiccups—transforming into a bear then back again, and a smile dancing on it's tiny lips.

Haile nods at Erebus as I begin to thrash against the shadow chains holding me in place.

That's the last I see of him before Erebus disappears in his blast of shadows.

I'm screaming again.

Screaming in pain and in rage, and I have never felt a brokenness quite like this. Nothing compares to the ache in my chest. There's emptiness in my belly where my child had grown, and now there is nothing.

My child.

My baby.

Empty.

And I am ripped into yet another memory.

Another birth, the same pain.

Again.

And again.

And again.

Each time, I feel that hole in my chest widen until it has consumed me completely. Erebus is always there. Always whispering sweet words, but there's a coldness in him that wasn't there at the beginning. After a while, I can't even bear to look at him.

When it's finally over...after dozens of babies are ripped from the realm they belong to, I'm back in the cave made of clouds, sitting with the very woman who endured hundreds of heartbreaks.

"I'm so sorry." These are the only words I can manage between the tears soaking my cheeks.

Astoria cups my cheek and wipes the tears away with her thumb. She wears a sad smile, and silver lines her eyes.

"Each time, I came here." She gestures around us, and stars come to life with the movement. "I tried to leave my grief. I suppose after enough time, there wasn't anything else left."

FORTY-FOUR
THE GAME
Erebus

THE SHADOW BOND BETWEEN my pet and I is stretched to its limits. Any tighter and it may snap. After following the pull, I find myself standing on the edge of the realm, staring at Helena while she holds an unconscious Aislinn in her lap. My shadows hiss and I pinch the bridge of my nose. I cannot leave that mortal alone for an hour without coming back to her unconscious or missing. When I got a new pet, I had not expected for her to be quite so untrainable.

There's a grotesque crunch beneath my boot, and I lift it to see a squashed insect, which is odd considering we don't have insects in this realm.

"What is this?" I ask Helena while pointing at the hundreds of carcasses ailing the ground in a circle around the two girls.

"Isela." She shrugs as if that one name was answer enough.

Just what I need, *more* gods interfering. I inhale deeply and on the exaggerated exhale ask, "Why?"

"She was stalking after us in the Imorti Woods."

"Must I really ask *why* again?"

She looks up and flutters her lashes. "I don't know. Go ask her."

I scowl. "And Aislinn?"

"Touched the barrier and her eyes rolled back. I think she's in a vision."

"Why are you two at the barrier at all?"

Helena bites her lip and looks as though she is deciding whether or not to tell me.

"Out with it, Helena."

"She uh...she portaled us here when we were swarmed by the bees."

I straighten the cuff of my suit jacket. "So Isela probably saw her portal? Which means it is very likely she told Haile already?"

Helena shrugs.

I run my hand over the side of my jaw. "Just one day, just one boring day is all I ask."

"You've had hundreds of years of boredom. Come on, admit you love this game just as much as the rest of us?" She smiles.

"I enjoy very little. The *game,* as you call it, is not on that list. Come now, sister, let us take the girl back to the Shadows."

"I don't think we should move her."

"Why not?"

"It feels like she's speaking to someone."

"Speaking to whom?"

Helena shrugs again. I shut my eyes while trying to rein in my frustration before I pluck every feather from her wings.

"Fine. We will wait here." I motion for her to hand Aislinn over.

"Get your grubby shadow fingers away from her! She doesn't need to wake up with any more unwanted marks!"

"What makes you certain they are unwanted?" I grin, and she recoils in disgust.

"As if she'd be interested in anything you wanted to give her when you stole her from her life!"

Her blow hit its mark. I've never struggled with a conscience before, except for when it came to Astoria and the things I've done to hurt her, but I find myself reflecting on the time before Aislinn came to stay with us and her first few days in the Shadows. I wonder what might have been if I'd gone about it differently, if I had been warmer, perhaps explained things better before she left the breeding ground she once called home.

A smile creeps along my face as I imagine it.

She wouldn't have liked me at all if I'd been warmer.

Whether she admits it or not, my little pet is just as dark as I am. She feels the draw. I see the struggle each time she's in the Shadows. She's comfortable there.

"Why does your face look like that?" Helena asks.

"He can't help it. It's just his face," Aislinn says from Helena's arms where she now stirs awake.

I'm flooded with a peculiar weightlessness that has me feeling good enough to ignore the jab. "What did you see?"

My little pet is staring at me in a way I've never seen before. It is rather uncomfortable, and my shadows stir at the uneasiness. "You're going to want to steady yourself before I tell you."

"I assure you, I could not be more steady. Tell me, Aislinn, what did you see?"

"I saw Astoria," she says.

"Saw Astoria what?"

Her eyes narrow, and I feel as though they're looking into the deepest corner of my being. "I saw Astoria herself. Her mind is torn—stuck in the barrier."

Stuck in the barrier... I gape at the invisible wall. Placing a hand to it. It is faint...but there is a hint of Astoria's power, a small pulse...how have I never noticed before?

Helena gasps. "How?"

"Because Astoria created the barrier. In the throes of grief, she wanted to be sure she never felt that pain again. After each child lost, she'd spend time here. Leaving the parts of herself she no longer wanted...her grief."

"All this time?" I ask, clenching my fists to hide my trembling hands, hide how close I am to falling off the edge. A heavy feeling sits on my chest as I think of my wife so broken she had to hide herself away. She hid this from me. When we shared everything together, she hid this from *me*.

"All this time. The barrier is a manifestation of the wall she put up to guard herself. She didn't mean to, but she's stuck there now."

"Fuck," I say under a breath with realization, "Isolvie peittviot y'taluolo kue."

"Split barrier, not whole?" Helena asks. "What kind of absolute gibberish is that?"

"Astoria said it in her sleep. She was trying to tell me. She was asking for help."

Now that I have blown off a bit of steam in the Abyss, I am ready to face the problem. My pet is safely tucked away in her chambers for the night, so I do not feel the need to continuously check in on her and am free of distraction.

Admitting I was wrong is not something I think I am capable of, but perhaps I was looking at the picture in the wrong light. Aislinn is essentially useless to me now. If she breaks through the barrier to tunnel the new shadows in, she may destroy Astoria for good. I'd rather watch this entire realm fall apart than take that risk. Knowing Haile, he will not put Astoria's life above his own ambition. He is not to be trusted with this new revelation until absolutely necessary.

My teeth crack against one another as I bite down and try to figure out a way out of this mess. It is delicate, this whole predicament. Should I have brought Aislinn here? Likely not. Do I regret it? No. Will I send her back? Also, no.

I cannot have the other gods talking. She is a part of my household whether she likes it or not. Those markings claim her for the Shadows as one of us. I could perhaps kill her mortal body sooner rather than later...but I do not know for sure if that would release Forbis from her vessel, and time-walking is still a viable option, but how far back do we go? To the last birth? The day we learned of the prophecy?

Astoria would have the answers I seek. My only trusted confidante...but if she were here, I wouldn't be in this position, would I? It does not sit well with me knowing that she hid her grief, not only from herself, but from me. Why did she not trust me with it? Did she not know how I grieved too?

When I round the corner to head to my library, Helena is leaning against the wall waiting just as I knew she would be.

"Helena." I walk by her and wait for whatever foolishness she wants to spill out.

"I think it's time, don't you?" she asks.

My eyes flare and I wrap us both in a vortex of illusion in case of spies. "Helena, discretion, we do not want you ending up like your mother, do we?"

She rolls her eyes. "I think we're past discretion. Can't you feel the shift in the air?"

"I feel it, but it is no concern of ours."

"No conc—Erebus! This realm concerns us. If it implodes, we go with it, as does the mortal realm. The king would ruin us all for pride."

"I will not release him from his punishment, Helena."

"He is one of the few that can kill a god with nothing but his own raw power. If there is ever a fight, it will be between the two of them. No one else would stand a chance, and you know it."

"Yes, I do know it."

"So *release* our father."

"He killed my mother," I say plainly.

"We all have dead mothers and evil fathers. Stop living in the past and use your stupid brain. The king can't keep on the way he has. You know the old word better than anyone. You know this is all wrong."

"Helena, I will not waste my energy on this right now. I have gotten some rather shocking news about my wife today, if you do not recall, and I need to deal with that before anything else."

She folds her arms across her chest. "Oh yes, how could I expect you to care for anything other than your precious *starlight*?"

"Careful, sister, I may tolerate your shenanigans, but I will not hesitate to put you in your place if you force my hand."

Helena looks as if she has a snide remark on the tip of her tongue, but her features soften at the flare of shadows and she changes course. "What about her?"

"Who?"

"Aislinn? What is your plan for her?"

"I have yet to decide. She is little more than a pet now that my plans have been thwarted."

Helena's eyes shift, and I doubt anything good will come of whatever thought she's had. All she says is a low "mmm" and steps out from my illusion. "Well, it's been a long night. Happy brooding."

She salutes me with two fingers above the brow and takes off, blowing back dozens of books. With an agitated breath, I catch them all before they hit the ground. That sister of mine is always stirring up trouble. One of these days, I'm not going to be able to save her from it.

FORTY-FIVE
A HUNDRED BURDENS
DeLuca

THE DAYS THAT I'VE been alone in this damp cave of nightmares has me questioning my sanity. I only see slivers of them, crawling along the walls to bring me food or water.

They want me alive, that much is clear.

They have not spoken.

I don't know if they *can* speak.

Each time the glow of their eyes becomes visible through the darkness beyond, I hear this song. This beautiful, captivating song that puts me to sleep, and when I wake up, a cooked fish and chalice full of fresh water are there.

The manacles they chained me to the floor with block my gifts, however, I do have full function of my limbs again. The creatures pulled out whatever poison-dipped needle was wedged in my spine, and thank Felix, the effects weren't permanent.

The cave floor is covered in a layer of water, I am constantly wet and without access to my fire. Never before have I felt cold like this. I'd almost rather them kill me than endure this a day longer. But I still have people counting on me, and death is not an option.

"You're awake," a female voice says. It's alluring beyond measure and dripping with its hypnotic waves.

"Who's there?" I ask against the darkness, fighting the seductive emotions being forced upon me.

"Hmm, an odd question considering you came to me...one I had wished to ask. Who are you? A man, yes, but no mortal, no. So how did you come to be here, *god?* Did Soren send you?"

"I wasn't sent. I came on my own volition, in search of a portal."

In a flash, two bright eyes the color of sea glass are before me. Her deep auburn hair is braided with various shells strung through it. With soft features, she looks to be in her late teens. She looks...*innocent*...but with a heavy energy liked she carries the weight of a hundred burdens.

"What makes you think you could use my portal?" she asks, running a sharp nail along the side of my face.

This must be Oonaugh.

If what Lysette said is true about her hating men, I need to tread carefully. "I have water magic. I thought I could trick it into thinking I'm you." I answer honestly, knowing full well that I am at a disadvantage.

She starts laughing so close to my face that I can taste her breath. It's intoxicating. Every bit of this girl is a trap meant to lure and entice.

"Silly man. You can not trick portals with magic. It would be too easy."

"Is there *any* way to get through?"

"The cruel irony is that you can only pass with the blood flowing through my veins, but I've been bound to this cavern. I cannot leave."

Despair and grief stir with the helplessness that already sat heavy in my chest.

My last shard of hope.

Gone.

"So you only came for my portal and not my body?" She pouts and rubs the wall beside me, releasing a bioluminescent light and revealing her naked body. She has scales the color of her eyes covering large patches, but not enough.

I avert my gaze instantly. "I have no interest in your body."

"No?" she questions with a sultry voice. "What about my isvitoks? Or I believe the mortals may call them *sirens*? What about *their* bodies?" She gestures behind her, and six women, also naked with patches of scales, walk closer and into the glowing light.

"I don't have any interest in any woman's body except one." My voice is firm with my conviction.

"I can taste lies." She hisses.

"I'm not lying. I need to get to the gods' realm to save the woman who means everything to me."

Her lip curves into a snarl. "So you hunt this poor girl then?"

"No. Like I said, I'm *saving* her. She was taken."

"Taken?" Oonaugh perks at this. The sirens behind her straighten their spines.

"Yes. Erebus took her, and I intend to get her back."

"Erebus?" She looks genuinely confused by this.

"Yes."

Oonaugh begins whispering to her creatures in Old Daeil. There's a flurry of hisses and wails between words I do not understand. Oonaugh finally turns towards me again. "We do not trust the words of men. They are tricksters. They are monsters. They take and they take. They feel entitled to our bodies and care little for our minds. When we deny them, they take it anyway."

It takes me a minute to unravel her words, and when I finally figure out her meaning, my blood boils—even without my fire. "I would never, *never*, force a woman against her will."

"I want to call you a liar like the rest." She pushes my hair back out of my face. "But *that* did not taste like a lie."

"Because it's not, and if I ever met a bastard who did, I would give them a slow agonizing death befitting their crime."

Oonaugh's eyes glow brighter as she smiles and reveals teeth sharpened to points. "*That* was also not a lie," she says with confidence. She turns back to her sirens and again converses with them in Old Daeil. The isvitoks seem angry, and Oonaugh appears to be trying to calm them, but considering I don't know Old Daeil, I have absolutely no idea what she is saying.

The sea goddess shushes the creatures and gives me her full attention. "We have decided to let you go to this woman who holds your heart, but be warned—I have many sisters hiding in this cave, all with poisoned barbs ready to strike if you move against us."

"Oonaugh, I'm not here to hurt you."

She sighs with an exhale. "Truth."

Oonaugh takes my shackled wrists in one hand, then gestures her other hand out as if she is expecting something. One of the isvitoks produces a key and places it into Oonaugh's opened hand. She unlocks the shackles, and they drop. The moment they are gone, I feel the stir of power swell beneath my skin. My shoulders roll as I adjust to it and let its familiarity wash over me.

"Since I am inclined to help you, *man*, I wish to know your name."

"DeLuca."

"*DeLuca.*" She squints. "Lie."

I sigh. "Half lie. I am called DeLuca by most...or Luc. My name is Rainier DeLuca."

She purrs out my name. "Rainier. That too, is not a full truth, but I suspect you do not know your truth." Oonaugh moves behind me, running those long fingernails down my neck. "I require a promise for my help."

"And what is that?"

"Mmm." She licks her lips and eyes me with a burning desire. "Two promises, I suppose."

"I will do anything. Name your price."

"Good. First thing, you find a way to retrieve my trident from the mortals in Rilyse so I can be rid of the curse binding me to the waters."

"Done." I don't even have to think about it. I'd give her the very air from my lungs if that was her price.

She moves in front of me and places both hands around my neck. "Second, you will bring me Soren. *Alive.* You may hurt him. In fact, I encourage it. But I want him alive."

"Why?"

She pulls her hands away with a snarl. "Because he is a disease among the living, and I want to watch him feel just as powerless as I did."

"The stories of old say that you became jealous when he took a mortal lover and that you turned her into a beast so no man would love her again."

She gives a half laugh that tells me she is in no way amused. "It never ceases to surprise me what mortals will believe. Writings by corrupt old men with agendas towards more power and control." She scoffs.

"Then what happened?"

"Do you care?"

"Yes."

She looks surprised to find honesty in the word. "Very well. Let's find a place to sit. The story is long and unpleasant, and I wish to not tell it in this damp cave."

She grabs my hand and leads through the dank tunnels until they open to larger passages. The spacious cavern's walls are lit with bioluminescent light. The deeper we go, the brighter and more colorful it becomes. We get to a carved archway and my breath ceases to exist as I take in the cove and all its splendor. Centered is a lagoon so blue it almost brings tears to my eyes. That same bioluminescence found throughout the passages covers every inch of the cave walls and floor, but beneath the glow, I can make out an opalescent sheen that is similar to the homes in Caeliss.

The six sirens jump in and my jaw hangs slack as I watch their feet transform into fishlike tails with barbed stingers at the end.

Oonaugh watches them with a grin as they swim under a bridge that leads to another room I cannot see.

She gestures to the water. "The water has healing properties. It can cure anything. It used to be a hidden doorway to the other realm, to their Lake of Eternal Life, but the door has long been locked. My portal isn't located within this watery prison. Being bound to the Lake of Eternal Life's water, I unfortunately can not reach it."

"How did you get bound?"

"By Isela, for daring to speak against her favorite son." She pats the ground beside her as she sticks her feet into the water. I sit and stick my feet in too. It seems to be singing to my body, and the Siphon Stone containing my water magic hums within my pocket. Oonaugh stares at the place where it hides with curiosity, as if she hears the call too.

"What happened to you, Oonaugh?"

"Hmm, so much, Rainier, so much. We will start at the beginning then." She tips her head back with her eyes closed. "I am the youngest of the Made-Gods."

"Made?"

Her chin drops and she looks me in the eye. "Made by Kato, of course."

"Ah." *Who the fuck is Kato?*

"I was *made* around the same time Soren was *born* To Haile and Isela. We were raised together and were so close that I had thought of him as a brother when we were young." She swallows. "Well, as time went on, I suppose he started to see me in a different light."

"Did you begin to see him in a different light as well?"

She shakes her head, and there's a small tremble in the motion. "No, but that didn't matter to him. I justified it to myself, told myself he loved me. That, perhaps, we were woven together. I didn't know what love felt like anyway."

"Oonau—" I start to speak, but she lifts a finger to quiet me.

"Do not interrupt. If I don't get it *all* out, I won't get any of it out. For years, I let him take my body in the ways he wanted. Each time, he left immediately after finishing. I would sit in the lake surrounding my home and cry for hours. He was not gentle, nor was he kind."

I'm overcome with the desire to hug her, but it feels inappropriate given the nature of her story, so I stay still and listen despite the fire aching to be unleashed.

"He went to the mortal realm often. This was before we had rules and stipulations about our comings and goings. One day, I followed him to a woodland village north of where the Obsidian Mountains now sit. The village is long gone, but it was beautiful. Their inhabitants were happy and filled with song. The village leader had a daughter, a daughter beautiful beyond compare by mortal *and* god standards. She was called Vristra."

Oonaugh licks her lips, catching the bottom with her teeth and exhaling slowly through her nose.

"I watched Soren try to seduce her. She continuously turned down his advances. She was promised to another and wanted to remain chaste for her betrothed. This was a time when such a thing was coveted and required for good matches. Soren threatened storms. He threatened to blow away the village. To strike down her father with lightning. She finally agreed."

The water my feet touches begins to steam as I lose control of the fire in my veins. "Agreeing under threat is *not* the same as agreeing."

A small laugh catches in her throat. "Right you are, and yet, the deed was done. He had no care for her comfort. She bled and couldn't walk for days. When her father came to her, angry for her falling prey to a man, she tried to explain about Soren. That she did it for the village and for his safety. Her father didn't believe her and he cast her out in disgrace."

"He cast out his daughter for something that wasn't her fault?"

"He did."

"Bastard. No wonder you hate men."

Her lips quirk into a tight smile that disappears quickly as she continues. "When I learned of what had happened, I sought Vristra out. Offered to bring her to live in my palace under my protection. She wanted nothing to do with the gods and she wanted nothing to do with men ever again. She begged me to make her hideous, into a monster. Over time, she became a sort of guardian for those who need protection. She can sense someone's intentions."

"Yeah, I've met her. She has quite the temper."

Oonaugh chuckles. "That was not my doing. She always had one."

"So how did you end up bound to this place then?"

"Eventually, I went to Kato, the Creator, and told him everything. He enchanted the gods' realm so that anyone forced into anything they did not freely choose would immediately burst into stardust, but this still left the mortals defenseless. Soren proceeded to get worse and worse in his treatment of beautiful women. More violent too. I continuously followed him and offered the women sanctuary and to change them into a form more powerful, one in which they would be able to defend themselves. Most eagerly agreed. They became my isvitoks—and my sisters. I finally had enough when he found a loophole to Kato's enchantment—if the person is asleep, they can not say no. He procured razinine, a sleeping powder that can even put a god into a deep sleep."

My eye begins to twitch as I hold back every obscenity on the tip of my tongue. She doesn't have to finish for me to know exactly what comes next in this story, but I don't stop her. She needs to tell it, and if all I can do for her in this moment is shut up and listen, then by gods, I'll cut out my own tongue before interrupting her.

"I woke up to him on top of me more times than I can count. At this point, Kato was gone. No one has seen or heard from him in eons. So, I went to his mother, Isela, for help."

Oonaugh grabs hold of my hand as if she's trying to steal some of my strength. "I was called to court before the gods. I thought I was there to give testimony. That was naive of me. I was there on trial. Isela went to Haile and told her I was building an army to overthrow him."

"No." My voice is hoarse as I can hardly believe what I am hearing, the pure injustice of it.

"Oh, yes. She brought a handful of my isvitoks and showed their teeth and claws. She made them sing and showed their power over emotions. It was all the proof he needed. I didn't get to speak. He took my trident and gave it to Soren to dispose of. Then he closed off the doorway with a seal made of aietal so that the isvitoks couldn't get through. He cursed me so that I may only be able to walk where the eternal life waters flow. Which, in the mortal realm, is this lagoon alone. I can, of course, manipulate the waters to stretch throughout the cave, but there's not enough of it to go further."

"No one came to help you?"

"No one dares defy Haile."

There's real fear behind her glassy eyes. I squeeze her hand and she blows out a loud breath.

"I will bring you Soren and I will find a way to break you from this cave. Even if you aren't able to help me. I will find a way. What was done to you was unjust and cruel. You did not deserve that. None of you did."

"Thank you, Rainier. But as I said, I *will* help you."

"How?" I try to stop the hope that spreads in my chest, but I can't help it—it blooms like an infinite flame refusing to sputter out and die.

"My portal, the one that leads to my palace, is located out in the ocean. I can send some of my isvitoks to escort you there."

"But you said I can't get through if I am not you."

"Wrong. I said you need my blood. Well, any bodily fluid would suffice. But, as you've stated, you're only interested in one girl. I thought blood-sharing might be your preference."

"Blood-sharing?"

"We will need to combine our blood so that the portal will allow you to pass." Without another word, Oonaugh takes the hand that she has been holding and slices it open with a jagged green-tinged knife. She then does the same to her own palm without so much as a wince. "Hold my hand, Rainier."

I do as told and feel a rush as our blood combines. There's a familiarity as the waves of water mingle with my fire. "I can feel you," I say under my breath while simultaneously trying not to moan in pleasure because the caress of her power feels so godsdamn good.

"And I feel you. You're stronger than any god I've ever met." Her eyes are dilated, taking me in as much as I am her.

Oonaugh finally pulls her hand away. "That should be enough. Kiri, Jonna," she calls two of her sirens over. "Take DeLuca to the portal." They nod and beckon me into the water. One with long blonde hair carries a sword with her but holds it like an offering.

I'm still breathless and staring at my hand when Oonaugh kicks me into the lagoon. When I come up again, she's smirking and points at her hand with raised brows. I look at mine. It's completely healed, but I still feel her swimming within my veins.

The isvitoks, Kiri and Jonna, tie a sword belt around my waist and slide the sword the blonde had been carrying into the sheath.

There is a pearly swirled design inlaid in the hilt. This sword isn't fit for royalty...it's fit for a god.

"Her name is Isoei Iseutda...Sea Storm. She is made of imperialite. She will not kill a god, but she will do more damage...and enhance whatever power you have."

"Sea Storm," I whisper, running my fingers over the intricate carvings. "I will treasure her," I say in way of thanks.

"Oh, and Rainier?"

"Yes?"

She tosses me the blade she used to bind us. I catch it and slip it into the back of my pants. "Don't lose that...it's aietal. I trust you know what it does."

I nod. "I do."

"Good...and don't lose it or that stone concealed in your pocket. The portal is on the ocean floor where two seas become one. It is a sacred place and, as such, is home to one of our fiercest guardians, Kylshin."

FORTY-SIX
LEGION OF LIGHT
Aislinn

THERE'S A STORM RAVAGING the woods surrounding me. The drops slap against the ground with fury. I feel her desperation radiating like a call on the wind, the woman hidden beneath a cloak. She's praying at a makeshift altar in a stone circle.

All alone.

A bundle of daffodils.

A bird's nest containing 3 eggs.

Eight butterflies, all in shades of orange.

She's praying to a specific god, not just praying—calling.

The hooded woman pulls a white dove from a cage beside her. She eases it out, holding the creature's wings snug against its side. A crack of thunder makes her almost drop the snow-white dove, and it struggles against her grip. Without haste, she pulls out a small dagger, plunging it through the tiny chest as she carves out the heart and places the carcass on the center of the altar.

An offering.

She is repeatedly murmuring something spoken in a language I don't understand, except Haile. I recognize the name of the king of gods. The next crack of thunder causes her to jump. She turns, and her hood falls.

Iris?

What in all creation is she doing?

"Aislinn?" a small child's voice says from behind me.

I turn quickly and find the young girl who so closely resembles me as a child. "Hadleigh...you shouldn't be here. I told you not to try to find me again."

"What's wrong with your eyes?" she asks me.

"My eyes?"

"They're darker and surrounded with a silver line."

"I—I don't know...Hadleigh, what are you doing here? It isn't safe for you!" I yell over the next crack of thunder.

The vision warps and turns until Hadleigh and I are the only two in it. We are standing near the Egora bog. There are legions of soldiers. Some with golden cloaks, some in mortal armor, some gods, some...dead.

"What is this?"

"It's a vision I keep having... Grandpapa keeps telling me not to worry. He keeps saying visions aren't always right. He says that we can't know for sure and that they change. But I keep having it. The same over and over."

My heart cracks, as does my voice. "Oh, Hadleigh..."

"I just want it to stop." She sobs while I hold her.

Something in our embrace sends my body alight. Like the feeling of being complete...of being whole. It makes my shadow sing and a calm rush over me.

I pull away quickly—knowing exactly what just happened.

"*What's wrong?*" *she asks.*

"*Hadleigh. I am so happy to see you...but I need you to never come to find me again. Never. We can't be near each other.*"

Her lip quivers. "*Why?*"

I shake my head and push her hair behind her ear. "*It's better if you don't know.*"

"*Don't you like me anymore?*"

Why, gods, why her? "*I think I like you more than anyone else I have ever met...even DeLuca.*" *I wink. She smiles at that.* "*It's for your safety. Don't trust anyone. Don't share the visions of the future with anyone...even Grandpapa*"

Her voice is small. "*Okay, Ailie.*"

"*Be brave, Hadleigh, you bear a great burden, but we are never given more than we can handle, and you will never be alone, not truly.*"

When I awake in the room I once thought of as my cage, I feel oddly at ease. I'm surprised to find the Child Blade still where I left it on the dresser and secure it to my thigh. The shift in energy is such a stark contrast to weeks ago when I was first brought to the Shadows. After my conversation with Astoria, I decided it was prudent to stay with Erebus for the night. I have a new sympathy for him. Not that it changes anything...but I have an understanding as to why he is the way he is. He calls me pet, yet *he* is more akin to an animal backed into a corner.

He's sitting with a leg crossed over his knee and writing in some old book with a smugness in his expression that makes me uneasy, especially paired with the oddly still shadows.

We need to talk about this and figure it out. Now is better than later once he's used all two strands of his patience. Today will bring many surprises, but I must get through this one first

I just need to let it out.

"The air is unsettled. Change is coming," I say as I enter through the large archway into the breakfast parlor that overlooks the Abyss.

"I know, pet," Erebus replies without looking up from his book.

I grab an apple-like fruit off the tray and sit down. "The barrier *will* eventually fall."

"I *know,* pet."

"Will she survive it?"

Erebus looks up at me, shadows swirling in his gaze. "I do not know."

My gut tightens as I prepare to share something with him that I haven't wanted to admit since waking up in Kaoket. It's not something that comes easily to me. Despite playing down my progress, this is one thing I haven't been faking. It makes me feel weak and worthless, an echo of how much of a disappointment I was to my parents. I can't access the very thing he needed me here for—my memories.

"I need to tell you something..."

He looks up curiously and sets his book on the table. "Well?"

My chest hurts as I prepare to admit my shortcomings yet again. "I have blank spaces in my memories. Like they were tampered with."

Erebus rubs his jaw. "Is it the Weavers' or Utikalo's doing?"

"I'm not sure...I think the Weavers. They seem to have some kind of agenda that I can't figure out...but it *feels* like I know it."

Erebus mutters under his breath. "*Fucking Weavers.*"

"I was going to go ask them about it when Isela chased us with bees."

"Mmm, yes, I have been meaning to ask you, my little pet, why is it that Isela, goddess of seasons and *queen* of the gods, sent a swarm of poisonous bees after you? It is very peculiar behavior, even for her."

Poisonous? Well, that makes sense. She did give me two options, and considering I haven't left the realm, I should have expected an attempted murder.

"Because I saw something she didn't want me to."

His gaze sharpens. "And what is that?"

"I will tell you. Just not now. I don't think you will handle it well after everything with Astoria last night and—" I gesture toward my head to imply my scrambled brain, "—this whole ordeal."

"Aislinn." His voice vibrates through my bones, full of command, especially around my marks.

"Are you sure you want to hear this? You can not un-know it once it's out, and trust me when I say it changes *everything*."

"Out with it."

Telling him today wouldn't be the worst timing. I could use something to distract him with. I sigh and sit across from Erebus, bracing myself for the outburst that will surely follow this information. "When I met Isela at Cintamarri's party, we touched, and I accidentally saw one of her memories. Isela was making Astoria a tonic, one she *said* was to keep her from falling pregnant."

"Yes, I know of the tonic. We have all been very perturbed as to why it did not work considering her skill with creating concoctions...in fact she is so skilled the humans started worshiping her and her alone, practicing her craft themselves."

I wince. "Well, the tonic actually did exactly what it was intended to...it was made with dust taken from the remains of the fertility goddess."

His brows are threaded together as he tries to process and the air goes completely still, like it, too, is holding its breath. "Are you saying that Isela was actively trying to get Astoria to conceive? Even when she knew what it meant for us? What it meant for her daughter?"

"Yes." I shrug a shoulder. "As she mixed it she said, '*Lets see who the favorite is now.*'"

I've never seen Erebus so void of emotion. The shadows appear to be frozen around him, but his outward stoicism can't hide the cataclysm dancing to his breaking point. They begin to whisper, slow at first. The whispers increase. Louder and louder until I'm drowning in their cries. Shadows skitter around the room. Erebus's face has gone a stoney gray with the swirl of shadows in his eyes. Then he's gone. Vanished to wherever in the realm he can release his storm.

"Told him he wouldn't handle it well," I say to one of the shadows left behind.

I planned on asking Erebus to take me back to Kaoket, but I can try myself. I've portaled twice now... I can probably do it again.

Most likely. Maybe. Possibly.

No, I can. I can do this.

I close my eyes.

Kaoket.

Kaoket.

Kaoket.

I repeat the name over and over. When I squint my eyes open, I'm still in the parlor, and lavender eyes are looking back at me.

"Your face looks off. Are you feeling okay? I know mortals get ill sometimes for no reason. Are you ill, Aislinn?" Helena asks.

My shoulders drop. "I was trying to portal to Kaoket."

"I don't think you were doing it right."

"No, clearly not."

"Do you want a ride?"

"Please."

"Say no more, uldoaka, hold on tight." Helena grabs me, and we are through the palace and airborne in half a breath.

I look behind her shoulder at the Abyss beyond the Shadows and watch the dark illuminate in blasts of blinding white.

"What's going on back there?"

"Erebus is losing his temper. Better in the Abyss than out here so he doesn't create another rift..." She shudders. "Or Oblivion."

"It's odd to see someone who appears as collected as he does to lose control in such a way."

She snorts. "Trust me, Ailie, grumpy goon is anything but in control. He's a trickster, remember? He's totally faking it." Helena drops me off at the doorstep to Millena's palace. "I wish I could stay and hang around, but I have a special date with the god of my dreams and a little airhead. Toodle-loo, lovely!"

She kisses the air beside my cheeks and takes off. Helena is a strange one, but she has grown on me.

Raising my curled fist, I prepare to knock, but before I have the chance, the door to the palace bursts open. Agnar is on one knee with his obscenely large hand on my shoulder and panic in his eyes.

"My child! Where in the realm did you go? I was convinced that nasty beast in the woods had gotten you!"

"I—ugh—well, it's kind of a long story, but I spent the night at the Shadow Palace."

That panic in his eyes turns to hate instantly. "With *Erebus*?"

"Well, not in the way *you're* insinuating, but yes, he was there."

"He is a corrupter. He darkens all that he touches." Agnar rises and punctuates his sentence by pointing to the marks visible on my arms and wrist. I cover them, now feeling too exposed in my short-sleeved athletic wear.

"I'd like to go back to the Shadow Palace. I've done what I can here...and beside that point, I came for my lesson, not a lecture."

I'm laying on the soft floor, catching my breath after a grueling training session with Agnar. He calls Chimmy in, and the little creature waddles up to us with a tray of water and plates with snacks.

Agnar takes the cups and pushes one towards me. "Drink."

I don't argue. I take the water and gulp it down quickly. When I've finished, Agnar grabs a plate from Chimmy before dismissing him. The odd glow of the food here always makes me pause. It's pretty, sure, but anything glowing like that can't be healthy.

"Why is it enchanted?" I ask while examining a grape-like fruit the color of the sun.

He's quiet for a moment, then offers his hand to help me to my feet. "Let me show you something."

I hesitate before I accept his offered hand. Agnar may be cruel to others, but now that my memories are entwined with his children's, I see glimpses of him as the father he was, the husband he was—so utterly and wholly in love with Millena. Sometimes it's hard to believe he is the same god that slaughters armies—and children—without batting an eye.

Agnar leads me out to a clearing in the gardens. "Have you figured out how to portal yet?"

I clench my jaw, my frustration turning to an ache of impatience. "No. I haven't." *Something I aim to remedy the moment I am alone.*

"How long will this take? I have somewhere to be."

He makes a sound in his throat as if he finds me amusing. "Not long, especially if we fly."

"Fly?"

Agnar smirks and rips his shirt off overhead. If I thought his stature was menacing before, it's infinitely worse now. He's basically a giant without a single pinch of loose skin. I'm pretty sure each ripple of his abdominal muscles is the size of my fist.

I can't help but notice the tattoo covering his side—a balanced scale, Millena's sigil. The pillar lines up from his hip to the top of his ribs with three stars above it. One pan comes to the front of his ribcage and has a sun resting inside it. He turns his back to me, giving me a look at the other side of the tattoo, which comes to the back of his ribs and carries a moon. I watch in amazement as enormous wings made of flame flicker out from his shoulder blades. They're probably the size of Helena's but without a single feather, just a brilliant symphony of yellows, reds, and oranges. Despite the flames, I don't feel a lick of heat from them.

I walk towards them, cocking my head to the side to examine them. "They're incredible."

"They are," he agrees proudly.

Memories slip past my shield of a time where Agnar's wings were always on display. "Why do you keep them hidden now?" I ask.

His eyes narrow as if he's trying to decipher some code I've spoken. "Because they're magnificent, and anything that is magnificent makes you a target here." He opens his arms to me. "Now, come."

"They won't burn me?" As soon as I ask, a memory surfaces and I know the answer already.

"Not unless I tell them to."

I nod, which is all he needs before he scoops me up. We fly over Kaoket, but instead of flying towards the Shadows like I'm used to, we fly over a lush land covered in colorful trees and palaces of all sizes. Everything seems to glow with that same strange hue as the plants in Kaoket. The air blowing through my hair carries hints of moisture as we fly over a lilac body of water and finally land on a bridge. Agnar places me firmly on my feet before letting me go and folding his wings back.

"A waterfall?" I ask as I watch the purple waters tumble over the edge of the realm.

Agnar chuckles and turns me around. We're overlooking a huge lake. My eyes widen as I take it in. To my right, I spot Cintamarri's palace as well as the beginning of the Shadows. A range of volcanic mountains surround it, sputtering at the top like they're angry to even be looked upon. To my left, everything is bright, too bright. There is another mountain range that glows gold and has an enormous castle nestled between peaks. It's bigger than any other palace I've seen here, which is saying something because you honestly could fit an entire village in any of them.

"Ahhh yes, the Auric Mountains. That one belongs to Haile," Agnar says as he catches my line of sight.

"Makes sense. He needs the extra space for his ego."

Agnar stills. The corners of his mouth twitch. I'm not sure if he's going to shout or be sick. My eyes widen as his face turns red, and just as I'm about to back away and run for it, he lets out a barking laugh with so much force it knocks me off my feet. He's doubled over, laughing hysterically, and even though the sound could bring down the very mountains we stared at, I find myself laughing with him.

When we finally find some semblance of control, I catch gold glittering around the outskirts of Haile's castle for miles. I squint, trying to figure out what could be causing the sea of sparkles. It's definitely not the same glow the rest of the realm has.

"Does Haile have a glitter fetish or something?"

"Or something," Agnar says under his breath. "No, dear one, that is the Legion of Light."

I'm not sure why, but those words tug at some invisible thread wrapped around my mind. "Legion of Light," I repeat more for myself than him.

"They are the protectors of the realm, under my command."

I vaguely remember seeing men in gold cloaks in some of my visions. "Are they gods?"

"No, they are mortal...or used to be. Sold themselves to Haile in exchange for eternal life. Though, their eternal life is spent serving him, I'm not sure it was a fair trade. Don't tell that to Haile though."

"But they're under *your* command?"

"I am their general. Haile is their king."

"So if it ever came between you and Haile, they'd pick—"

He finishes for me. "Haile, yes. But it would never come to such a thing. I am a loyal subject to the king."

"Mmm," I say while trying to pull on that thread of knowledge I have buried away.

"We're not here for the legion, child. We're here so you can see that." Agnar points directly across from us, past Kaoket to another body of water that ends in a wall of clouds and mist.

"Pretty," I say.

"Beyond the mist lies the Afterlands."

I gasp. "The Afterlands? Truly? Can we go?"

"Absolutely not. Only the best shadows and a messenger god can pass through to the Afterlands. Any kind of impurity will taint it and our realm will crumble. That lake beyond Kaoket is guarded by a serpent-like creature named Ormund. He guards the water entrance. The only other entrance is through Egon's palace. He—or I suppose Helena now—protects it with a series of wards and creatures."

"How is a shadow determined good enough to enter?"

"When a mortal dies, their shadow is sent to a kind of holding space. It's in a fold between our realm and the mortal realm. They stay there while they await their walk through Oblivion. The shadow god is the one who passes judgment. He reads the shadows during their walk. Watches memories from their lives, decides if they were good enough to pass through to the Afterlands or if they earned the Abyss. Their eternal punishment is determined by what kind of person they were. Erebus uses his trickster magic to send them illusions befitting of their shortcomings."

A small flood of memories comes back, my time in the mortal realm when Erebus had sent me a few visions. They were so unsettling, and I get the feeling they were mild compared to what he gives those he deems worthy of punishing. "I would not want to be on the receiving end of that. But I thought you said they waited in the Lake of Eternal Life?"

"Some do, yes. The ones who are harder to read or refuse their walk through Oblivion. But upon arrival, they're in a fold between our realms." His eyes find mine, and he says in a low voice, "On the other side of the barrier."

It all keeps coming back to the barrier. "So the ones deemed worthy, what does their eternal bliss look like?"

He looks at me puzzled for a moment, then realization hits him. "My child, eternal bliss does not exist. What awaits them in the Afterlands is nothing. It all just ends. They get to become a part of the realm, their essence feeding our magic and the ground we walk upon."

Another misplaced memory as the empty space in my mind itches for the information it once knew. "So the reward for living a good life is to just...cease existing?"

"The reward for living a good life is an end to suffering."

"That sounds like a load of bullsh—"

Agnar interrupts me again. "You asked why everything glows, why we use the enchantments. It's because ever since the barrier went up, we have been unable to get new souls to feed our lands. We have to enchant them just so the Olvi doesn't end up looking like the Shadows. Our realm is dying, Aislinn."

At last Haile's desperation and cooperation with Erebus makes sense. Haile is draining his abilities to keep the realm alive, which is failing because it lacks the energy from new shadows. I'm not sure what this information changes, but knowing the motive behind his behavior feels like an advantage.

Of course, this revelation will have to wait as I have to focus my energy into teleporting. I was hoping to have figured it out by now, and Erebus's attention is now split with his new knowledge of Astoria which gives me the perfect opportunity to practice on my own.

I look out over the water.

Inhale.

Exhale.

Breathe in.

Breathe out.

The Opari Stone vibrates beneath my skin. There's a disturbance in the realm. It's quick, a flash of power and nothing more.

Come on.

I can do this.

My attention shifts to a glowing ripple in the air. I push more intention toward it, thinking only of where I need to go. Everything else slides away. My body buzzes, not in a painful way but in a way that feels like release. My eyes flutter open in time to see the shimmering portal materialize before me.

Checking that the Child Blade is still secured to my thigh—I smile to myself, pride swelling in my chest, and step through the portal.

FORTY-SEVEN
AMONGST THE STARS
DeLuca

Oonaugh's sirens lead me through the web of passages in the Leviathan's Cavern. Some of the tunnels are completely submerged whereas others are much like the rest of the cave and covered in just a few inches of water. I've had to use the stone in combination with an air bubble of my own making in order to not drown. Would a god actually drown? I don't know, but I'm not willing to risk it when I'm so close to getting to Aislinn.

The sirens are unbothered by the long swims. They glide through the water as if they are a part of the waves. I have to use the Siphon Stone and air to propel me forward in an effort to keep up with them.

A silver glow from the moon lights up the water around us. It has a calming effect and stills my racing heart. Part of me wonders if Astoria is watching over us... Part of me doesn't want to hope for a mother who cares.

The sirens do not speak much, to me, at least. They seem to communicate to each other through a series of hisses and clicking noises. They gesture for me to follow each direction we should go.

The blonde one slows in front of me and I slow with her. She then stops and grabs hold of my arm beneath the water. I look at her with a questioning expression, only to find her face has gone ashen.

"What is it?" I ask. Her eyes dart down.

The other siren has stilled as well. Waiting. For what though?

As if it sensed my question, I feel the movement below, stirring the water around us. It laps over my shoulders and neck, hitting my face. A dark shadow moves below us.

"What is it?" I ask again, this time much quieter.

"Kylshin," the siren holding my arm says with a thick accent.

The other, the dark-haired one, adds with an equally thick accent, "Guardian."

"Friendly?" I ask.

The siren subtly shakes her head no.

Shit.

My heart palpitations send ripples through the water as we wait. As still as possible—hoping Kylshin doesn't notice us. Just as I think the guardian has moved on, and I breathe out a sigh of relief, the water is being sucked from below us. It's like we are being pulled into some great drain.

The sirens begin hissing erratically.

I send a blast of air below us, hoping to move us away from the beast.

Maybe not my best move because now he's angry.

A giant squid-like creature erupts from the water. It has two claws the size of a horse, tentacles filled with hundreds of round suckers, and a circular mouth full of sharp teeth. It lets out an ear-splitting shriek, and the sirens lunge for it, teeth bared and claws raised.

They're not enough.

Their scratches, which would tear the throat of any man, have little effect on such a beast.

Within mere seconds of their assault, the creature has its tentacles wrapped around them, binding their arms to their sides. They're hanging upside down so that the spikes at the end of the sirens' tails can't inflict any damage and render them all but helpless. My hands wrap around the hilt of the sword, and I draw it, angled to start hacking at a tentacle wrapped around the blonde siren. I get two hits in before I'm knocked away by another giant tentacle. The blow pushes me a couple feet back, and I return the sword to the belt.

Fuck!

Think DeLuca, think.

I could call upon my fire, but I'd risk burning the sirens. I could open the ocean floor below and have it swallow him whole...but again, that harms the sirens. Water won't do anything against such a creature...well, not *fluid* water...but maybe ice would.

I haven't ever tried to conjure ice before, but I've seen Dover do it, and it's the only way I have of saving the sirens without causing more harm. Clenching my fist tightly around the Water Stone, and thinking of my intention, I thrust my fist towards a tentacle. To my relief, the stone obeys. Ice captures the limb holding the dark-haired siren.

She bites the fleshy bit of tentacle still exposed and drops to the water. The Guardian screams in what can only be explained as a war cry as I hold each of its limbs hostage and free his prisoners. Once both sirens are freed, they motion for me to follow then point down.

"Door," one says.

I nod my understanding when we hear the crack that sends a rush of dread through my body.

Shit. Shit. Shit.

The ice is breaking.

The sirens again begin their frantic hissing. They are by no means weak, but they're not a match for this beast before us. I make a split second decision, and with a look of apology, sweep them in a water cyclone of my own making, propelling them back towards the Leviathan's Cavern. They're shouting so loudly that even with the wind whipping around violently, I can make out the frantic sound of terror. I am just able to disperse the cyclone when I hear the final crack of ice and roar of the guardian.

It's big.

But I'm fast.

And I have my power to help propel me.

Quickly, I cast a new air bubble around my body and dive below the water. It's too dark to see anything with only moonlight above, so I cast another bubble filled with flame to light the way. I still cannot see the bottom, but I *can* see the enormity of the creature. It has to be the size of a small mountain.

I waste no time and push air back so that I am racing towards the bottom faster than humanly possible. The movement of the water tells me he's close, but if I turn around, I'll lose my concentration. So, I push on, to the deepest depths of the ocean, half blind, and being chased by a damn monster.

I'm going to see Aislinn.

The beast's screech is even worse below water. I suddenly find myself surrounded in black goo. Even with my ball of fire, it makes what low visibility I had nonexistent.

The substance is thick like oil we use to light sconces.

Could it be just as flammable?

I don't have the time to second guess myself.

A quick look around doesn't tell me much. I have no idea where the creature is. I have no idea where I am. But I do know that if I'm right, despite being underwater, that if fire catches, so will the Guardian and everything else in close proximity.

Luckily, I don't burn.

With a smirk, I still, feeling the movement around me and knowing the beast is close. I wrap myself in a tight pocket of air which pushes away some of the black.

I wait.

He circles me.

Stalks me.

But he doesn't know that I am the predator here, and he is keeping me from the only thing in this whole fucked up life that I want.

The creature comes nearer.

Nearer.

Finally.

I let go of the bubble surrounding my flames, letting them loose, and watch it all catch fire.

The creature shrieks, even below water its deafening.

The fire barrels towards the surface, and I have to really fight against it to stay below. But when it finally clears, it's like there is a sky of oranges light above me, and below me is a door.

Well, a door of sorts. It actually looks more like a well. There's a discolored sheen above it like some kind of film acting as a shield or something.

I stick a hand through to test it. When I pull my hand back, there is a tingling, almost numb sensation, but it is fully intact.

This is it.

I'm finally going to get her back.

Without thinking too much about it, I push myself completely through the portal.

I feel like I'm dying.

And being reborn.

The portal tears and stretches my insides. My eyes and ears are bleeding, the drops turning from a deep red into a royal blue. The universe around me flashes and changes rapidly. It's like I'm swimming amongst the stars and being crushed by them all at once.

When I am finally spit out on the other side, my head is spinning. It takes me a moment to adjust to my new surroundings and to the feel of my own body—which somehow feels stronger now.

It's...It's nothing I have ever felt.

The only thing that comes close is after you've been sick for some time and finally get back to yourself.

Yeah, that's it...It's like coming back to myself, even though I never knew I was lost.

I'm treading in some kind of odd purplish body of water. Right in front of me is a castle—it must have belonged to Oonaugh, painted a gleaming lilac that matches the surrounding water.

There's a cove just up ahead that can only be described as majestic. I swim for it as swiftly as I can. When I reach the colorful shore, I pull myself out of the water and lay on my back, breathing heavily and staring at the strange sun while I begin laughing uncontrollably. My hand slides through the smooth gleaming gems surrounding me. They're like a mixture between sea glass and river stones and so godsdamn beautiful.

I fucking made it.

I laugh to myself again and some of the weight in my chest is lifted. Not all, but enough.

Okay, now to find the Shadows.

Kill Erebus.

Save Aislinn.

Perhaps not in that order, but that's the general plan.

A shadow moving in the odd sun's light has me hopping back to my feet and pulling out the aietal dagger. Just a few feet away is a weird little creature waddling toward closer. I'm not entirely sure what to do at this moment. It doesn't look as if it *can* do any harm, but this is not my realm, and looks can be deceiving.

"Master has sent Chimmy to fetch you," it says in the common tongue.

"Are you Oonaugh's?" I ask, wondering how the Haile she got word to it so fast.

The creature rears back with disgust. "Stars above, no. Come, follow Chimmy." It turns towards a tunnel in the cove I can only assume leads to the palace.

"I'm not following you. I don't know who or *what* you are. You could be an enemy for all I know." A very unintimidating enemy...the image of this cute little creature doing something diabolical almost makes me laugh. Yet, I should practice caution while learning these new surroundings.

The creature sighs as if exasperated. "Master had said as much." He waddles towards me with something in his claw-like hand. "Assurance Chimmy means well."

I take the object from him, and my heartbeat speeds. I have to swallow three times before I can find words. In my hand lies a tiny gold locket. I don't need to open it to know that there's an uncut ruby inside. This is Aislinn's. My fist tightens around it and my lips curl back. "What have you done with her?"

"Me? No, Chimmy is a loyal servant. Master said to be here to fetch you, so be here Chimmy is. Let Chimmy fetch you."

It takes a second to click, but I think...gods, I think Aislinn sent this creature. "She saw me coming?"

"Indeed."

"Is she being held somewhere? Why didn't she come herself?"

"She is free to come and go as she pleases...though many eyes upon her. Questions are best saved for her."

She's here.

She's alive.

I think I might float away without the burden of not knowing weighing me down.

It's all I can think as I decide to follow this strange creature against my better judgment. I put the dagger away and he leads me through the short jewel crested tunnel into the palace. There's a door, shimmering with the same sheen as the Leviathan's Cavern the opens easily for the creature.

My wet footsteps echo in the empty hall. The air is stale and has a sticky-salted quality to it. Whereas everything outside seemed to glow, the inside is pale and unkept.

Abandoned.

Even the shining fish scale wallpaper is peeling off each wall.

Seems they've forgotten this place just as they've forgotten Oonaugh.

My wet footsteps echo throughout the empty hallways. I keep one hand on the hilt of Sea Storm and the other clenched tight in around the locket as if it's a lifeline through this insanity.

The creature that called itself Chimmy points its tiny paws towards an oversized door with intricate waves carved into the silver frame.

"In there," he says before waddling off.

My heart is thumping so erratically I'm afraid my chest will collapse. My hands lay on the wood of the door, ready to push open. But I can't do it.

I rest my forehead against the door frame and breathe deeply, counting back silently and trying to smother the flames of hope that have begun roaring.

Without another wasted second, I push the door open.

My shoulders drop, and my heart aches.

She's not here.

That flame of hope just turned into tiny embers, holding on for dear life. I walk towards the large covered window and pull back the curtain. There's a view of a glowing mountain range. A sea of gold appears to shimmer around the castle that sits between two sloped peaks. There's a cold draft behind me that feels familiar, but it has to be a trick. It has to be.

"Luc?"

Tears prick the backs of my eyes. I can't turn from this window because no way...there's no fucking way it could be her. But that did sound like the sweetest song I have ever heard in my life—her voice.

"Luc?" she asks again.

With a shaking exhale, I turn and pause. Not sure if I can believe my eyes.

Aislinn.

Alive and well, from the looks of it, more than well.

She looks less tired than she usually is, and there is something else I can't quite put my finger on, but I don't fucking care because it's her. A small smile tugs her lips up, and I run towards her at full force, crushing her body to mine.

The kisses that follow are not as gentle as I'd imagined for our reunion.

They're frantic and messy.

My cheeks are wet.

From her tears or mine, I don't know. I don't care.

Because I can feel her. She is here.

"You're—okay?" I ask between kisses.

"I'm okay." she replies and pulls back. Her hands caress my cheek and I lean into it—still afraid that this isn't real. "You almost have an actual beard."

I can't help but laugh. "Lysette made me shave it before I came, but I ran into some trouble, and it came back."

"Lysette?" Her eyes widen. "Is she here too? I lost sight of her when you went into the cavern...you too, actually."

"No." I swallow. "No, she's in Rilyse with Petra Kaillen. She's safe. Lost sight? Actually, it doesn't matter. Tell me later." Aislinn nods, and I rest my forehead to hers. "I finally found you."

"I knew you would." Her next words open a pit in my stomach. "But DeLuca, you shouldn't have come here."

FORTY-EIGHT

LEADEN

Lysette

I MEANT TO ONLY wait an hour, I did. But an hour turned to two, and two turned to three. Before I knew it, the sun began to set over the vast ocean. It's far too beautiful for me to cry while watching it. When DeLuca left, I didn't expect to feel this ache in my chest. It hurts almost as much as losing Linnea. The difference is that I don't know if he's dead or alive. I don't know if I should hold on to hope.

With everything I had, I tried not to become attached to DeLuca. Not to let him in. I knew the risk of getting him to the gods' realm and my heart cannot handle losing yet another person I love. Yet, here I am mourning him as if he's already dead. Just like my mom. Just like my dad. Just like Orynn.

Just like Linnea.

The pain of his absence is something I'm just going to have to live with. This has been the plan since the beginning. I knew he was going after Aislinn. It shouldn't hurt so much.

And the only person I really want to see right now is across the nation, ironically in the same place I lost everything.

The remaining Guardians should be arriving to Rilyse soon, if Evander got the messages out as planned. I still have a part to play in this. DeLuca's mission is to save Aislinn. Mine is to save what remains of Stellera.

I can do that.

I can remain strong for my nation, for my people.

It's the very least I can do after my father played such a huge part in its demise. I wish I could ask him what the Haile he was thinking. Switching babies, genetic testing on pregnant women, the condition of Ashe—how could my father be the man who chased away my nightmares and embraced me with the warmest, most loving hugs *and* also be the monster responsible for such atrocities? It doesn't make any sense. Even reading his journals, I don't understand how he could be both of those men.

When the sun is nothing more than a memory haunting the edge of the sky, I turn back down the beach towards Rilyse. It takes me almost twice as long to get back as it took with DeLuca—partially due to my limbs locking up with the cold air, partially because I'm mentally preparing to mask the agony weighing me down. I pull DeLuca's jacket tighter around me. I've given myself this walk to feel the heartache and no longer.

I am needed. I cannot break. I *will not* break.

Hannah greets me once I make it back to Luppitier House. My legs are shaky with exhaustion, and all I want is to take a warm bath and go to bed. But unfortunately, the Kaillens were kind enough to wait for me to start dinner, so I must join them out of obligation. Not that I don't like them. Actually, I rather enjoy Petra's company. Her husband, however, gives off a sickening energy that I can only handle in small doses. I'm not in the mood for pleasantries and small talk. I will fake it for the sake of civility as all ladies are taught to do.

The table is set for the three of us. It looks strange given the enormity of the table. Petra has a finger rubbing her temple as she gazes absently at her husband who is going on about the rebels "spoiling" this nation as I am seated.

"Ah, nice of you to join us," Craven says with a sarcastic edge clipping his tone. That guy really gets under my skin.

"I apologize. The walk took longer than expected."

Petra looks at the empty entrance to the dining room. "So he made it then?"

"I believe he did. I waited as long as I could."

She nods. "Excellent."

"Can we eat now? I'm most excited about the dishes this evening." Craven asks, clapping his hands to signal the servs.

The young man dressed in the Kaillens purple and silver uniform is slightly trembling as he wheels in the cart with our meals. I wonder what has happened here to make him fear us so much. Petra smiles at the serv and nods as he sets the plate before her, then me, and finally Craven. The serv looks at me oddly before leaving, and it reopens the floodgates of guilt. How he must hate us. If ever I have the voice to influence change, I vow here and now to use it.

Dinner is surprisingly simple tonight. Some kind of stew that pairs perfectly with the chilly weather and warms my bones. Warms everything, really. The spice has my lips tingling, and the comfort it brings has me even more exhausted than I was before. In fact, I may even skip the bath and just immediately crawl into bed, if I can even make it up the stairs.

Gods, I really don't even know if I could make it out of my chair.

My body feels leaden. I have never felt this drowsy before, not even when running for my life after Obsidian was taken. The room begins to spin. It's as if someone has replaced my limbs with stones and filled my head with air.

Something is wrong.

Very, *very* wrong.

I look up and catch Petra's gaze. Her brows are drawn together tightly, and her skin is coated in a sheen of sweat. There's a small moment of panic that flashes across her face before she falls forward into her bowl. Stew flies up, spraying the wall and table. Her body is unmoving other than the slowed rise and fall of her back telling me she still lives.

Slowly, oh so slowly, I turn my head as much as I can to look at Craven. His wide grin turns my stomach. Or maybe that's something else. Slowly, I blink between Craven, Petra, my stew, and then back to Craven.

When I realize what's happened, I know I have to get upstairs to my bag of vials. I have to get to the hopea serum to expel this poison. It takes every muscle in my body to move from my chair, but even with all my strength, my legs still give out. I drop to the floor, barely retaining consciousness. My hand reachers for the dagger strapped to my leg but doesn't even make it. I can't even move my head to see whose feet are striding toward me. I try to ask for help, but the sounds that come out are incoherent croaks.

Then my arms are forced back, and hard metal captures them. Shackles. My consciousness slips into emptiness.

The scent of old seawater and sewage assaults my nose.

My wrists sting from the metal binding them together above my head. My head is pounding and my tongue feels like sandpaper. I wiggle on the chains securing me to the ceiling, but they won't budge.

What's worse, I can't feel my power *at all*. Not the little vines wriggling beneath my skin. Not the tremors in the earth. It's all gone.

"Well, thank Haile you're not dead." I turn towards the voice and find Petra chained in a cell beside me. Iron bars separate us and she looks just as bad as I feel.

"Who?" I ask through the pain in my throat.

"Craven," she says, and the raw gravel in her voice tells me it hurts her to speak just as much as it does me.

I attempt to swallow, but my mouth is too dry, and I just end up involuntarily whimpering. "Why would your husband lock you up?"

"There is no love between us. There has never been. We do not share a bed nor more words than are required. But this? I do not know nor could I guess."

Even in Obsidian we've heard of the cruelty of the Earh family. Of their "*games*." My father was invited each year. Thankfully, he was able to find an excuse to miss out, but many of the lords would attend the inhumane gathering.

"You don't think he's going to *hunt* us do you?"

Petra's chains rattle above her as she unsuccessfully tries to slip her wrist free. "For the sake of transparency, Lysette, I believe that might be exactly what he's doing."

"Why though? He knows that Guardians are on their way to meet with us!"

"I'm sure that has something to do with it. He despises Children. He despises the Liberators or anyone different. Our meeting would have surely aided both."

"Your staff will notice you've gone missing."

"They may. But in my absence, Craven is in charge. They will do his bidding as our laws command."

"What about your power? Can't you produce lightning like your sister?"

Petra smiles weakly. "I could, if we weren't shackled in aietal cuffs."

No, no, no. Oh gods. No.

My breathing changes as panic settles in my chest. This cannot be happening. This can't be real. "There must be *something*. There must be!"

"I'm su—" Petra is cut off by the sound of a heavy door opening and closing. We are both quiet, listening to heavy footsteps against the cold wet ground and a glowing light comes closer. It's almost *too* bright against the dimly lit walls of the cellar and momentarily blinds me.

"Hello, beautiful ladies," a man says as he approaches. He moves the light down so it casts its illumination over his face.

"Dom!" Petra's voice is full of hope. "Oh, Dom, I'm so glad to see you. Please tell me you found the keys to get us out!"

The hope in Petra's voice hurts my heart, because with one look at Dom, I know in my bones he is not here to help us.

Dom, the man who greeted DeLuca and me at the gate, smiles. "Sweet Petra, I couldn't possibly get you out when I worked so hard to get you in."

Petra gasps. "*You*? But, Dom...you really? Why?"

He drums his fingers against the bars of her cell. "We want things to remain as they are. We do not need revolution," Dom says with a shrug of his shoulders. "Rilyse is thriving."

"Dom, please. Whatever is going on, we can figure out a solution. It doesn't need to come to this," Petra says.

"We heard you, Petra, we heard you talking about turning Rilyse into a sanctuary province. We'd be no better off than the rest of Stellera if that were to happen."

"We? So Craven *is* in on this, then?" Petra asks.

"Craven, and the *entire* Rilyse council. We've all agreed. Your ideals no longer align with ours."

Anger stirs in my veins. "You're traitors to your nation."

"At least we're not *traitors* to our own brethren," Dom quips.

"So what? We're just going to rot here, so we don't challenge your regime?" I ask.

"Of course not, what kind of fun would a hunt be if the prey were chained in a dungeon?"

So we *are* to participate in Earh's games. I do my best not to see how rattled I am with that knowledge.

"How long?" Petra asks in a quiet voice.

"Less than a month," Dom says. "Servs will bring you down food and water. Do not try anything, or they will be punished." The way Dom's eyes spark to life says whatever punishment he is thinking of is a twisted thing of cruelty, one of which he enjoys bestowing.

I have no doubt that we'd be able to knock all these bastards on their asses *if* we had access to our power. Without it, we're all but helpless, and the only person who would notice my absence is in another realm. I don't want to be pessimistic, but it isn't looking good for us.

Dom sets his lantern by Petra's cell, a small gesture of kindness for an old friend, perhaps. As he turns away, chuckling, I'm overcome with the sense that this will be the last shred of kindness we receive in the weeks to come.

I watch the yellow light dance on the walls, trying to formulate some semblance of a plan, mentally going over everything father has told me about the Hunt and what I know about the Earhs.

"You're astonishingly calm," Petra says.

If she could only see inside my mind, she would know that is the farthest thing from the truth. "I'm trying to figure out a way out of this."

"You know as well as I do that so long as we are in these shackles, there is no way out of this."

I release a half laugh. "Yes, in this dungeon and in these shackles. But perhaps there is a chance when they take us to the woods in Nylen."

"Perhaps. Or perhaps they will kill us faster."

"So that's it, you give up?"

"I didn't say that. All I'm saying is that you're a smart girl, so don't make any foolish decisions."

I *am* a smart girl. If I could just clear my thoughts, something will come to me. Being a Bottinial isn't my only strength. I've been using it as a crutch as of late, but I am more than my ability.

And I am going to get us out of this.

Part Three

WHOLE

FORTY-NINE
FEELS LIKE HOME
Aislinn

"Of course, I came. I told you I would," DeLuca says.

The excitement in his eyes has slightly faded, which promptly forces a lump in my throat.

"I'm sorry, I didn't mean it the way it came out." I exhale and try to push aside the thoughts forced by the Utikalo memories. "I knew you would, but you being here endangers the stability of both our realms."

His brows furrow, and I realize what I've said too late.

"*Both our realms*? Ailie, *this* isn't your realm."

"I know...but...I don't know how to explain it, but it *feels* like...home."

I watch him swallow. "It feels like home, but you don't want *me* here?"

Gods, this is not going well. Why didn't I prepare some grand speech? Or do something romantic like leave a trail of flower petals?

I'm being pulled in so many different futures and memories. My mortal side is fighting with the parts of me that have become the Utikalo. Why can't I just tell him how happy I am to see him? Because I am! I'm so happy I almost don't believe it's real. He came for me despite all odds being stacked against him. But him being here is one of the last pieces of the prophecy. We have officially run out of time.

DeLuca must see the warring emotion on my face because he wraps me in his arms and drops his head to the crook of my neck. My mortal side wins as I hold him as tightly as I can—never wanting to let go again.

"It's not that I don't want you here," I say quietly. "It's that for some reason, I can't see. Our being here *together* will cause the realm to fall, and when it does, it will change everything...for both gods and mortals."

He pulls back so that our gazes lock. "Honestly, Ailie, I don't give a damn. Let the realm fall. Now that I've found you again, the only way I'm leaving your side is if I'm dead, and even then, I'll haunt you from the Shadows."

My heart swells, and before I can form words, his kiss snuffs them away.

Messed up memories be damned.

Let his fire consume me. I will happily burn with him.

I wrap my arms around his neck and press my body harder into his, only pulling my lips away to yank his shirt over his head. His skin is seconds away from catching fire, but his heat has never bothered me. I crave it. He cups the side of my neck while his mouth explores the other side just below my ear.

Gods, being this close feels so good.

So right, there's no way it can be wrong.

He whispers, "Burn with me." and then he's actually on fire...no...I'm on fire...at least, my clothes are. The flames dance along my skin but don't burn as my pants and shirt fall to ashes around us, leaving me in nothing but the garter securing the Child Blade to my thigh. He eyes it with an amused smirk and then his mouth again finds mine in a desperate urgency.

DeLuca backs me against the window. The shocking cold of the glass combined with his extreme heat sends pinpricks racing through my nerves, intensifying the feel of everything. He pulls away from my lips suddenly and turns me so that I am looking out the window towards the glowing mountains.

I'm caged in by his muscular body and can feel every ridge pressed against my back. With one hand, he captures my neck, lifting it so that my lips meet his again. The other hand is trailing down my breast. I'm panting against his lips as he toys with my peaked nipple, and I *swear* I could come undone from this touch alone. His hand moves on from the delicious torture, down the curve of my hip until it dips between my legs.

The warmth of his breath combined with his groan weakens my knees so that I have to press my hands against the glass to stabilize myself. DeLuca laughs, and I try to join him, but it comes out as breathy moans as his finger dips in and out of me, slowly at first until he adds a second finger. Gods...even his fingers are radiating heat. His body presses me harder into the glass, and his fingers move faster, his thumb stroking me in time. The tightening in my core becomes too much to hold back.

"Oh, gods, Luc...Luc, I'm going to—"

"Let go, baby. Let the realm know I'm here."

I get some kind of twisted satisfaction looking at the glowing mountain while DeLuca's name falls from my lips with my release.

Trying to catch my breath, I lean my head back against his shoulder. But he's not done with me yet.

I'm whirled around so that I'm facing him again. He takes his fingers into his mouth, then says, "I'll die tomorrow, happily, with the taste of you on my lips."

I laugh at the shared memory that seems so long ago. Then it's me crashing my lips against his. He responds instantly by pulling one of my legs up and over his hip.

As he goes to guide himself into me, I laugh again as he curses with the realization his clothes are still on. He burns those off too. A stone and dagger smaller than the Child Blade drops, and I smile, shaking my head. With one hand, he pulls off the sword belt and lets it clatter the ground.

He starts nudging at my entrance with a silent question in his eyes. I wrap my arms around him tighter and pull him closer with my leg wrapped over his hip. We both moan as he slides into me. There is no savoring this moment as we have in the past.

No. This is frantic, possessive, desperate.

We are so, *so,* incredibly *desperate* for each other.

I match his rhythm thrust for thrust, holding onto him as if I'll never see him again. And with the way things have been, I might not.

DeLuca has one hand bracing against the glass and the other holding my leg up by the thigh. I bounce up and wrap my other leg around his waist. He pulls me tighter against him. The friction of our bodies rubbing together is driving me absolutely mad with need. I'm torn between wanting this to last forever and wanting to succumb to the need for another release. With the way he's moving, I don't think I have much of a choice. I'm racing to fall off the cliff and I can only hope he will come with me.

"Oh gods!" I scream when I don't think I can hold off any longer.

DeLuca continues his punishing pace but pulls my jaw so that I'm looking at him. His eyes are narrow, as if reminding me exactly which god is bringing is responsible for this euphoria. "Who?" he asks.

"Luc," I correct myself with a raspy breath.

He grunts in approval and kisses me. He carries the air, the ground, the sea, the fire, in that kiss. It is the beginning and it is the end, but it's more than that, it's our forever.

When my breathing hitches and my screams of pleasure intensify, DeLuca pulls away to bite the sensitive spot on my neck.

That's it, my last shred of reserve. There's no holding back as the climax barrels through my body like a shooting star.

Luc's orgasm follows mine, slowing his motions to ride us both through the waves.

It's like fireworks erupting.

Literally, there are bursts of light swirling around us.

As if the very magic that lives in the air is celebrating our union.

And it's beautiful. There is no way something so incredibly beautiful can be as disastrous as everyone makes it out to be.

His head falls into the crook of my neck while we both try to remember how to breathe again, and it's in this small moment of vulnerability I decide I will not be without him. Not again. *Never* again.

Past lives and prophecies be damned.

He is mine.

And I am his.

In this life, the next, and whatever else there is.

He is mine.

DeLuca is drawing lazy circles along my naked back as we lay on the plush blue carpet in front of the window. Each time his fingers brush the space between my spine and shoulder blade, it sends a delicious shiver through my mark, almost like an itch being scratched, though I know he is being careful not to actually touch it.

When he stills, I know something is wrong.

"What is it?" I ask.

"How are you able to walk freely through the realm? I thought I'd have to storm a castle and break you free from chains."

The image of him playing white knight makes me giggle, and I have to work really hard to control my face as I answer. "The first few days I was confined to a single room in the Shadow Palace. But Erebus and I came to a kind of understanding and he slowly allowed me more freedom."

"I'm still going to kill him for all he has done. Everything he has taken and destroyed." DeLuca's grip tightens around my waist in a possessive way.

I chew the inside of my cheek. "You may want to talk to him first...I'm not excusing the things he's done...but he had his reasons...and I have mine."

DeLuca sits up. "You're defending him?! Ailie, he killed my parents. He took you. He corrupted Pierce. I could go on for days about the evils he's spewed into our lives."

"I know...I know...I'm not telling you to forgive him. Just hear him out. Some of us are chained to a life we were born into." I hope he sees the silent message in my eyes, the one begging him to trust me and conveying that I know what I'm doing. It's a lot to ask of him, I know.

He sighs and pushes a strand of hair away from my face. "No one is born a monster."

"I used to think that. But living among the monsters has changed my view a bit, and I have come to realize...nothing is inherently good or bad. There are many layers in between."

His gaze softens, like another thought has hit him. "Have you seen her?"

"Your mother?"

"Yes."

"Yes." I take his hand in mine. "There are some things you should know."

I proceed to tell DeLuca about Astoria's state of mind. About the barrier, the Afterlands, and all I've learned here. I tell him about being taken to Kaoket in the dead of night. The library and Oblivion. Aietal and imperialite. About the visions connecting me to Hadleigh. The creature in the woods. I tell him everything. All that I can without endangering my plan. After what he's done to get here, he deserves one hundred percent of the truth, and I will give him as much of it as possible. I know I don't have to hold back from him or keep secrets, but there are ears everywhere, and I can't risk being overheard.

DeLuca's rubbing at his stubble as he contemplates what I've told him. It has to be a lot to absorb. There's a deep furrow in his brow that is actually really cute. I'm tempted to smooth it out with my finger, but I know if I start touching him again, I won't stop. I have been so starved for him, I find I've become quite insatiable.

"So, this realm is dying?" He asks.

"Yes, according to Agnar. And with the way Erebus and Haile have been behaving, I am inclined to believe him."

DeLuca nods as if he's come to a decision. "All the more reason for us to leave. We have to go back to the mortal realm."

"We can't. The barrier prevents anything leaving unless the portals for specific gods are used at very specific times. Anyone else trying to use it or using it at the wrong moment will tear into flecks of scattered stardust. Not to mention, if this realm falls than so will the mortal realm."

"We can't leave?" He runs his hands through his hair.

I shake my head no.

"Fuck. I left Lysette in Rilyse. She's supposed to be meeting with the Guardians about picking up the pieces of Stellera. I know she's not counting on me to come back...but I have this strong feeling that she still needs me...needs *us*."

There's an uninvited slew of jealousy pumping through my veins, but I push it out, knowing it's misplaced. "There isn't anyone better suited to deal with the Guardians than Lysette. But, I can check on her...if you want me to?"

DeLuca nods. "Maybe just every once in a while so we know she's okay. I feel really guilty dragging her across the nation and leaving her to fend for herself. I should have at least found her an escort back to Caeliss or wherever she wanted to go."

A smile creeps across my face. My beautiful, thoughtful man. "I'll make sure she's okay. Give me a minute."

He holds me closer while he waits. I do as I've practiced many times over and search for my friend, convinced I'll find her thriving in Rilyse. Nothing can prepare me when I see her and what's happened. My smile drops and my heart races as I chase the vision back and see how she ended up there, withering and chained.

A cry sticks in my throat. It's an effort to keep the tremble out of my jaw. I don't want to tell him because I know exactly what it will do to his newfound calm. I know how close they've become and everything they've endured together.

How exhausting it must have been for the Utikalo, to always be the bearer of bad news.

I exhale and wrap my hand with his. "There's something you should know about Lysette." The color drains from his face and I place my free hand on his cheek to comfort him. "When she got back to the house, she was given something to put her to sleep. They have her in aietal cuffs in the cellar, along with Petra and a few others."

The heat around DeLuca becomes almost unbearable, and the bridge across his shoulders catches alight as he sits up. He takes many deep, seething breaths before he asks, "Who is responsible for this?"

"It seems Petra's husband has started an anti-rebellion movement, and they are also anti-Children. They're rounding up rebels and people with abilities to participate in one of their '*hunts.*'"

The marble cracks beneath DeLuca's fist, spider webbing throughout the room. "There has to be a way to get back! I got here and that shouldn't have been possible! There has to be a way, Aislinn!"

"Right now, there's not, at least not with the barrier and without a portal."

"How did Erebus come then? How did he talk to Pierce?"

"Gods can still be summoned. I'm not sure if they're there physically, but their essence is...and Erebus *has* a portal."

DeLuca looks like he's about to break all over again and there's a crack in his voice. "Is there no hope for her?"

"There's hope. Just because we can't help her doesn't mean we can't do something." I breathe out slowly. I really don't want to do this, but the alternative is letting my friend...no, my family...suffer a fate too cruel for even the worst villain. "I'm going to try to reach Hadleigh...ask her to deliver a message to Rett. I'm hoping he can go find Lysette. I can't say for certain as I don't see the future clearly and won't ask it of Hadleigh. She sees too much as it is."

DeLuca swallows and nods. His head hangs low between his shoulders. "I tried to keep Lys safe like you asked."

I put my forehead to his and whisper, "I know."

The swirls of my marks freeze as I feel his presence before he shows himself. Gods, not now, Please, just a few moments longer.

"Well, well, *pet*, what do we have here? A little surprise? For me? You shouldn't have." Erebus appears in a blur of shadows.

DeLuca rises and puts himself between me and Erebus, pulling the sword he brought free from the belt.

I scramble to pull the rug over my exposed body—much to Erebus's amusement.

DeLuca doesn't appear to not care about his own nudity. He stands firm as he confronts his father with his teeth bared. "Stay away from her!"

"Didn't you know, Delun? We're all friends now," Erebus says, though his expression is anything *but* friendly as he calls upon his shadows to wrap around DeLuca and me. When they dissipate, we are both fully clothed.

"We could never be friends. You have to be able to *trust* your friend," DeLuca says, not sparing a glance to his sudden appearance of clothing.

Erebus's eyes catch mine and a cruel smile forms on his lips. "Our Aislinn trusts me, don't you, pet?"

With a yell, DeLuca plunges the sword through Erebus's abdomen. Erebus's eyes widen and inky shadows slither out from the wound, now dripping with deep blue blood.

DeLuca twists the blade with nothing but pure hatred in his gaze.

Erebus smiles. "Oh Delun, so naive and impatient. If you wanted to kill me, you should have used the dagger strapped to our Aislinn's thigh."

DeLuca steps back, pulling the sword with him. "*I know.*"

I roll my eyes. "Cut it out, you two! There's no need for any of this."

Shadows skitter along the walls and floors in a way that sends a blanket of comfort over me.

Erebus lowers his voice. "There are spies everywhere, little lambs. You have not been careful enough, and soon word will get back to Haile that you're here."

"So we take him to court?" I ask.

"No, pet, think about it. Think about what you've seen. Think about what you *know*. Use that twisted little mind of yours."

The prophecy, killing Mari so the gods could no longer have babies, Astoria having to give up all her children...Agnar hunting them.

"Shit," I say under my breath.

"What is it?" DeLuca asks.

I turn to him with widened eyes. "If Haile or Agnar find out you're here, they're going to try to kill you."

FIFTY
KEYS IN PLACE
Erebus

IN THE MIDST OF telling Haile what I learned about his wife and her manipulations, I feel my pet's heart rate increase. Being as old as I am, it takes very little effort to keep the same bored expression I often wear in his presence. One of Haile's many gifts is that no one can lie to him, and if he knew what I sensed, he would no doubt go to her in my stead.

No.

My pet.

Something Haile can't corrupt with his perverse light.

Best to finish our business and then I will go to her.

I do, however, send a few shadows to find her just in case she's in danger. The shadows hiss their findings and it takes all I have to remain impassive.

The son of prophecy returns.

The son of prophecy returns.

The son of prophecy returns.

So, my wayward son has returned.

I had wondered when he would make his appearance.

Foolish boy.

487

Haile is not happy with the news I have brought to him. For once, I am grateful for his cruel affinity for punishments. Of course, I would love to be the one to bring Isela to justice, but as Haile's wife, I would be imprisoned and in no better position than my father. I am fairly certain Astoria is the only of his many children that he cares for, and he no longer has love for his wife. I have the utmost faith that Isela will suffer for her crimes this day. His rage is scarcely contained and shines through his gold markings.

In a flash of light, the king is gone—leaving me free to go to my pet.

I cannot put into words the emotions overwhelming me when I find her in the abandoned palace once belonging to the sea goddess, seeing her naked and intertwined with Delun. He should not be here. The carelessness. After everything I have done. Everything to keep the prophecy from fulfilling. Everything I've put Astoria through...these two are going to bring the ruination of this realm.

She looks so relaxed, so at ease with him. I want to shout at them for their idiocy, but the words die in my throat. My shadows skitter to the surface and I appear before them, conjuring clothing as quickly as possible. Not that it does much good for me...the clothes I conjure are nothing more than illusion, visible to everyone but I will *always* see through illusions. Not that I would ever tell them that.

"Why would Agnar try to kill me?" Delun asks Aislinn, ignoring me completely with blatant disrespect.

"Because he has hunted all my children." I supply the answer. I cast an illusion over my blood-stained shirt so it looks completely renewed. This seems to displease Delun. If only he knew how badly the wound actually stung... It is a shame my pride would never allow that...and my ability to walk through pain is unmatched.

"The prophecy I told you about," my pet adds.

"Right...right..." Delun looks as though he is piecing everything together. "So I'm going to have to remain hidden somehow."

"Yes," my pet and I say in unison. She looks at me, her eyes wide with a silent question, and for some reason I cannot even begin to contemplate, I *want* to help her.

I exhale sharply through my nose. "I will hide you in the Shadows."

"There is no way I'm going to hide in the Shadows." He folds his arms and his eyes narrow.

"Luc, please. It will be okay. It's not what you think it is. The Shadow Palace is the best place to hide you...and you can see your mother."

I still.

How dare she offer that?

Who does she think she is?

In Astoria's fragile state, who knows how she will react to his presence? After all, Delun was the one who broke her.

I pull at the shadows marking her skin so knows just how unhappy I am with her. She glares at me. It would be comical if we weren't on the precipice of disaster.

Delun's voice is quiet. "I want to see her."

"So, you will stay with us?" Aislinn asks. There's hope in her voice.

He nods, and the instant he does, we vanish in a cloud of shadow. My pet instantly excuses herself, kissing Delun, saying she needs to use *my* basin and oktalei to enhance her power. For what, I do not know. She has developed an inappropriate comfortability here. She is hiding something, and I have been too distracted to notice. Between the two of them, Delun is a bigger risk. I send a shadow along with Aislinn as my spy and stay with by his side.

"I want to see her now," Delun says.

I'm rubbing my temples, already regretting the decision. I should have just locked him up somewhere like I had when I first brought my pet here. So much easier to manage when they are restricted to one room.

"It's been a long and exhausting day," I say with a shrug. "Perhaps next week would be much better."

"I want to see her now!" His body trembles with the little control he has, and I watch as his shadow stirs with a colorful brilliance similar to watching fire's reflection off the sea.

My shadows tremble beneath the promise of his power, despite his inability to control it fully. I sigh. "Fine. But you shall not upset her, or we leave and I lock you away for the remainder of your time here." He nods his agreement and I shadow us into Astoria's skyroom.

I gesture for Delun to follow me into the skyroom. He's unsure as he steps onto the invisible floor. If this moment wasn't so tense, I might have laughed at the way he taps his foot around, feeling for solidity.

"Astoria, darling, come meet someone," I say, pushing Delun forward. I cannot dent my curiosity. Perhaps a reunion is just the thing she needs to lift her mood...or perhaps it will push her further.

"Suns snuffing out the light, all begins and all ends tonight," my beautiful moon goddess says as she strolls towards us.

Delun looks between us both with a questioning expression as though I can make sense of the nonsense my wife has just spilled.

"Your lovely mother speaks in riddles lately. I'm afraid I do not know what she is talking about."

He bites his cheek and nods. "I see. Well, it's not the first time I've had a mother speak in tongues."

That was a jab towards me. For whispering in his mortal mother's head. Driving her crazy. Trying to break my son before Agnar could kill him. I do not feel remorse for that mortal's life, nor the other things I've done out of necessity and meet his defiant stare.

Mortals are no better than cattle. Their only purpose is to feed our lands once they have expired, and most of them can't even do that because they allow themselves to become so corrupt.

"The keys in place, sun's embrace, the bridge formed, this realm forlorn." Astoria continues her nonsense. Like a moon in orbit, she walks around us aimlessly.

"Her consciousness is trapped in the barrier," I say quietly.

"Ailie told me," he says. Then his throat bobs. "I don't think I was prepared for this."

We share a look, and I know that despite our history, in this moment, we are united in our shared heartache. The silver of Astoria's body catches light as she moves through the room. It almost appears as if she is glowing...remnant of her past self.

I close my eyes and allow myself to relive those days for a short breath. She would want Delun here. She would do anything in her power to keep him hidden from Haile.

And as penance for everything I have robbed my wife of, I will do this.

I groan in annoyance, *knowing* this is a mistake. "This room is untraceable. It is suspended deep in the heart of the shadows and made entirely of illusion, making it the best place for you to hide. You are to remain here while I prepare one like it for you. Speak to her... Do not expect much though."

Delun nods without looking away from Astoria. I ignore the glassy look in his eyes and leave them. Another tug at emotions I don't recognize after seeing them together... Thoughts of what could have been flood my mind—unwelcomed—I flush them out with reality.

This never could have been.

It never *can* be.

Bursting into my library, I head straight for the scrolls I keep hidden behind illusions—the prophecies of the Utikalo. I have read them so many times, searching tirelessly to find any clue, any loophole, anything to bypass this prophecy, it's a wonder they're still intact. The Shadows can not fall. If they do, the entire realm will crumble behind it. I should not have dismissed the boy's resourcefulness. He is clearly enamored with my pet and has inherited his mother's determination.

He is also strong, much stronger than the last time we met and growing into his power. And what's more, now that we are in the gods' realm, I recognize his shadow. It's one I've been waiting a long time to see again. Delun may actually be the first of my children that Agnar cannot kill.

He might be the first to survive.

I run my fingers over the text in the scroll. *A child of moon and shadow will release the shadows.* Clear as the sky above. We have very few shadows remaining, and if we lose the ones we have, I will no longer have anything to feed the realm with.

The boy has to go.

My shadows scream beneath my skin, fighting and shredding, as they realize what it means—Aislinn also has to go.

I know Delun will not leave without her, not when he's fought so hard to get her back. Her presence here has proven to be useless.

She is so irreparably broken. The barrier must remain until Astoria is free of it. And my pet can not possibly fix my Astoria, not in this form. Perhaps I will revisit the idea in a few decades now that I have tethered her to me.

It is decided. I am sure of this new course. But why then? Why do I feel this incessant need to keep her here?

I'm missing something, I'm sure of it.

My shadows continue to wail as I keep searching through old texts and scrolls, looking for anything that might explain this bond I wish to sever.

"It is not for eternity," I tell my shrieking shadows to try and quiet them. "She is bound to the Shadows. She will be back in one form or another."

FIFTY-ONE
DARK AND DREARY
Aislinn

"I FEEL YOU WATCHING me," I say as I round the corner to the room with the isvipotale basin. "If you wanted to know what I was doing, all you had to do was ask."

The shadow that has been tailing me skitters along the floor, now in clear view instead of trying to be discreet. It takes the shape of a small animal that vaguely reminds me of a cat. I roll my eyes. It's like he doesn't know me at all even after all this time. My little follower trots along like I invited it and I shake my head while muttering a curse.

When I get to the basin, I slice across my arm and feed the bowl some of my blood—second nature, thanks to the memories that are not exactly mine. I pour the oktalei liquid in and focus on who I want to see—Hadleigh.

The colors in the bowl swirl and swirl until they turn into an image. A room covered in yellow with a bed and handmade quilt. A body, not quite dead yet not alive...Heidon.

"Hadleigh," I say into the bowl. The image blinks before me as if I am looking at it through my own eyes. "Hadleigh." I try again, and the image shakes as though someone is trying to clear their head.

Right.

Our minds are connected—I must be in her head.

"Hadleigh, it's Aislinn...blink twice if you understand me."
The image blinks twice, slowly. "Good. I need your help, Hadleigh.
I need you to find Rett. Tell him to go to Evander at the old manor.
Tell him Lysette is in danger. She is being held captive in Rilyse by
an Earh, down in the old cellar. She can't use her powers. Make
sure to tell him he plans to start the Earh Hunts again. Can you do
that, Hadleigh?"

She blinks twice.

"Thank you, you brave girl."

"Heidon," she whispers.

"I'll do my best," I say, though I know it is an empty promise.
His shadow is stuck in the in between while the barrier stands, but
I can't bear to break her heart. "I have to go, it's not safe for us to
keep this connection. Stay safe, Hadleigh. I miss you." I pull out
of the vision and shiver at the sudden rush to reality.

"Whatcha doin'?" I jump and find Helena leaning against the
doorway.

My hand flies over my heart. "Gods, you can't sneak up
on people like that." She smiles as if I've paid her the highest
compliment. "I was just enhancing one of my visions." I don't like
lying to Helena, but as much as I like her, I know better than to
trust anyone. Also, it's not exactly lying if I'm just omitting the
truth.

"Fine. Don't tell me." She pouts, clearly seeing right through
me. "I'm having a little get together in a few days. Very exclusive.

Only my favorite people. I wanted to hand-deliver the invitation."
She holds out a handmade invitation, specks of pink and black
glitter falling off as she does. It's so very *"Helena."*

"I'll try." I smile and shake some of the glitter off.

"Try? *Try?* What else would you be doing? Hanging out with
master of dark and dreary?" My laughter is cut short by the hiss of
the shadow in cat form. I stare at it for a second before I continue
on with my laughing. This time Helena joins despite her attempt
to seem annoyed. She's not a very good actress, it's a wonder she's
survived so long in the midst of the scheming gods.

"I'll be there," I finally say.

She accepts with a nod before her face drops and she rolls her
eyes which have an odd golden glow that I've never seen before.

"Ugh! I am being summoned. Probably Soren again. Duty
calls." She salutes, taking off so fast my hair blows back.

"How did it go?" I ask Erebus who is leaning against the wall
beside the basin room.

"As well as it could have. She was not disturbed by his presence
so I have allowed him to stay."

"How did DeLuca take her condition?"

"How should I know how *Delun* takes anything?" Erebus says with a bite in his tone. His face smoothes into a smirk. "With the exception of you."

"Don't be gross, Erebus."

He shrugs. "It was not I who was fornicating in front of a window with the tacky, yet perfectly functional drapes drawn open."

"It's even more gross that you had your shadows spying on us."

"I wasn't spying." He swallows and his voice comes out just above a whisper like it's painful to admit. "I felt your heart race."

I stop walking and stare at him for a moment. It didn't occur to me that this shadow bond would allow him to feel that. It probably felt similar to when I'm afraid...He sent a shadow to *check* on me.

"Erebus." I look at him with a question...although I'm not quite sure what I'm asking.

He shakes his head. "Tell me, who did you contact in the mortal realm?"

Right, he did just have a shadow spying on me.

"I had to get a message to someone. One of my friends is in danger. Held prisoner by a monster."

He snorts. "I suppose you relate to that, don't you, pet?"

"You're not the monster you think you are."

His eyes snap up to mine. "We'll see."

I suppose we will. "I have to ask you something."

His brows raise in mild amusement. "You're always asking me something."

"It's a favor."

"A favor? I would have thought you knew better than to ask a favor from a god."

"It's about my cousin, Heidon. The shadow you stole when I was still in the mortal realm."

"I did not *steal* anything. You *gave* him to me."

"Not purposely!" *Control your temper, Aislinn. Stay on his good side.* "Anyway, even with the barrier up, is there any way to release the shadow?"

He looks borderline annoyed by the question. As he used to when I first arrived. "No."

"What about a portal?"

"There isn't *any* way, pet." His voice is clipped, and I have to remind myself not to shrink beneath it.

My heart splinters knowing I will have broken my promise to Hadleigh and that Heidon is well and truly lost because of me.

"What if the barrier comes down?" I ask, making my voice as gentle as possible.

"I'm not willing to risk Astoria."

"Wh—"

"I. Will. Not. Risk. Astoria," Erebus says through clenched teeth, his shadows flaring like tentacles. If the look in his eyes wasn't enough to deter me from further inquiring, then the way he abruptly bursts away in a mist of shadow tells me all I needed to know.

Erebus will not help me.

FIFTY-TWO
PROTECTOR
Aislinn

THIS CAN'T LAST FOREVER, I know it can't...but the last few days
since DeLuca's arrival have been so good. We've had luck keeping
him hidden from Haile and the other gods. Helena has been extra
snoopy, hanging around the Shadow Palace more than usual and
asking strange questions...well...strang*er*. She is always a bit odd.

Astoria seems to enjoy DeLuca's presence. She still speaks in
riddles, but there is a sort of calmness over her that wasn't there
before. I've been half-tempted to bring him to the barrier to see if
he could see her as she was...but I also know Erebus would never
allow it and we are definitely already pushing his hospitality.

I've been spending as much time with DeLuca as I can without
raising suspicion from Agnar or anyone else, which is surprisingly
easy considering I bounce between Kaoket and the Shadows so
often.

Erebus surprised me by creating a room warded from the other
gods specifically designed for DeLuca. It's deep below ground and
could be considered a hospitable dungeon, but it's done its job
thus far. The interior is actually incredibly nice with deep reds and
dark wood. It fits his personality perfectly, not that I think he's
ever stopped to consider how he'd decorate a bedroom. That seems

kind of ridiculous to even think about. It's hard to believe I used to spend so much time thinking about it.

Erebus seems to avoid DeLuca at any cost, which is just as well. Each time they see each other, I'm constantly on edge waiting for one of them to stab the other. But Erebus *was* considerate while making his choices for this room. It's hidden and dark, illuminated by the illusions of stars. I stare at them as they sparkle on the ceiling and can't help but feel this part of the room was made more for me than for the god who's currently molded to my body like a personal blanket and breathing deeply with sleep.

So much has changed in a matter of months…I've changed since I first met DeLuca. It's hard not to wonder if he still wants this version of me. I know deep down I am not the same girl he met at the manor. Despite not knowing my own memories anymore, I have never doubted my love for him. I feel it as strongly as the need to breathe. Each glimpse I allowed myself to have of him while we were apart only solidified it, like a gilded shell around my heart. Impenetrable.

But there is something else, some other feelings I can't quite place. And the instinct that came with the invasion of memories that tell me to push him away, to protect the realms. That he, or maybe *we*, need to leave this place.

I'm so lost in thought that I don't notice the shift in DeLuca's breathing.

"When you're this deep in thought, you go wholly still. Sometimes I wonder if you're lost to a vision." He kisses my temple and I turn in his arms so that we're looking at each other face-to-face. "What's wrong?"

"I'm scared, Luc."

He traces a finger down my cheek. "Of what?"

I nearly crumple. The weight of everything I've been holding in is almost unbearable and I hadn't realized I was slowly being crushed by it. "So much. The prophecy. For the friends we left behind. Of myself and who I'm becoming...of this." My forehead rests against his, and our mouths are so close that our breath tangles between us. "Of losing this," I whisper.

"You're not losing this. I may not have walked through a thousand miles of fire like I said I would, but I crossed a nation, ocean, and fucking realm to get to you. You're not getting rid of me any time soon."

I don't notice the tear escaping my eye until DeLuca wipes it away with the back of his hand.

"I love you, Rainier DeLuca."

"I love you, Aislinn Theodora."

The kiss that follows feels more like a promise. A promise of a life to come if we stick together, if we can overcome the many obstacles we are about to face.

The life we dreamed of.

Simple and ours.

But as I feel that life slipping away, the kiss becomes more frantic, as if I'm trying to chase after it.

DeLuca hardens against me, coaxing a moan as it drives against my core. I want to be consumed by him and burn in his fire. I want him to burn with me. I'm now straddling him and ripping at my clothes. His hands come to grasp my hip, but I swat them away with a mischievous smile and start sliding down his body.

He sucks in a shaking breath, "Ailie...wh—what are you doing?"

Instead of answering, I pull down his pants and kiss his hip bone then drag my tongue to the other one.

"Fuck!" DeLuca says. He grabs a fistful of my hair with just enough pressure to encourage me but not enough to hurt.

I take his entire hardened length into my mouth and work it up and down a few times before I come up and grin at the complete chaos in his eyes. "I'm worshiping my god."

A full morning in bed was probably too much to hope for. If I had my way, we'd spend days in bed to make up for the lost time. Unfortunately, our current living situation comes with a lack of privacy and our host likes to remind us of this fun predicament at all times.

"House meeting. Now," Erebus says with a snarl as he materializes in his burst of shadow. He takes in the state of undress

DeLuca and I are both currently in and rolls his eyes. "Meet me in the parlor in fifteen minutes," he orders, and then he's gone.

I release the blankets covering myself and laugh until I look over and see DeLuca, stone-faced and nearly vibrating with anger.

"What?" I ask.

"I don't like how he just shows up whenever he pleases. You're naked!"

"I was covered." Probably not a good time to tell him how often Erebus alters my clothing.

"You know I had every intention of killing him when I got here, right?"

"Yeah, I know. But maybe that's the very thing that releases the shadows and kicks off the prophecy. We want to avoid that, don't we?"

He grumbles something inaudible and I kiss his cheek. "Come on." I mock Erebus's serious tone. "House meeting."

DeLuca grabs my chin and pulls my lips to his. After he kisses me, he leans in so that his voice is softer than the wind, "I'm still going to kill him."

As soon as we get to the parlor room, Erebus conjures us breakfast and gestures for us to sit. "It is clear you two have other things you'd like to be doing and the last thing I want is to waste my time, so I'll make this quick. Helena is having a party tonight."

DeLuca and I exchange a confused glance.

"I know, I was invited..." My eyes widen. "Wait...were you *not* invited?"

"You know better than anyone, I do not *need* an invitation, *pet*."

"What does that have to do with us?" DeLuca's hand finds a place on my upper thigh that sends a river of heat to my core.

"As my dear pet has pointed out, she is invited, meaning she will be occupied...as will many other gods tonight as Soren will also be hosting a *party* of sorts. One where Haile and Agnar will *both* be in attendance."

"For someone not wanting to waste time, you sure are dancing around the point of this conversation," DeLuca says.

Erebus's jaw cracks. "So, *Delun*, I have a little father-son bonding excursion for us to go on."

DeLuca's face scrunches. "Why would I want to do that?"

Erebus produces a cup of coffee in a swirl of shadow and hands it to me. "Because it's to retrieve an artifact to send you back to where you belong."

DeLuca and I both are stunned into silence. I nearly drop the cup, but DeLuca's hand is beneath it before it leaves my hand.

"No need for thanks," Erebus says.

DeLuca's hand moves back to my thigh, this time conveying a silent message. "I'm not leaving without Aislinn."

Erebus inhales deeply and exhales in a way that screams to his annoyance. "Yes, you may take my pet. I have decided it is counterproductive to have her here to save your mother when she may very well be the thing that destroys her."

"Wait...so...*I'm* leaving the Shadows?" I swallow and look out at the Abyss of darkness I've become so fond of.

Erebus seems to sense my hesitation and his eyes soften in a way only I can see. "For now."

The words punch harder than anything Agnar has thrown at me during training. I look back and forth between the two gods. Both represent an entirely different future, entirely different *life*. And I'm torn.

My head is not in it. Agnar swipes my legs out from under me and just before I hit the ground, he catches me by my shirt.

"Forbis! Pay attention! If you're in the training room, your mind is here with me." His command takes root and my thoughts clear instantly.

"How do you do that?"

"Swipe your legs?" He asks, his voice becoming gentle once more.

"No, how do you affect my emotions like you do? It's not always, but when we train and you shout commands, it's almost an impulse to follow your voice."

"Ahhh, well, I am the god of war. I wouldn't be of much worth if I couldn't keep the soldiers in line."

I grab water off the tray and take a large gulp. "It's more than that though, isn't it?"

Agnar doesn't answer. He just smirks and taps his nose. "You know, your observation skills are just as useful in a fight as anything I'm trying to teach you."

"Are you just trying to make me feel better because I'm not progressing?"

"Only partly. But really, you're not a very good fighter." He laughs.

I shrug my shoulders. "I never thought I'd have to fight."

Agnar grabs small daggers and begins to throw them at a target on the wall absentmindedly—hitting the center with each toss. "Don't mortals fight all the time?"

"They do, but highborn ladies rarely do."

He turns and looks at me with confusion. "Why not? They want to keep you weak? Complacent? Easily targeted?"

I think back to the governing families as Agnar's words hit a cord of truth. "Well, yes actually. There were many women in positions of power, but many of the nations had a suspiciously long lineage of male heirs, and it just happens that they are the very same families that believe servs are property."

Agnar makes a sour face and shakes his head as if I'm speaking in tongues. "Such a backwards realm. Okay, child, we're going to try something else today. It is clear to me that you will never have the skills of a soldier."

I glare at him, rubbing the sore spot on my arm from where I've already been repeatedly hit today. "I'm not sure if I should be offended by that or not."

"You shouldn't be. It's not a bad thing or a good thing, it just is. One of the best lessons you can learn from me is to adapt. Play to your strengths and what works for you, not what others can do." He looks down at the blade strapped around my thigh. "You have killed before, have you not?"

I wince and nod. No use in denying it.

"Tell me about it."

I swallow and shake my head. "I'd rather not."

"I'm trying to help you, Forb—" He pauses and exhales as he stares into my eyes. "Aislinn."

I don't know if it's the way he said my name, so genuine and kind, or the grief in his eyes that I know is formed from all the loss he's endured, but I nod slowly and sit against the wall, playing with the Child Blade on my fingertip while reliving those moments. "It wasn't anything heroic. None of them were."

"I don't believe in heroes," he says with a playful smirk.

I suppose, to the god of war, my crimes would seem insignificant.

"Alright, the first was a man who turned into a monster named Pierce Decatur. I jumped on his back while he was coming after someone I loved and stabbed him repeatedly in the chest." I look up at him, waiting for a reaction. When there is none, I continue. "The next was the same person I love's sister. It was her or us. So we chose us, and I wanted to spare him the pain of killing his own sister. I slit her throat while he held her down." Putting the Child Blade back in the leather strap around my thigh, I close my eyes and exhale. "The last was Audrina. My best friend. She betrayed me, traded my life for hers. She put the person I love in harm's way, and I went into a blind rage, then stuck a dagger in her chest. I looked into her eyes as I did it and was satisfied watching the light leave them."

I wait for the judgment, the reprimand, as I lay my own monstrosities before the god of war. None come. He stares at me with a deep contemplation and understanding. "So, you've only fought when you're fighting for your loved ones? You're a protector, Aislinn...a guardian."

I burst out laughing. "I'm no guardian, I assure you."

"For what it's worth, I think you'd be an excellent guardian." He offers me a hand, and I take it, rising to my feet, and blocking out the flashes of memories that come with it. They're his, and they're painful. He must be thinking about it now if I have to fight this hard to block them out. He really did love his children. While my heart breaks for him, I have to remember who he is and what he's capable of. He has murdered hundreds of Astoria's children. "Alright, from what you told me, you seem to be more reactive than proactive. I want to utilize that and use your small size, can you jump through portal yet?"

I'm distracted by my thoughts and murmur, "mhmm" before I process the question and silently curse myself for the slip. "I mean, I'm getting better. Close to doing it on command."

He doesn't appear to notice my attempt to cover the mistake. He nods thoughtfully and grabs tiny throwing knives off the wall. "No matter, I can help with that too. You're in for a long day."

FIFTY-THREE
WORTH THE FIGHT
DeLuca

THINGS IN THE GODS' realm are not what I expected, not by a long shot. I expected so much more hostility. I expected to save Aislinn from my deluded father.

But she didn't need saving.

Now I'm sitting in this weird as Haile library, staring at the eternal dark beyond. It's still a shock Erebus *wants* to send us home. After everything he did to get Aislinn here, it's hard to believe he'd just send her back. I don't trust him even if Aislinn seems to.

I pull a book off one of the many shelves in an attempt to occupy my time waiting for Aislinn to get back. The text changes too fast for me to read it, each word translating to a language I don't know. Every page is the same. I put it back and grab another—the words are the same.

Another.

Another.

Another.

Each and every one of Erebus's books are unreadable.

So much for learning about the gods' realm while I'm here.

As I make my way to the stairs near the foyer, the front door slams closed and Aislinn comes walking in as if she owns the place. There's confidence in her steps, and I watch a moment before alerting her to my presence. This realm has changed her. That fierceness I saw just barely breaking the surface before has finally shown itself. It's like she's becoming the truest version of herself, and gods, I love her more for it.

"Are you going to stay up there watching me all night, or are you going to say hello?" she asks, wincing as she places a hand on her hip.

"I was just admiring the way you shine here." I come down the rest of the stairs and kiss her cheek, right over a brand new fucking bruise. My blood begins to boil looking at it, but I know bruises come with training. Instead of losing my mind, I take a second to cool my temper and run the back of my finger along the mark. "You know, you could have asked me to train you."

She shivers beneath my touch. "I have a feeling we wouldn't get a whole lot done." There's a seductive edge in her voice, and I laugh because she's not wrong. I can't keep my hands off of her. Each time I get her alone, it's like every rational thought is replaced by a desperate need to be buried in her, and even *that* isn't close enough.

"At least let me kiss away all the aches." My lips move down her collar to another bruise on her shoulder. A little noise catches in her throat that has me almost burning off her clothes again.

"You know—" Erebus says from behind me. "Kisses do not get rid of aches, Delun, but this will." He produces a small jar of some sort within a swirl of shadow and tosses it at Aislinn. She catches it, flinching with the movement, and murmurs a thanks before he's gone again.

I open my mouth to say something, but she kisses me, swallowing whatever words were there and letting them evaporate on her lips. "Come on. If you behave like a good boy, I'll let you rub the cream in."

Aislinn is bathed, and each mark is gone thanks to whatever that cream was Erebus had given her.

But I remember.

I remember each mark that dared show on her skin. I plan to erase all evidence of it further with my own kind of touch tonight when she gets back from Helena's. For now, I just have to be sated watching her get ready like a *"good boy"* as she put it.

Seeing her apply her lip stain reminds me of where her mouth was just this morning and sends my blood rushing down. I smirk while wrapping my hands around her waist—purposely allowing my fire to rise in my fingers as I trail them along her stomach.

"You know, I've never claimed to be a *good boy*," I say against her neck, extra heat coming out with my breath. I twirl Aislinn around and press her into me so she can feel exactly what I'm thinking about as I kiss up the column of her neck. "You look beautiful. It would be such a shame if this scandalous little outfit was shredded to bits."

She pushes me away with a laugh. "You wouldn't!"

"I'm pretty sure we both know I would—and I wouldn't feel the least bit sorry about it."

Her eyes travel up my body in the mirror and the move makes me almost lose any kind of control as my need for her grows. Aislinn's breathing becomes ragged. Cupping her face and bringing it towards mine, I can nearly taste her, but, of course, this is the moment Erebus comes to collect me for our *bonding excursion.*

Ailie pulls away and folds her arms, scowling at him.

He looks Aislinn up and down with a frown. "You would let her go out in that?"

I scoff but it comes out as more of a snarl—the animalistic noise surprising even myself. "I respect her enough to not tell her what she can and cannot do. She can wear whatever she wants."

"Sure, sure. But there are some gods who will not *respect* her in the same way. I wonder how many will be to able control themselves, especially with such a tantalizing outfit?" He lifts a brow, and I admit his words make me hesitate. I'm not keen on Aislinn venturing around this realm alone...but she's navigated it up until this point without me...and considering my presence here has to remain secret, I don't see a way for me to escort her.

Just as Aislinn opens her mouth to say something to Erebus, she's wrapped in a vortex of shadow, and when she's released, her dark blue shift dress is about three inches longer and has an extra layer of gauzy fabric.

Aislinn looks down with a sigh but doesn't seem at all surprised and Erebus crosses his arms with a pleased smirk. She glares at him.

Instinct kicks in and I step between them, nudging Aislinn behind me. My voice carries a warning in the low tone. "What the fuck is your problem, Erebus?"

Aislinn touches my arm in a comforting gesture and shakes her head. "You get used to it."

"Used to it? How often does he alter your clothing?"

She pretends to count on her fingers. "Almost every day that I've been here."

I lunge for Erebus, but Aislinn wraps herself around me, and I melt into her scent. Fresh water and lunalilies...with a hint of something else that hadn't been there before. It's an ever-calming combination that I will never get enough of.

"It's not worth the fight," she says quietly into my neck.

"You're worth *every* fight," I counter, lifting her chin so that our eyes meet. A small smile tugs at her lips that she tries to hide, but I capture it in quick a kiss. "I love you, Aislinn."

"I love you too. See you tonight. Oh, and don't kill each other please. It would really complicate things." She laughs. The sound like a slow river rippling over stone.

"I make no promises," I say with a smirk.

"Nor do I," Erebus says, wiping the smile clear off my face before I'm dragged back and into a blur of shadow.

"A little warning next time," I say as we are placed in some kind of dead woods. My feet slide over some fallen leaves before I find my footing.

Erebus shakes his head as if I disappoint him. "I see being among the mortals *has* weakened you, Delun."

"My name is DeLuca. It's the name my mother gave me before *you* drove her to kill herself."

"Actually, I do believe she called you her 'little rainy rainstorm' and she would have died soon anyway. Mortals always do, especially the ones in that wretched town. I probably saved her from more hardships." He shrugs, and I begin to vibrate from holding back my fire.

"Mortal lives are worth more *because* of their fragility, not less. They live more. Love more. All this time you take for granted means something to them. It is precious." Smoke comes out of my nostrils as I speak.

Erebus cocks his head looking at the smoke. "I appear to have gravely miscalculated with you. All that I have done to quell your power has had the opposite effect. Most interesting. But you are obviously untrained. More of a danger to yourself than to me."

I'm about to retort when we hear a rustling in the dead woods around us. Erebus's shadows flail out like whatever the noise is *actually* concerns him. He stops walking—holding an arm out for me to do the same.

"What is it?" I ask.

"One of the many beasts that dwell in the Imorti Woods."

"I'm guessing it's not so friendly?"

"No. He is a guardian. Meant to keep trespassers from getting to the Shadows."

I should have guessed. "So he's yours then?"

"No." Erebus shakes his head. "Dureias no longer answers to any god."

As if the beast heard its name, a screech sounds through the woods. Its pitch is so high, I find myself unable to move other than to attempt to block out the noise. I look over and see Erebus is doing the same with a pained expression. My hands are wet, and I know if I were to pull them away, they'd be coated in blood. The screeching continues without rest until the giant beast appears before us.

Wings larger than any creature I've ever seen flap so hard the wind nearly knocks me down. I call upon my own wind to push against it and offer some reprieve, but it's a struggle as the gusts continue to push back. The creature resembles a sort of fairytale dragon. But instead of its skin being scaly and lizard-like, it is transparent, showing every bone and muscle beneath. Its eyes are the purest blue I have ever seen. The creature has horns in all different lengths jutting out from around his head, almost like a deadly crown.

"Do not move," Erebus says through clenched teeth.

Dureias finally stops its unbearable screeching and comes forward towards us. It moves on four legs like a lizard, but its grace reminds me more of a sea snake moving with fluidity through ocean waves. Flames flicker along my fingers and shoulder blades. The beast seems to notice, and his attention is now fully on me.

"I said *do not* move," Erebus says.

"I can't help it. Sometimes it just happens," I say with annoyance.

"How embarrassing for you." Even without turning my head, I feel the judgment radiating off of Erebus.

Dureias's snout flexes as if he is sniffing and his giant jaws lift, revealing rows of teeth the size of my arm. I tighten my fists and call fire below my skin to be ready for anything. Dureias inhales deeply, and on his exhale, releases a plume of smoke. He doesn't do anything else except stare at me...as if he's waiting for something.

He huffs—aggravated—and releases another plume of smoke, then does a gesture resembling a nod. His exhale blows my hair back and the smell of pure death surrounds us.

I squint while trying to figure out what the Haile is happening when he releases a third plume of smoke.

I exhale my own smoke through my nose the same way I did when Erebus pissed me off a few moments ago. Dureias's slitted eyes widen and he does this little hop that reminds me of an excited puppy—a very, *very*, large and deadly puppy.

"Huh. If you like that, watch this."

I create fire balls, floating them around the creature while he tries to swat at them with his nose and front claws. I start to laugh as I add in the other elements as well. Dureias rotates between each elemental orb, trying to bite them and roaring when I move it too quickly for him which makes me laugh harder. When I look over my shoulder, I find Erebus staring at us with an unreadable expression.

"What?" I ask.

"This is just quite an interesting turn of events. Dureias has only ever answered to one other."

Dureias doesn't like that I've turned my attention from him and nudges me with his huge head. I scratch a spot between his horns, and he leans into my touch with his eyes closed and an almost smile...if a beast such as this is capable of smiling.

Erebus whispers, "So very interesting," while looking at the beast beside me.

"He doesn't seem so bad to me."

"He is known as *Dureias the Destroyer*."

A laugh sticks in my throat as I continue to play with the giant. "I think he just wanted a friend, and all you gods are too busy vying for power to have considered it."

Erebus scoffs. "Gods do not have friends."

"Exactly my point about mortals being worth more."

Erebus looks as if he is chewing over my words. "Hmm. Well, say farewell to your *friend*. We have places to be and a schedule to keep. The others will not be kept busy for long."

I glare at him. "Fine." Turning to the beast and scratching a spot near his snout I say, "See you later, Dureias. I promise to come back with more fireballs."

The creature whimpers pitifully while he curls up around himself. Even wrapped up, he's as big as a large hill and horrifically terrifying. I don't know how I managed to stay on his good side, but I plan on staying there.

"Where *are* we going" I ask once we've walked a bit through the woods. There's a sickly crunch beneath each step I try not to think about too much considering this wood is full of dead things.

"To Haile's palace." Erebus replies as if it were the most idiotic question he has ever been asked.

"Why?"

"It's where he keeps the Orb of Opari."

He's insufferable. I don't know how Ailie has survived him and his vague non-answers this long.

"Which is?"

Erebus turns to me, a burst of shadows skittering around him. "You ask more questions than my troublesome pet!"

I bare my teeth at him. "Stop calling her that!"

Erebus smirks. "Would you rather I call her *'Ailie'*? Or how about *'baby?'*"

"Are you trying to make me lose control?"

"Is it working?"

I don't bother to answer. He knows it is. If not from my face, then from the lick of flames sputtering along my shoulders.

"We are going to a secret portal I have concealed that leads into the Auric Mountains behind the Sun Palace. This way, we do not have to go through his army of puppets."

"Why not just shadow-poof in?"

He raises a brow. "*Shadow-poof?*"

"Yeah." I wave my hand around to resemble his swirling shadows. "Your little shadow transportation thing you do."

The corners of his lips twitch, and it takes him a second to replace the scowl. "I can not *shadow-poof* anywhere near his palace without him being alerted. He can sense others' powers so we are both going to have to do this the mortal way."

"Good thing I have plenty of practice with that."

"The irony of you being a mortal spy is not lost on me."

We trudge through the woods until we come to a large hollow skeletal tree with branches twisting in all directions. Erebus waves his hand, and a portal made of complete darkness appears. He gestures for me to walk through, but I'm going to take that risk. What if this were all an elaborate plan to separate me from Aislinn so he could send me back to the mortal realm without her? Yeah, fuck that.

"You first." I fold my arms. Erebus sighs as if I am the most exhausting creature in this realm and walks in, disappearing in a ripple of black. I mutter, "*shit,*" then follow him through.

It's a strange sensation—walking through this portal—as if a thousand butterflies are dusting their wings on my skin. It makes me shiver when I come out on the other side.

The mountain is so bright. Not just compared to the shadows, compared to anything. It's near blinding and feels wrong. Erebus looks so out of place here, like a snowstorm in summer.

"I loathe this place," he says.

FIFTY-FOUR
IT'S ALL REAL
Rett

It's midday when Cass and Hadleigh come running out to our training field. I'm in the ring with Bones and have him on the ground with my knee in his back and his hand pinned to his shoulder blade, but the sight of those two girls distracts me enough for Bones to maneuver out of my hold and throw me off him.

"Time," I say, holding my hands in a t-shape before getting to my feet.

Cass is breathless by the time she gets to us, her golden hair blown wild from rushing over here. She takes a moment to push it out of her eyes, then looks at me pointedly.

Leighra is running for her, obviously sensing something wrong as I do. Out of the whole group, Leighra isn't my favorite, but she's not my least favorite either, especially after all the time we've spent together recently during *Mortal Combat*. I can't believe *that* name stuck. It started out as a joke, and we all just started calling it "MC" and despite the stupid name, it feels good to belong to something.

The breeze cools the sweat along my spine and brings goosebumps all over my body. I feel weaker today. My body drags. I'd like to think the sweat is from working hard in the ring...but it's been days of this and a headache to rival all headaches.

Cass rubs the young girl's back and urges her forward. I'm not sure I will ever be used to the uncanny resemblance to Aislinn. It's like looking at a memory. "Go ahead, Hadleigh, tell Rett."

"Me?" I look at Cass then Hadleigh l with confusion. "Is it Iris? Is she okay?" I fight off nausea.

"Not Iris," Hadleigh says while looking at her feet, and relief washes away the tension held in my shoulders. "It's...um...it's your sister."

My blood drains. I feel light as panic fills my veins. "Lysette?"

The small girl nods, curls bouncing with the movement, and she looks up at me with sad, sunken eyes. I drop to my knees in an attempt to get on her level, but I'm still tall enough that she has to look up. "Aislinn sent me a message."

"Aislinn?" My chest nearly seizes and that nausea comes barreling back through throat. Aislinn is communicating with Hadleigh? Thank Haile, she's alive...but what the fuck?

"Let her finish," Leighra says, grabbing Cass's hand.

Hadleigh nods. "Aislinn has been talking to me in my dreams, but this time, I was awake. I heard her voice in my head. She said to find you and tell you that someone took your sister and that the ear hunts are starting again."

"The ear hunts?" My brows meet in the middle, then I feel my expression widen as it registers what she means.

Holy fucking fuck. It can't be...it can't.

Mase laughs. "Ear hunts? Stelleran's are bizarre."

My breathing shallows. "Do you mean the *Earh Hunts*?" I ask and pray she says no.

Hadleigh nods again.

The wind seems to die, and everything in this once beautiful valley darkens.

Fuck. Fuck!

I close my eyes and try to block out the screaming desire to run to Iris. "What else did Aislinn say?"

"Aislinn said to go to Obsillian and find Evendor. He can help." Hadleigh says.

"Evander?" Evander is dead, isn't he? I jump to my feet, covering my face as I try to process.

Lysette.

Taken.

For the Hunt.

For *Earh's* Hunt!

It's a struggle to hold back the vomit now. I focus wholly on my breathing.

"What is it Rett? What is the Earh Hunt?" Dover asks.

I look at Hadleigh, then Cass, and silently convey it's not a conversation I want to have around a child. Cass gets the message and takes Hadleigh's hand. "Come on, Hadleigh. I'll make you some lunch." She smiles but glances back at us over her shoulder with worry pinched in her expression.

Once they're far enough away, I run for the nearest tree and puke. The bile burns as it comes up and the headache increases tenfold. My knuckles slip open on the bark of a tree as I punch it. I don't even feel it, but gods, I wish I did. I wish I could feel anything else right now.

"Rett?" Harlow's voice is laced with concern as she puts a hand on my back.

The "MC" circle around me, clearly expecting answers. I've been trained to endure some of the most high pressure scenarios our army could come up with. There's not enough training in the realm to prepare you for something like this, for it to be your own family. If it were war...well that's one thing...but this...this is something else. Something far worse. I exhale in an attempt to calm my panic so I can speak clearly.

"The Earhs are the most twisted of the governing families, only tolerated because of their wealth. They put all their value in male heirs and belittle women. They accumulated their vast wealth by hosting an annual 'Hunt.'"

"I take it this isn't a normal hunt?" Bones asks.

I slowly shake my head. "It's bad, guys. Worse than bad. It's the sickest shit I've ever heard of. They take people they deem lower than themselves, usually women, and keep them chained in animal stables. They make sure they're at their weakest and then begin testing them. The tests are observed, and those invited begin scoring the captives based on their likeliness to live through it. They take bets and the winners get their pick of whoever survives."

Davina clenches her stomach. "I think I'm going to be sick." Harlow holds her sister, but her face is just as pale.

"That's not the worst part," I say sadly.

"What's the worst part?" Mase says, anger splotching his skin in red patches.

"Once they make it through the 'games,' the real hunt begins. The captives are unloaded into a heavily wooded area enclosed by fences made of oxidous lines. They release the beasts that hunt them. Those forced into the Hunt have to survive three days in order to win, but even if they win, they're sold to the highest bidder."

"That's disgusting," Rik says as his tattoos shift into snake-like ropes up his arms.

I nod.

Leighra tucks a short piece of auburn hair behind her ear and asks, "And everyone knows this is going on?"

I nod again, chewing on my cheek.

"Why didn't anyone try to stop it?" Harlow shouts, fists clenched and shaking.

"My father tried, but unfortunately, the Stelleran hierarchy was corrupt long before the Earhs and only got worse with the following generations." I answer and take a deep inhale, realizing just how true those words are and, for the first time...truly understanding the Liberators.

"And that's who has Lysette?" Davina asks, tears in her eyes.

I choke on the word. "Yes."

"We need to go to the Elders with this now," Leighra says. The others nod in agreement.

"They'll let me go, right?" I ask her with real fear in my heart.

She places an arm on my shoulder. "I'll make sure they do. She's one of us."

Leighra agreed to be my Elder escort, even though she technically is not an Elder. The rest are too fucking old to withstand the journey. Alec could, but he's still in the shit house for everything that went down in the Silver Hills.

Dover also agreed to come, because of course he did. Dover is the best man I have ever known. I'm sure the others would if they could, but the Elders were hard enough to convince to just let the three of us go, so we didn't try to push it for Mase, Harlow, Rik, Bones, and Davina to come as well. Not that I'd ever want the girls anywhere near the Earhs, anyway.

"Bear, please, they can go without you. What if I have the baby early?" Iris pleads as I swing my rucksack strap over my shoulder.

"I have to get my sister," I say, my heart breaking at the hurt on her face and knowing I'm causing it. "You don't know these guys, babe. They make what happened at the wedding look like child's play. I'll be back as soon as I can." I kiss her swollen belly as she sips from her teacup. Placing my hands around her hips, I whisper to my unborn child, "Bye Emberlin. Daddy will be back soon."

"And does Mommy get a goodbye?" Iris asks with a pout.

"Of course she does." I set her tea down on the table by the door and dip her as far as I safely can while kissing her. Her mouth is warm and sweet from the tea still coating her lips, and I lick the remainder off.

She's beaming up at me, her eyes wide, and that crack in my heart splinters even more. "I'm going to miss you," she says with a sad smile.

The nausea I've felt for days persists, along with the headache. There is no fight left in me to use with Iris. I blow out a breath and run my fingers through my hair. "If Evander is actually there, then *maybe* I can trust him to get Lysette and can be here for you." Each word tears at my gut. It feels so wrong, but also wrong to stay away. I feel like I'm being ripped apart from the inside out.

Iris starts bouncing on her toes, pleased with my answer. "Oh bear, you're the best!" she says, wrapping her arms around my neck and standing on her tiptoes to kiss my cheek.

"I said *maybe*. It's not a promise. I can promise to see you soon though. Love you." I press her tight against me in a hug that will have to sate my need for her.

"Maybe is basically yes," she says with a wide grin. "We both know it. I love you. Come back soon."

I attempt a smile, but it fails and I nod before walking out to join Dover and Leighra at the entrance to Caeliss. That tearing in my gut doesn't get any better. In fact, it gets much worse with each step I put between me and Iris. It's physically painful, but I know I have to keep going. Lysette needs me.

It's already been two days since we got Ailie's warning. I'm not even going to begin to understand the connection she shares with Hadleigh. Everything has been so weird since discovering the Children. I feel like, at this point, anything is possible and to just roll with what comes. We should've left earlier. We wasted too much time having to go through discussions and approval. A full day.

Lysette's in danger. DeLuca let my sister get captured by monsters. He is by far the worst protector I have ever met. He lost them both, Aislinn and Lysette. Two for two.

Thankfully, Leighra was given a map with the exact location of the entrance to the tunnel, which probably shaved off half a day in the woods at least, if we even would have found it on our own. The hole looks like nothing more than an animal's burrow. Small and inconsequential.

I mess with the levers and buttons, cursing at how complicated they are, until I hear the groaning of gears and magnets sliding into place—telling me the transport is on its way.

Leighra and Dover both try to hide their awe, but don't do a good job as they examine the purple glow given off by the oxidous lights lining the railway. Do they know how close to death they are?

The pod arrives, and after a few minutes and a lot of angry words, I figure out which lever to pull. The three of us take our seats and I blow out a large exhale, trying to calm my scrambled mind. I feel so torn. Save Lysette, leave Iris. Stay with Iris, leave Lysette's fate in the hands of others, and that hasn't worked out too well for me so far. The gods must hate me.

"We'll get her back." Dover claps a hand on my shoulder. "We will, man."

All I can do is look at him and attempt a smile. It doesn't form though, so I end up swallowing and tilting my head back against my seat, keeping my eyes on the metal roof.

"This *Evander* guy, he's trustworthy?" Leighra asks.

"He is," I say. "We served together. He's my best friend."

"Then why didn't he come with you?" she asks suspiciously.

"We thought he was dead. I actually have no idea how he survived. How he's still surviving. I only know what you do, what Hadleigh told us."

"Remember, only what he *needs* to know to save Lysette. Nothing about Caeliss." Leighra's tone rubs me the wrong way, so I only scoff and nod in response.

"I'm going to go with him," Dover says.

I sit up straighter and stare at him as if I misunderstood.

"So that you can be of sound mind and stay until your baby is born, I will get your sister back." He puts a hand over his heart. "I swear it on my shadow."

"I couldn't ask that of you."

"You didn't. Lysette is my friend. The thought of her being with the people you described fills me with rage so hot I could boil."

"Thank you, brother. Thank you. Anything you ever need from me you only have to ask." I say and feel it in the depths of my heart.

"We're stopping," Leighra says before her eyes roll back white. A chill runs up my spine because every time she does it—it really fucking grosses me out. The doors open to an empty hall. If anyone were there all they'd see is an empty transport thanks to Leighra, but it seems the security in my old home is nonexistent. Leighra's eyes return to normal, and we make our way down the tunnel to the lift. I waste no time and put in the series of levers and buttons to get us to the fifth floor—to my father's office. Before I know it, I'm pounding my fist on the familiar door. Each knock a blow to old wounds.

"Enter." A voice beckons from the other side, a voice I know well and thank fucking Haile for.

"Rett?" Evander's eyes are wide as he takes me in.

"Ev." I mirror his disbelieving stare. "We don't have much time. There's so much to tell you. So much I want to know. But Lysette is in danger."

"Lysette?" I swear all the damn color drains from his face. He gestures to us to come in, then closes the door behind us.

"Yeah. The consort of Rilyse took her. He intends to start the Hunts again...Lysette being one of the hunted."

"The conso—Craven?" Evander turns red. His anger is visceral. "Craven in fucking Rilyse?"

I nod.

"Gods-fucking-damn it!" He shouts—standing up so fast the chair flies back. "Fuck!"

Leighra and Dover look at each other and step to the side, giving Evander space. I'm pissed, but I didn't quite expect this level of anger from him.

"You know him?" I ask with a raised brow.

"I just got back from Rilyse. I was supposed to meet Lysette there. She was gathering the Guardians to try and restore order to Stellera. Craven greeted me and said Lysette and Petra went off on some kind of mission, that all was well and the Guardians would sort it out." Evander runs his hands through his hair. "I'm a damned idiot. I should have known Lysette wouldn't take off without leaving some kind of message."

I put my arm on his shoulder. "You couldn't have known, Ev. You *couldn't* have. But I need you to save her. Iris is heavily pregnant and I can't leave her alone... I understand if it's too much to ask... but I have to ask it anyway...will you save my sister?"

"I was already mentally preparing to leave as soon as I walk out this door," Evander says.

His body language, his mannerisms...he has a stake in this too. I'm not quite sure I want to know about it. I just need to trust that he will do everything to get my sister back.

I exhale in relief. "This is Leighra and Dover. They're friends... well... Dover is a friend. He has offered to aid you in getting Lysette back."

"Then he is a friend of mine too." Evander and Dover clasp forearms, a silent agreement passing between them. The sight pulling a weight off me. I almost feel like I can breathe again...but not quite.

Dover and Evander stay behind in the study, studying maps and discussing their course of action. I have already said my goodbyes. Words will never express the gratitude. I absolutely have faith in the two of them to get this done.

There is one more stop I need to make—Iris's parents' room. I want to find something of theirs to give to her. Something special. If such a thing exists, I will find it.

Leighra waits for me by the lift, trying not to make eye contact with the dozens of refugees taking residence in the ruins of my home. The serv quarters are in bad shape. A lot of rubble...and old blood. I'm not sure if the smell of burning flesh is a memory or lingers from the wedding.

Mikail's quarters seem to be in decent condition considering the rest of the hall. When I open the door, it is clear the place has been ransacked already. It crushes my spirit, but I don't dare give up.

The head of security's rooms were nicer than the rest of the servs. He had a spacious living area and small kitchen. The door on the left side leads to his private bedroom.

Completely empty.

Not even his mattress remains.

Figures.

The door on the opposite side of the quarters leads to Iris's old room. I drag my palm along her closed door, thinking of the times we snuck in while the house was busy. The memory brings a sad smile to my lips. I miss those simpler times.

After a brief hesitation, I open the door. As expected, her room has been stripped bare. Her mattress is gone as well. I'm about to leave in defeat when I notice something beside her empty bed frame—a secret compartment in the wall, cracked open slightly. It is likely to have already been ransacked, but it's worth it to check.

I deflate when I see nothing but an old book.

Well. If it was worth hiding, it must be important to her.

I grab the book carefully as the pages are very old and don't seem to be bound together well. A silver chain with a bell-shaped flower charm hangs down in place of a bookmark.

Perfect.

Opening the book carefully so the old pages don't tear, I examine the bookmark. It looks handmade, and the small tarnishing around the joints makes me think it's pretty old—hopefully an heirloom if Felix is on my side. I'm about to close the book and stick it in my bag when words at the top of the page catch my attention: *Consuming Love.*

Okay, color me intrigued. Maybe this is how Iris got to be so godsdamn good in the sack.

For best potency, charge ingredients below the evening sun. Make sure to dose daily for effects to be most accurate and be the first thing they see as the tonic takes root in the subject's system.

Caution: the love felt while on this tonic is blinding, consuming, can lead to obsessions and changes in behavior. The target's mind will latch onto you and associate you with their only form of happiness. Not for long term use. Stop once subject exhibits signs of immunity. Do not increase dosage under any circumstance. Can pose a threat to mental and physical health of both parties.

Below that is a list of herbs and flowers, most of which I've never heard of.

Is this a godsdamn witch book?

I flip to the front. It's written in Roussian, but I recognize the symbol for the Followers of Isela. A sphere with two upside down triangles.

Witchcraft...fucking witchcraft...what the actual fuck?

There hasn't been a witch sighting in Stellera in hundreds of years. What the Haile is Iris's family messed up in?

The tea.

The room around me blurs. My heartbeat is so loud it drowns out all other sounds. I drop to my knees—dropping the book in the process.

The special tea Iris started giving me when I got back from the army to help with my mood... It's not possible...she couldn't have...wouldn't have.

The feelings I have for her are real.

The love is real.

It's all real.

But the love I had for Ailie...how did that just go away?

How was I able to betray her...to even look at Iris the way I did.

She fucking drugged me.

Iris. Fucking. Drugged. Me.

I slam the door closed and find Leighra leaning against the wall waiting for me.

"What's that?" she asks, eyeing the book.

There are no words. I'm too godsdamned angry. I'm fucking wrecked. There is no recovering from this. I thrust the book into Leighra's hand, and it seems as if she recognizes the symbol just as I had by the way her eyes widen.

"Why do you have something like this?"

With my head against the wall, I blow out the breath I'm holding. "Iris. She...it isn't...it's never been." My back slides against the wall until I'm sitting with my head between my knees. My heart aches in a way I never thought possible. It hurts more than seeing my family slaughtered and finding out my life was a lie. More than when Ailie was taken. It hurts more than anything. This betrayal cuts deeper than all of it because through all the tragedy this year has brought, I had her. I had Iris. It was us and we could handle anything life threw our way. But she was also a beautiful lie. "None of it was real."

Leighra purses her lips as she takes in my rambling and the opened page of the book. There's a flash of emotion over her features as she realizes. Then she lets out a breath dripping in pity. "That's really fucked," she says with what seems like the most empathy she can conjure.

"I don't know how I can face her," I admit.

"Then don't. Not like this. Go with Dover and Evander."

I sit up and stare at her in surprise. She is the last person I'd expect to say that.

She sighs. "Look, I know I seem aggressive at times, but I'm just trying to protect the ones I care about. It's not personal. I think you're a good man, and I *know* Dover is. Lysette is one of our own—we protect our own, and she's in trouble. Go with them. I'll deal with the Elders and tell Iris you needed space."

"Are you sure? She's not going to like it."

"Let me handle it."

I close my eyes and hit my head against the wall a few times. "Will you watch over her? Make sure the baby is okay if I don't make it back in time...and that she's okay?"

Leighra smiles. "This is how I know you are a good man. Of course, despite what she's done, she's one of us too. Although if I were you, I'd keep this book a secret. Witches and Children have notoriously had bad blood over the centuries." She knocks into my shoulder. "Want me to give her the book?"

"No. Burn it. It's nothing but manipulations."

She nods and her shoulders relax, closing the book and turning to stick it in her bag.

"Wait," I say and take the silver bookmark out from the pages. "Give this to her. Burn the rest...and tell her..." The words are like hot coals in my throat but they need to be said. "Tell her we are done. When I come back I will be there for our daughter, but Iris and I are done."

I can't believe I almost chose Iris over my fucking sister...my sister! I can't believe I chose her over Ailie.

Knowing that it was due to the influence of her potions brings a clarity I had no idea I was searching for. I'd never choose anyone over my family. I'd never choose anyone over someone I've been in love with since I was a child.

How the fuck did I not see this sooner?!

One thing I know for sure is this will never happen again.

No one will come before my family.

No one will ever turn my mind into something it isn't.

My destiny is not to be some house-husband, waiting on Iris's every need and sitting idle while I wait for her.

That was never a life meant for me.

I'm going to save my sister.

And then I'm going to rebuild Stellera.

FIFTY-FIVE
WITHERING AWAY
Lysette

I'VE LOST SENSE OF time.

I'm not sure I have ever been this thirsty.

This tired.

I'm so disoriented I'm not even sure I would be able to walk straight if I were released from these chains.

The other cells around us have been slowly filling up.

All women...only women.

The girl across from me is so young. She can't be more than fifteen. She hasn't stopped crying since they brought her in.

Most of the women do.

But not me.

I don't have the tears in me.

I'm withering away in this cell.

My consciousness ebbs.

In and out.

In and out.

In and out.

A rattling on the bars to my cell makes my eyes flutter open slowly.

"Hello, abomination," Craven says. His voice is filled with disgust, and spit flies on every syllable.

I try to speak, but the sandpaper feeling on my tongue makes me mute. Not even a whisper comes out.

Craven smiles triumphantly. "You're no better than a tavern whore." He tilts his head and crinkles his nose. "Actually...the whores smell better." He laughs at his own joke like he's the most clever asshole to walk this realm.

I scowl as best as I can with such little energy.

"I just thought you'd like to know how your little meeting went."

My eyes widen.

"The remaining families were upset by your absence, given you were the one who had called the meeting. I told them you were off with your little god on some kind of secret mission and my dear Petra went in aid. So no, they will not be looking for you."

Hope fizzles and dies inside of me, and I want to die with it.

"I should be thanking you. The houses have decided to help me rebuild Stellera. Get trades going again, put the low-born back in their place... Of course, once it is again sturdy, we will have to place some *real* people in their positions. Can't have a nation run by freaks."

I can't believe they all went along with it. That they all trust this bastard. How did they not see through him?

"Your friend, the lowly one, he was harder to convince than the others, but he left, back to his rebel trash. Don't worry, we have big plans for them too—and your Obsidian Manor."

I turn my head up with as much dignity as I can muster.

"Yeah. Your father thought he could look down on me too. Thought he was too good for our *Hunts*. Well, Magnus, look where you are now. Deader than fucking dirt and your only child left in *my* dungeon. I wish he were still alive, just so I could see his self-righteousness fall when he learns of my plans for you."

Craven moves to the cell next to mine, to Petra. "Beautiful wife, it pains me so to see you in such dastardly conditions."

Petra wheezes, her voice shaking. "Then...let...me...out."

"So you can conjure a storm to wipe out all of my friends? No. I think you'll have to stay put."

"Why did you come down here?" She asks with so much hatred I can feel it through the bars.

"We're moving. I came to check on all my assets. We're going to take a trip to Nylen, to our old hunting grounds. You never wanted to see it before, and I've been dying to show you."

Petra throws up. It's only bile, and the smell turns my own stomach sour, but there's nothing to bring up, not since they limited our meals to once every other day. But Petra throwing up tells me she knows all about the hunting grounds and all the horrors inflicted there.

All the horrors that will be inflicted upon us.

Because no one is coming.

And we are alone.

I watch the light dance off Craven's lantern and project on the walls. It reminds me of the sun, the very thing I miss most about life outside of these cellar walls. The warmth, the spark, the way it fills me with life. He continues to speak, but his voice is muffled by the plan slowly taking shape.

The likelihood of gaining access to my abilities is next to nonexistent. I am not foolish enough to believe they'd let us out of our cuffs. If I am to survive this, I'm going to have to rely on my mortal skills. I'm going to have to play their game—and win.

When I do, I'll rid Stellera of the vermin who'd find sport in the suffering of others. When I win, I'm going to level the hunting grounds until there is nothing left.

The promise is my oath.

My lifeline.

FIFTY-SIX
HOLD YOUR BREATH
Aislinn

EREBUS IS SO COMPLETELY and utterly annoying. I don't know what his obsession is with my clothing, but it is driving me insane, and by the look on DeLuca's face, it's making him downright murderous.

I examine the dress Helena gave me to wear tonight, now with the additional length and layers and sigh. Well, it's too late to get anything else now considering most of my clothes are actually conjured by Erebus, Agnar, or Helena, and none of them are here currently.

A small part of me is actually excited for tonight. The last party was a little...tense...but Helena said it will be small, and she definitely knows how to have a good time. The only thing that would enhance my excitement would be being able to bring DeLuca...I'm not sure when or if that will ever be a possibility.

The portal I create sparks around me like a silver pool. Being underestimated has always worked to my advantage, and this is no different. I thought for sure when I ended up at Oonaugh's palace that Erebus would question it. He must be thoroughly distracted to not have given it a second thought.

Thankfully, Agnar's last lesson gave me everything I needed to make my sudden emergence of ability believable. He worked with me for hours until my portals held sturdy and I could get from one side of the room to the other in a blink. He had me attacking the dummy from all sides and, I admit, that bit was helpful. I only wish I didn't have to waste time pretending I couldn't already do it. Haile will be coming, of that I have no doubt. As soon as he learns I can portal, he will ask me to get through the barrier. I only hope I can hold off long enough so that DeLuca and I can go...home? Yeah...home. There isn't a better option for us. Not right now.

I step through and onto Helena's palace's front steps. Mercifully, there aren't any other gods out here. My hand reaches for the iron knockers, but soon as my finger reaches the cool metal, the door opens. There's a moment where my fist is still in the air, ready to knock, and I put it down with an awkward smile. I'm greeted by Raza, the god of dreams and nightmares, as well as Aria, the goddess of air. I supposed I could have guessed Raza would be here, considering he and Helena seem to have a thing going on, but Aria I have not met yet. She's small. Not a child, but hardly taller than one. Her blonde hair is braided and wrapped around her head with blue flowers woven through.

"Welcome, Aislinn, we have been waiting for you," Aria says. Even her voice feels airy. She floats in front of me and Raza waits for me to go before following.

He stays just behind me.

I'm reminded of when I was flanked by guards being walked to Lord Magnus's office...when he didn't want me to run away, before he could tell me all about Rett's true parentage and stealing babies from Ashe.

Helena has set up a tea party, a true honest-to-gods tea party, complete with tiny cakes and dainty tea cups.

"Ah, my mortal friend! Guest of honor!" Helena yells as she runs towards me full-force, wearing some ridiculous jumpsuit that is coated with feathers below the knees and elbows. "What in the star-crossed fate happened to your dress?"

I open my mouth to answer, but she cuts me off. "Wait, don't tell me. Lord self righteous?"

I snort. "The very one."

She rolls her eyes. "You know it's an illusion right?"

"What is?" I ask in confusion.

"Nevermind," she says quickly, then points me to a seat.

When we're all sitting, she looks at Aria and raises her brows. Aria nods and casts air around us so that we are in a type of bubble. Raza flicks his fingers, and Helena's face drops on the table. Followed by Aria's.

Oh gods, he's poisoned them.

I've gone clammy as I look around, plotting my exit. But before I can move, my eyes grow unbearably heavy, and my head feels like it's weighted by stone.

Oh gods, he's poisoned me too.

My head falls, but I'm deeply asleep before it hits the table.

I'm surprised when I take in my surroundings to find that I am sitting at an exact replica of the tea party...except now, I also am wearing some ridiculous veiled hat and my dress is back to the way it was.

Helena, Aria, and Raza look at me expectantly, and it clicks.

We weren't poisoned. Raza put us to sleep and combined our consciousness so that we could speak freely. That means this is not in fact a tea party...but something else. Something I'm not sure I want any part of.

"Hey, best friend!" Helena smiles, and the three gods sitting before me sip on their tea as if nothing out of the ordinary has happened.

"What the Hai—"

Aria interrupts me. "Don't say his name!"

Raza shoots her a look that I think is meant to calm her, but I could be wrong. "We don't speak the name of any of the gods unless we mean to call upon them."

"Oh..."

"I'm so glad you made it." Helena beams.

"Helena... what the—" I glance at Aria who wears a stern look. "What is going on?"

Helena clears her throat. "Welcome to the 'Dream Team!'"

"We are not called the *Dream Team*." Aria rolls her eyes.

"Well, we don't have an official name, so the 'Dream Team' is what I call it."

Raza laughs and watches Helena with absolute adoration in his gaze. It would be cute if I wasn't so confused.

"What is the 'Dream Team?'" I ask.

"Well, lovely Aislinn, it is our secret club for rebellions!" Helena claps.

"We meet in shared dreams where we can be sure no one is listening or spying," Raza offers. "Safer to speak freely."

"Okay...and so what is *this* meeting about?"

"That sunny bastard of a king is planning something," Aria says. "We are on the precipice of change. The air whispers to me of fates and destruction."

"Can we not be cryptic?" I ask.

"We just need to know...are you or are you not going to take down the barrier?" Raza says.

"Not."

The three of them let out a collective breath of relief.

"You *don't* want me to lift the barrier?"

"No!" Helena shrieks. "The last time the king ran amuck on mortal lands, he incited a war that nearly took down the realms!"

"A war? Why would Hai—I mean *he* start a war in the mortal realm?"

"The more living beings pledged to him, the more power he has." Aria shrugs.

I ponder. "So the barrier being up—"

"Has weakened him significantly, yes." Aria finishes my thought.

"You wanted me to portal through the barrier though...that day with the bees, you begged me to try," I say, looking at Helena.

She rolls her eyes. "I wanted you to get out. No offense and all, but you being here puts us all at risk. Sunshine can not be allowed anymore power than he has."

I shudder to think about Haile with *more* power, considering what I've seen him do to Erebus. "But it's not just weakening him—the whole realm is dying."

"Right," Raza says. "We have an idea for that."

"So, my beautiful bestie, we were thinking...well, *I* was thinking, but they think it might be a good idea...it might be a good time for Egon to be crowned king of gods."

My brows knit so severely I'm afraid they will get stuck together. "Egon? Your father? The god of death?"

"That's the one!" she says brightly.

"I thought he was imprisoned?"

"He is," Raza and Aria say in unity as if they've had this conversation hundreds of times.

Helena stands and begins to pace in front of the large window framed by a pink frilly curtain. "Daddy is imprisoned in Oblivion. He can be freed...by someone pure enough to walk it."

"You think I'm pure enough?" I ask skeptically.

"Ehm, close enough at least. Anyway, I figure you could probably break him out considering you can portal, and if something goes wrong, you can just high-tail out of there. Once that's finished, he can take over as king." She smiles and folds her hands beneath her chin, her violet eyes alight with excitement.

I try to search the memories that aren't mine to find Egon, to figure out what sort of god he is and if he would actually be a better king, but there's nothing. Not a drop of him.

"I'm going to have to visit the Weavers before I make a decision. They're withholding some of my memories, and I don't know anything about Egon."

"Yes, yes," Helena says. "But do not breathe a word of it to anyone else. No one."

Raza stirs his tea with a finger. "You know, Egon was always meant to rule our realm. Two parts of the same shadow. One to rule the dead, one the living."

I did not know that. "So why didn't he?"

"They couldn't rule together. Couldn't view one another as equals, and it was the mortals who paid the price."

Mortals always pay the price.

Before I can ask another question, we are ripping back into consciousness. Our tea party is set exactly as it was.

Aria and Raza have their features in pleasant but vacant masks. Helena is...well, Helena is being Helena and is staring at me with eyes too wide.

"Well, great having you!" She winks. "Tea time's over. Best to go *weave* your way back home."

I wonder if the others dismiss her odd behavior as a personality trait. She is by far the worst conspirator I have ever met.

"Uhm...okay..." I say, grabbing a tiny sandwich shaped like a skull, because despite the tea party being a cover for the "*Dream Team,*" I actually am hungry. "I'll see you all later then?"

"Oh, you can bet on it! I'll meet you at my brother's sinister shelter in a few hours!"

Raza and Aria say pleasant goodbyes and I portal myself to Kaoket. Maybe I should have mentioned Erebus's plans to send me back to the mortal realm...but all these overlapping plots and schemes keep pushing mine.

I'm running out of time.

My sandal-clad feet crunch over the skeletal debris littering the Imorti.

Leaves.

Twigs.

Bones.

The bones make me wonder what other critters live in the Imorti Woods. Other than the "beast" everyone is always talking about. Also, I wish I had worn boots...and maybe a training outfit instead of this flimsy dress. That was poor planning on my part.

I wander aimlessly, waiting for the tug that never comes. The doorway could show up anywhere in Kaoket. I supposed it would be worth it to go to the other side. My stomach tightens in anticipation as I create the portal, readying myself for the headache that accompanies the constant ring in my ears when visiting the Vivatus.

I'm immediately greeted with a sense of wrongness when I appear through my portal. The odd glow that usually coats the plants seems to be sputtering in and out. Between the sputters, it looks as though rot has begun to fester.

Smells like it too.

It's nauseating.

I'm close to the edge of the forest when I finally feel that pull. The Opari Stone vibrates beneath my skin.

Took long enough.

I was beginning to think you were hiding from me.

I smirk to myself and follow the thread of fate tugging me towards the Weavers. The Opari Stone continues to buzz as I tap into its power. I welcome it like an old friend. I love the feel as it tangles with whatever power I already had.

There's an odd pinprick sensation at the base of my neck. It's the feeling of eyes watching me. Each time I turn around to inspect it, there is nothing there. But the feeling remains, and I quicken my pace to a light jog.

I don't think training with Agnar has made much of a difference. Even this small amount of exercise has me completely winded, but I trudge on, jogging through the false Vivatus and watching the rot spread around me like a disease. This is getting bad. If they don't figure out how to feed the realm soon, I doubt there will be much of a realm left, and if this realm dies...I don't even want to think about what will happen to the mortal realm.

The tingling at the base of my neck doesn't subside until I fall through the gate to the Weavers' fold. Out of breath and body on high alert.

The five cloaked figures immediately surround me, taking turns speaking.

"*Imposter.*"

"You have."

"Returned."

"What do"

"You want?"

Creepy.

I stand and dust off my bare legs. "I want my memories. All of them. I'm tired of being incomplete. Send me back into that lake of terrors and put the rest in. I'm next to useless with all these gaps in my mind."

The one in the middle comes forward, pulling back her hood and revealing the swirls tattooed on her forehead. "You ask for that of which we can not offer."

"What do you mean you can't offer it?" I put my hands on my hips.

"We can not offer what we do not have. Whatever memories are lost were taken...destroyed."

"By who?"

All five of them stare at me with blank expressions.

"The Utikalo?" I ask.

They nod. A chill makes my shoulders shake.

That familiar itch of vacancy where I should have a memory opens in my mind. What would the Utikalo possibly have to hide that's worse than being the child of prophecy to bring down the Shadows?

I know I probably won't get an answer, but I still have to try. "Why would they do that?"

"To"

"Protect"

"The"

"Future."

This is a waste of time. Obviously, the Weavers aren't going to be any help in this. I'd have better luck flipping through Erebus's tampered books. Unless...perhaps they may show me what the Utikalo lost.

"Can you show me the future you wove? The one that had the Utikalo tearing themselves apart?"

"We can only show Viitor, and *you* are *not* Viitor," the female with her hood down says.

I grind my teeth. "Can you tell me more about Egon, at the very least?" Maybe he really is the answer this realm needs.

The Weavers hiss as if I've cursed them.

"We do not speak of the Master of Death here. We do not want him to find us. To *use* us," one of the males says.

So, yes—this has been a giant waste of time.

"Can you tell me *anything* useful?" I ask with an irritated edge in my voice.

One of the other females smirks from below her hood. "*Hold your breath, imposter.*"

"Hold my bre—" I'm pushed from the fold before I can even finish my sentence.

Damn Weavers.

The second I open my eyes, I find two yellow ones looking right at me. A breath later and a familiar black dust is making its way into my lungs. There's a scream stuck in my throat. My vision blinks in and out, but before I lose consciousness, I see another pair of eyes poking out from a bush, followed by more and more until the entire bush is blinking at me. I'm thrown over someone's shoulder and then there is nothing.

FIFTY-SEVEN
MASTER OF SHADOWS
Erebus

THIS PALACE MAKES ME sick, the false light and sickly bright
sheen coating every surface. Haile's palace is just as inflated as
his self-conceit. Delun stays by my side. His feet are stealthy
and I am mildly impressed by the way he maneuvers with such
fluidity—despite his height and bulk. It is almost as if he is part of
the air he commands.

I lead him through a series of glistening halls with gold veined
white marble, past the many busts of each of his sons and the
statue dedicated to my Astoria, and finally down to Haile's private
chambers. Drops of deep blue line the hallway—sticking out
among the polished white and gold.

My body stiffens with realization.

Blood.

Gods' blood.

My shadows writhe, they sense it too. A disturbance in the
energies is making me especially anxious to get out of here. I am
not a fan of change, but I sense its arrival like an unwelcomed
visitor. We have a small window, and I do not want to miss this
opportunity. The realm is restless tonight. The enchantments are

fading in the Vivatus. If Haile's magic is declining this severely, he is no doubt becoming desperate.

I have seen him desperate before.

I am not eager to repeat that particular history.

"It's quiet," Delun says in a hushed voice.

"It would be, if you were not speaking."

He gives me a sidelong glare and I relish in it with a smug smile.

I open the gilded door marking Haile's private chambers and nod Delun inside. "Come, just through this door now."

This room is exactly as I remember, exuberant and dreadfully uncouth—everything a glittering gold or pure white. I don't hide the disgust from my features and let my nose turn up.

"What does it look like?" Delun asks.

"A clear sphere. About as large as your head. Very heavy."

He nods, and we begin our exploration, digging through drawers, careful to keep everything in place. The obvious hiding spots like the closets and drawers come up empty. Haile is comfortable enough in his power that he would not expect a thief. Wherever he keeps the orb would be easily accessed for his daily use.

Tapping my fingers against the top of a dresser, I stare at a large writing desk that is entirely overcompensating.

The most obvious of places. It's embarrassing, truly. I rifle around beneath the drawers until I finally find it a small lever. I flick it up with a finger, and with a click and heavy groan, part of the wall falls away—revealing the Orb of Opari. False security has brought down entire monarchies... It would seem gods are no better.

Delun rushes to grab the orb and I slap his hand away with a swish of shadow. He opens his mouth to say something I'm sure is meant to be intimidating, but I stop him by holding out a finger.

"You must not touch it with your hands. In order to transport it, we will need to wrap the orb."

He grabs a pillow off of Haile's oversized bed and wiggles the gold-silk case free of the insert. "What about this?"

"That might have worked, if it wouldn't alert him that someone had been here." I look him up and down. His clothing is incredibly dull. Nothing special. Not worth mentioning. Perfect. "It will have to be your shirt."

"*My* shirt? You have on layers. Why not *your* jacket?"

"*Mine?*" I recoil in disgust. The suggestion is appalling. "And walk around in half a suit? Absolutely not. You can remain without a shirt for a few minutes. I assure you, the inhabitants of this realm will not pay you any mind."

Delun's eyes harden as they lock on me, but it does not take long before he is pulling off his shirt. For the first time, I notice the scars marking his arms. An oddity for a god. Whatever is responsible must not have been of their realm. He wraps the orb in his shirt and ties a knot at the top.

"Let us get away from this dastardly disgraced palace." I motion for the boy to lead the way.

We just make it into the hallway when we hear a door slam.

I sigh at the inconvenience and I look at Delun, hoping he can read my silent command to remain quiet while we continue to slink through the halls. A woman's laughter splinters the silence. I'd know that high-pitch tittering anywhere.

Ravetta.

The laughter quickly turns to moans and then screams of pleasure. I can't say I'm surprised. Ravetta has been so far up Haile's asshole she probably is acquainted with each particle of shit that comes through him.

Delun lifts his brows and I shrug. I do not want to give half a thought to whatever kind of fuckery is happening below us. We walk by a large window, one that overlooks the kingdom, far past Kaoket. It is a pretty spectacular view, if you like shiny things. But as I squint, I see the shine fade in and out like a dying heartbeat. The enchantments are failing. We would be lucky if it lasted the week. Something else catches my attention...something far more concerning... Haile's army is missing.

"I never thought I'd be glad to be back here." Delun pants as we enter the parlor. I sent the orb to the isvipotale in a swirl of shadow. Once my pet returns from her outing, I will explain to them both how to use it. That way, I don't have to repeat myself.

I hate repeating myself.

Almost as much as I hate questions.

"Don't get used to it. You'll be back to where you came from soon. Out of my hair for good."

"For good?" He seems an odd mixture of suspicion and surprise. "Does that mean you're going to stop messing with my life?"

"Well, that depends."

"Depends on what?" he asks.

I shrug. "It depends on how this all plays out."

"I want you to leave us alone. I don't want you to watch me or contact me or interfere with anyone else in my life. *Especially* Aislinn."

"Now that, I can not promise." A corner of my mouth twists up in amusement. "You see, we are bonded, my pet and I."

His anger tinges the air with a smokey scent. "Bonded?"

I do wonder how far I can push until he loses control completely. The raw power flowing through the boy is wasted. His potential is limitless. "Shadow-bonded. She belongs to me."

"She doesn't belong to anyone but herself!"

Oh, this little angry god. He is too easily riled.

"You are so very wrong, Delun. I own her shadow. We are connected. As long as I rule the Shadows, she is bound to *me*."

Delun's flames dance along his skin, and I must admit he could have been something great if he were able to grow up in this realm where he belongs.

I get lost in my thoughts of what could never be and what was not, so when Helena flies in unannounced, I am thoroughly unprepared. She spots Delun immediately and her eyes bulge like the bug she is.

"I knew it!" she squeals.

"Shit," Delun and I both say at the same time—and in the same tone, which has us looking towards each other with furrowed brows.

"I knew I felt a rift open! But how? How did you get here?"

If it was going to be any god that found out our secret, probably best for it to be Helena.

He looks at me before answering. I give a slight nod in response to his silent question.

"Oonaugh's portal," Delun offers.

"Huh. Cool. I didn't know that one still worked...oh! I bet you met Kyle! Ugh, what a good beastie. He's one of my favorites!" she croons, and my shadows shudder thinking of that tentacled creature.

Delun looks confused and then I see a veil of realization flash over his features before they turn into something akin to shame.

Stars know what that was about.

My shadows begin tittering, and I look beyond Helena, expecting to see a dark-haired girl with emerald eyes following her in.

My stomach drops in a way I've never experienced before. The hall is empty.

"Helena," I say slowly, "*where* is my pet?"

Delun stills at that, turning his full attention to Helena, his eyes growing wild and dark.

"She will be back soon." Helena waves me off. "She went to see the Weavers to get the rest of her memories back. Don't be such a nervous naysayer."

I exhale in relief. "What are you doing here, Helena?"

She looks affronted and places a hand to her chest as though I have truly and deeply wounded her. "Waiting for my dearest friend, of course."

I raise a brow. "*Dearest* friend?"

"Oh yes, Aislinn and I are the best of friends. Bound by secrets." She wiggles her fingers to punctuate her words.

My youngest sister is exasperating...and yet, she is the only sibling I can tolerate.

A tingle through my shadows alerts me of a presence approaching. Without a word to the others, I travel in a burst of shadow to my grand foyer, opening the door to find one of the small creatures from Kaoket standing before me. Agnar uses these things as messengers, so I wait impatiently for it to relay whatever garbage Agnar has for me today.

"May Chimmy enter, Master of Shadows?" the tiny creature asks. I open the door a smidge wider and gesture for it to come into the foyer. He waddles slowly, agitating me further.

"What is it?" I ask.

"It is...sensitive... Chimmy could get in great trouble by being here. Great trouble, indeed," it says with a tremble.

"Well? Out with it, creature."

"Oh! Hello, Chimmy!" Helena squeals as she enters, Delun in tow.

"Madame Death." The creature bows for her, then turns to Delun. "Master."

"Good to see you again," Delun says to the lowly creature.

"On with it!" I've officially lost all my patience for this day.

The small creature's shoulders sag, and his head lowers. "It's about the Master Mortal... Chimmy has family that dwells in the Vivutus Forest, and they witnessed something. As soon as they send message Chimmy, Chimmy come here straight away for help."

"Help what?!" I shout.

The creature cringes away but takes a deep breath. "Ravetta has taken Aislinn. She blew a dust of sorts into Master Mortal's face that make her sleep, and the slimy one took her."

"That bitch!" Helena says.

"Not again," Delun says, squeezing his eyes shut and clenching his fists, which are fully alight.

I say nothing.

I do nothing.

I do not even breathe as I search for that tug of our bond.

It lays so still I almost miss it, but there it is.

A faint pull.

Found you, pet.

I throw my arms out, preparing to sweep all of us up in shadows. "No one takes what's mine."

FIFTY-EIGHT
NOTHING
Aislinn

COLD METAL BITES INTO my wrists and ankles, holding me tightly in place as I'm laid out on a hard surface. The cold brushes across my skin, leaving trails of goosebumps. The Weavers' words replay in my head: "*Hold your breath.*"

Thanks for the warning.

Could have been more specific.

I'm so tired of being taken places against my will.

Tired of being so easily targeted.

What happened to simply asking someone for their time? A simple, "*Hello, Aislinn, how are you? Would you mind conversing with me for a few moments?*"

Nope. Instead, they take. Take, take, take. Always taking and wanting more.

When I get out of this, I'm going to have Agnar train me twice as long. I don't care how hard I have to work. I will never be taken again.

A gust of air blows around me before I feel the drop of a thin blanket. Blanket may not be the right word, more like an oversized piece of paper.

Trying to open my eyes is like trying to swim with stones tied to my feet, but I feel as if I am being watched. When I finally win the battle to get them open, I find that I am strapped to some kind of golden altar. My captor's serpentine gaze sparkles, and her deviant smile sends rivulets of fear through my body.

"Ravetta?" I say groggily, still trying to shake the fog away. "Wh—"

"I'm going to save you the trouble of speaking. You're in a hidden room beneath Haile's palace," she says. Her venomous voice has a edge of excitement to it.

"Why did you take me?"

"Because my king asked me to, and I want to be a *good queen*, unlike the old traitorous bitch who used to hold that title."

I swallow as I try to understand. "Queen...used to?"

Ravetta smirks. I notice for the first time she has a dagger in her hand...my dagger... She uses it to point toward the far wall and I follow the movement. A gasp escapes my lips at the scene before me.

Isela's limbs are tied to wooden beams crossed like an "X." Shackles hold her in place as she bleeds out from the wound slashed from hip to hip. Her womb is nailed beside her bloodied face. The cuts are fresh, blue blood hitting the floor in a consistent drip. It doesn't look as if she's breathing, but it's hard to tell from where I am.

"I have you to thank for that, I suppose." Ravetta sighs. "If you hadn't told Erebus about Isela slipping bits of Mari to Astoria, we may never have figured it out. It's so twisted...actually made me respect our former queen a smidgen more."

I won't pretend I ever liked Isela, but the scene before me is so grotesque that vomit gathers at the back of my throat. No one could have deserved that. No one. Judging by the thousands of tiny cuts coating her naked body, they dragged out her suffering.

And from the look on Ravetta's face, they reveled in it.

"You and Haile did that to her?"

"No." Her smile creeps as slowly as the chill down my spine, "I'm just the deliverer. The dirty work was all Haile. He has a kind of *kink* for this kind of thing. Something about it really gets his blood hot." She brushes her hair away to show tiny little cuts along her collarbone.

"That's sick."

Ravetta's eyes flash, shifting from yellow to red, before quickly shifting back to that same yellow. "Don't speak about my king in such a way." She snarls inches from my face.

I drop my voice to one of understanding and compassion. "You don't have to let him hurt you just because he's the king."

"Oh, dumb mortal bitch, of course I do, because *I fucking love it.*"

Monsters made for each other.

Before I can tell Ravetta just how horrible I think she is, a door slams open, rattling the odd metal walls. Haile comes trudging toward us with a crazed look of delight.

Ravetta bounces to him, leaning up on her toes to kiss him. Not just a peck. That would be far too civilized for these two—they're sucking each other's faces as if it's their life source. Their bodies mold to fit each other's forms. Haile is pushing against her until they bump against the wall Isela is currently strung up on. Rivers of blue blood drips from their heads and down their faces, making them look utterly insane.

Just when I think I'm about to witness Haile fuck another woman beneath the still bleeding body of his wife, he pulls away. "Not now, my little savage. I have work to do. Run along and play."

She pouts. "But I want to play *now*, my king." Ravetta wipes a finger in the blood dribbling down Haile's face and swipes it across the top of her breast, pulling his focus to it.

Haile's eyes flare brightly, but he shakes his head. "No, I must be quick before they find out we have her."

"Let me help, please, my king!"

"This is something I must do alone. I need full concentration, and you are quite the distraction. Run along and keep watch. Come to me the instant you see movement in the Shadows." He kisses her, then licks the blood off her breast. Moaning in delight.

I gag, the noise drawing their attention. Ravetta winks at me, then blows Haile a kiss before walking through a fold and disappearing.

Haile takes a satisfied inhale before turning to me. "Hello, mortal."

"You know Erebus will come for me, right?"

"Yes. I have noticed how particularly fond of you my daughter's husband is. I find that interesting considering he doesn't seem to be fond of...well...anyone, so why is it he comes to your aid each time? Why is it that he harbors not only you but your secrets as well?"

"I don't know. You'll have to ask him when he comes for me." I keep it to myself that I know DeLuca will also come for me. But part of me hopes I'm wrong, because if he comes, he will expose himself and be in more danger than I am.

"Oh, I plan to." His smile would be dazzling if it wasn't so deluded.

I sigh and school my expressions to look bored as I've seen so many of the gods do. "Let's just get it over with."

"Get what over with, mortal?" Haile asks while twisting the Child Blade on the table beside my arm.

"Whatever it is you've taken me for."

Something flashes across his face like eagerness. "If you insist. Why haven't you brought down the barrier now that you have regained your magic and memories?"

This is his burning question? "You could have asked me this in a more civilized way, you know?"

Haile leans down so that we are nose to nose. "I could have, but it seems we have run out of time for civilized conversation. Now answer me, mortal."

"I don't have the full memories. They're filled with holes and choppy. As for the barrier, I don't think you'll want it down when you hear the reason." I smile knowingly, just biding my time before my rescuers charge in. I imagine it, how satisfying it will be to watch Haile get put in his place for once.

"Tell me." His jaw clenches as his patience wears.

"It's Astoria. She is the barrier...or a part of it. If you destroy the barrier, you pose the risk of destroying her. Permanently."

Haile draws back as if I have actually surprised him. He looks as though he's weighing different options and different plans, his upper lip curling back, and he finally says, "She has been gone for some time now. I suppose I will finally be able to mourn her properly."

"You'd do that to her? Your own daughter?!"

He spits in my face. The saliva burns like acid. "Do you know what devastation *your actions* have caused? Manipulating words in prophecies and sending us to chase after our own asses for millenia!"

"That wasn't me!" I try to wriggle from the bindings strapping me to the altar.

Zero budge.

I focus on creating a portal.

I could get myself free.

But any stirring of power has disappeared completely.

Even the ringing in my ears has gone quiet.

"The one responsible lives here beneath your skin." He slides the Child Blade down my arm, the one containing the Opari Stone Erebus had shoved beneath it. He doesn't press hard enough to draw blood—yet. "My only daughter lost everything because of *you.*"

"But she's not, is she?"

Haile's face hardens. "Not *what*?"

"Your *only* daughter." I smirk.

His joyless laughter causes my throat to tighten. "This is why you should have stayed dead, Utikalo. You *see* too much."

I clench my teeth so hard my molars crack as he digs the tip of the Child Blade beneath the Opari Stone—carving it free.

I scream.

I can't help it, even as I try to remain strong. The pain is unparalleled as he digs two fingers into my wound to pull out the stone. I'm shaking by the time he's done, and he is standing over me, looking like he's just been given the greatest gift in the realms.

"Good girl. See, not so bad."

I'm panting, trying to catch my breath, and unwanted tears trail down my cheeks. Trying to make my voice as firm as I can, it still cracks. "You got what you wanted. Let me go."

"I think not. One stone. I need all three to open the barrier."

My voice trembles. "I d-d-don't—"

Haile places the blade on my lips and leans in real close. "Shh, shh, shh, I know you don't have Viitor. I know, dear, but I was wondering if you know where it is." I shake my head no. Praying he doesn't hear my heart beating like a damn traitor.

"Mmm." He smiles. "Let's try again. Do you know where the Viitor Stone is?"

I feel his influence trying to pull the truth from me, but I shut him out and think of her. Her innocent face. Her bright eyes and smile. I can't give her to this beast.

"I'm waiting, *girl*. Where is the Viitor Stone?"

I bite my tongue so hard, my teeth break through it. Blood pools in my mouth and slides to the back of my throat.

A muscle in Haile's jaw ticks, and he plunges the blade into my shoulder. I scream out.

"Tell me!" He twists the knife in slow circles until I can't fight it off any longer.

"In Caeliss! It's in Caeliss!" I say with a cry, cursing myself as I do, but I couldn't. I couldn't hold it in. It's like he reached into my voice and pulled it out using forceps made of fire. I couldn't hold it back.

I couldn't.

"That wasn't so hard, was it?" He runs a finger along my cheek, wiping at the bit of blood that has slid out from the corner of my mouth. "Now, I want you to find it for me."

Haile unlatches my restraints with one hand and keeps me pinned by the throat with the other. He works so fast I don't have the time to even think about moving before he clenches the Opari Stone and presses against my forehead. In a flash of light, we are traveling through my memories of Caeliss. He sees everything. When we discovered our powers. All our friends. My new found family. Our homes. The celebrations and offerings. The Elders. And then he finds her. The little girl with brown curls and a splattering of freckles.

There is a strange vibration as Haile joins our bodies. We look through the same eyes, but he takes control of my voice.

"Hadleigh," he says through my lips. I try to bite them closed to keep him from speaking to her, but it's no use. A burning light tears through my throat. "Hadleigh," he says again.

She turns, eyes brightening. "Aislinn?"

I try to shake my head. To tell her to run. But I can't. I'm a prisoner in my own body. "Hadleigh, I found a way to save your brother," Haile says through me, and I realize what he's about to do.

I thrash in my own skin, fighting, clawing, screaming, but outwardly remain still.

"Heidon?! How?!"

"We need to create a bridge, Hadleigh. A bridge to join the realms."

Hadleigh's eyes grow impossibly wide with hope. "Can you do it?"

No! I try to shout but again am silenced and Haile's voice rings out as my own. "*We* can, sweet Hadleigh, we can."

"We can?"

"We can."

"How can I help?" she asks eagerly.

"Tell me, Hadleigh, did you know that we can portal?"

Her face loses a little bit of that light. "I don't think so."

"I can help you. Just let your mind relax. I'm going to show you an image, and I need you to believe that you are there. Can you do that?"

"I think so."

"Good. Good girl."

An image is pushed out around us. A familiar image. I know this place...I *know* this place.

The unfinished bridge.

The sickly green liquid spurting out

The Egora Bog.

The one bordering the Astoria province.

I can't speak. Still held captive inside my own head, but I damn near split it open trying. Trying to reach her. But it's too late. Hadleigh is there, at the bottom of the bridge, about to take her step up.

"That's it, Hadleigh. Come to me."

Haile. Please let her go. Leave her out of this. I'll do anything. I will take down the barrier and create portals. Please let her be.

"Why do that when I could control all three stones? I could have the power of the Utikalo for myself. I don't need you. You are *nothing*."

I want to argue, but how can I?

I can't even get him out of my own mind.

Can't fight back.

Can't save Hadleigh.

Can't remember anything useful.

I'm worthless.

I *am* nothing.

"Glad you finally see it," Haile says.

Get out of my head!

"Soon. She's nearly there now."

Hadleigh's hair whips wildly in the wind as she continues her trek across the broken bridge. The toxic bubbles fester and pop around it, the brave girl holds no fear on her face. She shows nothing but sheer determination to save her brother.

"That's it, almost there," Haile encourages as she gets to the end.

The stories were true.

The bridge is littered with skeletons, but they're not laying around bones as you would expect. They're standing, at least twelve of them, at attention—as if waiting for a command. When Hadleigh spots them, she freezes and lets out a whimper.

"Go on, go on, they will not harm you," Haile encourages using my voice. "They are Guardians, and you're uldoaka. They will know you are their friend."

"Uldoaka," Hadleigh says quietly, and all the skeletons turn their empty skulls towards her at once. She jumps back with a little scream and looks half a beat away from running back.

I feel Haile grow impatient. "Keep going, Viitor," he says through my mouth.

"Viitor?" she asks quietly.

"*Hadleigh*, you must keep going. Heidon is counting on you."

Her lower lip trembles, and she closes her tiny fists. "For Heidon," she says and continues walking. She whispers, "Uldoaka" under her breath, repeating as if it's her own special prayer to give her the courage to get to the end.

The skeletons' heads turn and watch as she passes, but to my relief, they do not move or try to stop her.

"Good girl, Hadleigh. Now I need you to open your mind's eye."

"My what?"

"Mind's eye. Feel your power. Feel it centered in your mind. Once you feel it, grasp it. Then picture me on this side. Imagine our threads, silver, iridescent, and gold, weaving together to form the bridge."

Whatever Haile is saying must be working, because once Hadleigh's eyes close, I feel a tug on that familiar thread, the one I always let guide me. It tugs from my core, and as it joins with the two others, that ringing in my ears turns into a song. The most beautiful song in existence.

It feels whole.

Euphoric.

And then Haile laughs, disturbing my bliss.

"It fucking worked," he boasts.

Before us, connected to the unfinished bridge, is a tangle of metallic colors forming a sort of path to a portal...but one large enough for an army.

"Okay, Hadleigh, stay there. I will be there soon to complete the bridge on my side. I need you to put your hand on the portal. Keep it there. Do not move it until I come for you. I'm going to need to leave your mind. I will see you soon...with Heidon," Haile says, again using my voice. The vision cuts out in a burst of light.

I'm sweating and exhausted. The pain in my arm and shoulder is now more pronounced since returning to my body fully. Haile is grinning, and it's the most terrifying thing I've ever seen.

"Okay, so now what? How are you going to open that portal? Take me to the other side of the bridge?" I ask.

His smile falters, and he looks down at me, still strapped tightly to the stone table, and sneers. "I'm not taking you anywhere. I told you, you are *nothing*."

"You can't open it without me! Can't hold the bridge without me!"

"On the contrary, I can do everything without you. All I needed was your connection and a stone."

"The stone is a part of me. It is bonded to my shadow." Despite the raging pain in my body, I find myself smirking up at Haile.

I am not *nothing*. He *needs* me.

Haile barks a laugh and drags his curved blade down my collarbone. "To be transparent, I don't need your stone. We've already rebuilt the bridge, and the portal will open for Opari and Viitor. I don't care much about what has already passed, I'm always looking towards the future. But a little excavation to find the Forbis Stone is too tempting to pass up...I do wonder; does it live in your blood the way gods' magic does?" He taps the center of my chest with the blade. "Now, let's see about freeing it from your unworthy body." His clovered-honey eyes glint with madness. He's deranged, completely and utterly corrupted.

I realize in this moment, that this is it.

No one is coming to save me.

I can't save myself.

I am nothing.

Not special.

I was never the child of balance from the prophecy.

It was always Hadleigh.

The life I so desperately wanted flashes through my mind. Me and DeLuca in a little seaside cottage somewhere in Astoria. His arms around my round belly and children with dark curly hair and bright blue eyes laughing behind us. It's so simple, so easy…yet, it's everything I can never have. Everything is about to change. A single tear slips out from the corner of my eye.

I'm not leaving this place alive.

FIFTY-NINE
BEAUTIFUL NIGHTMARE
DeLuca

EREBUS SWEEPS US IN his shadows and deposits us somewhere near that same gold mountain we were at earlier. This time, I don't complain. Helena, however, gives him a string of curses. Apparently, the shadows ruffled her feathers or something. I don't know, and I don't care. Because another fucking god took Aislinn from me, and he is going to burn for it.

Unfortunately, if I want to find her quickly, I have no other choice than to follow Erebus since he shackled her to him like some kind of animal. The only fortunate outcome of that connection is that it acts like a tracker, and in this moment, I'm grateful for the direct link.

We're moving quickly to Haile's palace, our determination mirrored until Erebus stops suddenly.

He's gone completely still. Then the very air vibrates around him before shadows burst from him in an explosion like a dying star.

Helena and I get blown back by the blast. I rise to my feet and stalk toward him. "What the fuck, Erebus?"

His jaw locks as he grinds out the words slowly and with agony in his voice. "She is hurt."

She is hurt.

Aislinn.

Is.

Hurt.

The words echo in and out, repeating in my head as my heart pounds painfully. At first it feels like falling into a void, and then the anger pushes me back out again. There's no use in trying to hold back the flames as they engulf my body. At the very least, I have enough control that they do not burn—it's moreso like bursts of pure energy. I'm not going to have any semblance of calm until I get Ailie back to where she belongs.

With me.

"She's hurt?" Helena comes rushing to our side. Worry replaces the usual mischief in her eyes.

Erebus nods tersely. "I felt her wake from a deep sleep. Then I felt a spike in her heart rate...and now, I don't feel her at all."

"Not at all?" My flames flicker, as if those words are trying to drown them.

"Not at all, but it is the same when she portals or has a vision. Perhaps she portaled herself back to the Shadows," Erebus says and then whispers to some of the shadows swirling around him. They speed off as soon as he finishes speaking.

"They will report back to me. If she is at the palace or anywhere else under my domain, they will find her." There's something off in the way he says it.

"You don't truly believe she's there, do you?"

"Haile has his own reasons for wanting her. Only a fool would underestimate him, and I am no fool."

No, but I am for letting Aislinn out of my sight. "Where would they take her?"

"He would know we are coming," Helena says. "Here near the Auric Mountains would be the safest against Erebus and his shadows. There's no way Agnar would aid him in this."

"Where?" I don't care if they hear the desperation in my voice. I *am* desperate. I didn't come all this way just to lose her again.

I can't lose her again. I won't survive it.

"Last I felt her was in the palace," Erebus says, looking as if he is fighting some internal battle. "That is where we will begin. Calm yourself, or your temper will lead to our ruin. We will search his palace until we find her."

Calm myself? He can't seriously expect me to remain calm at a time like this. If he does, then he doesn't understand what it is to have love and to risk losing it.

"I'll take to the skies, look for any sign," Helena says.

Erebus grabs her arm to stop her. "No one else, Helena."

She nods, the gravity of the situation holding us all on the edge of its blade. She flies off so fast I hardly see her move.

"Come, Delun, we will go in the same way we did earlier."

I follow him, unable to speak, unable to feel anything but the desire to get to Aislinn. My stomach is clenching, and I find it hard to breathe.

I failed her.

Again.

We search for too long. My flames around me are unrelenting, but I retain enough control to not burn everything I touch. I'm just about to suggest we find Helena when Erebus stills again.

"I feel her."

"Where is she?!"

"It's muffled, as if it's pushing against a veil of reality. The connection is straining. My little pet is fighting it. She's trying to reach me, but it's like screaming below water, and the only reason I can feel any of it at all is—" His eyes dart to me. There's real concern there, or as close to it as the shadow god gets.

I growl in frustration, running my hand through my hair. "Is what, Erebus?"

"Her pain is excruciating."

There is no stopping it now—I erupt. The air sweeps up my flames, burning all the rooms behind us. The godsdamned ground trembles beneath my wrath. A vicious wind fills the halls, carrying flame and debris along with it.

"Delun!" Erebus shouts from behind a shield of shadow, and I prepare for him to tell me to calm down again. To my surprise, he doesn't. His gray eyes flicker with understanding. "She's below ground."

I don't waste a single second. At my command, the floor we stand on splits, dropping us to the lowest level. We land on our feet as if we'd only taken a step rather than dropped multiple floors. Pieces of the palace begin to rain down on us, but I create an airshield to block it out.

A goddess with yellow serpentine eyes appears seemingly from nowhere and laughs a menacing cruel laugh while dancing in the chaos surrounding her.

"Where is she?" I shout.

She stops her dancing, then leans against a cracked pillar, examining her nails. "Whomst?"

Erebus is on her in a second, his arm pushed against her throat and shadows wrapped around her hands. "Tell him, Ravetta!"

"Oh, Erebus, you do remember our time together! How else could you know I love it when you bind my hands like this." She blows him a kiss in the air.

"You're with her?!" I ask, feeling my blood boiling further.

"Not in thousands of years," Erebus says while still glaring at Ravetta.

I look between the two, trying to decipher the truth, but I really don't fucking care. "Aislinn?" I shout.

"Aislinn this, Aislinn that. Every god wants to talk about *Aislinn*." The goddess rolls her eyes and it pisses me off so much that I send a bolt of fire directed at the eye closest to me. She shrieks in pain as it melts from the socket, and I suppose Erebus is also caught off guard because he loosens his grip enough that the goddess escapes.

Erebus curses and points to a hallway. "Go! Delun, go now! I'll go after Ravetta."

I crash through the doors, ripping each along the corridor off their hinges and tossing them aside like they weigh nothing. "Aislinn?" I shout over and over while stalking the halls.

I'm at the last door, and I blow it off with one small clench of my first. The first thing I notice is a goddess strung up on the wall, bleeding rivers of blue and unmoving, but I do not know this woman, or goddess, whoever she may be.

My breath halts before my eyes have time to find the center of the room. It's like I know before I see. I feel it in the deepest depths of my hollow shadow. She's there, on the golden altar. Her arms are split open and dripping crimson blood onto the otherwise pristine tile below.

Drip.

I wince at sound, closing my eyes to try and block it out.

Drip.

Drip.

Each drop hitting the floor hammers at my breaking heart.

Drip.

Slowly, I open my eyes again. My vision blurs, but there is no mistaking the scene before me.

My flames sputter out, as if they, too, cannot bear to exist without her. I rush to her and scoop her limp body into my arms before falling to my knees. The bastard carved open her chest and left her open and bare. My fingers tremble over the locket, now splashed in red, then trace a shaking finger over her cheek. He didn't touch her face, but everywhere else is...unrecognizable. I've never seen a body so badly mutilated. He enjoyed this. It's evident in the way he sliced like brush strokes on canvas. This is his art.

I try to focus on her face, smoothing her blood-soaked hair off of it.

So still.

So pale.

All the light drained from those emerald eyes I love so much.

She's cold.

Someone is shouting so loud I can't hear anything else.

Oh...it's me...I'm shouting.

Thick tears slide down my face.

I crush her broken body to mine, breaking with her.

Not just breaking.

Shattering.

Crumbling.

Dying.

I'm dying a thousand times over, and fuck, I pray I really am just to end this pain.

Erebus and Helena rush in and take in the scene. Helena falls to her knees, wings tumbling across the floor and hands clasped over her mouth. But Erebus, that fucking cruel asshole is smirking. He starts walking towards us and something in me snaps.

"Get the fuck away from us!" My fire returns as I shout, erupting around us so that we're shielded by the flames. Erebus's shadows recoil from the light.

The glow of the flames shines over Aislinn's face, and her voice fills my mind as I'm transported to a memory. We're in the Silver Hills, her head against my chest as she whispered, *"If you do end up burning, I will happily burn with you. When we are nothing more than ashes in the wind, we can return to the stars together. Forever together."*

I kiss Aislinn's forehead, my lips quivering with each excruciating word. "Forever together, baby. Let's return to the stars." I let go of the control and allow the fire to consume us. Her body catches. I could snuff it out, I almost do, but I'd rather us burn together than for her to rot away alone. So I let it burn. I feed the fire my rage until it grows hotter. Willing it would obliterate me as well, though I already know it won't—that will be done by the dagger hidden behind my back. I hold her tighter to my chest, waiting for her to crumble into nothing, accepting this as our last moment.

"Delun. Let her be," Erebus says, his voice slithering into my mind, past my wall.

"I won't leave her!"

"Son, let go of the fire. Trust me."

"I could never trust you."

"Then I will come in and help you."

"You can't."

"I can. I am immortal. It will hurt like sunlight, but I can if need be." To prove his point, Erebus takes a step forward, walking into the flames. I can see the pain he tries to mask, and his shadows scream so loudly even I can hear their cries.

"Fuck." I reluctantly drop my shield of fire, looking down at the charred remains of the girl I love and shattering all over again.

Erebus is by my side, his hand on my shoulder. Helena behind him sobbing. "Look." His voice is softer than I've ever heard as his gaze falls to Aislinn's chest. Beneath her charred skin, glowing embers die out as a smooth smoke-like shadow weaves between the wounds.

That tiny spark of hope I can never seem to smother ignites somewhere deep down within me. "What are you doing to her?" My voice is hoarse and breath hard.

Erebus smiles. "Wrong question. You should be asking what I *did* to her."

Helena wipes the tears from her violet eyes and gasps with realization. "*Harbinger.*"

Aislinn's wounds all pull close. The skin remains gray like little rivers of shadows running across her skin. She begins to stir, and that damned flame of hope begins to pull together the shards of my heart. She starts convulsing, foaming at the mouth. Her back arches so deeply, I fear it may break. An invisible force lifts her in the air high above us. Large black shadows erupt from her back and spread like a cloud of darkness. It temporarily blinds me as a combination of shadow and stardust drapes over the room.

When I can see again, I am sure I must be dreaming. Before me Aislinn stands—completely healed with a hazy sort of glow around her and black wings that swirl like smoke. Her once emerald eyes are now so dark they are almost black and lined with a ring of silver. This woman is crafted from some kind of beautiful nightmare.

I swallow the lump in my throat before approaching her. "Ailie?"

She smiles, but it doesn't quite reach her eyes. It's pained despite her best attempt to hide it, but she tries, and I know it's for my benefit. "Luc."

"You're—" My words stick to my throat, like if I voice them, this illusion will fall.

She reaches for my hand and places it on her cold face. "Alive."

The noise that comes out of me is a shaking breath I hadn't dared to let out until this moment. My thumb strokes her cheek. "Alive." Our lips brush in not quite a kiss, but they linger there as we inhale one another. Her scent has changed. Rather than freshwater and lunalillies, it is like a frosted meadow. Icy and sweet.

"I'm so sorry, Luc," she says against my lips.

I laugh against hers and pull back to look at her. "Sorry? *You're* sorry? Aislinn Theodora, you have nothing to apologize for. I should be on my knees begging for your forgiveness. I never should have left your side. I'll never make that mistake again. I swear it on my blood."

She looks up at me, the silver of her eyes nearly glowing as they fill with tears. "We don't get a say over our fate anymore."

"What does that mean?"

Erebus steps into my peripheral vision. I'd forgotten he was here. He smirks down at us. "Yes, pet, tell us what that means."

"I'm changed," she says, her voice so heartbreakingly small. "My mortal body has died... *I* died."

"Ailie." I grab her face with both hands so she has to look at me, to see how deadly serious I am. "I don't care what you are as long as you're you."

Erebus laughs, and Aislinn gives him a heated look. She exhales and shuts her eyes. "I'm the harbinger of Death, Luc. Anywhere I go, Death will follow."

"I. Don't. Care. You're still Aislinn Theodora Delphia to me. You're still mine."

"Actually," Helena pipes in, "she belongs to the Shadows now."

My spine straightens, and I realize it moments before he says it. What it means. What Aislinn is trying to tell me.

Erebus's mouth twitches with amusement. "She's mine."

SIXTY
UNNATURAL
Leighra

THE ELDERS ARE GOING to kill me. Not literally...hopefully, but I know I majorly screwed this up. It was my job to ensure the newcomers followed our rules and bring them back to Caeliss. This is the second mission I have failed, and I'm positive my good standing will disappear the moment they realize I not only let Rett go, I encouraged him.

The rules are outdated and implemented in a time of war against our kind. If what Rett has told us is true, I suppose there may still be a bit of animosity towards Children. But also, if things are as bad as he and the others say, maybe *we're* the ones who are wrong for staying hidden for so long when we have the capability to help. My moral compass is spinning and I have no clue which direction it will land upon.

A small pile of snow falls from the trees above and lands in my hair. I'm glad we don't have to deal with this stuff in Caeliss. There's hardly any on the ground, and it's still managed to make this little trip infinitely more miserable. At least I'm almost there now. About another hour or so and I should be wrapped around Cass in front of a nice fire, preferably nude.

That is if I can avoid the Elders first.

With a sigh, I shake my head.

I fucked up. There's no getting around it.

Maybe I can catch Alec or Priestess Alis on their own and explain it all. Lysette is one of us and needs help. He's her brother.

I'm not sure if I should reveal Iris's connection to the craft. There are those who hold on to their superstitions a bit *too* tightly.

Oh gods. Iris.

I'm going to have to deal with her too.

Gods, this is a mess.

I step onto the mossy log bridge that rests over the Aeikpo Bog with careful steps. There's movement beneath the pungent liquid and I smile at the Guardian below. "Morning Vristra."

The spines along her back break the surface before her head does. Even with the disfigurements of her eel-like body, I can tell she was once beautiful. Her pointed teeth show in what's almost a smile, if Vristra is capable of such a thing. She starts waving her hands and talking quickly in Old Daeil. "Po yeitsi uldoaka, etalo eivit isevitis yvieiuis etalviis aeiso," she says—warning of a disturbance in the realm.

"I'm sure it's just chaotic energy from so many coming in and out of Caeliss lately. Do not worry. The Isoots would see danger before it reached us."

Vristra huffs and clicks her tongue before diving below the murky waters again. Although, now that I think about it...there is a weird sensation in the air. The sun is shining a bit brighter than usual and my skin is buzzing. I thought it was nerves about failing the Elders, but now that Vristra has said something, I wonder if it could be more. My stomach knots and instincts kick in. I palm the knives sheathed around my thighs and take off into a sprint.

My feet are quick and my body agile from all the days of training with the boys in our circle. The closer I get to the guardians, Ismat and Edwige, the more my heart flutters. I pant out "uldoaka," and they lift their silver spears, allowing me access to Caeliss. From up here everything looks as it should be, but that feeling in my gut won't give, so I continue sprinting. There's only one person on my mind—Cass.

The streets are filled with our people. They're searching for something or someone, but all I can think about is getting back to her. I have to see her. Make sure she's okay. I continue to sprint past the panicked people, my anxiety only growing. I finally make it after running through the maze of streets.

Cass's sobs are loud enough to hear through the door, and I almost rip off the hinges to get to her. She's curled up on her side in the middle of our sitting room tucked into a ball. I don't know what's wrong. I can't even begin to guess. All I know is she needs me. I drop my bag and my knives then curl myself around her on the floor, holding her as she shakes with each loud cry.

"What happened, dasi eivit?"

There's a rattle in her chest as she tries to take a breath like she's trying to take in the strength from the air around us. "H-Hadleigh is g-gone. She went m-missing sometime in the n-night."

"No," I say in disbelief, tightening the hold I have around her. Not Hadleigh. That poor girl has already been through more than any nine-year-old ever should. More than *any* kid should. I know it's possible she's hiding out somewhere, but the feeling in my gut makes me fear the worst.

"N-no one can find her, not even a t-trace. She vanished." Cass continues to cry. "I can't. I can't lose her too. Leighra, what is happening to this place?" She holds my arm into her chest and shakes.

"We will find her. I'm sure Maegora is already using her sight to look."

She sniffles. "Aunt Maeg has been trying all morning. There's some kind of block or shield she can't break through."

"What about—" My next words are drowned out by the sounds of the summoning bells. I look at Cass. I've never seen her light so dulled in my life. With a kiss to her shoulder, I say, "You can stay here. I'll go find out what's happening."

"No. No, it could be about Hadleigh. I should come and see what they've found out." She moves to a seated position before I help her stand despite her shaking legs.

Golden hair is stuck to her cheek in the places that her tears have already dried. Carefully, I push it off her face and motion for her to turn around. When her back is to me, I begin quickly braiding her hair. Running my knuckles along her jaw, I kiss her temple and grab her hand so that we are together in facing whatever comes next.

The chaos in the streets has not subsided, but at least they're all headed in the same direction now. The path to the temple is crowded, but they make a room for us—likely do to my position with the Elders. People get quieter as we get closer to the temple's entrance. Anticipation makes my heart thunder, but I stay firm for Cass. She needs me and I would die before I let her down.

We make our way through the crowd, and when we get to the front, Cass's eyes widen, and she instantly falls to her knees with a gasp. My focus is entirely on her, so when someone comes and falls on top of her in a crushing hug, it takes me much longer than I care to admit to register who it is. But when I do, the blood drains from my body and I collapse on top of them.

"Holy shit, Heidon," I say breathlessly.

"Did you guys miss me or something?" He laughs as if he wasn't just in a four-month long coma.

"So much," Cass says with a half-laugh-half-sob.

"How?" I ask, getting off them and helping them to their feet.

"I don't know. One minute we were in the Silver Hills, and the next I was waking up in the healing center." He runs a hand through his overgrown hair. He looks fine, better than fine. "Where is everyone else?"

I motion for them to head to the temple. The crowd's eyes have begun to fix on us, and we don't need an audience right now. "There's a lot to catch up on, but maybe with not so many ears around."

Cass looks around and nods. "Is Aunt Meag inside already?"

Heidon winces. "Yeah, she's kind of a mess right now. Between me and Hadleigh, I'm not sure if she will recover from the stress or let either of us out of the house again. Hadleigh is going to be in so much trouble when she turns up."

"You're not worried about Hadleigh?" I ask.

"Nah, I used to disappear all the time before she was born. I think it's a kids-with-visions thing. Thankfully, as I got older, they got less intense. She'll turn up."

The people continue filing into the temple, but that feeling from earlier is still creeping beneath my skin. Cass and Heidon follow the others into the temple, but I'm still leaning on the railing and staring at the horizon. That feeling hasn't subsided, and it is making me hyper vigilant. Mase, Harlow, Rik, and Bones make their way up the steps and stand beside me.

"Do you feel it?" I ask them.

They nod and give me questioning looks.

"What is it?" Rik asks.

"It feels like...raw power," Harlow says. "It's like when new life sprouts below the dirt, and everything around it is disturbed—but magnified by the thousands."

"Whatever it is, it feels wrong," I say quietly.

They murmur agreements.

The ground begins to shake violently, and I have to hold onto the rail to keep from falling.

"What the fuck?!" Mase shouts over the thunderous noise crackling in all directions.

"Earthquake?" Rik asks.

"No, this is something different. This is unnatural," Bones says, skin ripping apart as he shifts into his animal form.

I go to reach for my knives and curse silently when I find my thigh bare. I never picked them up again after dropping them at the house.

All the Children who had just gotten settled into the temple come to investigate the commotion. Cass's hand slides into mine, her other holding Heidon's. The sky splits open with another loud crack. That same strange glow that seemed to be surrounding the sun grows. It looks as if it's coming right for us.

It *is* coming right for us!

"Everyone back inside!" I shout over the panicked chatter. The others begin to echo my command, shuffling the others back into the temple, but we're not quick enough. The falling sun makes impact near one of the fields outside of the main village. Then dozens more splashes of light follow until Caeliss is completely surrounded in sea of gold.

A large man comes into view along the road leading to the temple. In his arms, a young girl with a head full of brunette curls is cradled to his bare chest. He also seems to be covered in golden light. It's engraved into his skin and ever-changing. The closer he gets, the clearer it all becomes.

"What...the..."

Priestess Alis pushes past us with a gasp, then falls to her knees, signaling the rest of us to follow.

"Haile."

Keep in Touch!

Find out all the latest in JB's world & writing!

**You can find her on Facebook under *JB Wright*
as well as Instagram and TikTok under
HeyJ.B.Writes!**

**Join the discord for early updates and news -
JB Wright Books & Things
or to connect with more amazing authors join *The Book Hive* on discord.**

It Took a Village.

I am beyond blessed Tears of Astoria was received so well and getting Son of Astoria out was definitely a labor of love but watching all of you fall in love with the characters helped push me forward.

First, as always, I need to thank my husband and children. Their patience is never ending and I have felt nothing but supported and encouraged while chasing this dream. Also my WHOLE FAMILY. I am so blessed to have all the support from everyone around me.

Perci Jay...you saved my ass on this book. Thank you for always being daddy's biggest supporter and such a great friend. It has been so fun growing you on this journey.

Jessica, thank you for being the first hype girl for SoA, I honestly don't think I would have gotten it done without your encouragement and all the help!

My alpha readers, oh my gosh, thank you. Y'all were such a fun group! I loved watching your banter in the group chat.

Utikalo, girrrrls. Dani, Danna, and Coco. My boo-thangs. Your energy gives me life.

Lauren, Meg, Willow, Riki, Cruz—and Holly by proxy, thank you for all of your help and support while ready early drafts and pointing out all my faults while simultaneously boosting my morale.

OH MY GOSH, my ARC team!!! Over 200 of you. It's unreal. I can't even wrap my head around it. I had 30 for Tears of Astoria and now there are over 200. I am blown away.

Booktok, specifically IndieBooktok, thank you for giving me a platform and actually taking a chance on a wee little indie such as myself.

My artists, Zoe, TL, and Rachel, thank you for bringing these characters to life!

Samantha-freaking-Norbury and Sean Chausee...what can I even say? At the time of writing this, the audiobook has not been produced but every clip you've sent has been incredible and I am absolutely incredible and I know magic is about to happen!

I can't even articulate how thankful I am for you all. So many people made this possible.

GLOSSARY

Old Daeil

Ada - I am
Aeikpo - Danger
Aeisi - Day
Aeitli - Dark
Aviiskaisis - Discuss
Dailotta - Mother
Dao - Me
Dasi - My
Daviko - Mine
Dauteiol - Mortal
Dauuk - Moon
Etaleiki - Thanks
Eteiggoa - Trapped
Ei - A
Eika - And
Eikvidalis - Animals
Eivit - Air
Etalo - The
Etalviis - This
Eu - To
Goloeiyuo - Please
Guiseiolis - Portal
Iseilo - Safe
Iselota - Stellera
Isetuko - Strong
Isevitis - Stirs
Isoie - Seer

Isoie - Seer
Isoot - Seer
Isolvie - Split
Istaleia - Shadow
Isukis - Sons
Isvipotale - Sight
Isvitok - Siren
Kataleis - Chaos
Katalvia - Child
Katalviatok - Children
Katoeieut - Creator
Kaoket - Center
Koy - New
Kue - Not
L'roo - Free
L'vikeiol - Final
L'vito - Fire
Lolluy - Fellow
Lut - For
Lutowot - Forever
Oeorkeiol - Eternal
Okavikpo - Ending
Oka - End
Oktalei - Enhance
Olviko - Lightning
Olvipo'at - Light

Olvilo - Life
Oluwo - Love
P'toeietal - Breath
Peik - Ban
Peittviot - Barrier
Po - Be
Po'oluy - Glow
Poeietalot - Gather
Potoevikpois - Greetings
Pouais - Gods
Putk - Born
Taleioll - Half
Talewok - Haven
Taloeite - Heart
Talog - Help
Teisi - Ray
Tuiiso - Rousse
Uko - One
Ukolsi - Only
Utikalo - Oracle
Ul - Of
Uldoaka - Friend
Viisoleika - Island
Viisolo - Isle
Viklivieo - Infinite
Wuvia - Void
Wviisvieut - Visitor
Y'taluolo - Whole
Yeitk - Warn
Yeitsi - Wary
Yo - We
Yutalo - She

Pronounciations

Aislinn - Ae-s-lin
Rainier - Rain-eer
DeLuca - De-lu-kah
Lysette - Liz-et
Lys - Liz
Soleil - So-lay
Leighra - Leer-rah
Helena - Hel-e-nah
Haile - H-ale
Erebus - Air-e-bus
Cintamari - sin-tah-mar-ee
Luppitier - Loo-pe-teer
Katoeieut - Kat-toy-eet
Oonaugh - Ooh-nah
Eikvidalis - Eye-k-vid-al-e
Aietal - Ae-tal

Gods / Guardians / Power

Kato - The Creator

Haile - Life / King of Gods

Egon - Death

Kaliel - Fury

Erebus - Shadows and Trickery

Astoria - Beauty and Night

Millena - Balance

Agnar - War and Hunt

Cintamarri - Desire

Felix - Luck

Edwissa - Love and Art

Merri - Fertility

Isela - Seasons

Ravetta - Chaos

Helena - Messenger / Reaper

Aria - Air

Sana - Health

Raza - Dreams and Nightmares

Soren - Skies and Storms

Oonaugh - Seas

Delun - Vengeance... ?

Utikalo - Oracles
- Forbis (past)
- Opari (present)
- Viitor (future)

Vrista - Aeikpo Bog

Ismat - Caeliss

Edwidge - Caeliss

Kylshin - Egonus Sea / Balliera Sea

Ormund - Lake of Eternal Life

Weavers - Fold of Kaoket

Skeletons - Egora Bog

Legion of Light - Haile's army

Chimmy - Kaoket

Nymphs - Cintamarri's Palace

Dureias - Imorti Wood

Isoot - Seer

Bottinial - Botanical

Eikvidalis - Speaks to Animals

Grounder - Control of Minerals

Elemental - All Elements

Gale - Wind

Shifter - Varies but can transform

Voda - Water

Sanguist - Blood Control

Aurer - Energies

Illusionary - Casts Illusions

Whisperer - Influence through whispers